This book should be returned to any branch of the
Lancashire County Library on or before the date shown

it's one that I'm going to be recommending'

BOOK ADDICT SHAUN

'A superbly written crime thriller... I cannot recommend it

D0294496

HOPE TO DIE

David Jackson is the author of two series of crime thrillers. *Pariah*, his debut novel featuring New York Detective Callum Doyle, was Highly Commended in the Crime Writers' Association Debut Dagger Awards. *Cry Baby*, a later novel in the same series, was an Amazon top ten bestseller and listed as one of Amazon's Best Books of the Year. David works as a lecturer in a university science department in Liverpool, the setting for his new crime series featuring DS Nathan Cody. He lives on the Wirral peninsula with his wife and two daughters, and can be followed on Twitter as @Author_Dave.

HOPE TO DIE

David Jackson

ZAFFRE

First published in Great Britain in 2017 by

ZAFFRE PUBLISHING
80-81 Wimpole St, London W1G 9RE
www.zaffrebooks.co.uk

A CIP catalogue record for this book is available from the British Library.

ISBN: 978-1-78576-112-6

also available as an ebook

1 3 5 7 9 10 8 6 4 2

Typeset by IDSUK (Data Connection) Ltd

Printed and bound by Clays Ltd, St Ives Plc

Zaffre Publishing is an imprint of Bonnier Zaffre,
a Bonnier Publishing company
www.bonnierzaffre.co.uk
www.bonnierpublishing.co.uk

For Lisa, Bethany and Eden

1

The beauty and majesty of the place only add to his fear.

Despite the poor visibility, the building ahead of him is unmistakable. Looking as though it has been carved out of the black sky and then suffused with its own light, it demands his attention. He has seen how even the godless are awestruck when they approach, mere specks in its presence.

He knows that this is a place of superlatives. That this is the largest Anglican cathedral in Europe and the fifth largest in the world. That it has the world's heaviest and highest peal of bells. That it has the country's largest organ. That it even has its own constabulary.

But they are all inconsequential tangibles. It is the sheer spirituality here that he finds overwhelming. If God is anywhere, he is here.

The sense of having been dropped into a mystical land is heightened by the weather. It is late afternoon on the first Saturday of December, but Christmas has come early for some. Snow fills the air. Huge, plump flakes swirl and glide before adding their contribution to the thickening white carpet below. It has created an unearthly silence here, and an unsettling change to the ambient light.

It's a sign, he tells himself. A warning. I should go back. I should get out of here right now, while I still can.

But he presses on, stepping up his pace so as not to fall too far behind the jabbering couple ahead of him. There is some slight comfort to be gained from being in their proximity – some sense of safety in numbers – but he knows it will be short-lived.

The snow crunches and squeaks beneath his boots. The hood of his coat is up and his hands are buried deep in his pockets, but still he shivers. Yet he knows there are beads of perspiration on his forehead, and his palms are clammy. His breathing is shallow and fast, and seems not to be bringing enough oxygen into his body. He feels on the verge of fainting, or at least dropping to his knees to spill his guts onto the pristine whiteness.

At the black iron gates he halts. Oblivious to his actions, the garrulous couple continue their plod towards the West Porch, and his fear mounts with each yard they add to their distance from him.

He looks behind him. Peers through the dense snowfall towards the street.

He is being followed.

He wishes it were not so. Wishes that the dramatic change in the weather would have been enough to provoke a change of plan. But no. The figures are there, and heading his way.

He doesn't have much time.

Facing forward again, he wonders what he should do. He catches sight of the huge statue of the Risen Christ, suspended above the entrance to the cathedral. He would like to imagine it wearing an expression of reassurance, of comfort, but from here it looks stern and disapproving. As if it is cautioning him not to tarnish this holy place with his troubles.

It occurs to him that it has always been this way. There will be no offers of guidance here. No signs from on high, pointing the way. He will have to find his own path.

The path he chooses is to his left. It takes him through another iron gateway and plunges downwards, as if towards the very bowels of the city.

The route could not be more evocative of death and what lies beyond it. On either side, the path is lined with faded and weather-worn gravestones. Countless numbers of them stand shoulder to shoulder against the high stone walls, their inscriptions speaking lovingly of the departed souls of past centuries. And, if further clues were needed as to the earlier use of this land, over to the left stands the Oratory – now forsaken and derelict, but once a thriving mortuary chapel.

He pauses again. Takes a deep breath. The freezing air stings his nostrils and sends a shiver through his body.

He walks on. Reaches a point that always chills him, even on a bright sunny day. It's a tiny triangle of land enclosed by tall headstones. One stone is missing, allowing entry. It worries him that someone, some dark malignant creature, could be hiding in there, waiting to jump out and attack him.

He tells himself not to be afraid, but his inner voice sounds hollow. There is *every* reason to be afraid of what is coming.

And then he reaches the tunnel. Its mouth is a black hole in the solid rock. He knows the passageway is only short, that he will quickly be on the other side, but still it fills him with dread. The headstones continue on into that tunnel. They stand to attention as if waiting to pass judgement on whoever dares to pass through the narrow space between them.

He knows he has to go on. He has no choice.

He quickens his pace. Hears the echo of his steps as his feet move from fresh snow to unyielding stone in the enclosed tomb-like space.

And then he is through, and he can breathe again. Can feel the freshness of the snowflakes as they push under his hood and melt against his skin.

He stops here, declining to follow the line of gravestones that bends to his right, through St James' Gardens. It's a small but pleasant park, with its own mineral water spring. At its centre is a monument to William Huskisson, former MP for Liverpool, his accomplishments in that position somewhat overshadowed by his fame as the world's first railway fatality, knocked down by Stephenson's Rocket.

But right now this stretch of land shouts at him of its grimmer past, as the final resting place for sixty thousand people across the ages. He feels he can still sense their presence, as if some trace of their souls has been eternally chained here.

He shudders. And it is not only because of the ghosts.

The moment of decision is upon him. Fight or flight. He feels his stomach tying itself in knots, his intestines clenching and unclenching. He wants to vomit and defecate at the same time. His mouth has dried out and his heart hammers against his ribcage.

I could run, he thinks. I could race through the park and to the far side of the cathedral. I'd be gone before they got here. They'd never know.

But he stands there dithering for too long. They have arrived. He can hear them. He will have to face his fears.

When he turns and heads back into the tunnel, it is as if his body is no longer under his conscious control. It seems to him as though he is simply a passenger in a vehicle, wondering where it will take him.

He sees them, their shapes outlined against the canvas of white beyond the other end of the tunnel. Panic floods his system again, and he dips his hooded head, hiding his face.

I could squeeze past, he thinks. In this darkness, I can't be recognised. I could walk straight past and keep on going, and nobody would be any the wiser.

And then it's as if the knowledge that he has some control over the situation emboldens him. As he draws level with the other occupants of the confined space, he finds himself stopping. Finds himself uttering a word he hasn't heard himself voice for a long time.

It has the desired effect. He registers the confusion, the puzzlement it causes. His pursuers become less than the demons he dreaded, less than the monstrous troll with its Cerberus-like hound. They become what they really are.

A middle-aged woman with her small pet dog.

And so he strikes.

It is all so fast. A blur. His hand leaves his pocket. His fingers curl tightly around the heavy lump hammer as he swings it at the woman's head. But she is fast, too – unexpectedly so – and she manages somehow to get a forearm in the way, and she makes it all go wrong, ruining his aim, getting that limb smashed to pieces instead of her damn head. And then she is screaming, for help and in pain, and the dog runs off barking, and it seems to him that this is all going to shit, and that he has to bring this to an end, has to fix things. And so he takes another swing at the source of all her noise, and this time he feels the hammer connect with her jaw, and her shrieks cease instantly, but now things become even more terrifying because even in this darkness he can see what she has become. He can see that she is now a slack-jawed zombie-like creature, pushing herself away from the gravestones behind her as if she has just crawled from a coffin beneath the ground, and that useless jaw just hangs and swings, showing him its broken teeth and its bleeding gums and saliva strands as she makes strange keening noises. And it is all fear now, it is life or death for him, it is kill or be killed, and so he leaves it to his body to save him from this apparition, to hit out again and hear the cracking apart of her cranium before she falls, still alive and murmuring and slobbering and drooling, and he has to pound her again and again, grinding that bone and turning that head to mush beneath his righteous blows.

When he is done, when his arm aches with its efforts and his chest heaves for oxygen, he rests against the wall and looks down at his handiwork. Looks down at the still pile of rags that once enveloped a living, breathing force.

Movement catches his eye, startling him. But it is not from the woman's corpse. Sitting in the mouth of the tunnel is a small dark shape, staring back at him, its eyes gathering what little light there is and firing it back at him in twin concentrated beams. He would like to imagine it as some tiny malevolent sprite, released from the unwitting host that has just been vanquished. But he knows it's only the dog. It sits amid the swirling flakes and waits patiently for its owner, seemingly unaware that all around, the snow is turning dark with her blood.

He chuckles silently at the extent of his own fear. All that wasted emotional turmoil. Telling himself he couldn't go through with it. Convincing himself it would go so badly wrong. Desperate for some higher power to intervene and prevent it happening.

Well, now it's happened.

And for once, God seems to have been on his side.

2

Detective Sergeant Nathan Cody pulls his collar up around his neck. Crunches through the snow and then up the half-dozen cathedral steps.

He likes churches. Religion, not so much. He has been an atheist for as long as he can remember, but he sometimes wonders how he would have reacted if he had been a believer a year or so ago, when he and his partner were having bits cut off them by a sadistic maniac. Would he have managed to find it within him to hold on to his faith after such an ordeal? He doubts it.

At the top of the steps, DC Neil 'Footlong' Ferguson is cradling the victim's dog in his arms. Some kind of terrier, Cody guesses, no expert on canines. He grimaces as he watches the dog licking greedily around the lower half of Ferguson's face.

'You should bag and tag that thing,' he says.

Ferguson pulls himself away from the dog and looks down at his sergeant – not a difficult feat for this beanpole of a man even though Cody has now reached the top of the steps.

'Eh?'

'It could be evidence,' says Cody. 'You might be contaminating it. It's certainly doing a pretty good job of contaminating you.'

Ferguson turns to the dog again. 'Don't listen to him. He's just a mean, grumpy man. You're lovely, aren't you? Yes, you are.'

In return, the dog resumes exercising its tongue.

Cody says, 'Do you have to let it do that? Doesn't seem very hygienic.'

'To be honest,' says Ferguson, 'it's the closest I've come to snogging for weeks. Got to get it where I can.'

Cody grimaces again. 'You're a reprobate.'

Ferguson puts the dog down, but holds on to its lead. The animal sits and looks up at him with wide brown eyes.

'You've got to admit, she's cute, isn't she?'

'I'm more of a cat person, me,' says Cody.

'Really? I'd never have guessed.'

Cody thinks there's an insult hidden in there somewhere, but he lets it slide. He moves to stand alongside Ferguson. Joins him in staring out from this vantage point in front of the West Entrance.

'I'm starting to feel all Christmassy,' says Ferguson. 'The snow, the cathedral, the old street lamps over there, the Georgian buildings . . .'

Cody adds, 'The police cars, the blue flashing lights, the uniformed officers, the CSIs in their white suits . . . Oh, and that woman with her head caved in.'

'Killjoy,' says Ferguson. 'You'd make a great Scrooge, you know that.' He pauses, then says, 'You had a gander at her yet?'

'Yeah. Not pretty. Someone wanted to make damn sure a couple of paracetamol wouldn't sort her out. This was vicious.'

Ferguson chin-points to the hive of activity below. 'They find anything of interest yet?'

'Nah. I'm not sure they will, either. Too much to-ing and fro-ing. The vic was found by another dog-walker, then some people leaving the cathedral came for a look, then the cathedral constables were all over it, then some paramedics ... And there's only one narrow little path leading down to the crime scene. It'll be a miracle if they find any useful forensics there.'

'Well, if it's miracles you want, this is the place for them. Speaking of little miracles, what do you think about Wibbly coming back?'

Cody snaps a look at Ferguson. 'Webley? When?'

'Tomorrow, is what I heard. Just in time to join the fun on this case. You mean you didn't know?'

Cody shakes his head. Looks back across the city. But now he's thinking only about DC Megan Webley.

Ferguson says, 'I thought you'd know more than me about it. Haven't you two kept in touch?'

'Not recently,' says Cody. Which is being a little disingenuous, he thinks. The truth is he's hardly seen her at all since she was hospitalised. And now she's coming back, and he'll have to deal with it.

Ferguson clears his throat before issuing his next words. 'You, er, you never did tell me the full story about what happened on that roof.'

It seems like an age ago to Cody now. Seems unreal. He was on the verge of sacrificing his life to save hers. She, in turn, almost did give up her life to save his. And all this taking place after Cody revealed things about himself that he has never told anyone else. It should have been one of those happy-ever-after moments: after forging such a powerful bond, they sail off into the sunset to spend the rest of their days together. But life's not like that. Life is complex and murky and affected by external forces that don't give a shit for fairy-tale endings.

'Nothing to tell,' says Cody, although he knows that Ferguson won't be convinced.

Two men come walking towards them. One is a uniformed police officer. The other is an overweight balding man in a hi-vis jacket.

The policeman says, 'This is the cathedral constable who was the first to be called to the scene.'

Ferguson is quickest to respond. He beckons the man up the steps, like a king granting permission to approach the throne.

When the man gets to the top, he glances at the dog, then proffers his hand to Ferguson.

'You must be Sergeant Cody. I'm Al Glover.'

Ferguson accepts the handshake, but gives an unsubtle tilt of his head in Cody's direction.

'Sorry,' says Glover as he switches his gaze to Cody. 'Don't know why I thought that.'

Cody knows. It's partly a height thing. For some strange reason people always seem to equate height with rank. But the main reason is that Cody has such a boyish face. He looks as though he could be a university student – not a seasoned detective sergeant on the Major Incident Team.

'No problem,' says Cody. He takes the man's hand. Finds it clammy, despite the freezing conditions. There's a faint tang of alcohol on the man's breath, too. Cody guesses he's had a tot of rum or Scotch to calm his nerves after what he's seen here tonight.

'I suppose you fellas come across a lot of this type of thing,' says Glover.

'A fair amount,' says Cody.

'Sure. Goes with the territory, doesn't it? Most people don't appreciate what we do, what we have to put up with.'

'No,' says Cody, smiling inwardly at Glover's sudden switch from 'you' to 'we'.

'No. And there are some right weirdos knocking about.'

'Weirdos? You had any here recently?'

'Oh, we get 'em all. Drunks, druggies, homeless – well, you know what I'm talking about, don't you? Our jobs are similar in lots of ways.'

'Anyone in particular, though? Someone who might be connected with the homicide here tonight?'

'Well . . . In particular? Well, nobody in particular. But we get 'em here, all right. All sorts.'

'I'll tell you what,' says Cody. 'Why don't you make a list for us? Local smackheads, regular nuisances – that kind of thing. Could be that one of them was here tonight.'

'Naturally,' says Glover. 'I was already thinking along those lines. I'll get right on it.'

He digs into his pocket and pulls out a packet of cigarettes.

'Either of you . . . ?'

Ferguson shakes his head. Cody says, 'No, thanks.' He watches while Glover brings the cigarette to his mouth with trembling fingers and lights it.

Says Cody, 'Tell me what happened here tonight.'

'Yeah. Okay. Well, the first thing I knew about it was when a bloke knocked on the door of the lodge.' He points to his left at a small building used to house the cathedral constabulary. 'He said a woman had been found on the path down there. Said she was badly hurt. Maybe even dead.'

'Do you know who this man was?'

'No, but he's been talking to one of your guys. He didn't strike me as the suspicious sort. You kind of get a nose for it after a while, don't you?'

'Was he the one who found the body?'

'No. That was a much older bloke. He's being interviewed too. I made sure he hung around. Common sense, really. Some of the younger lads, they wouldn't—'

'Okay, so you get told a woman's been hurt. What do you do next?'

'Well, I go over there, don't I? I grab my torch and I go and have a look. We're trained to deal with every kind of situation. This might be a place of worship, but you'd be surprised at what goes on here sometimes.'

'I can believe it. So you go to the woman, and . . .'

'And she's there, all right. Blood everywhere. Her head . . . Well, have you seen it? She's a mess. Dead, obviously.'

'Obviously?'

'Yeah. I mean, I checked for vitals. Of course I did. That's textbook, innit? But she was gone all right. You could tell that just by looking at her. Nobody could survive that.'

'Did you recognise her?'

'Not at first. Not sure her own mother would recognise her the way she is now. But I had my wits about me, and I realised who it was.'

'What made you realise?'

Glover gestures towards the dog. 'Her. She was just sitting there, only a couple of feet away. She was cold, shivering.'

'You'd seen this woman walking that dog before?'

'Every morning and evening, regular as clockwork. Sun, rain or snow. I keep an eye out, see. Pays to be vigilant in our game, doesn't it?'

'Ever speak to her?'

'A few times. Only to say hello, nice day, that kind of thing. I didn't know her name.'

'What about where she lived?'

'Not sure. I've seen her coming up Duke Street, but that's it.'

'Ever see her talking to anyone else?'

'Not that I recall. I got the impression she was a bit of a loner. Even went to the services by herself.'

'The services? In the cathedral?'

'Yeah. I think she was often in there. I mean, I didn't go looking for her or anything, but I often saw her going in or out.'

Cody looks at Ferguson, then back to Glover. 'Thank you, Mr Glover. If you could put that list together for me? And one other thing – you've got CCTV here, right?'

Glover nods. 'Inside and out.'

'Good. Dig out whatever recordings you've got, would you? I'll send someone over to collect them.'

'Ahead of you there. Already on my to-do list. Not surprising, really, I suppose. Given how similar our jobs are, I mean.'

'Exactly what I was thinking, Mr Glover. Good work.'

Glover smiles and nods. Heads unsteadily down the steps and back to his lodge.

'Enjoying the view, you two?'

The voice booms from behind the detectives, causing both of them to jump. They turn to see the large and imposing figure of Detective Chief Inspector Blunt. Cody guesses she has just come through one of the cathedral doors rather than materialising out of thin air, but he's putting nothing past her.

'We've literally just finished interviewing one of the cathedral constables, ma'am,' he says.

'I see. And did he tell you anything useful?'

Cody gives her a summary, and watches the effect on Blunt as she digests the information. He likes his boss, despite her fearsome aspect. And he knows that she likes him too. Not in any kind of weird sexual way – her attitude is more of a mother hen as far as Cody as concerned, although he has no idea what he has done to deserve the singular attention.

'Interesting,' says Blunt. 'It could be that our victim chanced upon something she wasn't supposed to see. A drug deal, for example. On the other hand, if she took the same route every evening at exactly the same time, then anyone who knew her could have just waited for her to turn up.'

'Meaning it was planned,' says Cody.

'Could be. If it was, somebody must have really hated her. You saw the body. There was a lot of pent-up aggression in that attack. Knowing more about what this woman was like might give us some clues as to who could hold such a grudge. And don't be fooled by the fact that she was a regular church-goer. Sometimes they're the worst.'

Blunt seems to notice the terrier for the first time. She bends at the waist and stares at it. The dog tilts its head as it looks back at her in confusion. Ferguson glances at Cody, who shrugs.

'Hmm,' says Blunt, and straightens up again. To her detectives she says, 'Well, what are you waiting for? Find out the victim's name and address, then get over to her place and find out what made her tick.'

Says Ferguson, 'Er, I'm not sure how we can do that at the moment, ma'am. The CSIs couldn't find anything on the body that could be used to identify her.'

'All right, then, ask her dog.'

Ferguson glances at Cody again before replying. 'Ma'am?'

'The dog, Neil. It's a prime witness. It saw everything that happened tonight, to its living owner, for God's sake. Don't you think it wants to help us find whoever did this terrible thing?'

Ferguson opens his mouth, but no words find their way out. Even Cody thinks the cold must have got to her brain cells.

'Bloody hell, Neil,' she continues. 'Call yourself a detective? Every time I've seen you tonight you've had that animal in tow. Take another look at it. Properly, this time. You'll see that it's wearing a collar, and on that collar is a tag, and on that tag is the name "Trudy" and a telephone number, presumably of its owner. Are you with me now?'

'Ah,' says Ferguson as it all clicks into place. 'Right. Give me a minute.'

Sheepishly, he retreats into the shadows, where he digs out his radio and a notebook and pen. Cody watches him go, thinking about his plans for taking the piss later on.

'What are you smirking at?' says Blunt.

Cody affixes a suitably solemn expression. 'Nothing, ma'am.'

'Hmm. You've heard the news, I suppose?'

'News?'

'DC Webley is rejoining us tomorrow. Clean bill of health and raring to go.'

Cody wishes everyone would stop feeling the compulsion to impart this piece of information to him. It's as though they're testing him. Sticking a pin in him to see how he reacts.

'Great,' he says. 'It'll be nice to have her back on the team.'

'Don't cock it up, Cody.'

The advice takes him by surprise.

'Ma'am?'

'She's a promising young detective, with a heart of gold. She just wants to get on with the job. You, on the other hand, have a tendency to make everything more complicated than it needs to be.'

'I have no idea what—'

'Good. Keep it that way.'

Cody isn't sure what more he can add to this conversation, and is glad when Ferguson returns, triumphantly waving a bit of paper as though he's Neville Chamberlain.

'Got it,' says Ferguson. 'The number is registered to a Mary Cowper. She's got a flat on Duke Street.'

'Amazing what we can learn from more primitive creatures,' says Blunt, in such a way that Cody isn't quite sure she's referring to the dog. 'Don't let me keep you.'

Cody and Ferguson head down the steps, back into the snow. Cody feels the flakes on the back of his neck, and pulls his collar up again. As they approach the gates he turns to Ferguson.

'Er, we're not a K9 unit, you know. You need to get shut of that thing.'

Ferguson shoots him a horrified look. 'She's not a *thing*. She's Trudy. And she just gave us our first lead.'

'Yeah, well, hers is one lead you need to let go of. I'm not going down Duke Street with that mutt. We'll look a right pair.'

Ferguson frowns, sighs. But he walks over to a uniformed officer and puts the dog lead in the bemused man's hand.

'Here. And remember, she's not just for Christmas.'

3

It takes them less than five minutes to walk to Mary Cowper's flat. On the way, they cut across the end of Rodney Street, where Cody's own apartment is. It strikes him that he may well have passed Mary on his travels without even knowing it. He often goes jogging in this area, sometimes even in St James' Park. He may even have said 'hello' or 'good morning' to her, with not a thought that she might end up in a victim case file on his desk.

It's still snowing heavily. The huge ceremonial arch at the entrance to the oldest Chinatown in Europe is just a dark, unremarkable shape through the shifting white veil. Cody is glad to get to the converted Georgian building where the woman lived until a few hours ago. He rings the bell for Flat 1. Gets no response. Presses the button again.

'Try another one,' Ferguson suggests.

Cody looks at him. 'Never would have thought of that. I was just going to walk away.'

He leans on the bell-push for Flat 2. Thinks, I need to get inside. Anywhere that's warm and dry.

The answer over the intercom is almost immediate: 'Hello?'

'We're police officers. Do you mind if we come in, please?'

'Police? Why police?'

It is clear to Cody now that the voice belongs to a foreigner. Eastern European or something.

'Nothing to worry about, sir. We'd like to talk to you about one of your neighbours. Flat 1? Mary Cowper?'

'Mary? Okay. Come, please.'

There's a buzz and a loud click as the door unlocks. Cody pushes his way inside. Feels relieved to be out of the wind and snow. He flaps his jacket to shake off the flakes. Wipes his feet on the welcome mat.

Ahead of them is the stairway, and to the right of that a wooden door with a shiny '1' screwed to it.

'Worth a try,' says Cody. 'Maybe the doorbell's not working.'

Ferguson steps up to the door and raps loudly on it. There is no answer, and no noise from inside.

'She is not there?'

The voice comes from the top of the first flight of stairs. A man is looking down at them.

'No,' says Cody. 'She isn't. Does she live alone?' He sticks to the present tense for now. No need to alarm the man just yet.

'Yes, alone. Yes. You say you are police?'

Cody approaches the stairs, pulling out his warrant card as he goes. He holds it in the air, even though he knows the man won't see it properly from there.

'I'm Detective Sergeant Cody. This is Detective Constable Ferguson. Do you mind if we come up and speak to you?'

The man beckons to them. 'Yes, please. Come. We can speak in my apartment.'

The detectives trudge up the stairs, then follow the man who beckons them into his abode.

'Please,' says the man. 'Take off coats. Have seat.'

Cody smiles and nods. 'Thank you, Mr . . . ?'

'Demidov. Yuri Demidov. Like spaceman.'

'Spaceman?'

'Yuri. Yuri Gagarin. You know him?'

'Ah, yes,' says Cody. Here, in the warm light of the living room, he gets a better look at their host. He is a thin man with a fat head. Or, rather, his head is widened by an explosion of dark curls that lends him the overall shape of a microphone. He looks to be in his mid-forties. He grins almost incessantly, his cheeks bulging and red as if from the constant facial exercise.

The flat is a mess. Not dirty, but untidy. Papers, books and folders dropped almost at random, it seems, across the room. Texts on complex mathematical topics cover the coffee table. Propped up on the mantelpiece are a couple of cheaply produced certificates for 'Best Paper Award'.

'Would you like some tea?' says Demidov. 'I have real Russian samovar. You know this, samovar?'

Cody sees the puzzled look on Ferguson's face, but decides not to get into explanations now.

'No tea, thank you. We'd like to talk to you about—'

'And cake. I have special cake from the Asda. You know this place, the Asda?'

Cody can't help smiling at Demidov's adoption of the Scouse manner of putting the definite article in front of the supermarket's name.

'Mr Demidov. Do you mind if we talk about Mary Cowper now?'

'Mary. Yes. Please. She is wonderful lady.'

'You know her well?'

'Not well. I live here only few months. I am visiting professor at university mathematics department. This is my first time in UK. But Mary, she is very kind to me.'

'Kind in what way?'

'She brings me pies.'

'Pies?'

'Yes. Apples pies. She cook them herself. She is very good cook. And she takes parcels for me, when I have deliveries. She is—'

He stops speaking suddenly, and his grin drops away as if something has just occurred to him.

He says solemnly, 'You have bad news, yes? In Russia, policemen at your door is always bad news, but I thought may be different here.'

Cody doesn't like to tell him that the police turning up at your door is usually an ominous sign here too.

'We've found the body of a dead woman. We believe it may be Mary Cowper.'

Demidov sits back in his chair and looks up at the ceiling. 'Oh, my God. Oh, my God. This is terrible. Such a wonderful lady. A good woman.' He looks at the detectives again. 'You are sure?'

'We're fairly certain.'

'Oh, my God. That is so terrible. How did she die?'

'We believe she was murdered. Her body was found in the grounds of the cathedral.'

'Oh, my . . . Who would do such things? She would hurt nobody. Nobody. I do not understand this.'

'We don't understand it either, so we were hoping you could tell us more about her.'

'All right. Yes. I will try.'

'You said she lived alone. No husband or children?'

'No. Nothing. Wait! She has dog. Trudy. Did you find her?' His eyes flicker in mild panic between the two detectives.

'Don't worry, Mr Demidov. We found the dog. She's perfectly safe.'

Demidov relaxes a little. 'Mary, she loves animals. She gave money to them.'

'I'm not sure what you . . . She gave them money?'

'Yes. Animals charity, you know? RPCSA, or something like this.'

'I see. But other than the dog, nobody else lives in Flat 1?'

'No. Nobody. She likes to be alone. She loves her dog. That is enough for her. But still she is kind to me.'

'When did you last see her?'

'Today! I see her when I come back from doing shopping. She is going out with Trudy. This is normal for her, you understand? I do not think this is last time I will see her. Oh, my God.'

'Please,' says Cody. 'Try to stay calm. Just a few more questions, okay?'

'Yes.'

'Good. What was Mary wearing when you saw her earlier?'

Demidov brings his fingers to his temples in concentration. 'I think maybe long brown coat. And – how you say . . .' He makes a circular wrapping motion around his neck.

'A scarf?'

'Yes. Scarf. Many colours. That is all I remember.'

'That's very helpful,' says Cody. 'Thank you.'

The description matches what the victim was wearing. Long brown coat and tartan scarf. Worth checking. Cody would hate to discover later that the corpse is that of a completely different woman, even though the dog was sitting next to it. It's an unlikely possibility, but he has known of worse blunders in the past.

He says, 'Tell me more about Mary. Did she have any close friends? A boyfriend? Any family?'

Demidov shakes his head. 'I do not know this. There is a man. Sometimes he comes here. But I do not think he is boyfriend.'

'Do you know who he is?'

'No. I have not seen him. I have only heard man's voice in her apartment.'

'How often does this man come here?'

'I do not know. Maybe not many times.'

'Okay. What about Mary's job? Do you know where she worked?'

'Yes. Mary is schoolteacher.'

'Do you know which school?'

'I forget name. It is in Wall-ton, I think. Girls only are allowed.'

'Walton? Oakdale Girls?'

Demidov stabs the air with his finger. 'Yes. Oakdale. That is right. She teaches religion. She is very religious woman.' He frowns before correcting himself: '*Was*. She *was* religious woman.'

Ferguson jumps in at this point. With both feet. 'But nobody's perfect, right? I mean, she must have had some vices.'

'Vices?' says Demidov. 'Explain, please.'

'Well, some people drink too much or take drugs. Some gamble or have wild orgies or—'

Demidov looks as though he's about to go into apoplectic shock. He straightens his spine, digs his fingers into the arms of the chair. 'No! Mary would not do any of those things. She is good woman always. Church woman.'

'I think that what DC Ferguson was trying to get at,' says Cody, anxious to defuse the situation, 'is whether Mary might have inadvertently upset someone. Even the nicest people in the world can sometimes irritate others.'

Demidov drags his gaze from Ferguson and focuses it on Cody instead. His mood softens, and there is a glint of wetness in his eyes. 'She make apples pies for me,' he says, as though that's all the eulogy she needs.

Cody obtains the phone number of the landlady from Demidov, then gives her a call. As she is currently entertaining a male friend, she is reluctant to bring the key over, but quickly changes her mind when Cody tells her not to worry, he'll use his own key – a massive red one that will take the door off its hinges.

He also calls in some CSIs, most of whom come directly from the cathedral. This isn't a crime scene – at least as far as anyone is aware – but if the attack on Mary was planned, then there is the possibility that the murderer may have at some point been in this apartment. Cody wants to make sure they gather any forensic clues to identity that may have been deposited here.

While the CSI team do their thing, Cody and Ferguson carry out some snooping of their own. Unlike Demidov's flat, Mary Cowper's place is spick and span to the point of obsession. In the kitchen there is not a spot of grease to be found, even on the oven. No plates or cups have been placed in the sink unwashed, or abandoned to dry on the rack. Grocery items in the cupboards are arranged neatly in categories rather than thrown in at random. It's not so extreme as to be classed as OCD – it's not as if the tins have all the labels facing outwards and sorted into alphabetical order – but Mary Cowper did like to be neat. Even the dog's bed looks to have been recently vacuumed.

It's a similar story in the living room. No dog hair or coffee-mug stains or films of dust here, thank you very much.

Cody is drawn immediately to the bookcase in one of the alcoves. He's a bibliophile, and believes he can tell a lot about people from the contents of their bookcases.

Mary Cowper was a woman after his own heart. She liked the classics – Dickens, Hardy, Brontë – but whereas Cody will admit to reading the occasional pulp thriller, there is no evidence of that here. Certainly nothing racy, either: not so much as a single Shade of Grey.

On the lower shelves are her reference books. Some are concerned with the various world religions, although those on Christianity dominate. There are also tomes on history and art. Next to those is a stack of school notebooks, presumably waiting to be marked or returned to her pupils. Cody picks up the top one and flicks through its pages. Finds that the most recent essay is on the importance of religious leaders.

Cody moves to the television stand in the other alcove, then crouches to study the row of DVDs. He finds *Mary Poppins*, *The Sound of Music*, *Les Misérables*, *Fiddler on the Roof*, and a number of recordings of ballet performances and other musical shows. Nothing from the *Saw* franchise, nor anything by Tarantino.

There is only one book on the coffee table, its edges square with those of the wooden surface below it. It's a copy of the Bible, big surprise. Cody picks it up in his latex-gloved hands, notices that it contains a bookmark. He flips the book open.

Romans 1. Cody's eyes scan quickly down the page. They alight on verse 18: 'For the wrath of God is revealed from heaven against all ungodliness and unrighteousness of men, who hold the truth in unrighteousness.'

Is that what happened? he wonders. An act of vengeance, in payment for some perceived 'unrighteousness' by Mary?

Cody returns the Bible to its position, then resumes his search of the flat. On the bedside cabinet in Mary's bedroom he finds another Bible, without a bookmark this time. A carved crucifix hangs above her bed. On the chest of drawers are two framed photographs. The first shows a woman – presumably Mary – accompanied by a small group of pupils at Oakdale School. In her hands is a large cheque (both physically and financially) made out to the Children in Need appeal. More evidence of her good works, thinks Cody.

He spends some time staring at the image. It's the first time he has seen what Mary looked like when alive – when her head wasn't spread across an area of several square feet. He guesses this is a very recent photograph: the birth certificate in her desk drawer puts her age at forty-two, which looks about right here. She was fair-haired, with twinkling blue eyes and an attractive smile. He tries to remember whether he has ever seen that face in the area, but no occasions come to mind.

He turns to the second photograph on the chest of drawers. He thinks at first that it shows a smiling Mary standing next to a similar-looking younger woman – similar enough to be her own daughter. But then he looks closer and realises that Mary is the daughter in the picture. She must have been in her early twenties when it was taken. The mother looks much older – at least sixty.

Cody wonders why Mary hasn't put on display a more recent photograph of the pair of them together. Did her mother pass away? If not, she would be in her eighties now. The news of her daughter's tragic death could break her heart.

He takes a step backwards to look again at the first photograph. Thinks to himself, Who are you, Mary Cowper?

You are profoundly religious. You love animals. You give money to charity. You bake pies for your neighbour. You keep your home spotless. You attend church services regularly. You love your mother. You are well educated. You avoid trash in what you read and what you watch. You are in the noble profession of teaching.

And yet the violence used to end your life spoke of hatred as pronounced as any I have ever encountered.

Are you too good to be true, Mary?

4

Cody walks home. His car is still at the station on Stanley Road, but he decides there's no point in going all the way over there just to drive it back again. He'll get a taxi to work in the morning.

The snow falls much more lightly now, but is still crisp underfoot. Rodney Street is eerily calm and still. Frozen in a past century. It is not hard to imagine this night as a Georgian Christmas Eve, or something straight from the pen of Dickens. To picture huge wreaths on each of these glossy doors. And, inside, wealthy parents drinking nightcaps as they joyfully fill their children's stockings and prepare for the festivities and excesses of the following day.

And then Cody gets to his own building, his own door. He stares at the brass knocker and sees it mutate into the angry, despairing face of Jacob Marley's ghost. In Cody's head the carol singing fades, and the mournful moaning starts up. And it's with a heart as heavy as lead that he takes out his key and lets himself in.

Inside, he listens to the whispers and the creaks and the tiny scrabbling noises of the building and its unseen inhabitants, and he wonders how much of it is real and how much is conjured up by his fevered brain.

Because, yes, his mind isn't as well as it should be. He's got problems, and he accepts that. But there's hope now. Light at the end of that long, sanity-constricting tunnel.

He moves through the hallway. Past the doors to the dental reception area and the surgeries. They are closed now. Locked up tight. The doors keep hidden the instruments of torture, the memories of pain and decay. The smells linger, though. Those nauseating antiseptic odours that are always associated with places of healthcare.

At the bottom of the stairs he pauses, as he often does. He considers going right to the end of the hallway, to that door behind the stairs. The door he fears most. It leads down to the cellar. It's always locked at night, and he doesn't know why it frightens him so much, but it does. Sometimes he stands with his ear against that door, listening for whatever might lurk on the other side. And sometimes he is convinced he hears things. Scratches and groans and possibly even murmurs. He tells himself that it is mice or the boiler or the wind finding its way through the grates. But he's never fully convinced.

Tonight he decides against that particular episode of self-amusement, and heads straight up the stairs. At the first turning he glances out of the curtain-free window. The snow in the walled rear yard is pristine, untouched.

Except . . . Are those footprints? There, leading towards the yard door. No. Can't be. Just a trick of the light.

On the first floor he passes more locked doors on to abandoned surgeries, then stops at his own. He finds his keys on the dimly lit landing, then unlocks the door with a clatter that reminds him of the chains shackling another of the ghosts that confronted Ebenezer Scrooge.

'Bah, humbug,' he mutters to himself, then smiles and pulls open the door, wincing as its hinges squeal in complaint.

He locks the door behind him. Ascends another set of stairs to his flat on the top floor. Instantly he feels more relaxed. The world outside is closed off. He can be himself, with all the things both good and bad that it entails.

It is late and he is exhausted and he needs sleep. But he also knows that sleep will elude him for a while yet. His mind is too occupied.

For one thing, the current case has gripped the analytical centre of his brain and refuses to let go. The figure of Mary Cowper he has floating around in there seems a bit like Mary Poppins, drifting with the breeze as she clutches her umbrella. Was she really that goody-two-shoes? Or was there a much darker side to the woman, yet to be discovered?

It occurs to Cody that well-meaning religious zeal is often only a stone's throw from its flip side. Entering his living room, he walks over to one of several well-stocked bookcases there. He scans his own section of books with religious associations. Realises that they are so unlike Mary's. Whereas hers are full of light and optimism and the joy of discovering God, his own are mostly questioning, damning, scornful and dark.

He takes down his copy of Dante's *Inferno* and flicks through its pages, wondering what Mary would have made of it. What would her reaction have been to the souls of the uncommitted, eternally stung by wasps while maggots and other foul insects drank the cocktail of their blood and tears? Or the gluttons, condemned to writhe for ever in vile icy sludge?

Cody looks out of his window at the snow blowing past it. Thinks of it finding its way into the dark tunnel concealing Mary's corpse. Thinks of her streams of blood flowing out of her tomb and melting the white carpet beyond into a pink slush.

Were you gluttonous, Mary? Some other deadly sin, perhaps?

He puts the book back into its position on his shelf. It's a long time since he has read any of it, but one quote is not easily forgotten.

Abandon all hope, ye who enter here.

The Anglican cathedral sits at one end of Hope Street. The street of hope.

No hope for you, Mary. Not now.

He flops onto his sofa. Tries to divert his mind to other things in an effort to relax.

Megan Webley makes an entrance into his thoughts. It doesn't help to calm him.

They have worked one case together since she joined the team. One case. And yet they seemed to pack a lifetime of events into that short period. Didn't help that they had prior history. They were an item many moons ago. Wasn't easy to forget that, even though they have both forged other relationships since then.

And tomorrow, Webley returns.

That's not going to be easy. Going to be bloody difficult, in fact.

Why did it have to be Webley?

And why did he have to go and tell her?

He told her, see. About his problems. Not that she couldn't grasp for herself what was happening to him. She turned up at the Major Incident Team just as he was entering his worst patch ever. She could see him disintegrating before her eyes.

But still . . .

Anyone else, and he wouldn't have said a word. Only Devon, his ex-fiancée, knows how bad he's been. He could have refused to say anything to Megan.

But he told her. Told her all about the clowns who mutilated his body and fractured his mind.

Not clowns as in bumbling fools, but clowns as in terrifying pasty-faced insanely grinning perpetrators of evil. Four of them, there were. A leader, whom Cody christened Waldo, and his three hench-clowns.

He told Megan what they did to him, back in the day when he was an undercover cop and the operation went tits up. Told her how the clowns tied him to a chair and took off his shoes and socks and . . .

Yes, say it, Cody. Think it. They used a pair of garden loppers to cut off the two smallest toes from each foot, didn't they? You still feel the agony of it, don't you? You still hear the crunch of your bones and your screams filling that warehouse.

And you remember what happened next, don't you? You told Megan about this, too. You told her about what the clowns did to your partner. You told her about how they turned on him next. About how they cut off his . . .

Say it.

SAY IT!

His face! All right? They cut off his fucking face!

Cody jumps up from the sofa. Wipes the beads of sweat from his brow.

It comes upon him like this sometimes. Usually when he's least expecting it. Or at night, when he's desperately trying to succumb to the sweet unconsciousness of sleep.

And that's the real secret he told Megan. The facts of his torture and his partner's death are a matter of record. DCI Blunt knows all about the events of that night.

But the extra piece of information he revealed to Webley was how he is still living that nightmare. He still hears the screams, still sees the clown faces, still smells the tang of blood on the air.

Sometimes it gets so bad that he simply snaps. He loses control. He lashes out. Webley has seen that side of him. She knows what he is going through.

But things have been better recently. Much better. Sleep hasn't been great, but he hasn't had a meltdown on the job since working on that last case with Webley. There have been occasions when he has come close – looking at the crushed face of Mary Cowper tonight was the most recent – but each time he has managed to keep it together.

He believes it's partly because of his admission of his illness to Webley. Credit where it's due. She acted as his sounding board, his amateur psychotherapist. He would never tell all this to a real shrink, of course. The force would never let him carry on doing the same job in his mental state.

It felt good to tell Webley, though. A massive weight off his shoulders. He's still not sure it was the right thing to do – it could still go horribly wrong – but for now he's grateful for the part she has played in keeping his sanity intact.

But it's only a part.

Something else happened. Something totally unexpected. He's still not sure what it means, but he clings to it for support like a baby monkey to its mother.

The phone call.

He's been getting mysterious calls for months now. Usually in the middle of the night. No caller ID. Not even a voice. Just silence.

Sometimes Cody speaks to his unknown caller. Asks a question or makes a joke. Sometimes he spits foul-mouthed abuse down the line.

And then came the one call that was different from all the others. A voice, yes, but it was Cody's own voice. It was the sound of him screaming and pleading and crying as he and his partner were tortured on that day that has been for ever seared into his memory.

Which means that somebody recorded the whole thing.

Which suggests in turn that the anonymous caller was there at the time, or else knows the person who made the recording.

The caller knows something. Knows a lot, probably. And now that fact is being revealed to Cody.

Why?

He has been asking himself this for the past two months. Why is the caller showing his hand in this way? What's he trying to prove? And what was the deal with all the silent calls prior to that?

Cody sometimes thinks he imagined it. Not the silent calls – he's had enough of those to know they're real. But he's aware that his mind is perfectly capable of playing tricks on him. He's had bitter experience of that. What if that last call was another figment of his imagination – another undigested bit of beef, as Scrooge put it?

He shakes his head, dismissing the notion. It was real, he tells himself. I heard it. I wouldn't have made that up.

He needs to hold on to that. When he had his heart-to-heart with Webley, he told her of his belief that the one thing capable of bringing his mental torment to an end would be the capture of the gang who tortured him. Only justice would bring him closure.

He still believes that. And the phone call brought him hope. A suggestion that the circus was back in town, and therefore within reach of the long arm of Cody's law.

Problem is, he hasn't had another weird call since then. Not even one filled with silence. He's beginning to worry that there will be no more – that the screaming he was forced to hear was a parting shot.

He can't accept that. Snatching away his hope would be an unbearable addition to the suffering he has already endured.

And then Cody remembers the quote again.

Abandon all hope . . .

When it happens, it is as he is lying in bed, thinking about religion and its hold on people, and about how people delude themselves into believing that their prayers are answered even when they are not.

It's only later, when he finally realises this, that the irony strikes him hard.

The phone rings.

This is the middle of the night, when only one person ever calls him.

Well, unless it's an emergency call to action by one of his superiors on the force.

It'll be that, he tells himself. Another murder. Or a significant break in the current case. Something far more mundane than my sanity.

In which case, why am I not answering it?

Cody continues to stare at the phone on his bedside cabinet. Continues to tell himself that it's a call to duty. As if he doesn't want to build up his hopes, for fear of having them dashed.

Finally he snatches up the phone. Sees that the caller ID is unavailable.

His heart is suddenly banging on his ribcage. As if it's saying, *Answer the fucking phone!*

He clicks the answer button. Brings the handset to his ear.

Silence. Blessed silence. A thousand words, a thousand songs in that majestic cacophony of nothingness.

It's him, thinks Cody. He's back.

When the call ends and Cody replaces the phone, he whispers a thank you into the darkness, and a single tear slides down his cheek.

And then he sleeps.

5

Sunday morning and the bells are ringing.

Or so it seems. It's like party time in here. Everyone hugging and kissing and smiling and laughing. There should be music and party poppers and champagne.

She looks good, Megan. Full of life. Hard to believe that said life was almost extinguished.

Cody watches the festivities from his desk, then feels guilty for keeping such a distance. He gets out of his chair. Heads over to stand quietly at the fringes of the small crowd. Waits for her eyes to alight on him.

When she sees him, he notices how her smile wilts a little. Notices how emotional pain darkens her eyes.

She could turn away then, and he wouldn't be surprised. But she doesn't. She's bigger than that. Instead, she forces her mouth back into its smile and moves towards him.

'Welcome back,' he says.

He throws his arms wide, inviting an embrace, possibly a chaste peck on the cheek.

She puts her hand in his. Shakes it firmly. 'Thanks, Sarge. Good to be here again.'

Sarge. Not even 'Cody'.

And then she's gone again. Back into the throng. Back to the genuine celebrations.

Cody sees Ferguson looking across the room at him with a concerned expression. He throws his friend a fleeting smile: *It's all good.*

But it's not good. He feels like a spare part – a spring or a washer from a reassembled appliance that seems to be working perfectly well without it.

He's glad when Blunt shows up and restores some order and formality.

'All right,' she barks. 'Save the backslapping for when you've solved this case. There's work to be done. Welcome back, by the way, Megan.'

Webley smiles and nods, accepting that it's the best she's going to get from her boss.

'You've come at the right time,' Blunt tells her. 'A nice, juicy murder. Talk to Cody later. He'll bring you up to speed.'

Cody looks round to see that this time Webley's nod is not accompanied by a smile. In fact her lips couldn't be clamped together any tighter. He also catches Ferguson raising his eyebrows at him as if to say, *Uh-oh, what have you done?*

'Tell you what,' Blunt continues, 'you can do your catch-up when you both attend the post-mortem later.'

Great, thinks Cody. The morning has just gone from bad to worse. The last time he was at a PM with Webley was an unmitigated disaster.

'So,' says Blunt. 'Progress. Plans. Where are we up to? Cody, what do we know about Mary Cowper?'

Cody gives her a rundown of the previous night's investigation. Ends up by saying, 'So, looks like she was as pure as the driven snow.'

Blunt pulls a face. 'If that's the best pun you can come up with, you need a humour transplant. And besides, it's bollocks. Nobody is that godly – not even the Pope. Mary Cowper may not have been a porn star, but she had some dirty secrets. Just like the rest of us, eh, Cody?'

He's not sure how to respond to that. Not sure if she's innocently cracking a little joke of her own, or if she's having a subtle go at him.

Blunt has her suspicions about him – he knows this. She has read the accounts of what happened to him and his partner. What she doesn't know – because he has always refused to tell her – is exactly how the events have affected his mental health. But she suspects, and she will never turn down an opportunity to remind him of that.

'Do some more digging,' she tells him. 'Under that driven snow you're bound to find some shit.'

Apparently pleased with her riposte, she addresses the squad as a whole: 'Right, what else?'

Ferguson pipes up next. 'We've been talking to people who visited the cathedral yesterday. We've started interviewing neighbours, owners of local restaurants, shopkeepers, and so on. We've also started rounding up and putting pressure on druggies and prostitutes from the area, just in case they know something. Forensics haven't found anything obvious yet, but we'll keep pushing them along. Oh, and we've tracked down

Mary Cowper's mother. She's in a care home in Huyton. Cody and I are heading over there later to talk to her.'

'What about love interests? Any sign of those in Mary's life?'

Ferguson shakes his head. 'Nothing as of yet. No old Valentine's cards or keepsakes in her flat. Everyone we've spoken to so far has only seen her alone.'

Blunt snorts. 'What, not a single romantic fling in her whole life? Forty-two, wasn't she? There must have been someone – if not now, then at some point. And I don't just mean Jesus. This male visitor the Russian neighbour told you about – do you know who he is?'

Ferguson shakes his head. 'Not yet.'

'Well, find out. He could be important.' She pauses. 'What about motive? Any thoughts?'

Cody says, 'Nothing gone from her flat, by the look of things. A purse was found in her pocket, so it doesn't look like robbery, although there was no bag found at the scene, so maybe her attacker ran off with that.'

Cody hears a discreet cough from somewhere behind him, but he presses on. 'I'm starting to wonder if she was really just in the wrong place at the wrong time. She takes her dog down to the gardens, just like she always does, only this time she crosses the path of some scumbag high on crack cocaine or whatever, and he stoves her head in. Probably doesn't even remember doing it now.'

Another cough, louder this time.

Heads turn. Cody looks round to see a hand raised timidly at the back of the room. The hand belongs to a bespectacled young woman with lank brown hair.

'Yes?' Blunt invites. 'It's Julie, isn't it?'

'Grace.'

'Yes,' says Blunt. 'Grace. What is it, Grace?'

Grace Meade is the newest member of the team. Arrived just a few weeks ago, and has stayed pretty much unnoticed since then. She's an Intelligence Analyst – a civilian role. She came here with a top-class degree in computer science. Obviously a very bright girl, but somewhat lacking in social skills. Cody doesn't know much about her. He has said hello to her on occasion, but never had an in-depth conversation. He gets the impression that Grace doesn't do in-depth unless it's about computers, which is probably why she is already a bit of an outsider.

Grace's voice is barely audible: 'I, er, I don't think it was a spur-of-the-moment crime. Or robbery, for that matter.'

Blunt seems taken aback. 'You don't? And why is that, Grace?'

'I've, er . . . While you've been speaking, I've been going through the recordings.'

'The recordings?'

'The CCTV footage. From the cathedral. I think I've found the killer.'

6

There is a profound silence. Everyone glancing at each other, trying to confirm that they have just heard the same thing.

'I'm sorry,' says Blunt. 'You've got the killer? On video?'

'Yes. I think so. Would you like to see?'

'Too bloody right I would.'

Blunt starts moving towards the back of the room. Everyone else rises from their seats.

'I, er, I can put it on the large TV screen,' says Grace, pointing to the front of the room. 'If you prefer.'

Blunt looks at the TV, then back at Grace.

'You can do that?'

'Yes, it was just a configuration setting. One of the first things I did when I got here.'

Blunt continues to stare in surprise. In all the time this squad has existed, nobody has considered that it was even possible to route individual computer displays to the large monitor at the front. Until now, the detectives have all gathered around a single desk to view material. The television has been reserved for watching news bulletins, and occasionally a football match when Blunt isn't in the vicinity.

'Right then,' says Blunt. 'Off you go.'

Grace rises from her desk. Starts to move towards the front of the incident room. Every pair of eyes is on her, some as if for the very first time. Cody detects a shakiness in her walk, notices the way she licks her lips as though she has just lost all the moisture in her mouth.

Grace stands next to the large screen and presses a button on the remote in her hand. The set flares into life. Cody thinks there's a problem with the display at first, then realises he's looking through the lens of a camera in a snowstorm.

Grace says, 'I've created a brief compilation of the most interesting bits I've found so far. Obviously I'll check the rest of the material too.' She gestures towards the screen. 'As you can see, the images aren't great. It was dark and it was snowing heavily. A few seconds later, though, we get this . . .'

She clicks another button. Three figures come into view from bottom left. They are small and indistinct, but it is just possible to follow them as they head up towards the cathedral gates.

'Wait,' says Blunt. 'Who are these people?'

'I believe one of them is the killer,' says Grace. 'See the one at the rear? How he hangs back slightly from the other two? I think he's trying to pretend he's with them.'

'Why?'

'My guess? He knows there are cameras on him, and he feels that he's less likely to attract attention if he's thought to be part of a group.'

Blunt nods, her face grave. If Grace's guess is correct, then it suggests the killer is a clever bastard.

'Now watch,' says Grace.

She lets the video run on. The team members watch as the trio approaches the iron gates. At that point, the trailing figure stops, allowing the other two to keep going towards the cathedral entrance. A few seconds later, the lone assailant takes a left turn down the path towards St James' Gardens and disappears from the camera's view.

Grace pauses the recording. 'I'm still checking the cameras from the gardens. So far, there's no sign of our guy. Either he stays in the tunnel, or he doesn't go very far after coming out the other side.'

'What about Mary? Did you find her? I assume she bumped into her killer coming the other way.'

'Er, no. Mary hasn't arrived yet.'

Cody notices the surprise on Blunt's face, and he suppresses a smile. It's not often that anyone manages to wrong-foot his boss.

Grace runs the video on. 'We see Mary coming into view . . . here. As you'll see, she's not carrying a bag.'

Everyone leans forward. Some squint. Cody can just about make out a figure with a dog. It's a weird feeling knowing that he's observing the final seconds of someone's life. He wants to shout at the screen, to say, 'Turn around, Mary! Don't go down there!' But he continues to watch, mesmerised and powerless, as Mary Cowper walks inexorably to her death.

It occurs to Cody that, if people of stronger faith than his are correct, then there is a power that could have prevented Mary's death. A cathedral, of all places, is surely a stronghold for its flock. Why was this allowed to happen?

'I've skipped the next bit,' says Grace, 'but it's only a couple of minutes. Here's our killer again . . .'

The dark, mysterious figure reappears. Heads back out of the cathedral grounds. He doesn't run – doesn't even seem in much of a hurry. It's as though he's on a gentle stroll, without a care in the world, without any regrets about having just smashed the brains out of an innocent woman.

Grace says, 'There's footage of him going away from town and up into the Georgian Quarter, but we lose him after that. As you saw, Mary wasn't carrying a bag, so robbery probably wasn't the motive.'

Cody senses the wave of relaxation as it moves across the room. As though everyone has been on the edge of their seats watching a really tense scene in a movie. Everyone breathes again.

'Okay,' says Blunt. 'So our killer is up to something else in that tunnel. Maybe he's shooting up. Maybe he's already high. Whatever. Mary comes along, sees what he's doing, perhaps there's an argument—'

She stops when she sees that Grace has a finger in the air again.

'Grace?'

'Sorry, but I was just wondering . . . I mean, what I'm suggesting . . .'

'Spit it out, Grace.'

'Well, what if the killer was waiting for her? What if he went into that tunnel, knowing that Mary wasn't far behind?' She starts pressing buttons on her remote again. 'There was a bit here . . . I don't know if anyone else noticed it, but if I zoom in and then slow it right down . . .'

The heads in the room all crane forwards once more. Cody sees the killer at the gates again – just after he has dropped back from the couple in front. Although much larger now, his image is highly distorted and pixilated. Despite what television would have us believe, the magnified picture is not magically filled in with detail that was never there in the original.

But still, this is the killer. Hidden underneath that dark padded coat with its capacious hood is the man who is about to steal away the life of Mary Cowper.

Who are you, you bastard? thinks Cody. Come on, show us your face. Just a glimpse.

As if in response, the figure starts to turn. But not towards the camera. It turns back towards the road. Remains looking that way for just a slowed-down second before straightening up again and moving off down the path.

'I've done some rough calculations,' says Grace.

Blunt looks as puzzled as Cody feels. 'Calculations?'

'Yes. I've factored in the angle of the killer's head, the time at which he turned, and the position that Mary Cowper would have been in at that time, based on her walking speed and working back from when she first becomes visible on video, and while we have to bear in mind that—'

'Grace, cut to the chase, please.'

'Well . . . I think he was looking directly at Mary. I think he was checking to see where she was.'

There is a stunned silence while everyone considers the ramifications of what Grace – who is not even a detective – is telling them.

'You're sure about that?' says Blunt.

'Not a hundred per cent, no. There are too many variables. But there's something else, too.'

'Which is?'

Grace looks around the room, and seems a little intimidated by all the pairs of eyes burning into her.

She says, 'The weapon. Am I right in thinking that Mary was struck with something large and heavy?'

Blunt looks to Cody for confirmation.

'That's right,' he says. 'We'll know more after the PM, but the pathologist reckons it was probably some kind of hammer or other blunt instrument.'

'But no such weapon was found at the scene?'

Cody nods. 'Also correct.'

Grace points at the screen again. At the frozen image of the killer, his hands thrust deep into his pockets.

'He's not carrying a backpack or anything. That suggests he's got the weapon in his pocket, ready to use, and that he brought it away with him again. If he's just looking for a quiet place to shoot up, why is he walking about with a massive hammer in his hand?'

It's a good point. An excellent point. She might not realise it, but Grace Meade has just impressed the hell out of everyone in this room.

'Thank you, Grace,' says Blunt. 'Good work.'

Coming from Blunt, it's a massive compliment. Cody watches as Grace Meade walks quietly to her desk at the back of the room, her head bowed. She seems unaware that her insight would put many a seasoned detective to shame, let alone other analysts. And Cody has the sneaking suspicion that this is nowhere near the end of her ability to surprise.

'Right,' says Blunt. 'Now we know. This was planned. Malice aforethought. Which means our killer knew Mary Cowper, and knew something about her that got right on his wick. If we're to find him, we need to know more about Mary, so get out there and find out who the hell she was.'

7

They are shown into the small sitting room by a woman called Babs. She looks to Cody like a farmer's wife: big, beefy arms and a ruddy complexion. Her voice, though, is surprisingly tiny and high-pitched.

'Phyllis is just getting herself ready,' she tells them. 'Can I bring you some tea while you're waiting?'

'No, thanks,' says Cody, expecting Ferguson to follow suit.

'I'll have a brew,' says Ferguson. 'It's bloody parky out there. Splash of milk, no sugar, ta. Oh, and if you've got any biscuits, I'd be happy to relieve you of them. Especially if they're chocolate.'

Babs smiles and walks out of the room. Cody stares as Ferguson lowers himself onto a high-backed chair and adjusts the cushions until they are to his liking.

'What?' says Ferguson when he realises he's the focus of attention.

'Biscuits?'

Ferguson shrugs. 'It's an old people's home. It'll be crammed full of biscuits. Those and Werther's toffees.'

Cody shakes his head, then takes the chair opposite Ferguson. Between them is a small wooden table, atop which is a copy of the *Reader's Digest* and a printed A4 list of impending Christmas events, including a 'Top Prize Festive Bingo Night'. Leaking through the wall is the sound of a television quiz show, the low drone of indiscernible banter occasionally punctuated by a buzzer or a blast of inane laughter.

'So,' says Ferguson. 'Nice to have Wibbly back on the job, eh?'

'Yeah,' says Cody. 'Couldn't be more pleased.'

'I could tell. The pair of you were practically skipping around the incident room. For a second there it was looking like you were about to catch her in the air, just like in *Dirty Dancing*.'

'It's . . . complicated.'

'That's what I always used to say about my maths homework. Didn't do me any good, though.'

'There isn't a formula for Megan. I can't plug this into a spreadsheet. It needs the human touch. A bit of diplomacy.'

'Well, that's you stuffed then, isn't it? Do you want to talk about it? Over a pint, maybe?'

For a second, Cody is tempted. It's been a long time since he's been for a drink with any of the lads.

'Nah. It'll blow over. I'll clear the air with her when we go to the post-mortem later.'

'Is that wise? I mean, with all those sharp implements around?'

The door opens, and Babs walks back in with a tray supporting a steaming mug of tea and a heaped plate of biscuits. Ferguson raises his eyebrows at Cody as if to say, *See, I told you this is the biscuit centre of the universe.*

As Babs sets the tray down, the door opens again. Another carer comes in, closely followed by a white-haired, slightly stooped lady who looks as though she's expecting someone to jump out at her.

'These are the gentlemen I was telling you about,' says the carer. 'You don't mind having a bit of a chat with them, do you, Phyllis? I'm sure they're very nice.'

Phyllis gives her a glare. 'Shows what you know about men. They'll have the clothes off you soon as look at you.'

Cody wonders whether to state categorically that he has no interest in whatever lurks beneath the elderly woman's baggy cardigan, but decides it might be best not to get embroiled.

The carer laughs in a way that suggests she wouldn't if nobody else was here, then leads Phyllis over and seats her at the coffee table. Phyllis fixes Cody with a disconcerting eye as the two members of staff withdraw to busy themselves with jobs elsewhere in the building.

'Hello, Phyllis,' says Cody. 'I'm not sure how much you've been told, but we're police officers.'

'Yes,' says Phyllis. 'He said you'd be coming.'

'I'm sorry, but who said that?'

'Him! The other fella. That other policeman.'

Cody looks to Ferguson for assistance, but gets only a shrug.

'Which other policeman?'

'That detective fella. You know. The inspector.'

Cody smiles encouragingly, then tries another tack. 'Oh, you must mean Inspector . . .'

He waits for Phyllis to fill the gap, but she doesn't accept the invitation, and Cody gives a sidelong glance to see a growing smile on Ferguson's face.

'So what did he say, exactly?'

'He asked some questions, and then he said that his sergeant would be along later to take down some details. You're the sergeant, aren't you?'

'Yes,' says Cody, feeling a little flustered now. 'Yes, but how did you—'

'Morse! That's his name. The inspector bloke.'

'Inspector Morse? I see. And you think I'm . . .' He looks again at Ferguson, who now seems to have found a spot on the wall of immense interest.

'No, Phyllis. I am a sergeant, but my name isn't Lewis. My name's Cody, and this here is Detective Constable Ferguson.'

Ferguson tears his eyes from the wall and sends Phyllis a curt nod of greeting. In return, Phyllis studies him intently, then lowers her voice as she says to Cody, 'Is he all there?'

Now it's Cody's turn to smile. 'Sometimes I wonder about that myself.' He leans forward in his chair. 'Phyllis, there's something I need to tell you.'

Seemingly oblivious to the gravity in his voice, Phyllis shifts her focus back to Ferguson, who is sipping from his mug of tea.

'Are you drinking that?' she asks him.

Ferguson looks mystified. 'Yeah. Shouldn't I?'

'They wee in it, you know.'

'What?'

'Them. The staff. They wee in the water when they make hot drinks. They think I don't know, but I do.'

Ferguson's face is a picture of disbelief, but Cody notices that he slowly replaces his mug on the table nonetheless.

'Phyllis,' says Cody to regain her attention. 'This is important. It's about your daughter. About Mary.'

Phyllis looks back into his eyes for a long time. And then she says, 'She's dead, isn't she?'

Cody holds her gaze. Tries to hold back his surprise too.

'Yes. She is. How did . . . how did you know?'

Phyllis keeps her rheumy eyes on him for a while longer, then suddenly lowers them. 'You can have the biscuits. They're safe. They don't do anything with them. Not the tea, though.'

Cody tries again. 'Your daughter Mary . . . well, she didn't have an accident or an illness. We believe she was murdered.'

'Sometimes I wonder about the dinners. I'm never quite sure about them. But you've got to eat, haven't you? You've got to survive. You can't just give up on life.'

'Phyllis, can we talk about Mary, please? We need your help.'

She narrows her eyes. 'Help?'

'Yes. We'd like to know more about Mary. We want to catch whoever did this to her. Will you help us?'

'Me? How?'

'Well, to begin with, when was the last time you saw her?'

'Quarter past eight.'

Cody's shoulders slump. He turns to Ferguson for help again. No amused shrug this time, but a slight shake of the head to indicate that this is a lost cause.

'I'm afraid that's not possible, Phyllis. Mary was killed yesterday at about—'

'It was quarter past eight! In the evening. Seventeen years and four months ago.'

Cody wonders whether this is another fantasy, but something in the woman's tone tells him it's not. She was too quick to answer, her numbers too precise. It also fits with the age of the photograph on Mary's chest of drawers.

'Seventeen . . . You haven't seen her since then? Can you tell us why?'

Phyllis tilts her head back and closes her eyes. Her lower lip quivers. It takes Cody a few seconds to realise she's praying, and he decides it's best not to interrupt.

When she's done she gives the Lord a quick nod. On opening her eyes she seems startled to find she still has company, as though her wish for the detectives to have vanished away has not been granted.

'I'd like to go back to my room now,' she says. 'There's a cookery programme coming on, and I like to be reminded of what nice food looks like.'

It occurs to Cody to ask whether she has just consulted God for the TV listings, but he thinks better of it.

'Just a few more minutes, if you don't mind, Phyllis. We won't keep you long. Just tell me a little bit more about Mary. Why hasn't she been to see you?'

'Nobody comes to see me, and I don't want them to come.'

'Not even Mary? Your own daughter?'

'Especially not her. I told her. I warned her. She wouldn't listen. That's why she's dead.'

'Warned her about what? Was she in trouble?'

'Oh, yes. Trouble, all right. I told her. I want to go back to my room now.'

Cody sees her agitation building, but he can't leave it like this. He needs to know, needs to get at the truth buried deep beneath her confusion.

'Did somebody want to hurt Mary?'

A laugh of derision. 'No. Not back then. But it was always going to happen. I'm surprised she lived this long. I want to go now.'

Phyllis stands up, then begins walking unsteadily towards the door. Cody and Ferguson follow her.

'Please, Phyllis. What did you mean, it was always going to happen? Why did you think she had a short time to live?'

Phyllis gets the door open, then pauses for a second. She turns and looks at Cody, and it seems to him that there is a touch of fear in her eyes.

'It was her heart.'

'Her heart? She had a heart problem?'

Phyllis nods. 'The biggest problem you can have. The Devil. The Devil had come to live in her heart.'

And then Phyllis departs, tottering down the hallway and leaving two mystified detectives in her wake.

8

Cody has the car heater on full blast, but it still seems frostier in here than it does outside. Although that might have something to do with the ice maiden sitting next to him right now.

'This is nice,' he says. 'Just like old times.'

'It was only October,' says Webley. 'And we worked one case together.'

Cody nods. 'Yeah, but . . . it was a cracker of a case, though, wasn't it? One to remember.'

'Actually, I'm trying to forget about it.'

He glances in her direction. She continues to stare straight ahead.

'How are you now?' he asks. 'Health-wise, I mean.'

'Are you just making conversation, or are you genuinely interested?'

'I'm genuinely interested.'

'Okay. Well, I've got a bloody big scar across my chest, which makes me cry when I look at it every single morning. You know, the scar I got after the doctors sliced me open. The scar I ended up with because, fool that I am, I risked my life to save somebody else's. That somebody being you, Cody. Other than that, I'm fine, thank you for asking.'

Cody nods again. He doesn't want to lapse into silence, but he has no idea how to turn this into an amicable conversation. His own fault, of course. He deserves the discomfort.

'Everyone seems really happy to see you back at work.'

'Everyone?'

'What do you mean?'

'Most people are happy about it, yes. But what about you? Are you happy I'm back?'

'Of course I am. What kind of question is that?'

'So you're glad I'm here? Not just on the team, but here, sitting in a car with you, working on a case with you? You're happy about that?'

'Yes. Absolutely. Why wouldn't I be?'

'Just checking.'

Cody pulls the car up at a red traffic light. He has an inkling that this journey is about to feel much longer than it actually is.

Says Webley, 'I nearly didn't come back, you know.'

'Today, you mean?'

'No. I mean I almost decided I didn't want to come back to MIT at all.'

'Why? Was it that bad?'

'At first, no. Murder investigation was what I'd wanted to do for a long time.'

'But then you got hurt.'

She turns to face him, and he can tell that she is searching his face for hidden meaning.

'In more ways than one,' she says.

Don't rise to this, he tells himself. Change the subject. Ask her about her plans for Christmas. Anything but—

'How do you mean?'

No, you idiot! Now you've done it.

He can feel her eyes burning into him. Senses that she's building herself up for what's to come. He braces himself.

'Cody,' she says. 'It wasn't just about getting shot in the chest. That was bad enough. It hurt like hell, and I could have been killed, and it was really scary. But I got over that. I'm tougher than you might think. It hasn't stopped me wanting to go back out there and catch some really dangerous people. But you know what really did hurt?'

Here it comes.

'You, Cody. You. It was like you weren't even aware of what I was going through. Or you knew but didn't care, which is even worse. Why didn't you come to see me?'

'I did. I came to the hospital a few times—'

'A *few* times. When?'

'Well, I was there just after they operated on you, and—'

'Wait! I don't remember that.'

'Well . . . I didn't actually get to see you then. Your family were there, and your boyfriend. I didn't want to get in the way.'

'I see. And the other times?'

'What?'

'These *few* times that you came to the hospital. When were the others?'

'You don't remember? There was that time when Footlong knocked that jug of water all over your bed. That was funny.'

'Yes,' she says. 'I remember. I remember everyone crowding into the ward when there were only supposed to be two visitors per bed. I remember Footlong and Oxo and Blunt and the others, all making jokes to cheer me up. And I remember you, standing at the back like you thought I had Ebola or something. I remember you hardly saying a word. And I remember thinking, I wish all the others would get out of here so that I can have a good heart-to-heart with Cody, because that's what I really needed then. That's what would have helped to take away the pain in my chest. Only that didn't happen, did it? You left with all the others, and it was just like you'd never been there.'

In the silence that follows, he dare not look at her. He knows there will be tears in her eyes, and he knows that the sight of those tears will cause him to crumble into tiny pieces.

'And that was it, Cody. That's the only time I saw you at the hospital.'

'I came to your house as well.'

'Yes, you came to the house. And when Parker told you I was asleep, you handed your flowers over to him and then left again.'

'I . . . I didn't want to disturb you. You were recuperating.'

Her voice becomes suddenly shrill. 'What did you think was going to happen? Did you think I was going to wake up and go into cardiac arrest at the sight of you? I wanted to see you, Cody. I wanted you there. I needed to talk about what we had just gone through together. Jesus Christ, if anyone should understand the need to talk about the effects of a traumatic event, it's you.'

She's right. He knows she's right. That long evening they spent together is crystal clear in his memory. He poured his heart out to her that night. Told her all about his fears and his pain. She was there for him. In fact, she came looking for him to tease out his unhappiness.

And since then? Where were you, Cody? Where were you when Megan Webley needed your help?

'I thought it was for the best,' he says.

Again he doesn't glance her way, but her stunned silence feels like a yell.

'The best,' she says. 'I see. Nathan Cody, the man who can't even deal with his own problems, knows what's best for me. Wonderful.'

There's nothing more to be said after that. Cody knows that any further contribution from him is just going to make the situation worse.

He's glad when they get to the hospital. Relieved to break the spell that binds them and yet separates them in the car.

'Let's go and see what Stroud has in store for us, then,' he says, mainly just to fill the emptiness.

'Sure you can cope?' Webley says. 'As I recall, you were a bit green around the gills last time.'

She's putting it mildly, and with anyone else he would lose his temper. But, again, he knows she needs to release some of her anger after the way he has behaved.

They say nothing else to each other on the way to the mortuary. Once there, however, the ever-buoyant pathologist immediately gives them cause to reactivate their voice boxes.

'DS Cody,' he says. 'And DC . . .'

'Webley.'

'That's right. DC Webley. How the hell are you both?'

'Could be worse,' says Cody.

'Could be better,' says Webley.

'Good, good,' says Stroud. 'And how is the lovely Stella? Still as perky as ever?'

'Perky' is not a word that Cody would ever use to describe DCI Blunt, and he's tempted to answer that she has changed little since Stroud last saw her, which happens to have been only the previous evening at the crime scene.

'She's radiant,' he says instead. 'Asked us to pass on her regards to you.' Which she didn't, but Cody knows that Stroud has a thing for her.

'Splendid, splendid,' says Stroud. 'Tell her she should pop over some time for coffee and cake. Speaking of which, can I get anything for you before we begin? I've got some incredible Scotch eggs in my bag.'

Rory Stroud likes his food, and is of a shape that attests to that fact. It comes as a surprise to many to learn that his expansive girth does not appear to be an obstacle to success with women, for whom he also has a hearty appetite.

If there's one thing that would never cross the mind of Cody when about to witness a post-mortem, it's a Scotch egg. He doesn't think he could look at one right now, let alone eat it.

'We're fine, thanks,' he says, then wonders whether he was right to answer for Webley too. In her present state of mind she might cram a whole Scotch egg into her mouth just to spite him.

'Your loss. Right then, let's rock and roll.'

Stroud leads the detectives out of the anteroom and into the post-mortem theatre. Cody swallows. He's nervous about this, because of what happened last time he was accompanied by Webley.

It'll be all right, he tells himself. You can do this now. You've come a long way since then.

He looks down the row of shiny steel tables. The white, naked body of Mary Cowper is laid out on one in the middle of the room. Even from here Cody can tell her head is not a conventional shape. He swallows again.

Webley seems unperturbed. She strides towards the body like the professional she is. Determined not to allow her to show him up, he picks up his own pace. It becomes almost a race to get to the corpse.

'No need to rush,' says Stroud. 'I don't think she has plans to leave any time soon. She's not dressed for it.'

When he gets to the table, Cody forces himself to take a proper look. He half expects to break into a cold sweat, or even to start seeing things that are not really there. Moments of even mild stress can be a trigger like that sometimes.

But it doesn't happen. He surprises himself at how composed he feels. Many would baulk at the sight of Mary Cowper. It was bad enough when her head was flattened against the ground, but now that it has been turned to stare up at the ceiling its grotesque proportions and rearranged features give it a nightmarishly cartoon appearance. It's like looking at the inspiration for a Picasso portrait.

It's the phone calls, thinks Cody. That's why I feel so okay about this. Whoever is making them probably intends to scare me, but they're having the opposite effect.

Call again, he thinks. Talk to me. Let me know what—

Bang!

The noise almost results in two more bodies on the autopsy table, their hearts stopped with the shock. Cody whirls round to see Stroud wielding the short, stocky lump hammer that he has just crashed onto the counter, causing the instrument trays to leap into the air.

'Jesus!' says Cody.

Stroud raises the hammer skywards. A poor man's Thor.

'Behold the murder weapon,' says Stroud. 'Or something very much like it. This one's from my personal toolbox at home. Last time I used this I was knocking plaster off my bedroom wall.'

Cody says, 'Too many cracks in it from all the headboard action?'

Stroud smiles, but refuses to be diverted. He moves closer to the body. Brings the end of the hammer to within a millimetre of an indentation in Mary Cowper's deformed skull.

'See how well it fits? And these marks on the neck . . .'

He indicates large circular bruises. Demonstrates to the detectives how well the hammer overlaps them.

Cody watches and nods. He thinks about Grace Meade's assessment earlier in the incident room.

He stretches a hand towards the hammer. 'May I?'

Stroud hands over the implement. Cody hefts it, feels the weight and solidity. Grace was right: you wouldn't secrete something like this on your person unless you had the intention of imminently assaulting someone. For self-defence you might carry something small and easy to conceal – a knife, perhaps – but this was intended as an instantaneous means for disabling and then destroying the victim.

'How many blows?' says Webley.

An intake of breath from Stroud. 'Hard to determine, exactly. I'd say at least half a dozen.'

A weapon like this, thinks Cody, just a couple of whacks would have done the trick. There was hate in this killer. A thirst for obliteration rather than a mere desire to end a life.

Says Stroud, 'But we're getting ahead of ourselves. Shall we begin the formal proceedings?'

Stroud takes the hammer back from Cody, then turns on the overhead microphone. He slips into his precise and objective scientific language as he starts his external examination of the deceased.

Cody stands there observing for as long as he thinks it takes to convince Webley that he's not going to freak out. He waits until the body has been sliced open and for Mary Cowper's internal organs to be scooped out before flashing a smile at Webley. She doesn't fire one back at him, of course.

He wanders off then, deep in thought. He suspects that the post-mortem will not turn up anything else of relevance. He'd bet his salary that Stroud isn't about to announce that the victim was pregnant, for example. Although her name *was* Mary, and it *is* getting close to Christmas. Do all three of the people here count as wise?

He stops at a table on which Mary's clothes and possessions have been laid out in evidence bags. Little of interest here, although Mary seemed to have been in the habit of stuffing all kinds of junk into her pockets: twelve pence in copper coins; a comb with several missing teeth; two biros; a cheap-looking teardrop-shaped pendant with no chain; a brass button with a sailing ship on it; an empty tissue packet; a mirror that could have come out of a Christmas cracker; an appointment card for the dentist; a half-empty bag of dog treats; and a shopping receipt from Asda – or *the* Asda, as Yuri Demidov called it.

It seems a desperately sad and incomplete summation of what Mary Cowper was.

So what's missing?

9

He remembers . . .

He is five years old. Just five. An age that should be filled with innocence and joy and blissful ignorance of the problems of the world at large.

But he is filled with paralysing fear. His milk-white legs tremble beneath the dark wooden slab of the kitchen table.

He is waiting, because that's what he must do at mealtimes. He must not rise from his chair. Must not question. Must not make a squeak that could be interpreted as any form of dissatisfaction with this simple but unbreakable ritual.

His mother has her back to him, but he can sense the all-too-familiar rigidity in her frame. She has been getting like this more frequently lately. The aggression building up, waiting for any excuse to be unleashed. He doesn't know what causes her to be this way, but he can always sense it when it's there. He has learnt to tread softly on these occasions – to make himself as small and unnoticeable as he can be.

But today is especially difficult. He feels sick. Has done since lunchtime. He doesn't know why. He's too young to reason about food poisoning or viruses. He just knows he's unwell.

Worst of all, he knows he will be unable to eat the food his mother is about to place in front of him. The thought of how she might react is making him even sicker.

He goes alternately hot and cold as he sits here. He slides his clammy hands along his bare legs, trying to smooth away the goose pimples. His intestines clench painfully, then slacken with an audible gurgle. The smell of the beeswax on the table makes him want to retch.

His mother brings a casserole out from the oven. She strains to lift the cast-iron dish in her gloved hands. When she removes the lid and places it on the hob with a clang, steam billows into the air and rolls across the kitchen.

He holds his breath for as long as he can, and when he can contain it no longer he tries breathing in through his mouth rather than his nose. But still the food odours manage to announce their presence with little subtlety, and he wants to cry with the effort of holding their effects at bay.

He tries thinking of other things. Nice things. A cartoon he watched earlier on the television. A picture book he likes to look at in bed. His favourite toy car.

Gradually, the waves of nausea subside. He hopes this is the end of it. He's okay now. He can get through this without incident.

And then his mother brings the food over to him. Sets a huge plate on the raffia placemat before him. It's running with thick chicken casserole, mounded with creamy mashed potato and green beans. He doesn't like green beans at the best of times. Right now they are but one tiny element of the torture.

He feels her eyes burning into him, and he manages to dredge up a weak smile of gratitude to appease her. When she turns away to plate up her own meal, he twists his head to divert his senses away from the cause of his discomfort.

The relief is short-lived. His mother returns, and he knows he must act as though all is well.

As usual, she announces that she will say grace. He bows his head, bringing his nose even closer to the steaming food, but it at least gives him the opportunity to close his eyes for a short while, to pretend that it's not there.

And then it's time to eat. He can avoid the inevitable no longer.

His mother tucks in, her every movement graceful, precise. He picks up his knife and fork. Starts to herd together some chunks of chicken. He feels the heat rising within him again, the perspiration beading his brow.

It doesn't take long before she asks him what's wrong, and when she does it's delivered in a sharp, accusing tongue that spikes him.

'Feel sick,' he tells her. But his voice is small – internal almost.

'What? Speak up, lad!'

'Feel sick. I can't eat my dinner.'

What he would like now – what he desires more than anything else in the world – is the sympathy only a mother can give. Isn't that what should happen here? Isn't this where she cuddles him and strokes his hair and tells him everything will be all right?

But that's not what he gets. What he gets is a venom-filled stare and sub-zero voice that tells him to 'Eat. Your. Dinner.'

And now he wants to cry. He knows this is just the beginning. He has been here before. It is an impasse. He so wants to do her bidding. He craves her approval. Needs her love. But he physically cannot execute her command. His body won't allow it, and he hates the fact that he is in this impossible situation. He doesn't know how to deal with it.

He is only five.

'Can't,' he says.

The clatter of his mother's cutlery being banged onto the table makes him jump. She follows it up with a barrage of questions. What, she asks him, will Jesus think of this? Do you know how important food is? How difficult it is for some people to get enough to eat? Have you heard of the starving people in Africa? All those pot-bellied little children sifting through rubbish heaps and drinking dirty water? Do you know what they would give for just a spoonful of that mashed potato? Do you even care? Well, do you?

He hears the words being spat at him from across the table, and now the tears are flowing and his whole body is trembling. He really doesn't want to upset his mother, and he doesn't want to upset Jesus, but he doesn't know what to do. He has no answers, because this is too hard, life is too hard.

His inaction is the trigger for his mother to come around the table. His impulse is to get out of there, to run away. But he knows from experience that it would only make things worse. She would chase after him and she would catch him and she would drag him screaming to an appointment with her leather belt.

She stands behind and to one side of him. Waits there for what seems an age. He sits on his hard chair, pale and tense, quivering at the thought of what she is going to do to him.

'Eat,' she says, her voice quiet but dripping with the threat of retribution if she is disobeyed.

'Mummy. Please. I can't.'

A hand reaches out in front of him. Grabs his dessert spoon. Uses it to scoop up some mash.

'Eat it.'

He shakes his head. 'I don't want to, Mummy. I feel—'

Her free hand grabs a hunk of his hair. Twists it savagely so that he cries out. And as he opens his mouth she rams the spoon into it.

'You will eat,' she says, 'because the Lord is watching you. He has provided this food and you need to stop being so ungrateful.'

And if that were the end of his lesson, he might be able to cope. But she doesn't stop there. She fills the spoon again, crams it into his mouth, and he is trying to swallow it, trying not to choke, trying to breathe, but she has found the fervour of her mission now, she is accelerating in her zeal, calling out the name of Jesus as she piles mash and chicken and mushrooms and those hateful green beans into his overflowing mouth, yelling at him about the poor little babies of Africa as she suffocates him with sustenance, drowns him with her beneficence. The shrillness of her voice assaults his ears, cutting off the sound of his own muffled cries, which don't seem as important to God. Only *her* voice counts. This is God's will. She tells him so as she spreads the gelatinous mess across his face, blocking his mouth and his nostrils and his eyes.

And then his body can take no more.

It erupts.

A geyser of food and vomit and saliva and snot shoots out of him. It catches his mother's hand in mid-delivery. Lands with a heavy splash on his plate and fans out across the table.

He falls silent after that. He wants to sob, to bawl, but he is too afraid. He knows he has done a terrible thing.

But his mother is silent too, and for a brief moment he wonders if she has come to her senses. Perhaps she realises now that he really is ill, and that he doesn't deserve such meanness. Perhaps she is sorry for her actions.

'Go to your room,' she says, her voice calm and quiet once more.

He hears her, but doesn't quite catch the emotion behind her words. Could that be pity? Affection, even?

He turns to get a look at her face, to search for the truth in her eyes.

'Sorry, Mummy. I didn't mean to—'

He is stopped by the sudden contortion of her features. The mutation of her mouth, her eyes, her whole face into a mask of utter contempt and fury. She draws her hand up to the opposite shoulder, as if in readiness to backhand him across the face, and he feels her hot breath and spittle on his skin as she roars at him.

'GET TO YOUR ROOM!'

He doesn't need telling twice. He is off that chair faster than if it were red hot. He flies across the kitchen and up the stairs as though his life depends on it. And when he gets to his bedroom and flings himself onto the bed, he pulls the covers up to his neck and cowers, his eyes and ears on the door in case she might be following.

Feeling sick and feverish and alone and unloved, he cannot prevent the tears flowing more freely now. He wipes his eyes on the sheet, but when he pulls his face away he sees that he has smeared the white cotton with dinner and vomit and mucus, and that makes him even more afraid, even more tearful.

Why is this happening? Dear God up there in heaven, why is my mummy always so angry with me? Are you angry with me too? I didn't mean it. I'm trying to be good. I promise I am.

He prays then. Long, intense prayers while he sniffs and cries. Prays for all the things he is supposed to pray for, including all the starving little children in Africa who have never tasted chicken casserole.

Eventually he falls asleep, still fully clothed.

When the nightmares come to him – this time in the form of a two-headed serpent that keeps coiling itself around his legs and pushing its forked tongue into his mouth – he wakes up shivering and drenched in sweat. The blackness of the room is oppressive, and he thinks there might be other demonic creatures lurking in the corners, and so he begins crying again.

'Mummy,' he calls softly. Then louder: '*Muuummyyy!*'

But she doesn't come.

He is only five years old, and there is an unbearable ache in his chest for the need of his mother.

But she never comes.

10

She waits patiently for her moment to shine.

Putting herself centre stage does not come naturally to Grace. Her stomach churns at the prospect of it. But she will force herself to do it, just as she did earlier in the day. It's the life she has chosen.

She nearly backed out of it this morning. She listened to all these seasoned detectives discussing the case and she thought to herself, I am not one of them. I am just a civilian. Not one of the elite. They don't want to hear my voice, my views.

She could easily just have knocked on Blunt's door. Presented her findings in private, quietly and without ceremony, and then left it to Blunt to use them in whatever way she saw fit.

But she has decided she needs to be more assertive, more attention-seeking. She deserves respect. She is worth that much.

Still, that walk to the front of the incident room seemed to take an eternity. She almost threw up when she got there. All those eyes on her. She dreaded making a mistake, of giving them an excuse to laugh at her.

But afterwards! The exhilaration! She had stunned them with her performance. Left them speechless with admiration. It was worth every second of the gut-twisting anxiety.

And she will do it again. And again. Keep doing it until they see her as one of their first ports of call when they need help in solving a case. She has skills they cannot even imagine.

But it won't be easy. She is a wallflower. One of life's unseen. She blends into the background, disappears from people's vision. Her presence is dismissed almost as soon as she is introduced to others.

That's how she feels. That's what needs to change.

I can be interesting, she thinks. I can be fun. I can be a friend. Just give me a chance. Say hello to me when you come in the door. Look in my direction when anyone has a question they can't answer. Ask me what I'd like to drink when you're heading out for coffee.

She's had a lifetime of being left out.

Not sporty enough for many. Too clever for the rest. Always the last to be picked for any team.

Computers became her obsession at a young age. They were her way of exploring worlds few others could visit. She could see and discover things denied to most. That power was the antiseptic to her daily pain.

At school, she soon discovered how to hack into the internal servers. She peeked at the reports that teachers wrote about her and other students. She read internal memos. Discovered that one teacher had gone off sick after a nervous breakdown. Learnt that another had left after being accused of sexual misconduct.

She could have looked at exams and tests in advance, but never did. She didn't need to cheat to excel academically. What would be the point?

She was never malicious either. She never altered or corrupted data. Never deleted files or infected the system with viruses. She saw herself as a 'white hat' hacker – her mission being to find ways of improving rather than destroying.

Well, except once.

It was in the sixth form. She discovered that two girls were posting things about her on Facebook. Saying that she was a man in drag, that she killed cats for experimentation at home. Nice things like that.

She cried for days.

And then she got even.

She hacked into the computers of both girls. Found out that one of them had already had sex.

So Grace posted out that information. Using the other girl's account.

The pair didn't remain friends for long after that. For Grace, it was a pleasure to watch the relationship disintegrate to the point of physical blows. Grace was no longer of interest to them. It was exactly what she wanted.

She hoped things might improve at university. Hoped for an elevated level of intelligence and liberal thinking that would provide the ideal environment for her. She envisaged herself holding court with a large cohort of friends as they chewed over matters of global importance and scientific relevance. Perhaps she might even enter into a romantic relationship or two.

She was to be disappointed.

It was little better than school. The vast majority of her contemporaries on the computing course were male, and it wasn't difficult to work out that most of them viewed her as far too nerdy. Even the geeky lads had interests that differed from hers. Try as she might, she could not summon up the same level of fascination as they did for online gaming and *Star Wars*.

And so here she is now. At the home of the Major Incident Team. Wearing her 'white hat' with pride, and about to take the next step in proving to her colleagues precisely what that signifies.

She studies the police officers with detached scientific interest from the back of the room. She is fascinated by the interplay, the dynamics, the body language.

She thinks that DCI Blunt has superb leadership qualities. Her word is absolute. Nobody dares defy her. Save perhaps for Sergeant Cody, but then there's an oddness to that relationship that Grace hasn't yet figured out. Blunt grants him a leeway that isn't afforded the others, and Grace is sure it isn't just because of his rank.

There's a peculiarity in Cody's relationship with DC Webley, too, Grace has noticed. A history that goes beyond being mere teammates.

Yes, he's an interesting one, is Cody. Grace noticed how much attention he was paying her when she was putting on her little show this morning. She doesn't for one moment think it's anything remotely connected to her appearance – that would be ridiculous – but could he have been just a little bit in admiration of her intelligence? He's certainly more erudite than most police officers she has encountered. She has even seen him reading classic novels on his lunch break. Whatever next?

Well, okay, DS Cody. Let's see how you react this time . . .

She listens to Blunt describing the outcome of the Superintendent's televised appeal for witnesses. Waits for her to make a final request for updates from her own small audience. And then Grace raises her hand. Adds a cough for good measure.

She notes with satisfaction the look of surprise on Blunt's face.

'Grace? You've got something to add?'

Grace lowers her hand as she rises from her seat, unaware that the synchronised actions make it appear as though she is lifting herself in the air with an invisible pulley.

'Yes.' She points to the front of the room. 'May I?'

A suggestion of a smile from Blunt. 'Be my guest.'

Grace grabs her remote control and threads her way between the desks. She feels the eyes on her again. Thinks it's the closest she'll ever get to being on a catwalk.

She halts alongside the flat-screen TV. Thumbs a button on the remote. The first video frame of the killer walking up towards the cathedral appears.

'In its raw form, this video doesn't tell us a lot about the killer. The camera never zoomed in on the target, and most of the video is distorted by snow on the camera and in the air.'

'Yes,' says Blunt, 'but I'm sure you haven't taken the witness box just to point out how little we know about the murderer.'

'No,' says Grace. Here goes, she thinks. Time to blind them with science.

Another button press. The video begins rolling. A few seconds later, the form of the killer is overlaid with a set of rectangles, turning him into a crude cartoon version, while dotted lines shoot out from the figure and highlight nearby geographical features as he moves. Down the right-hand side of the display, a panel containing an array of numbers is updating constantly.

'What the hell is that?' says Blunt.

'The rectangles on the killer's body are there to help the computer analyse his gait.'

'His what?' says one of the detectives.

'His gait. His way of walking. The numbers on the right here can tell us whether he has a limp or other unusual characteristic in the way he moves around.'

'And does he?' Blunt asks.

'No. Nothing significant. It does tell us he's almost certainly male, though. The probability score is nearly ninety-eight per cent on that. Even a woman trying to walk like a man to throw us off the scent would find it difficult to get near that score, especially when faced with unsteady terrain such as thick snow on the ground.'

Unable to resist the opportunity, Ferguson says, 'Can I get a copy of that software? I've had a few near misses in nightclubs recently.'

He gets a laugh from most, a look of contempt from Blunt.

'What are all those dotted lines?'

'I was coming to that. The computer is comparing heights with surrounding objects. Which isn't as straightforward as you might think. It has to allow for the foreshortening caused by the downward angle of the camera, and also the perspective created by things being in different planes.'

'How do you know the heights of the other objects?'

Grace smiles. 'I went out and measured them in my lunch break.'

Raised eyebrows again from Blunt. 'So what does all this tell us?'

'That he was certainly no shorter than five-eight and no taller than six foot. And that's being conservative. A good bet would be that he's between five-nine and five-eleven.'

'Rules me out, then,' says Ferguson.

'Yes,' says Grace. 'To be honest, I was hoping it would rule out a lot more. If we knew our killer was less than five feet tall, for example ...'

'Yeah,' says Ferguson. 'Those killer dwarfs are a menace.'

'All right,' says Blunt. 'This is excellent work, Grace. We know a lot more than we did before, so thank you for that.' She turns to the squad. 'Now, if there are any other—'

'There's more,' says Grace.

'More?' says Blunt, as though she's the beadle being asked by Oliver Twist for some extra gruel.

Grace clicks again, back to the magnified view of the killer. It's just a dark blurry mess, recognisable as a person but nothing beyond that.

'As you can see, there's no discernible detail here, and the more we zoom in, the more pixilated it will become. Other still images in the video share the same problem. There's nothing to enhance in an image because the detail simply isn't present.'

'So if it's not there ...' Blunt says.

'Well, it's not there in a single image. But this is a video, remember. There are lots of images of this guy, all with slightly varying pieces of information about him. What I've done is to bring all those different pieces of data together to form one composite image that is better quality than any of the individual frames. This is what you get . . .'

Another click, another view. She notices Sergeant Cody leaning forward at his desk, squinting to see the differences.

'I know,' she says to him. 'It's hardly earth-shattering. But take a look here . . .'

She points to a six-inch diagonal grey line high on the sleeve, then another where the killer's hand is thrust into his pocket.

'I think those are zips,' says Grace. 'A lighter coloured material has been used for contrast where the zips are present. And if you look here too . . .' She traces her finger along the figure's neck, where the hood joins the body of the coat. 'More contrast stitching.'

Cody continues the line of thinking: 'So if we find a suspect who has a coat exactly like that . . .'

'I might be able to help you there,' says Grace.

She thumbs the remote again. The dark fuzziness is instantly replaced by the gaudy brightness and colour of a website. And in the middle of the web page is an image of a coat exactly like the one the killer was wearing – contrast stitching and all.

'I tracked it down. It's made by a company called FirmWear, and there are only half a dozen outlets for their clothes on Merseyside.'

Blunt becomes suddenly animated. She points at one of her detectives. 'Get on it. Contact the shops. Get hold of any information you can about sales of this coat.' She turns back to Grace. 'This could be really valuable information. Thank you again for—' Her expression suddenly changes. 'You're still not done, are you?'

'Not quite,' says Grace. 'If that's okay.'

She hears the muted sniggers from the audience. But she knows they're not mocking her. They are lapping this up. They are actually rooting for her.

'The mic's all yours,' says Blunt. 'Sing away.'

'Well, this is more of an announcement of work in progress, really. I've been going through some of the CCTV footage from around the cathedral. I don't think we'll get anything useful from the recordings of last night, because the conditions were too awful, but on other days the cameras have picked up some really clear pictures. Anyway, there's a heck of a lot of video, so to speed things up I've automated the search using facial-recognition techniques.'

She sees the blank look from Blunt. 'I'm not sure I . . .'

'Basically, I feed in a digital image of a face, and the software searches for it in the video files.'

'I don't see how that helps. We don't know what the killer—'

'No, but we can look for anyone who we think might be connected with this case. For example, I gave it the photo of Mary that was found in her flat.'

She turns her attention to the TV screen again. All eyes follow her lead.

The view this time is of the cathedral's main doors. It's daylight, and people are filtering out of the exit.

'There,' says Grace. The video pauses, then zooms in on the figures. A red ring appears around one of them.

'That's Mary, coming out of the cathedral last Sunday morning. She may appear in other footage too – I haven't got that far yet. The point is, I can get the software to search for anyone. If you've got a suspect, I can scan his photo and look for him in these videos. If we can use that to break his alibi, or perhaps to make a connection between him and Mary in some way . . .'

Grace allows her voice to trail away, leaving the ramifications of her work percolating through the minds of her onlookers.

It's good, solid stuff. She knows it is. But do *they* know it? Or is it all just techie mumbo-jumbo to them? Are they thinking, Yeah, this is all well and good, but it's not real police work, is it? Has all this effort been a waste?

But then DS Cody breaks the silence: 'That's pretty bloody cool.' And the nods and murmurs from everyone else in the room tell Grace that she has done it. She has made her presence felt.

Blunt says to her, 'And you did all this in one day?'

'Yes.'

Blunt turns to her squad. 'This is the kind of progress I like to see. Work with Grace. Go to her with any intel you find. You just never know what she might be able to do with it.'

End of show. The curtains come down. Grace steps out of the spotlight.

And it's as if the blood rush in her ears is a huge and enthusiastic round of applause.

11

This is lovely, Megan Webley tells herself.

Sunday night in a smart Italian restaurant with my fiancé – what could be more perfect than this? Sparkling Prosecco, sparkling conversation, sparkling eyes of the man I love – everything so damn twinkly it's like being a princess.

So why does it feel like it has all been smeared with excrement?

You want to know why? I'll tell you why. It's because of an arsehole called Nathan Cody. The man who seems determined to disrupt my life, to the extent that I'd be overjoyed if he disappeared from it for ever.

'More wine?'

She finds a smile for Parker, because he deserves nothing less. Nods at him to refill her glass. She's in the mood for getting hammered tonight. Feels like getting pissed and then giving Cody a piece of her mind.

Except that Cody's not here. He's not here physically and he shouldn't be here in your mind either. Forget about that no-mark. Concentrate on enjoying yourself.

'Busy at the hotel today?' she asks.

Parker is a hotel manager. She doesn't really know what that involves, but she does know it can be stressful at times.

'Not too bad. Had a weird woman in last night, though. She wanted one of the staff to come into her room and read a bedtime story to her.'

Webley laughs. 'Is that all she wanted?'

'I don't know. I got to the end of the first chapter of a *Paddington Bear* book and then I fell asleep.'

She laughs again. She likes Parker's sense of humour. An ability to put a smile on her face comes high on her list of desirable attributes in a man. Cody could do with some lessons in that regard. She doesn't know what effect he's hoping to achieve with his bizarre behaviour, but it's certainly not tickling her funny bone.

'Anyway,' says Parker, 'what's more important is how your day went. First day back, and all.'

She goes to sip her wine. Decides on a long swig instead.

'Yeah, it was okay,' she says.

'Just okay? I thought you were really looking forward to it.'

'I was. I just . . . Never mind. I think I expected too much.'

'They didn't make a fuss of you?'

'It's not that. I got a great reception. Everyone was really pleased to see me.'

Everyone except Cody, that is.

'Okay. So . . . What's the problem?'

'Nothing. It . . . If you must know, it's Cody.'

'Oh. Him.'

She expects this from Parker. The two don't even know each other, but what Parker does know is that Cody used to be her boyfriend. He also knows that she tried to help Cody through his problems, and he made it all too clear at the time that he wasn't happy about it.

'Yes,' she says. 'Him.'

'What's he doing now? Does he keep asking you to tie his shoelaces for him? Drive him to the zoo?'

This is the less funny side of Parker. He exhibits a cruel streak sometimes.

'He's not a bloody inmate. I told you, he's been suffering from some kind of stress disorder. He went through a lot.'

'You've been through a lot too, and you're not a basket case. Or are you about to tell me you've boiled my pet rabbit?'

'You don't have a pet rabbit.'

Parker pretends he's about to burst into tears. 'Is this how you break it to me? All these years with little Fluffy, and you—'

'Stop it, you idiot. Anyway, let's change the subject. I don't want to talk about work.'

'That's fine. What would you like for Christmas?'

This takes her by surprise. Parker seems far too keen to go along with her idea of dropping the subject of Cody.

'What?'

'Christmas. When people give each other presents. What would you like?'

'I . . . I don't know. I haven't thought about it.'

'Then you'd better get your skates on. I'd like a new watch, if you're asking.'

'A new watch? Er, right. Okay.'

She glances at the one he's wearing. Parker has expensive tastes.

'I'll put some money towards it,' he says, as though reading her mind.

This annoys her, and she knows it shouldn't. He's trying to be helpful, practical, and she's taking it as though it's an insult.

I can't help it if I'm on an average wage, she thinks. And I don't have rich parents, either. I'm doing the best I can with what I have. And if that's not—

No. It's not about that, is it? You're still thinking about Cody. That's what's got your back up.

'Arsehole,' she says.

Parker splutters into his wine glass. 'What? Charming!'

'Sorry. Not you. Cody. He's acting like a complete arsehole.'

'I thought you didn't want to talk about work?'

'This isn't about work. It's about a person I work with, which isn't the same thing.'

'So he's being an arsehole. Can't you just stay out of his way?'

'No. No, I can't. He sits a few feet away from me. We work on the same cases together. We drive around in the same car together. Plus, he's my sergeant. He can tell me what to do. I can't just ignore him.'

Parker leans forward in his chair. Takes her hand in his. 'What, exactly, is he doing? Is it something you need to report to his superiors? If he's doing something which is inappropriate . . .'

She thinks about this. Yes, what exactly is Cody doing? Is he really being an arsehole, or is he just trying to keep their relationship on an even, professional footing? Why should she expect him to act differently? What more does she want from him?

More importantly, why hasn't she told the full truth of it to Parker?

She remembers the moment vividly. On that cold, grey roof. Cody offering himself as hostage in exchange for her. His life for hers.

Nobody has ever done that for her before. It's not Parker's fault, of course. That would be ridiculous. How many times do you find yourself caught up in a life-threatening situation anyway?

But it's not quite what she told Parker. She told him that the exchange was the hostage-taker's decision – that it was out of Cody's hands. Seemed preferable, somehow. Safer, for all concerned.

But it doesn't seem right that she's withholding it from him. They are engaged. They are going to be married one day. And already she is deceiving him.

What does that say about their relationship? What does it say about her?

'It's nothing inappropriate,' she says. 'Don't worry about it. I'm sure it will all work out.'

She clutches his hand tightly. Smiles reassuringly.

'Tell me what kind of watch you'd like.'

12

Cody spends a long time staring at the phone in his hand. He has the contacts open at 'Devon'. Which is not Devon the place – he tends not to put entire counties in his phone book – but Devon the person. More specifically, Devon the woman who used to be his fiancée.

Of course, that was before he tried to kill her.

Well, he didn't exactly try to kill her, Your Honour: he wasn't responsible for his actions at the time. He woke up in the middle of the night and put his hands around her throat. Thought she was a clown, you see. No, he doesn't make a habit of assassinating such makers of mirth and merriment, but this particular clown . . . well, it's a long story.

He doesn't blame Devon for deciding to call it a day after that episode, which was the culmination of a long period of erratic behaviour on Cody's part. She wanted him to do something about his illness – the 'something' meaning seeking psychiatric help. Knowing that such an act would lead to a change in his police duties – probably flying a desk in a dusty back room somewhere – he rejected her ultimatum. After that their relationship was doomed.

He misses her terribly.

What makes it worse is that Christmas is drawing near. He would like to buy her a present. He would like to take her to see a Christmas movie. He would like to go shopping with her. He would like to decorate a tree with her while they eat mince pies and listen to carols. That's what they do together at this time of year. Removing all that just isn't right.

It's not as if he has a half-decent alternative. Enjoying the festivities with his family is out of the question. He'd be lucky to get through the front door, let alone get a sniff of the turkey. His dad somehow forgets the true meaning of Christmas when it comes to Cody. Cody's brother, meanwhile – the one who makes his money from activities the legality of which Cody can only guess at – will enjoy pride of place at the table. Funny how that works.

So it's starting to look like Christmas on his own, then. That'll be fun. At least he'll be sure of getting the gift when he pulls a cracker with himself. Yup, there's always a silver lining.

He doesn't want to spend Christmas by himself. Doesn't want to exploit the charitable nature of others, either. Footlong, for example, would be more than happy to invite him over for Christmas dinner. But Cody isn't going to tell him about his predicament.

He continues staring at the name on his phone. Wonders what he could say to her. He's not planning to suggest they spend a lot of time together. Doesn't even have to be on Christmas Day, although that would be nice. He would just like to see her for a few precious hours. Exchange gifts, have a glass of wine or a cup of tea. Something, damn it, to take away this dread of being alone and miserable. Something to convince him that Christmas really does bring 'Joy to the World'.

But she's not going to agree to that. She has made it plain that she doesn't want to spend time with him unless he does something about getting his head back into shape.

And yet that *is* happening, isn't it? Not through his own doings, admittedly, but still . . .

He contemplates telling her about the phone calls. Telling her about his inkling that this is the start of something big. Of something that could be the solution to all his problems.

But she won't fall for that, either. Why should she? It sounds bloody stupid. He can't even rationalise it to himself. All he knows is how much more in touch with the world these phone calls have made him feel, but he can't explain why.

Besides, he's not convinced he wants to let anybody else know about the calls. Unscientific it may be, but he has the uneasy feeling that talking about them will jinx them. They'll just stop, permanently, and when his mind accepts the truth of that, it will step back off the minimal safety ledge holding it above the quagmire of insanity.

And then Cody decides he's thinking about this too much. Analysing it too deeply.

Go ahead. Call her. You were engaged to the girl. She knows you better than anyone else in the world. She'll understand how to talk to you, even though you don't know what to say. Above all, you still love her. Isn't that reason enough to just press the frigging call button?

He presses the call button.

He hears the ringtone. Feels his pulse racing. Don't fuck this up, he thinks.

The ringtone goes on for ever.

And then he hears a click, and he is almost on the verge of babbling like a teenager on his first date, and he hears a voice saying hello.

But it is not Devon's voice.

It is the pre-recorded message of the answering service.

He loses his nerve then. Ends the call without uttering a word. He doesn't want to deliver a monologue to empty space. He needs to know she's there while he talks. Needs to know how his message is being received and interpreted as he delivers it, so he can mould it if necessary, tailor it to her mood.

Crap. He really doesn't want to go through this angst again, just to make a stupid phone call that will probably do nothing but depress him. Where is she at this time of night anyway? Not that it's any of his business what she does with her time. Maybe she took one look at the caller ID and decided she didn't want the hassle of dealing with him. Not the most welcome of thoughts, but better than thinking she's out on the town with another guy.

Sod this, he thinks. I should go to bed. Another busy day tomorrow. Another day of dealing with the other woman complicating my life.

He gets up from the sofa. Wanders over to one of the huge windows. Much of the snow outside has gone, but it's still piled up on his windowsill and on roofs across the street and on the edges of the pavements below. It has turned to that hard, icy snow, rather than the soft, fluffy stuff. Makes him shiver just to look at it. And these original, single-glazed sash windows don't help matters. He can hear the frames rattling slightly, the wind whistling through them. He can feel the faint draught on his cheek. Yes, definitely time for snuggling up under a thick duvet.

The phone rings.

Devon, he thinks. She has checked her phone. Seen that she has a missed call. She wants to talk.

He bounds across the room. Finds the phone where he left it on the sofa. He grabs it and answers the call before she changes her mind.

'Devon?'

Silence.

And then he realises. It's his mysterious caller again.

What does he get out of this? What is he hoping to achieve?

'Talk to me,' says Cody.

He expects nothing. He has tried initiating conversation on numerous occasions, but it never works.

'Come on,' he says. 'Talk to me. Tell me what's on your mind. Tell me about . . . tell me about the clowns.'

He has never asked this before. Never been so specific about the events of the worst day of his life. He's not even sure why he's bringing it up now. But somehow it seems appropriate. The time seems right.

And then he hears it.

The music.

It's tinny. Mechanical. As though from an old-fashioned musical box or a wind-up toy.

Half a pound of tuppenny rice, Half a pound of treacle . . .

Cody hears the words in his head as the tune continues.

That's the way the money goes, Pop! goes the weasel.

And then it starts from the beginning again. Slightly faster now.

Half a pound of tuppenny rice . . .

Cody hears it through to the end. Listens to it play again, and again. Each time faster than the last, until it sounds as though the toy could break or burst into flames with the abuse.

The halt is abrupt, the ensuing silence more pronounced after that cacophony.

But the caller hasn't quite finished yet.

A voice. For the first time in these calls, a voice that is not Cody's own. He doesn't know whether it is talking in real time, or if it's recorded, or if it has been generated by a computer, or disguised by some electronic device, or even if it belongs to the caller. But at least it's a voice.

It has a sing-song quality to it, but disturbing rather than cheerful. The voice of Jack Nicholson saying 'Here's Johnny' in *The Shining*. Or the voice of the Child Catcher in *Chitty Chitty Bang Bang*. A voice to bring the frost into the very heart of this old room and chill Cody's bones.

He will hear this voice in his head for a long time. More than that, he will hear the words. He will study them, turn them upside down and back to front for their meaning. Wonder what terrors they promise for him, but also what understanding they might presage.

Four simple words that act as a door into a whole new world of the unknown:

'Nearly time to play.'

13

The name of the headmistress is Corinne Laplace, which to Cody sounds as though it should belong to a movie star. He wonders if her husband is French. Wonders, too, how many times people read her name and pronounce it like the two English words 'lap lace'.

She is tall and slim and refined. Cody imagines that she puts her little finger out when she drinks tea. He thinks she is probably one of those people who is older than she looks. He guesses at fifty, but she could pass for forty. Her accent is neutral, her vocabulary extensive.

Next to her sits the deputy head. Tony Beamish. Mid-thirties. Smart suit and neatly cropped beard. Traces of a Scouse accent that he tries to suppress. Acts as though he thinks he's on the same level as Mrs Laplace, but doesn't quite have the *savoir faire* to pull it off.

They are in the head's office. It's early in the morning – before the bell for school assembly. Makes no difference to Cody: he wasn't getting any sleep anyway. He's not sure whether he'll ever manage to sleep again after that phone call.

'This is awful,' says Mrs Laplace.

'Terrible,' says Beamish. 'Dreadful.'

'Mary was so kind. So gentle.'

'A wonderful woman.'

'Why would anyone want to hurt her?'

'Doesn't make sense.'

Cody believes that Mrs Laplace is genuinely upset. His opinion of Beamish, on the other hand, is that he is going through the motions, more concerned with pleasing his boss than expressing his own thoughts.

'That's exactly what we need to find out,' says Blunt. 'And since the school was obviously a key part of her life, I'm sure you can understand why we need to talk to everyone here.'

'Yes, of course,' says Mrs Laplace.

'Naturally,' says Beamish.

'But I would hope,' says Mrs Laplace, 'that we can conduct this in a way that isn't going to traumatise any of the girls in the school. Some of them are already quite upset by the news of Mary's death.'

'We have to put the welfare of the students first,' says Beamish.

'Absolutely,' says Blunt. 'Our aim is not to shock anyone. I don't intend to go into detail about the murder, and I'm certainly not going to describe the crime scene. You have my word on that.'

Mrs Laplace nods, apparently satisfied. Catching sight of her gesture of approval, Beamish nods too.

'Tell me about Mary,' says Blunt. 'Was she a good teacher?'

'Yes,' says Mrs Laplace. 'Very good. She came to us from Abbotsleigh Primary, with outstanding letters of recommendation. She could be quite strict with the girls, but I think they respected her for that.'

'How strict? Strict enough to make someone hate her?'

Mrs Laplace blinks in surprise. 'Surely you are not suggesting—?'

'I'm not suggesting anything at the moment. These are questions I have to ask. If a pupil bore a grudge, perhaps, or a girl's parents . . .'

'No, I don't think there was anything like that. I never received a single formal complaint against Mary. She was firm but fair. Everyone, the students included, knew that and accepted it.'

'All right. No formal complaints. But what about informally? Any rumours that someone might have threatened Mary, or wanted to hurt her?'

Cody can see that Mrs Laplace is starting to become irritated by this line of questioning.

She says, 'I don't know what kind of school you think we run here. This isn't St Trinian's. Our girls don't walk around with flick knives and betting slips.'

'They're good students,' says Beamish. 'Like any school, Oakdale has its difficult cases, but I think we'd know if we had any murderers in our classrooms.'

Which is just the problem, thinks Cody. People have this idea that murderers are easy to spot in a crowd, when often it's the least likely ones who go on to kill.

'So, as far as you know,' says Blunt, 'Mary had no enemies. She never fell out with anyone? Never had any arguments with another member of staff?'

'Hard though it might be to believe,' says Mrs Laplace, 'I can honestly say that the answer is no. Mary did not get into fights of any kind. And again, I hope you're not thinking that one of our staff may have had anything to do with this.'

Cody knows that his boss is thinking along precisely those lines. At least, she is not ruling out the possibility. There is a fundamental ABC of police detective work: Assume nothing, Believe nobody, Challenge everything. Until such time as every staff member in this school can be ruled out, they are all potential suspects.

Says Blunt, 'I'm just trying to build a picture of Mary and the life she led. What nearly everyone seems to be telling us is that she was in line for a sainthood. And yet somebody hated her with a passion. I promised I wouldn't go into detail, but believe me, what was done to her could not have been more vicious. Now why would that be? How do those things fit together? If we are to have any hope of catching her killer, we need to answer those questions.'

Cody sees the discomfort in the headmistress. She shifts uneasily in her seat. Her hand toys with her necklace. Cody guesses her mind is conjuring up images of a beaten and battered Mary, and trying to come to terms with that.

'I-I'm sorry,' she says. 'I hadn't realised it was as . . . as violent as that. I thought . . . Well, I don't know what I thought. But this . . . It makes it worse somehow.'

'Murder is never easy to deal with,' says Blunt. 'It's the ultimate act of aggression. That's why we take it so seriously.'

'Yes. Yes, I can see that. Please, ask us whatever you need to.'

'Anything at all,' says Beamish, causing Cody to think about throwing a cloth over this parrot of a man.

'All right,' says Blunt. 'Then tell us about Mary's personal life. What did she get up to in her spare time? Did she have any friends?'

Mrs Laplace looks at Beamish, who shrugs, then back at the detectives.

'To be perfectly honest, I don't think any of us knew her well enough to comment on that. Mary was dedicated to the school. She was always one of the first in, and usually the last to leave. As the head, I work pretty long hours myself, but Mary could put me to shame.'

'And outside of school?'

'I don't really know. She was very religious, and I think she devoted a lot of time to that. I understand she did a lot of work for charity, too, especially the RSPCA. She got involved in various fundraising events . . .'

'What about friends?'

Mrs Laplace thinks about this one, then shakes her head. 'I can't say I ever met any. Not that I can remember, anyway.'

'Were *you* her friend?'

'Me? Well, I . . . I wouldn't say *friend*, exactly. A colleague, certainly. And we had many chats together, but I don't know whether—'

'Ever see her outside school?'

'Well . . . We never met up to socialise or anything, if that's what you mean.'

'I'm not sure what *you* mean. Did you see her outside school or not?'

'No. Yes. I took her home sometimes. She didn't drive. Relied on public transport. Occasionally, when she worked late and left the building at the same time as me, I would offer her a lift back to her flat.'

'How often was that?'

'Not very. As I say, it was occasional. Is it important?'

'Did you ever go into the flat with her?'

'Yes. Sometimes I'd have a quick cup of tea. I'm sorry, but is this really—?'

'But you wouldn't class her as a friend?'

'No. We had very little in common. I don't think we discussed anything other than work.'

Cody finds it interesting that Mrs Laplace seems extraordinarily keen to distance herself from Mary. He wonders whether Beamish is going to ape her in that regard too.

He decides to test it out.

'And you, Mr Beamish,' he says. 'How would you class your relationship with her?'

Beamish seems a little thrown by the question. 'What? How do you mean?'

'Well, did you think of her as a friend?'

'We . . . we were friendly enough to each other on school premises, if that's what you're getting at. But nothing beyond that.'

'Ever go into her flat?'

'Good God, no.'

Beamish sees the raised eyebrows before him and adds a hasty follow-up: 'I mean, we weren't as close as that. We had totally different interests, different outlooks on life. There was never any reason for our private lives to overlap.'

'What about the other male teachers here?'

Beamish gives him a mystified look.

Cody says, 'One of Mary's neighbours told us that she occasionally had a male visitor. We were wondering if it might be someone she worked with. Do you know of anyone it might have been?'

Beamish and Mrs Laplace exchange glances, and it's not clear to Cody that he's going to be supplied with an answer.

But then Beamish says, 'Possibly Andy. Andy Puckleton. He's one of our maths teachers. As far as our staff go, I'd say he was the closest to Mary.'

'Close in what way? Romantically?'

A snort from Beamish. 'I doubt it. I don't think either of them could have—' He stops himself, then, as though realising he was about to make an inappropriate joke. 'What I mean is, I think their mutual interests went beyond the physical.' He casts his gaze upwards towards the heavens.

Cody finds himself looking that way himself. He doesn't expect to find any answers there.

No divine revelations are inscribed on the ceiling of the assembly hall either.

As a pupil, Cody never could concentrate during school assembly, and this one is little different, despite the seriousness of the subject matter being discussed.

Mrs Laplace controls the proceedings. She stands at the front of the stage, while Cody sits behind her, alongside Blunt. Webley and the other detectives have already begun interviewing members of staff.

The hall is huge, with additional seating in a gallery at the rear, but even so it has been difficult to cram every pupil into it. They sit listening in rapt attention, some of them already visibly distressed. Mrs Laplace begins by confirming what the girls already know, and doing her best to scotch any rumours based on what they don't know. She moves on to deliver a short eulogy for Mary Cowper, during which some of the girls become even more upset.

It's at this point that Cody's attention starts to drift. He has a different voice in his head. The voice from last night.

Nearly time to play.

What the hell does that even mean?

Play what?

And what was meant by 'nearly'?

There was no way Cody was going to be able to sleep after that. 'Nearly' could have meant in the next few minutes, or even seconds. How could anyone relax knowing that some momentous event, foretold by a faceless and ominous caller, was imminent?

He tried telling himself that 'nearly' could also be measured in hours, days or even weeks. It's all relative. Didn't help him sleep, though.

The announcement wasn't setting up a fixture for a game of chess or football or tiddlywinks. It was something far more sinister – of that Cody is certain. And that's making him edgy. All morning he has felt as though he needs to be constantly checking over his shoulder. He has looked at everyone he has spoken to today in a different light, wondering if they might have something to do with this game into which he has been dragged.

Mrs Laplace sits down. Blunt gets up. She introduces herself and Cody to the pupils. Tells them in plain and measured terms what she and her team of detectives are doing here today. Assures the girls that there is no need to be afraid. Invites them to come forward if they feel they know anything – anything at all – that might be relevant.

Cody hears only a fraction of her actual words. Important though this case is, he wants to be elsewhere. He wants to be at home, waiting by his phone. Waiting for it to ring. Waiting for the information he craves.

He knows this was the same caller as before. The one who sent him each and every eerie silence. And the one who broke that silence with the sound of Cody's own blood-curdling screams.

It has to be the same person. And he will call again, with more pieces of the puzzle, more rules of the game.

Cody knows he cannot refuse to play.

More worrying is the realisation that he cannot afford to lose.

14

Webley resents everything this morning. Resents the fact that she had to get into work so early. Resents the fact that she did so after getting so little sleep. Resents the fact that Cody is occupying so much of her mind at the moment. And, to top it all, resents the fact that she seems to be getting the shitty end of the stick when it comes to the interviewing allocation.

She wasn't fair to Parker last night. It wasn't right to keep going on about Cody like that. But, at the same time, she needed to get it off her chest. Parker does the same when something has bothered him at work. We all do it.

He seemed okay with it, bless him. Didn't lose his temper. Didn't yell at her to stop going on about her bloody ex-boyfriend. He could easily have twisted things that way. Made it into something it wasn't.

And it certainly wasn't. About Cody being an ex-boyfriend. It was about Cody being an arsehole of a police sergeant, and that's different. That's just a moan about a work colleague. We all do that.

Cody looks different this morning.

She's finding it hard to be so angry with him, and she wonders why that is. It's almost as though there is something worrying Cody. Something of immense importance to him.

But why should I care? she thinks. I've tried caring about him before, and look where it got me. If something is bothering him, he can sort it out himself. He's a grown man, for God's sake. And if it's about his mental problems, he can seek professional help. I don't want to hear his confessions. I don't want to jeopardise what I have with Parker, thank you very much.

And anyway, why does he get the cushy number this morning? Why does he get to sit in a warm, comfy office with a teacher, while I'm stuck in a poky little workshop with the lowest of the low?

She looks at the caretaker's assistant seated across the table from her. Jamie Morgan seems barely old enough to have left school himself. His navy-blue overalls look several sizes too big for him. Two pencils protrude from the breast pocket, and Webley thinks she can also see the outline of a cigarette packet there.

She glances at the electric heater which seems to kick out more light than heat, then she sighs and begins her questioning.

'You work here as a caretaker's assistant, is that right, Jamie?'

'Yeah.' He smiles, as though pleased to get off the starting blocks without stumbling.

'Who do you assist?' As she asks this, she wonders if it should be 'whom', but reckons that Jamie is unlikely to pick up on it. Cody would know, of course, smartarse that he is.

'Well, everyone, I suppose. The whole school.'

'No, I mean who's your boss?'

'Oh. You mean Colin. Colin Daley.'

'Yes. Mr Daley. He's the one who tells you what to do?'

'Er, yeah.'

'And what sort of things would they be?'

'Er, well . . .'

It seems to Webley that she is demanding too much of Jamie's mental faculties, so she decides to make it simpler for him.

'Take today, for example. Has Mr Daley already given you a list of things to do?

'No. No, he hasn't.'

'But I assume he will do at some point later in the day?'

'Er, I'm not sure . . . exactly.'

It suddenly hits Webley that Jamie might not be as stupid as he makes out, and that there is another possible reason for his difficulty in being forthcoming.

'Jamie, do you mind if we just get one thing straight from the start? I'm not trying to trip you up or anything. You're not in any trouble. I just want honest answers to perfectly reasonable questions. Okay?'

He seems to relax a little. 'Okay.'

'Right. So at the moment you're not sure what jobs you'll be doing today, and the reason for that is . . .'

'He's away. Col, I mean. He's off sick today.'

'I see. How do you know that?'

'What?'

On the other hand, thinks Webley, maybe he really is thick. She says, 'That he's off ill. Did Mrs Laplace tell you?'

'No. Col called me direct.'

'When?'

'First thing this morning. He said he felt awful, and that he wouldn't make it in today.'

'What's wrong with him?'

'He didn't say. Just that he felt bad.'

'Does he often call in sick at the last minute like that?'

'No. Not often.'

'Okay. So today you're running the show by yourself, is that right?'

'Yeah. But . . .'

Webley gives him a second or two, but Jamie seems to have run out of steam.

'Go on.'

Jamie flinches, as though he has just been poked with a sharp stick. 'Well, Col doesn't like me doing anything without him being there to supervise.'

'Why's that?'

'Health and safety, mostly. Gotta know what you're doing. Even in a school it's surprising how easy it is to end up dead if you're not careful.'

Webley can't stop her eyebrows jumping up in surprise. She studies Jamie's face carefully for signs of irony, but it seems as though he really isn't aware of what he's just said.

'What's it like working here, Jamie? Do you like it?'

He shrugs. 'S'okay.'

'Is it a bit weird being in an all-girls school? All those female hormones floating around?'

'That's true enough. I can't get my head around it sometimes.'

'Get your head around what?'

'Just the way they are with each other. They can be right bitches sometimes.'

'Really? In what way?'

'Like, if a couple of lads fall out with each other, they have a punch-up and then they're the best of mates again. Doesn't happen like that with girls. It can drag on for ever. They start spreading nasty rumours. They post things on the Internet. They try to turn friends against each other. It's psychological warfare here sometimes.'

'They talk to you, then? The girls, I mean. They talk to you about their problems?'

'Well . . . not really. Some of them do. But I've got eyes and ears, haven't I? I can see what's going on. Because I'm not a teacher, they don't care what they say when I'm around. They don't need to cover it up.'

'So you hear things they wouldn't say to a teacher?'

'Sometimes.'

'Do they ever say anything *about* the teachers?'

'Too right they do. Some of them use language I've never even heard before.'

He laughs at that, although Webley suspects that Jamie is not so easily shocked.

'Like what? What kind of things do they say?'

'Just . . . swear words. You know. Insults.'

'About who? The head?' Again, Webley questions whether it should be 'whom' here. And again, it irritates her that know-it-all Cody springs to mind.

'Any of them. Especially the strict ones. The ones who give detention or shout in class.'

It has been a bit of a meander, but Webley gets to her point. 'What about Mary Cowper? Ever hear any of the girls say anything about her?'

Jamie hesitates. 'Miss Cowper? No. Can't say I have.'

'Are you certain about that? I've heard she could be quite strict.'

'I don't think it was the same. From what I heard, the girls had more respect for her. I don't think any of them would have wanted anything bad to happen to her.'

'And you?'

'What about me?'

'What did you think about Mary?'

'She was all right.'

'All right in what way? Did you like her?'

'I could take her or leave her.'

'She wasn't a friend, then?'

'I wouldn't call her that.'

'Ever ask her out?'

Webley isn't sure what caused that question to jump from her lips, but she's pleased with it. Sometimes it's useful to deliver a curve ball, simply to assess reactions.

Jamie blinks, laughs. 'Are you serious?'

Webley keeps her own face impassive. 'Why wouldn't I be?'

Jamie straightens up in indignation. 'Why the hell would I be getting together with Mary Cowper? She was old enough to be my mother.'

'It's not so ridiculous. She was a good-looking woman. Ever see *The Graduate*?'

'No. What's that?'

Webley sighs inwardly. 'Never mind. So you never met Mary Cowper after school?'

'No. Absolutely not. She's not – *wasn't* – my type.'

'Never went to her flat?'

Jamie's voice steps up an octave. 'I don't even know where she lived. I had zero interest in the woman. I hardly talked to her in school, never mind outside it.'

And then Webley decides it's time for another tricky throw of the ball. She hasn't forgotten the difficulties Jamie seemed to experience in the early part of the interview; now, while Jamie is becoming increasingly agitated, seems a good time to capitalise on that.

'What about Colin?'

The sudden shift has the desired effect on Jamie, who appears slightly stunned. 'What?'

'Colin Daley. Your boss. How did he get on with Mary?'

'How d'you mean?'

'Well, did he like her? Hate her? Did he complain about her?'

'He never spoke about her.'

'What, in all the time you've worked here, Mr Daley has never once mentioned Mary Cowper?'

'No,' says Jamie. But then he seems to realise how absurd an answer it is. 'Well, yeah, of course he *mentioned* her. But only when it was about doing jobs for her.'

'Jobs?'

Jamie waves a hand to indicate the workshop. 'Work. The stuff we're paid to do.'

'Can you be more precise?'

'I dunno. The usual. Move furniture. Change lightbulbs. Fix the heating. That kind of thing.'

'Nothing out of the ordinary?'

'Like what?

'Get her car started?'

'She didn't drive.'

'Go round to her flat and change a lock or fit a door?

'Not as far as I know. Anyway, why are you asking me so many questions about Col?'

Because you're hiding something, thinks Webley. And you're not clever enough to keep it hidden.

'You'd rather I didn't?' she asks.

'I'd prefer it if you asked him yourself.'

'He'll tell me the same, though, won't he?'

'What do you mean?'

'What you just said about him having no interest in Mary Cowper. He'll confirm that, won't he?'

'I didn't say . . . Look, I was just giving my opinion, okay? I don't know enough about him or Mary to say anything for definite.'

No, thinks Webley. But you know something, don't you, matey?

You know something.

15

Cody is glad they have been split up. Much though he likes Webley, he can do without her quizzical looks and burning glares at the moment. The others have picked up on the tension between them – he's sure of it. Perhaps not Blunt, though. If she had, she would probably have paired them together on this interview just for the perverse satisfaction it would give her. She has a habit of throwing little tests of emotional stability his way whenever she has the opportunity.

He is seated in a tiny office used to advise pupils when they need to discuss things in private. Opposite him, Andy Puckleton looks to be only in his early twenties. He is thin, with pronounced cheekbones and dark curly hair.

Cody sends Puckleton a welcoming smile. The man looks as though he needs it. He keeps fidgeting nervously. He adjusts his tie, his cuffs, his watch strap. He smooths his hair, tugs on his earlobe, rubs his tongue over his teeth.

Cody wonders if he is always as anxious as this, or if there is something in particular that's bothering him.

So he begins his questioning.

'Mr Puckleton, isn't it? Mind if I call you Andy?'

'Yes. I mean no. I don't mind. Andy's fine.'

'Okay, Andy. So you're a maths teacher?'

'Yes.'

'I was never much good at maths. English was my forte, if it's okay to mix my languages like that.'

'Mix your . . . Oh. Yes. I see what you mean.'

This is going to be hard work, thinks Cody.

'Have you been at the school long, Andy?'

'No. Just over two years.'

'And this is your first real teaching job?'

'Yes. In at the deep end.'

Puckleton offers a smile, but now Cody is less inclined to keep things light.

'The deep end? Is it that bad here?'

Puckleton recoils at the serious way in which his interrogator has responded. 'No. I didn't mean . . . It's just a figure of speech. Some schools are much worse than this.'

And now Cody returns a smile. A bat-and-ball approach. Keep the interviewee confused about your real thoughts and intentions.

He says, 'I know. You couldn't get through a day at my school without someone breaking someone else's arm, or mugging them for their lunch money – and that was just the teachers! I suppose it helps being an all-girls' school. Or does that make it more difficult?'

'Difficult? In what way?' Puckleton seems genuinely mystified.

'You tell me. I've never worked in a girls' school. I imagine it brings its own challenges, no?'

Puckleton thinks about it. 'Well, yes, I guess so. Emotions can run high sometimes.'

'Among the staff, too?'

Puckleton's mouth opens and closes a couple of times. 'I'm sorry, I'm not sure what—'

'I'm simply asking if things ever get emotional among the staff here. Arguments, perhaps? Affairs?'

'I . . . I wouldn't know about that.'

'Hmm,' says Cody. He writes in his notebook. A meaningless squiggle, but Puckleton won't know that. 'Tell me about Mary.'

'What would you like to know?'

'Was she a nice person?'

'Yes. Yes, I'd say so.'

'Maybe more than that? A lovely person?'

'I . . . She was a *good* person. I think that's the best way to describe her.'

'Good?'

'Yes.'

'But not lovely?'

Puckleton pulls at one of his sideburns. 'Look, I'm not sure what you're getting at.'

'Did you know her well?'

'Not really.'

'You wouldn't call her a friend, then?'

'She was a . . . a *colleague*.'

Cody sends Puckleton a discomfiting stare. It is starting to irk him that everyone in this bloody place seems to want to distance themselves from Mary. *Great teacher?* Absolutely. *Highly moral?* Of course. *Close friend?* On your bike.

It also irks him that nobody appears willing to break ranks regarding how nice Mary was. Nobody, that is, except her own mother. Could that be just because the old woman is undoubtedly doolally? Or is she really the only person aware of just how dark Mary's heart was?

But then again, why is it that nobody else seems to have become aware of Mary's sinister side in the seventeen years since her mother spotted it?

He says, 'So, then, you never spent any time with Mary outside of school?'

Puckleton looks appalled by the suggestion. 'No. Never. We didn't have that kind of a . . . I have a girlfriend.'

To Cody, the reaction seems defensive and exaggerated. Why not simply reply with a calm 'no'?

'A girlfriend?'

'Yes. Laura. She's a secretary.'

'Here? In this school?'

'Yes. We've been going out for almost a year.'

'I see. But that wasn't my question, Andy. I asked if you ever spent any time with Mary outside of school.'

'I . . . I'm sorry, I thought you meant—'

'So did you?'

'No.'

'You didn't socialise at all?'

'No.'

'Never went for a drink after work, or call at her flat?'

'Never, no. I don't think I even know where she lived.'

Cody nods. Puts another couple of squiggles in his notebook. Out of the corner of his eye he sees Puckleton poke a finger into his collar, as if to allow a build-up of steam to escape.

Cody scratches his chin. Tries to emulate the ragged detective Columbo when he is about to catch a suspect in a lie.

'See, Andy, there's something I don't quite get here.'

Puckleton purses his lips. 'What's that?'

'Well, one of the other members of staff told us that you and Mary were quite close, and that you knew her better than anyone else.'

'No. That's not right. I have a girlfriend.'

'Yes, so you said. But, with all due respect, you've misinterpreted my words again. It's perfectly possible to have a friend who is female and is not your girlfriend.'

Just look at me and Webley, he thinks.

'I see what you mean,' says Puckleton. 'Well, I suppose it's true that I chatted with her more than most.'

'What did you talk about?'

'All kinds of things. We had similar interests. History, religion . . .'

'Are you religious, Andy?'

'Yes. Is that such a bad thing?'

'Not at all. But these discussions were all in the grounds of the school, is that what you're saying?'

'Yes.'

'Never in Mary's flat?'

'No. I've already said—'

Cody decides it's time to take off the gloves. 'All right, Andy. Just to keep you in the picture, what we'll do at some point is to take fingerprints and DNA samples from you. Then—'

'What? Why?'

'To rule you out. There's a lot of forensic evidence in Mary's flat. We need to confirm that none of it belongs to you. We'll probably also take some recordings of your voice. One of Mary's neighbours heard someone talking to her, so again we need to make sure it couldn't possibly have been you.'

Puckleton's eyes are darting now, as though he's looking for a way out of this room that he seems to find so stifling.

Says Cody, 'That's all right, isn't it, Andy?'

'Look,' says Puckleton finally. 'Supposing I did go to Mary's flat?'

That's better, thinks Cody. 'Are you saying you did?'

'I . . . yes. Occasionally.'

'How occasionally?'

'Not very often at first. Lately it's been once, maybe twice a week.'

'Twice a week? That's quite a lot.'

'Do you think?'

'Don't you? Twice a week. I'd say that was quite a lot. How long did you stay each time?'

'About an hour. No more than that.'

'I see. And what did you do in that hour?'

'Nothing.'

'Nothing? You visited Mary Cowper in her flat, twice a week for an hour, and you did nothing?'

'I mean, nothing . . . sordid. I have a girlfriend.'

Change the record, thinks Cody. 'So what was it you did?'

'We talked.'

'What about?'

'All kinds of things. Like I said, we had a lot in common.'

'I see. And what did your girlfriend think about your visits to Mary's flat?'

Puckleton's gaze drops to the floor. 'She ... she had no opinion on the matter.'

'You didn't tell her, did you?'

'No.'

'Why not? Why didn't you tell your girlfriend?'

'I, er, I didn't think it was important.'

'Not because you thought she would misunderstand?'

'Well, maybe. Perhaps she would have got the wrong end of the stick.'

'Andy?'

Puckleton raises his head again. 'Yes?'

'I'm going to be straight with you here. I don't think you're being entirely truthful with me.'

'Why? What makes you say—?'

'You visit an older woman, alone in her flat. You spend over an hour with her, twice a week, and you don't tell your girlfriend about it. And all you're doing with this woman is having a cup of tea and a casual chat about nothing of any importance. Is that really what you're asking me to believe?'

'When you put it like that . . .'

'There's no other way to put it, Andy.'

'No. I suppose not. All right.'

'All right what?'

'I'll tell you the truth.'

'I think that would be best,' says Cody. He keeps his voice level, but inside he's hoping for all kinds of juicy revelations. He's thinking, Okay, Andy, here's where you tell me about your secret love affair and how Mary threatened to expose you or blackmail you, so you bashed her head in. Go ahead, Andy. Let it all out.

'She was helping me,' says Puckleton.

Right, thinks Cody. Not exactly my definition of 'juicy'.

'Helping you how?'

'She . . . she listened to me. She understood what I was going through.'

'Which was?'

'I was having . . . doubts.'

'Doubts? About being a teacher?'

'No. I love teaching. I'm talking about my . . . my faith.'

'You mean your religion? Your belief in God?'

'Yes. I mean, I want to believe, but . . . well, I'm just not sure I can any more.'

'Why's that?'

'Nothing particular. A whole load of reasons. The state of the world. The cruel things that happen in it. Lately I've just been finding it really difficult to reconcile that with the existence of a God who loves us and cares about us.'

'And you discussed this with Mary?'

'Yes.'

'But not your girlfriend?'

'No. Actually, that's not true. I tried, but I don't think Laura really appreciated what I was going through. Religion isn't her thing.'

'So you approached Mary instead?'

'Yes. Mary is – was – very open about her Christianity, and very certain in her faith. I needed to understand where that certainty came from.'

'So all of these meetings at her flat – they were about religion? Why didn't you just tell me that up front? Why make me drag it out of you?'

Puckleton's lower lip trembles, as though he is ready to burst into tears. 'Because you wouldn't have understood. Nobody understands. You would have thought it was a ridiculous story, and that I must have had something to do with Mary's murder. And then it would have got back to Laura, and she would have thought I was doing something sordid. Nobody would be prepared to accept that this has been an extremely trying time for me. I needed to talk it over, and Mary was the only one willing to listen and give her views without being judgemental. In a way, she has been my therapist. And so I . . .'

He halts, and now there is a definite glint of wetness in his eyes.

'What?' says Cody.

'I'll really miss her.'

Cody nods slowly. He looks at the wreck of a man in front of him, devastated by grief at the death of his only confidante.

And he wonders how much of it is an act.

16

It couldn't last for ever.

Webley is surprised it lasted this long. It's Thursday now. The murder seems an age ago. For most of the week she has managed to avoid having to spend time alone with Cody. When she had to communicate with him there were always others in the vicinity. Made life much simpler. She could keep things formal. She could avoid having to concern herself with his screwed-up attitudes and bizarre behaviour.

But it's more difficult to do that right now, when it's just her and Cody, cooped up together in a tiny unmarked hatchback.

She didn't have much choice in the matter. It was an order from Blunt. 'You two,' said the DCI. 'You're making fuck-all progress here, so make yourselves useful by talking to that missing caretaker bloke. If we're going to come up empty-handed, we might as well be complete about it.'

So that's what they're doing. Ticking another box. Fulfilling another action. Proving to future scrutinisers how thorough they were in failing to find a murderer.

She is physically unable to accompany someone in complete silence, even when she is fuming. Her nature won't allow it. So she tries filling the yawning void with perfunctory conversation. Tries asking Cody if he watched *Coronation Street* last night. Tries asking him when he last had a night out. Tries telling him about the Christmas decorations in Liverpool ONE this year.

Oh, fuck it, she thinks.

'This is bloody ridiculous,' she says.

Cody, who is driving, takes his eyes from the road for a second. 'What is?'

Webley flaps her hand in the space between them. 'This! This whole situation. You and me.'

There is a long silence while she watches Cody trying and seemingly failing to grasp her meaning. Typical bloke.

He says, 'I'm not sure what—'

'We're not being ourselves, Cody. We're not being normal people. Correction – I'm not being normal, and you're not being whatever you usually are. Which, by any definition of the term, can never pass for normal.'

'I thought we were doing okay.'

'Bollocks.'

He shoots her another glance. 'I think we've been working quite well together the past few days. There haven't been any arguments, any tantrums, any—'

She stops him with a raised palm. 'Before we enter the minefield of which of us has been resorting to childish behaviour, the point is . . . Well, the point is that you're missing the point.'

'I'm glad you've made that clear.'

She takes a few seconds to gather her thoughts. To put them in some kind of rational order so that she has some chance of getting them through the thick skull of the idiot sitting next to her.

'When I started working for MIT,' she says, 'it came as a massive shock to find you were working for them too. To be honest, I thought it would all go tits up. But it didn't. We got on okay. And when you needed someone to talk to, I was kind of . . . honoured that you chose me. It was nice to know that we could still relate to each other on a personal level.'

She watches him for a reaction. Gets nothing more than steady nodding.

'But now it's different,' she continues. '*You're* different.'

'In what way?' he asks.

'I don't know. I can't put my finger on it. Did you go near any giant alien seed pods while I was in hospital?'

'Not that I recall. Are you sure it's not you who's different? Maybe all those drugs the doctors gave you scrambled your brain.'

She ignores him. 'When's the last time you wigged out? I mean properly, like you did when we worked on that last case together.'

He mulls it over. 'I haven't. I've had a couple of wobbles, but that's been it. I haven't beaten anyone up, if that's what you mean.'

'Okay, good. And what about the nightmares? Still having them?'

'Yes, Dr Freud. Afraid so.'

'As often as before?'

'No. Not as often. Not as intense either.'

She slaps him on the bicep. 'So you *have* changed! Jesus, this is like getting blood out of a stone. Now, next question. Think about this carefully. *Why* have you changed?'

He opens his mouth, and she raises her palm again. 'I said think about it carefully. Don't just blurt out the first thing that jumps into your head. You know that never ends well with you.'

Cody stares ahead for a while. Checks his mirrors. Drums his fingers on the steering wheel.

'Well,' he says. 'Maybe it's because . . .'

'Go on. And if you say "I'm a Londoner" now, I'll batter you.'

'Actually, I was about to say that maybe it's because of you.'

And now she is suddenly sorry she asked. This isn't supposed to be about her. She doesn't want it to be about her.

'Me?'

'Yes. It's like you said. You were there for me. Other than Devon, you were the first person I ever told about the problems I've been having. Getting that off my chest was massive for me. I can't tell you how much it helped.'

She wants to cry now. This is a bit of the old Cody. The honest, truthful, trustworthy Cody.

But only a bit.

'Bollocks,' she says again.

'Excuse me?'

'That's not it. There's something else. Something you're not telling me about.'

'Why do you say that?'

'Because of you not coming to see me while I was away. If talking to me is so bloody good for your health, why would you want to stay away like that? It doesn't make any sense.'

DAVID JACKSON | 125

'Wait a minute. You're talking about two different things now. We've already discussed my reasons for keeping my distance while you were sick. That has absolutely nothing to do with me having nightmares.'

Webley feels her irritation building with this man. 'First of all, you didn't really explain why you didn't come to see me. That's still a mystery to me. And secondly, if you're saying the two things aren't connected, then you must have a reason for saying that, which implies you *do* know why you've gone all weird lately.'

Cody furrows his brow and shakes his head. 'You've lost me now. This is getting far too complicated.'

'Only because you're being so bloody cryptic about everything.'

She folds her arms in indignation. Turns her head to look out of the side window, searching for distractions that will enable her to switch channels in her mind.

But her mind refuses to be drawn away from the compelling drama.

She turns back to Cody. 'When we were on top of that building . . .' she begins, not entirely convinced she wants to continue.

'Yeah?'

'What was going through your mind? I mean, what was your plan?'

Cody shrugs. 'To get everyone out of there, alive and in one piece.'

'No lies this time, Cody. The chances of that happening were minuscule, and you knew it, didn't you?'

'I . . . Somebody had to do something. Somebody had to get up there and establish a line of communication.'

'Stop talking like a cop, Cody. Speak to me like a human being. You were intending to die up there, weren't you?'

'Well, "intending" is putting it a bit strongly. I never—'

'All right. *Expecting*, then. You were expecting to die. You had no clever plan whatsoever. In fact, it was downright primitive. A straight swap. Your life for mine.'

'Megan, I . . .'

'Oh, my God. I'm right, aren't I?'

No response from Cody, but his face says it all. She has suspected it for some time, but never had the vanity to accept it as unquestionable truth – to believe that her own life could ever be considered worth more than another.

'Why?' she asks. 'Why would you do that?'

Another shrug. 'Seemed like a good idea at the time. You said it yourself – my brain doesn't always work like everyone else's.'

'And that's it? That's what you're telling me? It was just another malfunction? Just another fuse blowing in that old junction box between your ears?'

He takes his gaze off the road again. Stares searchingly into her own eyes, as if trying to gauge how much reality she can cope with. As though making up his mind, he faces forward again.

'Don't try to read too much into it, Megan. Don't try to build it up into something it wasn't. It was a knee-jerk reaction – trying to make the best of a bad situation. Luck was on our side, but it could easily have gone the other way.'

The words sting, and she knows they shouldn't. She had hoped he might say it was something much more meaningful than a 'knee-jerk reaction'. Something more profound. Something related to the important things in life – the things that matter, the things in which they share an unbreakable belief.

Perhaps even – dare she think it? – something about love.

But this is better. This makes it easier for both of them. This shakes no apples from the tree, creates no waves in the pool. Their lives can continue to run on separate rails, with no danger of future collisions.

'Fine,' she says. 'I won't ask again.'

Good one, Cody, she thinks. You gave the right answer there. Even though she doesn't believe a word of it.

17

The house is a modest terraced property close to Wavertree Playground. The playground is actually a small park, bequeathed to Liverpool Corporation at the end of the nineteenth century by a donor whose name was never revealed – hence the park's nickname of 'The Mystery', or often just 'The Mizzy'.

Cody thinks he could do without another mystery in his life right now. There are lots of things he could do without right now, not least of which being Webley here with all her intimate questioning.

Feeling on edge, Cody rings the bell, then immediately raps the doorknocker.

The door is answered by a boy of about twelve years of age. He is wearing the white shirt and charcoal trousers of his school uniform, and appears to be caught up in the whirlwind of puberty. A thin wisp of hair sits precariously above his top lip, and runs down into a beard of joined-up acne. When he speaks, he does so in a strangulated voice that wavers alarmingly in pitch.

'Whatever you're selling,' he says, 'we've already got one. Sometimes more than one.'

'Is your dad in?' says Cody.

'No,' says the lad. 'My dad's dead.'

Instantly forgetting his problems with Webley, Cody throws her a questioning glance, then pulls his notebook from his pocket and flips through its pages.

'This *is* the house of Mr Colin Daley?'

The boy is silent for a few seconds, and Cody realises that he's staring at the Merseyside Police logo on the front of the notebook.

'Who wants to know?'

Cody reaches back into his jacket to find his warrant card. 'We're from the police. I'm Detective Sergeant Cody, and this is Detective Constable Webley. We just need to have a little chat with your dad. Nothing to worry about.'

The boy chin-points at Cody's ID. 'How do I know that's real? My mate Jez has got some ID that says he's eighteen, and he's the same age as me.'

'Why would we be making it up?'

'I dunno, but neither of you look like detectives to me.'

Cody can't stop a smile creeping onto his lips. 'What do detectives look like, then?'

'Older. Fatter. Less hair. And with a better car than that tiny Corsa.'

'We'll take the first three as a compliment. I agree with you about the car, though. All they had left today, I'm afraid. If I go over to it and switch the siren on, will you believe me then?'

The lad studies Cody's face, then Webley's, then seems to reach a decision.

'Dad's in the shower.'

'Alive?'

'Yeah, judging by his singing. At the moment, he thinks he's Rihanna.'

'So why did you tell us he was dead?'

'Dad's orders. For when cold-callers turn up at the door. You know – Jehovah's Witnesses, charity workers, people trying to get you to switch energy providers. They're never sure what to do when I tell them that everyone in the house is dead except me.'

Cody smiles again. 'I'll bet. Mind if we come in while you fetch your dad?'

The boy looks uncertainly into the dark hallway. 'I suppose.' He pulls the door wide open and allows his visitors in, staring at them intently as they pass.

'In there,' he says. 'Don't sit on the cat.'

He shows them into a small living room at the front of the house. A battered and faded sofa and a matching armchair are arranged in an L-shape in front of a huge television. In the bay window a dark wooden table is strewn with paper, textbooks, pencils and a laptop. On a ledge in one alcove sits a fake Christmas tree complete with colourful flashing bulbs, while the smiling lit-up face of a plastic Santa stares down at them from above the fireplace. In the other alcove is a display cabinet, on top of which is a framed photograph of a grinning man holding up a huge ugly fish.

The middle seat of the sofa has been claimed by a large tabby cat, curled into a ball and apparently fast asleep. As Cody and Webley sit down on either side of it, the cat wakes up and takes an immediate interest in Webley, much to her apparent discomfort.

'I'll fetch my dad,' the boy says, and disappears from the room.

Webley's frown turns to disgust as the cat clambers onto her lap. 'What's it doing?' she asks.

'He's being friendly,' says Cody. 'Give him a stroke.'

'The only one having a stroke here will be me. You know I don't like cats.'

'Actually I'd forgotten. Just relax. He'll settle down in a second.'

'I don't want him to settle down. I want him to piss off.'

Oblivious to Webley's antipathy, the cat gyrates a couple of times on her lap, then curls up again and goes back to sleep.

'It's heavy,' says Webley. 'And hot. And I bet it's got fleas. If I come away from here with bites on my legs, I'm blaming you.'

Cody laughs. 'Do you want to reword that last sentence?'

She throws him a glare. 'You're not helping, Cody.'

The boy comes back into the living room. 'Dad says he'll be a couple of minutes. He says I have to talk to you till then.'

Cody watches the lad traverse the room and sit at the table where the books and notes lie open – presumably his homework.

'Is this about the murder?' the boy asks. His voice is matter-of-fact. As though this is the sort of question he asks all the time. At his age, maybe he does.

'What makes you think that?' says Cody.

'Dad said it would be. He said the police have spoken to everyone else at his school. Only a matter of time before you came to speak to him too.'

'It might be,' says Cody. 'What's your name, son?'

'Ewan.'

'All right, Ewan. Know about the murder, do you?'

'I've heard things.'

'What kind of things?'

'Like about the woman. The way she was killed.'

'Uh-huh. And what way was that?'

Ewan leans forward in his chair. 'The killer chopped her to bits. Cut her legs and arms off, then swapped them about. Cut her head off, too, and put it between her hands.'

'Who told you that?'

'My mate Jez.'

'He knows a lot of things, your mate, doesn't he?'

'Yeah. He reads up on that kind of stuff. He likes weird things. What's the weirdest murder you've ever worked on?'

Cody looks to Webley for help, but after the episode with the cat, she's leaving him to fend for himself.

'Er, I'd have to think about that one. Most of them aren't as weird as you might think.'

'Is it true,' Ewan asks, 'that it's impossible to strangle yourself?'

'What?'

'Jez says you can. He says you can strangle yourself to death, but I think you'd pass out before you died. Which is right?'

Cody catches Webley staring at him, her eyebrows raised as she waits to hear his expert reply.

'I, er . . .'

The door opens and Colin Daley breezes in. Cody is grateful for the interruption to his interrogation.

'Right, lad,' Daley says to his son. 'Take your work upstairs, will you?'

'Oh, but Dad . . .'

'No buts. Up you go.'

Sulkily, Ewan gathers up his belongings and trudges out of the room.

'Nice lad,' says Cody.

'Most of the time,' says Daley. 'Asks too many questions sometimes, as I'm sure you've found out. I've got enough to do around here without trying to find answers to everything he wants to know.'

'Just the two of you living here?'

'Yeah. My wife died a few years ago. Cancer.'

'Sorry to hear that.'

'S'all right.'

Colin Daley is a slim, wiry man. He has thrown on a white T-shirt and grey jogging pants. His thinning hair is still damp from the shower. He doesn't take a seat, but stands in front of the fireplace, bouncing on his heels and rubbing his hands together.

'So,' he says, 'you're the police?'

'DS Cody and DC Webley,' says Cody. 'How are you, Mr Daley?'

'Fine, fine,' says Daley, but he looks puzzled by the question. 'A bit tired, but I'm okay.'

'So you've recovered then?'

It takes Daley a while to catch on. 'Oh, you mean because I was off work on Monday. Yeah, I'm over that now.'

'What was the problem?' says Webley.

'Dunno. Something I ate the night before, probably. Trust me, you wouldn't want to have been in this house on Monday. It wasn't pleasant.'

'But the school were okay about it?'

'Oh, yeah. I'm hardly ever off, me.'

'Must make it hard on your assistant, though, eh? When he has to fend for himself, I mean.'

'Well, he's not stupid. He's perfectly capable of holding the fort.'

'Yes,' says Webley. 'I spoke to him.'

She pauses at that point. Cody knows that she is trying to unsettle Daley by hinting that she might already know more than she is divulging.

Daley thrusts his hands into his pockets. 'Does that . . . I mean, is that anything to do with why you've come to see me?'

Webley pauses a few seconds longer. 'No, not at all. We're just covering all the bases by making sure we speak to every member of staff at Oakdale.'

'That makes sense. Yeah. Understood.'

'In particular, we're trying to build up a picture of Mary Cowper. Trying to find out why she would be attacked and murdered.'

Daley nods along vigorously. 'Yeah. Okay.'

'So how well did you know Mary?'

'Me? Ooh, not very well at all, to be honest.'

'No?'

Cody hears the feigned surprise in her voice, and again he knows that she is trying to catch Daley out by suggesting that Jamie Morgan may have intimated otherwise.

'Well, we had the occasional brief chat, I suppose. But only when we bumped into each other, or I was doing a job in her form room – that kind of thing.'

'Ever discuss her with Jamie?'

'Not that I recall. She was never really on my radar, if you know what I mean.'

'Ever see her outside school hours?'

'What do you mean?'

'Did you ever socialise with her?'

'No. Mary wasn't exactly a party animal. She didn't even go along to the staff Christmas meal.'

'Ever go to her flat?'

'Why would I do that?'

'Could be any number of reasons. Maybe she asked you to fix a leaky radiator or something.'

'No, nothing like that.'

'What about the other members of staff? Did she mix with them?'

'I guess so. You'd have to ask them. The thing you have to understand is that there's a bit of a hierarchy in a school – bit of an "upstairs downstairs" mentality. The teachers are in one gang, and we're in another.'

'We?'

'The caretakers, the cleaners, the dinner ladies, the lab technicians . . .'

'Okay, but you must *see* things. You must *hear* things. Didn't you ever hear anything bad said about Mary?'

'Can't say I did. Nothing serious, anyway.'

'What about personal relationships? Anything you can tell us on that score? Anyone that Mary was particularly close to?'

'Well . . .'

'Yes?'

'I don't want to drop anyone in it.'

'It's all right, Mr Daley. We don't reveal our sources.'

'There's Andy Puckleton, I suppose.'

Cody sees Webley nodding along, but she can't hide her disappointment. She was obviously hoping for a juicy new titbit, but this is stale news.

'Yes,' she says, 'we've already spoken to Mr Puckleton.'

'Then you know about the problems he's been having. His beliefs.'

'Yes. Doesn't look like he's made a very good job of keeping them private. Do you know him well?'

'No. Why do you think that?'

There's a touch of anger in Daley's words that puzzles Cody.

'I just wondered how you'd heard about Puckleton's issues, if it wasn't directly from him. Was it from his girlfriend?'

'His what?'

'Laura. One of the school secretaries, I believe.'

'Is that what—? No, it wasn't from her. To be honest, I can't remember how I found out. Like you said, I hear things all the time. Some are true, some aren't.'

Again Cody is puzzled. Daley was about to say something, then suddenly changed tack.

'Mr Daley,' says Cody, 'is there anything else you'd like to tell us? Anything you know that might help us to find Mary's killer, even if it doesn't seem particularly important?'

Daley shakes his head slowly, but his foot is tapping on the carpet at a much faster pace.

'Nope. Sorry, I don't think I've been much help.'

Cody stands up, leaving Webley to work out how to remove the animal still occupying her lap. He thanks Daley for his time.

He's not sure why yet, but he's not as convinced as Daley that this has been such a wasted journey.

18

Friday night is party night.

Or perhaps not. Not for Cody, anyway.

He has an excuse. He's busy trying to solve a baffling murder, which means that tomorrow is just another working day for him.

But that's not the real reason. He doesn't like to dwell on the real reason. He doesn't like to remember that it wasn't much more than a year ago that he would have been perfectly happy spending his nights at the bars and clubs, knocking back pints and telling bad jokes and strutting his stuff on the dance floor.

And look at me now, he thinks. Friday night and I'm reading a book and sipping a glass of orange juice. Woo-hoo.

He doesn't go out much now. He finds it difficult to get in the mood. He's tried it several times, but while his mates get increasingly pissed and find everything increasingly hilarious, he just gets increasingly anxious and depressed.

Sometimes he thinks he'd like to jump off the wagon again. He'd love to get so stupidly shit-faced that he ended up climbing a lamp post with a traffic cone on his head. But it's a trade-off, you see. Alcohol brings more of the bad guys into his head at night. Oh, yes – those maniacal, leering, homicidal clowns like nothing better than a booze-addled brain to make them feel welcome. Gives them all the encouragement they need to wreak their blood-drenched craziness.

So he hasn't touched a pint in months. Well, save that one time with Webley, and look where that led.

Trouble, is where it led.

He dropped his defences, and now she knows far too much about him. She's inside his head, which is a dangerous place to be right now.

She isn't about to give up on finding out why he stayed away from her while she was convalescing. She isn't quite past the anger stage of dealing with that, but she has at least created room for the dogged detective in her to pursue the matter.

It shows she still cares. And it's for that reason he wishes he could give her a more truthful answer. An answer that wouldn't wound her more than he has already.

She also knows that something has happened in his life recently. It's not just a suspicion that he can shake her out of; it's a solid belief.

And of course she's right. The difference in him is obvious to her. But he can't confirm that. He can't let anyone know what's happening until he understands it himself. It's like trying to appraise a book having only read the cover blurb.

And that's the other thing. The other reason why he's spending his Friday night alone in his flat.

For what must be the hundredth time tonight, his gaze drifts to the telephone. A small piece of technology that could be capable of changing his whole life. But his willpower alone cannot cause that phone to ring. Somebody else must do that.

Someone who carries a key to Cody's fate.

Friday night is party night.

But not for Grace Meade.

Wouldn't that be a thing? Grace Meade out on the town. Getting drunk. Dancing on a table. Snogging the face off some random stranger. Flashing her knickers. Throwing her guts up in an alley.

Don't be ridiculous.

It's not me, she thinks. Wouldn't want it to be me. I'd die of embarrassment. People would make fun of me. I'd be a laughing stock. Or some disgusting man would take advantage of me while I was drunk. I could never live with myself.

Although occasionally . . .

She thinks it would be nice to be able to let her hair down now and again. More than nice. It would be . . . liberating. She has watched with envy how other women of her age can simply enjoy themselves without worrying what others think of them, and sometimes she wishes she could be like that. Sometimes she wishes she didn't spend so much time caught up in her own thoughts and worries.

Like tonight, for example.

She is sitting on her bed, in her dressing gown. Her legs are pulled up and she is hugging her knees.

This was supposed to have been her week. Her opportunity to shine. To make an impact.

But it hasn't worked out like that, has it?

The software is good. It does what it is supposed to do. It works.

But if what she hoped to find isn't out there to be found, there's nothing she can do about it.

She worries that she got too cocky, that she expected too much. She was really hoping at some point in the week to make a major announcement. To say to everyone in this room, 'Look. Here's your man. This is your killer.'

Wouldn't that have been brilliant? A room full of trained detectives, and little Grace Meade solves the case. Wouldn't that have been such a feather in her cap?

But it didn't work out. Things never work out. Doesn't seem to matter how much effort she puts in, how many hours, how much enthusiasm – it never pays off.

And now she's in the doldrums. This is how it always happens. She gets excited and optimistic, and then her dreams get dashed, and the gloom descends. It's as though the black clouds are always waiting in the wings – waiting for their cue to roll in and rain down on her.

It isn't fair.

Life isn't fair.

I try my hardest – I really do – and all I ask is a little bit of recognition, a little pat on the back, but for that I need some success, and the success never comes for me, and why is that? Why is it that everyone else, most of whom don't have a fraction of the qualifications and intelligence that I've got, always come up smelling of roses? I don't want money, and I don't want fame, and I don't want a million friends or a big house or to be better looking. I'm a good person and I try hard and I want people to see that, and to let me know that they've seen it. And yes, maybe then I will get up and dance. Maybe then I will cry some happy tears instead of these sad ones. Maybe then my life will be what I want it to be.

She stops thinking then, because it hurts. And it's not just mental pain.

She raises one hand. Sees the blood on her fingertips, the skin under her nails.

She looks down at her legs. At her thighs, just above the knees.

She sees the long scratches and gouges she has made, and the rivulets of blood running down onto the sheets.

No short skirts for me tomorrow, she thinks.

Everyone count your blessings.

19

He remembers . . .

Six years old now. Still incredibly young, but the memories are more persistent. The impressions formed by his surroundings, his experiences, his mother are more deeply etched. They will not be easily erased, and later in life he will wish they could be.

His mother, in particular, looms large. He is torn between seeing her as the person who nurtures and protects him, and as the person who scares him more than anything else in the world. Already she is fracturing his mind.

This is a school morning. The end of the week, so he is tired. He oversleeps. This is unusual for him. Normally the sounds of his mother moving around will wake him, and fear of appearing slothful will keep him awake.

But not today. Today his eyes flicker open only when he realises his mother is already in his bedroom, fussing and clucking.

He realises something else too. And it is not good. In fact it is so bad he wants to cry. He has only just started his day, and already he is beginning to tremble.

She cannot know. He must keep it from her somehow.

She flings the curtains open. Praises the Lord for such a fine morning. Her words are those of someone who relishes life and is grateful for all the comforts that have been provided. But he sees through that. Even at six he detects the instability below the surface. All it takes is a shove in the wrong direction.

She bustles towards him, lecturing him on the perils of allowing this precious gift of time to be wasted.

He grips his bedclothes tightly. Keeps them bundled under his chin. Please don't let her find out, he thinks. Please, Lord, if you love me, keep me safe. Don't let her hurt me.

He tells her that he will get up in a minute. Tells her that she can use the bathroom first, if she wants. Anything that might buy him some time.

But she is not easily fooled. Not easily diverted from her mission.

Nonsense, she tells him.

And then she is taking hold of the sheets. Pulling them from his grasp. Yanking them across the bed to reveal his tiny, hunched-up, whimpering form.

And now she knows. Now she sees.

He has wet the bed.

Soaked the undersheet, his mattress, his pyjamas.

He is already telling her how sorry he is. Pleading with her not to be angry. He didn't know. He didn't feel it. He would have gone to the toilet if he'd known.

She stands in thunderous silence for a few seconds, but he knows it is only because she is in shock. This is the calm before the storm.

And then she erupts, as he knew she would.

The vice-like grip around his wrist. The feeling that his arm is about to come out of its socket as she pulls him up and off the bed. The whip-crack sounds and the intense stinging as she fires the slaps at his legs.

And throughout it all, her voice as she somehow turns this into a defiance not only of her, but of God. Words and phrases that he does not understand, but whose message is unmistakable. He is a sinner, and the Lord God is mightily displeased with him, and why would he want to go against all that the Bible teaches about respect and obedience and living according to the teachings of Jesus? Why would he do that unless he has the Devil in him?

And if that were the end of it, he could probably cope. He could get himself cleaned up and he could massage his red-raw legs and he could cry until he left the house, at which time embarrassment would take over and stifle his sobbing. He could go to school and he could allow himself to be distracted by the lessons, and when he returned home it would be to a better, calmer situation, and he and his dear mother could begin again, and perhaps optimism for future happiness and love would eventually sneak its way back in.

But his mother has other ideas. His mother is concocting further punishment that only much later will he come to label as psychological torture.

When he begins to strip off his pyjamas, she asks him what he's doing.

They're wet, he tells her. He needs to get changed for school.

And he thinks, but he's not sure, that he sees a smile on his mother's face as she tells him he will do no such thing. She tells him that he will wear those urine-soaked pyjamas all day, under his school clothes, because how else is he going to learn, hmm? How else is the lesson going to sink in that he needs to control his bodily functions? How else will he remember in future that soiling his bedclothes is a rebellion, a smack in the face of his poor mother who works so hard to keep this house clean and tidy? Honour thy parents. Do you understand what that means? Well, do you?

He doesn't understand. Not those exact words. Not at the age of six. But what he does appreciate is that this is the worst punishment ever. This will be an ordeal that will last all day. This is nothing less than sheer cruelty.

But he does as she commands, because he knows that the alternative is much, much worse.

He dresses as she stands and watches. Pulls on his smartly ironed trousers and shirt and pullover. And already he can see the damp patches forming. He can smell himself. And if these things are so obvious to him, they will turn him into a beacon at school.

He tries one last time to plead his case, but she is having none of it. This is his own fault, she explains. Reap what you sow.

He thinks that she might change her mind at the last moment. That, at the school gates, she will drag him back home to change, saying something like, 'Let that be a lesson to you.'

But that is being far too hopeful. His mother is a woman of her word, and of God's word.

And so at the school gates she simply ushers him into the playground as she always does. As if this is a day just like any other. She waits until he is in the midst of the other children, when it is too late for him to escape. And then she disappears, leaving him to his fate.

And it does not take long for it to start. The sniggering and the pointing. At that age children don't hold back. The questioning becomes direct. Have you wet yourself? they ask. And when he doesn't answer, they assume the affirmative, and their laughter becomes uproarious, and they begin the teasing.

And when he takes his seat in the classroom, the boy next to him makes a show of pinching his nose and shuffling his chair away from him, much to the amusement of the other children.

He wants the floor to open up beneath him. He wants to disappear for ever, to go somewhere far away, where nobody makes fun of him, where nobody hits him or screams at him. Where people are nice and friendly, and show only love.

But it seems to cure his bed-wetting. Give his mother her due, she has managed to perform that minor miracle. Destroyed a part of her son's mind in the process, but everything has a price, eh?

He sleeps on a knife edge after that. Snaps awake at the slightest feeling of fullness in his bladder, then goes to the toilet to empty it. Refuses to drink anything before bed, just in case.

And people wonder why he is always tired, always yawning in class. Don't you get enough sleep? they ask.

About six months later, recovering from a debilitating bout of flu, he gets plenty of sleep. Too much sleep. He is almost in a coma, it seems. And when he awakes in the middle of the night, he is mortified to feel the wetness again. Mortified and scared witless.

His solution is a long session with a hairdryer. He switches it on at its lowest setting so as not to make too much noise, and then he blows air onto his pyjamas and his sheets. He continues to do this for as long as he can – until it is time to get ready for school again, in fact – just so that he can be sure that his evil, unforgivable deed will not be detected.

But still he is left with the guilt. He has deceived his mother, and God is fully aware of this, and ultimately he will have to face his punishment.

He must live with that burden.

That is what his mother has taught him.

20

She eyes up the muffins. The blueberry ones in particular. Then she weighs up the calories and decides she had best stick to her usual but less exciting order of a cup of tea. The man behind the counter of the Piazza smiles as he serves her. It seems genuine enough. Not one of those 'I know what you do' types of smiles she sees all too often. So she throws him a smile back. It's the Christian thing to do, and this is certainly the place for that.

She carries her tray across to a comfy-looking armchair she's been coveting since she came in from the cold. As she threads her way between the tables, a uniformed copper seated at one of them looks in her direction and says, 'All right, Cassie. How's things?'

She recognises the policeman, but she's not sure where from, and right now she doesn't want to get into a conversation with someone who may once have arrested her. So she gives him a smile too, then presses on.

When she is seated, she immediately opens up the free copy of the *Metro* that she picked up at Lime Street station. She knows the copper is watching her, so she stares intently at the paper until she is sure he has lost interest in her.

She relaxes then. Actually starts to read what is in front of her. Sees that the police are still no closer to solving the murder of that woman at the Anglican – the poor cow.

Cassie has never really understood what people see in the Anglican. Okay, it's more cathedral-like, and yes, it's pretty impressive for what it is. But it's so Gothic-looking. So gloomy and spooky. Especially on dark nights like these.

She'll stick with this one, thank you very much. The 'other' cathedral. The Catholic one. Even though she's not a Catholic and never has been. This cathedral is just so much more modern and funky. It makes you happy just to look at it. That woman would never have been killed here.

Cassie lifts her eyes from the newspaper. The copper has gone, thank goodness. She looks out through the huge windows of the café. No sign of him there either. Just a couple of back-pack-toting tourists taking photographs of the impressive sight in front of them.

She takes her time supping her tea. There's no hurry. She has all the time in the world.

She gets to the back page of the paper. She's not that inter-ested in sport, but it's good to see that Everton are playing at home today. That means a healthy crowd of drunken fans hitting town tonight. Which in turn means a better chance of custom.

When she's finished, she grabs her bag and exits through the glass doors. The biting wind hits her, and she turns away from it.

But then the building fills her vision, rising in stark outline against the leaden skies behind it, and all thoughts of the cold are forgotten.

Its proper name is the Metropolitan Cathedral of Christ the King, but it also has several colloquial names, derived from its unique shape. One of the most apt descriptions is that of a huge upturned funnel, and so it is sometimes referred to as the Mersey Funnel, which is also a pun on the Mersey Tunnels that connect Liverpool with the Wirral peninsula.

It is also often called Paddy's Wigwam, although Cassie is never entirely sure whether that term is slightly racist – more so against the Irish than the American Indians. It definitely bears a resemblance to a circular tent of some kind, however, the flying buttresses looking like thick guide ropes tethering it to the ground.

Cassie has her own way of describing the cathedral. It always reminds her of the central console in Doctor Who's Tardis. It could easily be something that was left here by alien beings.

She finds a real smile of happiness now, and almost bounds up the concrete steps. She glances briefly at the gardens to her right – a lovely place to sit and contemplate life in the summer months, but deserted at the moment.

She enters the building beneath the immense vertical slab of concrete that houses the bells. Pauses as she always does to gaze around the interior while she soaks up the peace and tranquillity.

Unlike the Tardis, it seems smaller on the inside. The altar is in the centre of the circular space. Above it hangs a spiked, metallic structure that is said to be symbolic of the Crown of Thorns. Above that again, the tower that forms the 'stem' of the funnel is lined with stained glass that, on a bright day, casts magical beams of colourful light onto the worshippers below.

Cassie turns to her left to begin her customary tour of the circumference. She once read an article claiming that most people unconsciously turn right on entering a large space, and that shop owners who are aware of this lay out their wares accordingly. But Cassie always goes left. She likes to be different.

She walks slowly past the various chapels, occasionally stepping in to study an exhibit or read a note of remembrance. She is not easily moved to tears, but finds some of the messages heartbreaking – particularly the ones from young children.

She completes the circle almost before she's aware of it. As she reaches the baptistry, she turns and heads along one of the aisles between the benches surrounding the altar. Most of the benches are unoccupied, so she chooses one at random and takes a seat at its end.

Her prayers follow no well-defined structure. Most of her life has been spent without religion in it, and so she has no idea if there is any protocol here. The only thing she remembers from her school days is the Lord's Prayer, but even that doesn't seem relevant to her any longer.

So she does her own thing. Generates a stream of rambling, unspoken thoughts that she would like God to hear.

What she wants him to know above all else is that she is trying. She is not perfect, and she makes mistakes, and she doesn't always fulfil her promises, but she is at least trying to be a good person.

When she has finished praying, she sits for a couple of minutes more, her head bowed and eyes closed. Because it's peaceful here. There is no drama here, no danger. If she could stay here for the rest of her life she would.

Maybe I should apply to become a nun, she thinks. Ha – wouldn't that be a turnaround?

Finally she gets up. There's a reality to be faced out there.

She goes outside. Pulls her collar in against the wind as she stares towards Hope Street.

I wonder if there's hope for me, she thinks.

She doesn't retrace her way down the steps the way most people do. Instead, she turns to her left and goes around to the side of the cathedral. Her aim is to cross the grounds at the rear, then descend the steps near the crypt doors on Brownlow Hill.

It's devoid of people here. She suspects that many of the cathedral visitors don't even know you can come this way, or where it leads.

She halts. Gets out of the wind by stepping into an alcove beneath one of the buttresses. She digs into her pockets. Finds an almost-empty packet of cigarettes. Lights one up and stares into space as she savours the nicotine hit.

Forgot to say, Lord, she thinks. I've cut down on these too.

She flicks ash on the ground. Wonders how convincing she is to God. Wonders if her life will ever change.

A figure comes into view.

He's male. Wearing a big black coat with the hood up. Hands stuffed in the pockets. She wishes she had a coat that's as warm as his looks.

She blows out a cloud of smoke. Watches as the figure slows down, turns towards her slightly, starts to come over.

She wonders if it's a punter. Someone she's been with before. They don't usually recognise her in the cold light of day, especially when they've sobered up.

As he gets nearer, he pulls one of his hands from his pocket. She sees what he's holding.

A cigarette.

Poor bloke's dying for a fag, and hasn't got a lighter or a match. She smiles. She's been in that predicament many times herself.

'Got a light?' he mutters hoarsely.

He keeps his head down as he says this, and his hood hides his face. There's something about his voice, she thinks. But . . . Ah, to hell with it. Light him up and let him get on his way.

She digs in her own coat pocket for her lighter.

And then he punches her.

At least she thinks it's a punch. But the pain is immense, and pinpoints of light are exploding behind her eyes, and she seems to be having trouble staying on her feet. And when she blinks the world back into some kind of focus, she sees that it wasn't a fist that caught her but a hammer. A large, heavy-looking hammer that swings into her face a second time. And she wonders why he's doing that, and she decides to ask him. But her mouth isn't working properly. The words won't come out. Just meaningless noises. And something else. Her teeth, she thinks. Teeth and blood. All crunchy and wet inside her mouth. And now she doesn't know what to do. Doesn't think there's anything she can do. Her body isn't responding properly, and her attacker is still there in front of her. She can see his face now, though. Confirms what she thought, but that makes no difference. He's not going away. If anything he's coming closer. He's raising his fist too. Not the one with the cigarette but the one with the hammer. He's going to hit me again, she thinks. This one won't hurt, though. I won't feel this one.

God will look after me now.

21

Cody has never been so glad to see Blunt.

Not because he's expecting a hug from her or anything. He just wants to get out of this bloody freezing wind. He and the other detectives have pretty much done their bit up here, and have only stayed because Blunt ordered them to until she got there from her meeting.

But now she's here, marching towards them like the lady of the manor confronting trespassers on her land.

'I should warn you,' she tells them all, 'that I am not in the best of moods. Sometimes I could swear that the higher-ups in the force have completely forgotten what it's like to work outside an office. So I want some good news. If this is another squeaky-clean, whiter-than-white—'

'It's not, ma'am,' says Cody. 'The victim was a prostitute.'

This throws Blunt. She stares at Cody, daring him to confess he's pulling her leg.

'A what? Are you sure?'

'Yes, ma'am. Cassie Harris. She's well known to the local bobbies.'

Without another word, Blunt walks away to get her first look at the corpse.

Cody exchanges glances with Ferguson, who is stamping his feet on the ground in an effort to keep warm. Webley, meanwhile, seems unwilling to look at either of them.

A cup of tea, thinks Cody. A nice steaming mug of tea in the café downstairs – that's what we all need right now.

Cody looks up at the evening sky. It comes as a shock to see how black it is. He has become accustomed to being in the tiny bubble of brightness created by the cathedral's external spot lamps and those set up by the police. The white light bounces off the cathedral stone and the plastic awning erected over the body to protect it from prying eyes.

Blunt reappears after a couple of minutes. Picks up where she left off. 'So what's she doing here? Strange place to be touting for business. Mind you, when you think about some of the things Catholic priests get up to . . .'

'We don't think it was business, ma'am. Apparently she was a regular here.'

'A regular? You mean *inside* the cathedral? You mean she came here to pray?'

Blunt's quick-fire questions are rattled off as her mind takes her in the direction she was probably hoping to avoid.

'Yes, ma'am.'

'And she was in there today?'

'Yes. The woman at the reception desk remembers her.'

'Shit! You're telling me this is definitely connected to the death of Mary Cowper, aren't you?'

Cody nods. 'It's looking that way.'

'Shit. Has Stroud been here yet?'

'Been and gone. His preliminary opinion is that Cassie was probably battered to death with a hammer or some such.'

'Just like Mary.'

'Yes.'

Blunt takes a moment to look around. She turns to look along Hope Street towards the Anglican cathedral.

'What is this?' she muses. 'Two cathedrals, with a murder at each. An attack on the Protestants, and then the Catholics.' Her eyes widen in alarm. 'Bloody hell. If there's even the slightest indication that there's a Muslim behind all this . . .'

She lets the thought trail away. It's too early to be making wild and unfounded conjectures, and she knows it.

'All right,' she says. 'Let's get to work. Talk to everyone you can find who may have seen something. That includes people in the cathedral, the gift shop and the café.' She gestures vaguely across the street. 'It's a Saturday, so most of these university buildings will probably be empty, but knock on doors anyway. And see what you can do about grabbing any CCTV footage.'

She pauses, her face grave.

'We have to go through the motions, but my guess is that we'll come up with nothing. Unless last time was a fluke, our killer is careful. He knows how to keep his identity hidden. Our best bet is to figure out what makes him tick. So when you're done here, I'll see you back at base. Make sure you've got your thinking caps on.'

'When you're ready, Grace.'

The signal comes from Blunt, standing at the front of the incident room. Grace notes that, of all the people in the room, only DS Cody turns to look at her, an expression of mild surprise on his face.

He realises, she thinks. He is aware that it's after ten o'clock at night, and that I don't have to be here. I'm a civilian. I probably won't even get overtime pay for this. I could be at home in my slippers, drinking cocoa. Or ripping my legs to shreds.

Cody smiles his appreciation at her, and she feels weak at the knees. She throws him a hesitant smile back. Nobody else notices or cares.

Responding to Blunt's request, Grace hits a key on her computer. A close-up image of Mary Cowper appears on the large monitor in front of the squad.

Oh, yes, she thinks. They love their screen now. Now that they've got someone who knows how to work the thing. They should give me a pay rise just for that.

'Mary Cowper,' says Blunt. 'Age forty-two. A schoolteacher. Kept herself to herself. Deeply religious. Regular churchgoer. Charity giver. Very few friends, and apparently even fewer enemies. Other than her dog, no loves in her life, but then no obvious haters either.'

Blunt nods towards Grace, and Grace hits another key.

I need to teach them how to use the remote, Grace thinks. If they're just going to see me as a glorified button-presser . . .

'Cassie Harris. Age twenty-eight. Sex worker. Arrested numerous times for prostitution and drugs offences. This is the most recent mug shot from her arrest file. In her line of work she will have come into contact with all kinds of unsavoury characters. Some of them may have been psychos, or crazy on drugs. Some of them may have beaten her up before. She may have owed money. Sad to say, but the death of a prostitute is less of a surprise than the death of Mary Cowper. So there we have it: a saint and a sinner. What links the two?'

There is a silence of a few seconds. DC Webley is the first to speak.

'To be honest, we're not yet sure that this is the same killer. What if it's a revenge killing? Someone kills a Protestant, so a Protestant takes out a Catholic?'

'She wasn't a Catholic, though,' says Ferguson. 'The story we got from the clergy at the cathedral was that Cassie just liked to go there to pray.'

'The killer might not have known that, though. If you want to find a Catholic to kill, pick someone who's just been praying in a Catholic church. Most times that'd be a pretty safe bet.'

'True,' Ferguson admits. 'In which case maybe all this background work we've been doing on Mary Cowper has been wasted effort. Maybe all that was wanted was a Protestant – any Protestant. Same goes for today. In fact, maybe all that matters is that they're religious. Our killer, if there is just one killer involved, could have reasons for wanting to murder people who have a strong belief in God.'

Blunt nods. 'It's possible, but I hope it's not true. It's going to make our job a hell of a lot harder if it's as random and ill-considered as that. For now, let's work on the assumption that there are deeper reasons for these homicides. Any other thoughts?'

DS Cody speaks up next: 'You emphasised the differences between the two women, ma'am, but there are also similarities.'

He turns and faces Grace again. 'Grace, could you put the two photos up side by side, please?'

He asks so nicely, she thinks. Such boyish charm. How could I turn him down?

A couple of key presses later, and his request is satisfied.

Says Cody, 'Okay, so they'd hardly pass as twins. But they're not a million miles apart, either. Similar height, weight and build. Shoulder-length fair hair in both cases. I know that Cassie was only twenty-eight, but she had a hard life. She looks close to Mary's age in these photos.'

'You're saying our killer has a preference? A type?' Blunt asks.

Cody shrugs. 'Maybe. I just think we should be aware of it.'

'Agreed,' says Blunt. 'Another similarity is the method of killing, of course. Which is another reason to suspect that this is the work of one man. We haven't released details of Mary Cowper's injuries, so how would anyone know to kill Cassie that way? Taking a lump hammer to the head and face of both victims can't be coincidence.'

Webley joins in again: 'While we're on the subject of similarities, there's something else we should consider.'

'Go on.'

'Time of death. Both women were killed late on a Saturday afternoon. Maybe that tells us something about the killer. Maybe he works during the week, and Saturday is his day off. Or maybe he has a Saturday job in the Hope Street area.'

'Good thinking,' says Blunt. 'Go with that. See if you can come up with anything else that might put a person in that area at exactly the same time each week.'

Blunt points up at the screen. 'We need to look for connections between these two. Did they ever meet? Was one of the teachers at Mary's school also a client of Cassie? There's got to be something there.'

Says Cody, 'We can't ignore the religious angle, either. That's got to be key to this. Cassie was a prostitute. She was used to getting in cars and being alone with strange men. Our killer could have chosen any one of a thousand places to bump her off without any risk of being seen. But he chose the cathedral. Why was that? Did he even know how easy it would have been to meet up with her elsewhere, and in complete privacy?'

'I can answer that.'

She says it quietly, but it's picked up by the others. As the heads turn, Grace feels the familiar churning in her stomach.

'I, er, I've been doing some research,' she says. 'It wasn't hard to find this . . .'

She presses some more keys. The monitor at the front changes to show an online version of a newspaper article. It makes use of a stock photograph of a woman standing on a street corner at night. Next to that is the headline, 'Our job is in the sex trade, but we're people too.'

'This appeared in the *Clarion* several months ago,' Grace explains. 'It was written by a reporter called Martin Dobson. Some of you may have heard of him.'

She sees the reaction on everyone's face, especially Cody's. They won't forget 'Dobby' in a hurry.

'But that's by the by,' says Grace. 'The article contains interviews with several prostitutes, and tries to show that, once you get past the nature of their work, they're normal people just like everyone else. Some have kids. Some have other jobs. And then there's this bit . . .'

Another key press. The screen zooms in on a small section of the article. Grace reads it out:

'Cassie, 28, has plans to get out of this life, and has turned to God for help. Although not a Catholic, she turns up at the Metropolitan cathedral most Saturday afternoons in the hope that her prayers will be answered.

'"I'm not expecting miracles," says Cassie. "I know I have to do the hard work myself to make changes in my life. But all of us can do with a little help now and again to put us on the straight and narrow. In my case, that help comes from God."

'As it does for many women in her position, drug addiction complicates the situation for Cassie. But it's a vicious circle, as Cassie explains:

'"What I do on the streets is a quick and easy way to get money for the drugs, but it also means the money is gone in the blink of an eye. I can't save up for anything else. I can't buy nice things. Sometimes I don't have enough left over to pay the rent. What I've realised is that I can't keep going on like this for ever, and with God's help, I won't have to."'

Grace looks around at all the faces staring at her, attentive to her every word.

'Her photograph isn't in the paper,' she says, 'but I imagine it wouldn't be that difficult to single her out from the people who turn up and pray at the cathedral every Saturday afternoon. The killer may even have followed her previously, just to check.'

'So,' says Blunt, 'the question is – *was* Cassie Harris singled out? Was she targeted by someone who may have read this article? If our killer needed a religious sinner, then Cassie certainly fitted the bill. Or was she just in the wrong place at the wrong time? Find me some answers, folks.'

22

It was useful information, but not the breakthrough Grace was hoping for. She hasn't exactly cracked the case. She knows that anybody with a smattering of computer know-how could have found that newspaper article.

And what has it told them, other than that it may have aided the killer in finding a suitable prey?

No, not good enough. I have to do better than this, she thinks. I *can* do better than this.

But she observes the proceedings of the next couple of days with growing dismay. Sees, too, how the MIT detectives become increasingly frustrated.

They talk to a seemingly endless array of prostitutes, clients of prostitutes, and known drug dealers. Some of those brought into the station for questioning are characters whom Grace would definitely not like to encounter in a dark alley. They look as though they'd cut your throat for a couple of quid.

And after all the questioning, all the footwork, all the paperwork, they seem no further forward in the case. Nobody knows why Mary Cowper or Cassie Harris were murdered, let alone who did it.

This would be an ideal time, thinks Grace. These detectives are hungry, desperate for information. If I could give them something – anything to help them . . .

And then she finds it.

Again it's not huge. It doesn't crack the case wide open. But it's important. Boy, is it important.

She has her recognition programs to thank for this. With many of the buildings around the cathedral closed on Sundays, it's Monday before images from CCTV cameras in the area start coming in. Without delay, Grace puts her software slaves to work.

When she presents her findings in the incident room, she feels her confidence flooding back. It goes like this sometimes. Waves of depression and self-loathing interspersed with bouts of euphoria.

This is one of the peaks. Hardly Everest, but still a moment to remember, to savour. She can feel the electricity in the room as all heads focus on the single image she has displayed on the monitor.

It shows a figure on the steps of the Metropolitan cathedral. A man wearing a dark padded coat with pale grey contrast stitching over the pocket zips.

They finally have their confirmation that the same person is responsible for both homicides.

Webley wonders how to broach this.

It's a tricky subject, and so she is distracted. Most of what Parker is saying to her goes unheard. She just nods and smiles.

She has made him a shepherd's pie. At least, she thinks she has. She can never remember the difference between shepherd's pie and cottage pie. If it's lamb, it must be shepherd's pie, she reasons. Because shepherds look after sheep, right? Whereas beef would have made it a cottage pie, because . . . because what? Cows live in cottages?

Whatever, it's his favourite. He always says so. This man who is so used to wonderful hotel restaurant dining really enjoys this meal. Couple it with an expensive red wine, and he'll be putty in her hands. That's her thinking.

She's not convinced it's going to work.

She's not even sure she should mention it.

More wine. For both of them. Soften some of those sharp edges the situation seems to have.

'Lovely,' he says.

She's not sure whether he's referring to the food or the wine or her or this opportunity for blissful relaxation. But 'lovely' is a good word. Shows he's in a contented frame of mind. Receptive to unusual propositions, even.

So here goes . . .

'You mind if I ask you something?' she says.

He waves his wine glass in the air. 'Anything,' he answers.

'Anything' is also a good word. Invites her to open the door.

'Okay, so you know I was talking to you about Cody the other day?'

Parker looks up at the ceiling, as though casting his mind back.

'Arsehole.'

'What?'

'I think you called him an arsehole, if I remember correctly.'

'Yes, yes, I did, but, well, I've been thinking.'

'And you've thought of a better word than arsehole?'

'No, that's not what I've been thinking about.'

'Okay. So what's on your mind?'

'Cody . . . he's got problems.'

'Yes, I know.'

'And he's been acting really strange lately. Stranger than usual, I mean.'

'Right.'

'And I have to work with him. I mean, I have to get on with him. And, deep down, he's a really good bloke.'

'Megan, can you get to the point?'

She takes a breath. 'All right. I want to ask Cody to come round for dinner.'

Silence, of course. She expected the silence. Expects a bit of a fight now, too. She knows she's asking a lot.

'You want to invite Cody to come to dinner?'

'Yes.'

'You don't mean Christmas dinner?'

'No. Just dinner. Ordinary dinner. Some time in the next few days.'

'Here? At your house?'

'Yes.'

'Just you and him?'

She reaches out and grasps his hand. 'God, no. This isn't meant to be anything weird. I want you there. The three of us.'

Another pause.

'Why?'

'Why what?'

'You just said it's not meant to be anything weird, but don't you think it *is* weird, just a bit?'

'Well . . .'

'You want me, your fiancé, to sit down and have a meal and make polite conversation with your former boyfriend. Right?'

'Yes, but . . . but please stop thinking of him as my ex. He's a friend. And he's having problems. I want to help him. I want us both to try to help him.'

'You were furious at him the other day. What's changed?'

'Nothing. He's still being a knob. If it was anyone else, I wouldn't have anything to do with them. But I started thinking to myself, what if it's not his fault? What if there are things going on inside his head that are making him act that way? I can't just stand by and watch him suffer like that.'

'If he's that bad, should he really be working on high-profile murder cases?'

It's a good question. One she has asked herself many times. Is she merely compounding the problem by keeping quiet about Cody?

'I don't know. I don't think it's my call to make. Cody is still a good copper. He's doing a good job, and that's all that matters.'

'Until he freaks out again. He's got away with it so far, but what if he does something that puts one of his colleagues in jeopardy?'

She doesn't want to answer that too directly. Doesn't want to tell Parker that she has already experienced one or two close calls of that nature.

'All the more reason for helping him. Please, Parker. He's a good guy. Give him a chance. I think you could get to like him.'

Parker sighs. 'It means that much to you, does it?'

'Yes. Yes, it does. But only if you'll be a part of it.'

Parker drains his glass. Places it carefully on the table.

'What's for dessert?' he asks.

'Is that a yes?'

He smiles. 'It better be chocolate fudge cake, now that you owe me.'

She leaps out of her chair. Throws her arms around her fiancé. Tells him she loves him more than anything in the whole world.

Now all she has to do is to get Cody to agree.

23

The call comes at just after one in the morning.

Instantly awake, Cody sits bolt upright in bed. He fumbles for the switch of his bedside lamp. Turns it on. Blinks in the brightness as he grabs the phone from its cradle.

'Hello?'

He doesn't know what to expect. Not any more. The game has changed so much recently.

But it seems this is a retrograde step. We're back to the silent treatment.

Cody listens intently. Hears only his own pulse in his ears.

Am I expected to say something? he wonders.

Nearly time to play.

But what are the rules? Am I supposed to make the first move? How do I do that?

'What is it you want?' he asks.

Silence.

'Maybe if you told me why you keep calling me, we could move this on.'

Nothing.

'You were there, weren't you? At the warehouse. Were you one of the clowns?'

Click. And then a hum of electronic indifference.

Cody replaces the receiver. He doesn't know whether he has done the right thing, but the last occasion on which he asked directly about clowns appeared to set things in motion. It seemed only sensible to press harder on that line of questioning.

Did I push too hard? he wonders. Was that not the right move?

He considers this for a long time, then turns his lamp off and settles down in the bed. He suspects that sleep will elude him now, but he will make an attempt to hunt it down.

The next call comes at 3.15. Cody isn't sure whether he dozed off again or not. He knows only that his head is filled with confused, abstract thoughts, and for a moment he isn't even certain whether the ringing noise is real or imagined.

As he comes to his senses, he finds himself angry at this latest intrusion, and is tempted to let the phone go unanswered. How dare they play games with him? How dare they mess with his sleep patterns and his emotions and his life? Well, fuck 'em. They can go to hell.

But he puts the lamp on and answers the call anyway, as he always knew he would.

'Hello,' he says. 'Hello? He—'

The music cuts him off. The jack-in-the-box again. *Pop! Goes the Weasel.*

As before, it plays on repeat, each time faster than the last. It becomes a frenzy of tinny notes. And then . . .

The eerie, sing-song voice. But now a slightly different message: 'Time to pla-aay.'

And then the line goes dead again. Cody brings the receiver from his ear. Stares at it as if attempting to divine the meaning of the cryptic message it has delivered to him.

What the hell?

The game has started? How? What am I supposed—?

A loud buzz startles him. The intercom, out in the hall.

Cody leaps from the bed. Strides out of the room. In the hallway he switches on the light and then goes to the intercom console. He thumbs the talk button.

'Hello? Who is it?'

The reply is instant. But it's not intelligible speech. This is far more terrifying.

The scream reverberates around the hall, chilling Cody's blood. He recognises this scream. Knows exactly the pleading and crying and more screaming that is to follow.

This is his voice. This is a recording of him when he was being tortured. When his toes were being snipped from his body. It has been played to him before, over the telephone. But now it's here.

At his door.

The realisation hits Cody with the force of a thousand volts.

He's here. My attacker is here!

Cody is suddenly wracked with indecision. He can't unlock the door – can't allow whoever is out there to come in. What if there is more than one of them? What if they are here to torture and maim him again? What if their objective this time is to finish off what they started?

But, at the same time, he cannot simply do nothing. He needs to know.

And then he is running. Back into the bedroom first, where he picks up his extensible police baton from the bedside table. And then down the stairs, two at a time – flying down those stairs. His momentum carries him crashing into the door to his flat on the first floor of the building. He fumbles for the key. Unlocks the door. Out into a dark hallway. Find the light! Then down more stairs and more stairs – why do there have to be so many fucking stairs? – and then he is in the lobby, racing for the front door, on the other side of which is . . . what? Who is out there?

But he can't worry about that. Not now. It's too late to back out. He doesn't care about his safety any longer. Everything in the past few months has been building towards this moment. He has to face it. Has to find out.

And then he's unlocking the huge front door. Flinging it open as he raises his baton, ready to strike at whatever hateful apparition is waiting for him – come on, you fucking clown bastards, come and get it!

And then he's staring into space. The cold emptiness of a deserted city street. There is nobody here.

Panting for breath, Cody steps outside. Looks both ways along Rodney Street. The street lights reveal no figures, no moving cars. Whoever was here has pulled night around himself and disappeared.

The icy fingers of winter clutch at Cody, providing him with an uncomfortable reminder that he is wearing only shorts and a T-shirt. But still he is reluctant to retreat into the building. The answers are out here, defying him to find them. If he goes inside he will have given up; he will have resigned from a game that has only just begun.

But when his body begins to shiver, he realises that standing here is fruitless.

He turns and faces the building. Pictures a figure at the gloss-black door, pressing on the intercom buzzer. But the figure is fuzzy, indistinct. Cody's brain can superimpose no recognisable features on it.

Who was here? And why? What is he trying to tell me?

Cody trudges back into the building. Closes the door after one final peek outside. Making a decision, he slides the chain into position – something he wouldn't normally do because it stops the dentistry staff from getting in on his days off. The echoes of the rattling chain seem to him not unlike those heard in a prison cell block.

It makes him wonder which is worse: allowing the sinister forces outside to pay him a visit, or incarcerating himself with only the ghosts of the house and his mind as cellmates.

24

To Cody, the day seems weird enough without Webley doing her utmost to make it weirder.

Every time he raises his head from his computer, she looks across at him and throws him a smile. What is this? Be-nice-to-Cody day?

He'd go over and ask her, but he has weightier things on his mind. The events of last night, for example.

Now that was more than weird. That was downright surreal. That was how the Devil himself might play Postman's Knock.

Cody has replayed the episode in his brain thousands of times. Wondered on many of those iterations whether it was all the product of an overtired brain.

Could he have imagined it? Is it possible that the intercom never buzzed in the night? That there was no screaming? That there never was anyone at the door?

He has to admit it's possible. It wouldn't be the first time he'd had such vivid hallucinations.

But no, he thinks. This was real. I'd stake my life on it. Someone came to my door and called me on the intercom and played my screams to me in the middle of the night.

I was close. So close to finding out more.

Maybe if I'd been just that little bit more decisive. If I'd run down those stairs a bit quicker, or raced along the street when I got outside. Maybe the guy was just crouching behind a car, or hiding around the next corner. I should have gone a bit further, explored a bit more, instead of worrying about how cold it was. I mean, what kind of wimp am I? Why am I such a—?

Damn.

There I go again with the self-recrimination. I have to stop that. It is what it is. No point regretting it. Next time I'll be better prepared.

If there is a next time.

What if that was it? What if that was my once-in-a-lifetime opportunity, and I blew it?

No. Can't be. Whoever called last night was taking a big risk. Why go to all that trouble unless you intend it to be the start of something? There has to be more on the way.

Which is more chilling than exciting.

Cody needs there to be more. He needs there to be some kind of forward motion, some hope for closure. At the same time, he knows that what is to come isn't going to be a barrel of laughs. Less of a funfair, and more of a freak show. There will be probably be clowns involved. Roll up, roll up, and have the shit scared out of you, folks. Our clowns have serrated teeth and bad breath and rotting flesh and a penchant for inflicting pain and death. Start ordering those catalogues for artificial limbs now, folks, because you're gonna need them. Oh, and don't expect your sanity to remain intact either. Because it won't.

Not quite the truth, perhaps. The reality is likely to be far, far worse.

So that's something to look forward to.

Webley grabs him as he goes on his lunch break.

'Hi, Cody,' she says. All bright and breezy.

Cody eyes her with suspicion.

'All right.'

'Where ya going?'

'It's lunchtime. I was going to get some lunch.'

She nods sagely. 'Ah, lunch. Lunch is good. I think lunch is one of the best meals of the day.'

Cody keeps walking, with Webley dogging his footsteps.

'Yeah,' he says. 'Of the many and varied meals that I have in a day, lunch is right up there in my top three.'

'Really? What would come first? In a ranked list of those meals, which one would you put at the very top?'

'I'd have to say breakfast.'

'Not dinner?'

'No. Definitely breakfast. It's quick and it's simple and there's no palaver about it.'

'Oh. Well, I think palaver is good. Meals should have a bit of palaver about them. They serve an important social function, don't you think?'

Cody halts so abruptly that Webley crashes into him.

'Megan, what is this about?'

'Meals. More specifically, dinner. You're invited.'

'I'm invited to dinner?'

'Yes. You can RSVP here and now, but it has to be a yes.'

'I need clarification first.'

She nods. 'You may ask for clarification.'

'I'm invited to dinner. With you.'

'Yes. Precisely. Now that we've cleared that up, if you'd just like to—'

'What about Parker?'

'Who?'

'Parker. Your fiancé with the funny name. Does he know about this?'

'He does. He has been consulted on every aspect of the planning.'

'And what does he say about it?'

'He is wholly in agreement that it should proceed.'

'He is?'

'Absolutely.'

'And where are we having this dinner?'

'My place. You probably don't remember, but I'm a pretty good cook. I was thinking a roast. You okay for that? Or would you prefer fish? I do a fantastic—'

'Wait. Slow down. We're racing past the bits that need clarifying.'

'We are? I don't see how it could be made any—'

'Parker. I want to clarify Parker's role in this.'

She glances up at the ceiling. 'Hmm? What was that?'

As evasive techniques go, it's the worst. Things click into place in Cody's mind.

'This dinner. Who'll be there?'

'You. And me.'

'And?'

She stares at him for some time. Then her shoulders slump in resignation.

'Okay, and Parker. But that's it. Just the three of us.'

'So let me get this straight. You're inviting me to dinner with you and Parker. You want your ex-boyfriend to come to dinner with your fiancé.'

'You've got it. Now about this RSVP . . .'

'Why?'

'God, Cody. Why are you making this so frigging complicated? Parker and I are inviting you to dinner because it's a nice thing to do. That's all you need to know.'

'That implies there are other things I don't need to know.'

'No. That's not what I meant. You're reading far too much into this. I'm inviting you to dinner, not testing you to see if you're suitable to join MI5. What's the problem?'

'The problem is that this is a sudden change of tune. I haven't exactly been your flavour of the month.'

She sighs. 'No, you haven't. But that's because I've been selfish.'

'Selfish? In what way?'

'I expected you to act like everyone else. You know, when I was ill, I thought you might show up a few more times. Bring me grapes and shit. And when you didn't, it really pissed me off. But you're not like everyone else. You have your own issues going on. I should make allowances.'

'I'm not disabled, Megan.'

'No. I know you're not. But I do think you need more friends around you. You need to get out more.'

'This dinner – you're not planning to turn it into some kind of therapy session, are you? I don't want any touchy-feely nonsense.'

Webley's voice goes up a notch in both volume and pitch. 'Look. How many more times? It's dinner. Are you coming or not?'

'When?'

'Whenever you like. No, on second thoughts, let's pin you down. Sunday, seven o'clock. The best day for a roast. And don't say you've got something else on, because you haven't.'

'Why do I feel like I've just been insulted? Okay, you're on.'

Her eyes widen in astonishment. 'You're accepting?'

'Well, now you ask . . .'

'You're accepting. Great. Bring some wine. If you're going to be like this on the night, I'll need at least a gallon of the stuff.'

She walks away, muttering to herself, 'Jesus. Why didn't I just leave an invitation card on his desk?'

25

It's Cody who takes the call. He listens, says 'uh-huh' a couple of times, then tells the desk sergeant to send the guy up.

Cody stands up. Starts crossing the room. On his way past Webley, he raps his knuckles on her desk.

'You might want to be in on this,' he says.

Webley shoots him a puzzled look, but gets out of her chair and follows anyway.

'What is it?' she asks when she catches up with him.

'Young guy you interviewed at the school? Jamie Morgan?'

'The caretaker lad, yeah. What about him?'

'He's just come in. Wants to talk to us. Says he's got some important information, apparently.'

They reach the top of the staircase. Jamie Morgan, still in his work overalls, sees them standing there, and slows his ascent.

'Come on up, Jamie,' says Cody. 'We don't bite.'

Morgan continues up the stairs. Cody nods at him to follow, then leads him into an interview room. The three of them take seats at the single table in the centre of the room.

Hoping to ease the young man's obvious tension, Cody puts on a smile.

'I'm Detective Sergeant Cody,' he says. 'I believe you've already met DC Webley here.'

Morgan's gaze oscillates between the two detectives. 'Er, yeah. Hi.'

'The officers downstairs have said that you've got some information for us.'

Morgan sits hunched over. He slides his hand along the edge of the table.

'Maybe. I don't know. It could be nothing. I just thought . . .'

'Thought what, Jamie?'

Morgan bites his lip. It's clear he's struggling with the idea of imparting whatever he knows.

'Look, maybe this is a mistake. It's probably nothing. I should go home.'

It's Webley who speaks next.

'Where's home, Jamie?'

Cody notices how Morgan is able to lift his head and look Webley in the eye. She has a way with people, he thinks. She could probably even get this lad to come to dinner with her fiancé.

'West Derby,' he says. 'Just off Eaton Road.'

'So this is a bit out of your way, then. Do you drive?'

'Yeah. I've got a little Fiesta I bought off my dad. It's a few years old, but it's in good nick.'

'Did you come here straight from work?'

'Yeah.' He tugs at his overalls. 'Still got my gear on.'

'So you must have thought it was pretty urgent, then. Something that couldn't wait.'

Morgan studies the table again as he thinks about this. 'I suppose so. I just don't want to make a mistake, you know?'

Webley leans back in her chair. Folds her arms. Smiles. In another setting she could be mistaken for the lad's big sister, offering her insights into the workings of the female mind.

'Jamie, why don't you let us worry about that? We're pretty good at working out what's important and what isn't. Sometimes a piece of information that might seem trivial to someone else can be vital to us. It's much better that you get it off your chest. I take it this is something to do with the two murdered women?'

Morgan looks at her, then at Cody, then back to Webley.

'That's the thing,' he says. 'With it being two. It was hard enough when it was one. But if this is the same guy . . . And if it happens again . . .'

Cody wants to leap in at this point. Wants to demand that Morgan spits it out. But he knows it's best to leave it to Webley.

'What is it, Jamie?' she asks. 'What is it you want to tell us?'

'I . . . I don't want to get him into trouble . . .'

'Who? Who might be in trouble?'

'My boss. Colin Daley. It's probably nothing. But I didn't want you to think I was covering something up. Especially with this second woman being killed.'

'Okay, Jamie. You're doing the right thing. What is it your boss has done?'

'It was when you came to talk to us in the school. I saw you arriving, so I asked around and found out you wanted to interview everyone. That's when I told Col.'

Cody can't contain himself any longer. 'You called him on the phone?'

'No. He was in the workshop.'

'Wait a minute. You told us that Mr Daley was at home, and that he phoned you to say he was ill.'

'I know. I'm sorry. At the time I thought it was just a little white lie, and it probably still is, but—'

'Okay, so you tell your boss about the police arriving. What happens then?'

'Nothing, really. Col just accepts it. He doesn't seem particularly interested. But just a few minutes later he tells me he's feeling really sick, and that he thinks he'll have to go home again.'

'Did that come as a surprise to you?'

'Yeah. A big surprise. Col is never off sick. And he seemed right as rain when he first came in to work.'

'All right. So he tells you he's feeling sick. What then?'

'Well, then he asks me a favour. He asks me if I'd mind changing the story just a little bit. He says that if anyone asks, he never actually came in to work that day.'

'Did he say why he wanted you to do this?'

'Yeah. He said it would look suspicious if he went home as soon as the police turned up, even though he had nothing to feel guilty about.'

'Did you believe him?'

'At the time, yeah. I could understand his point about it looking like he was doing a runner. A slight change like that didn't seem such a big deal.'

'But now? What do you think about it now?'

'I don't know. Maybe I'm making a mountain out of a molehill, you know? But it's been bothering me ever since. And when this other woman got killed, it bothered me even more. I've been losing sleep over this. Like I say, it's probably nothing. Col probably was ill, and it was just coincidence that it happened when it did. But I don't like lying for people, especially when it's something as serious as this. So I thought I should come in and tell you the truth. That's right, isn't it? You want the truth?'

Cody nods. 'Jamie, if everyone told the truth, our job would be a hell of a lot easier.'

26

The boy again. Ewan. Standing at the door in his school uniform and a triangle of buttered toast in his hand.

'You're back,' he says.

'We're back. Is your dad there?'

'More questions?'

'More questions. Is he there?'

'Has my dad done something wrong?'

'We just need to ask him a few things.'

'That doesn't answer my question.'

Cody turns to Webley, inviting her to take over.

'Hi, Ewan. Would you mind getting your dad for us, please?'

Ewan takes a bite out of his toast. 'Can't.'

'You're not going to tell us he's dead again, are you?'

'No.'

'So why can't you fetch him for us?'

'Because he's not home yet.'

'Will he be long?'

'Probably not.'

'Okay, good. Mind if we come in and wait?'

Ewan chews. Cogitates. Shrugs.

'Okay.'

He turns and walks away. Cody and Webley follow him in. Back into the living room with its cheap Christmas cheer.

They all sit down simultaneously. Ewan bites his toast and stares.

He says, 'Is this about the other woman who was killed?'

Cody shakes his head. 'No, it's not about that.' Which is true, as far as he knows. No point filling the kid's head with scary possibilities.

'My mate Jez says she was a prozzy, this woman.'

'Does he now? Your mate Jez sounds like someone we should talk to. He seems to take a strong interest in these cases.'

'He loves things like that. Murders and stuff. Is it true she had a crucifix through her heart?'

Cody wants to smile, but at the same time he doesn't want to destroy the boy's innocent faith in his best mate.

'We're not allowed to talk about details of current investigations.'

He sees the disappointment on Ewan's face. Quickly, he adds, 'I had a think about that question you asked me, though. The one about the weirdest case I've ever worked on. I can tell you about that, if you like.'

The boy's eyes widen. 'Go 'ead.'

'Okay, so there was this bloke. His name was Jack. Bit strange, he was. He wasn't very good with people, so he was never in a job for very long. He lived alone, tried to keep himself to himself. The problem was, he had a really nosy neighbour. The woman next door. She had a husband and five kids, but she spent most of her time looking out of her window at Jack. Every time he stepped outside, he'd look up, and there she'd be, just staring at him. He couldn't mow the lawn or take the bins out or go to the shops without seeing this woman's face at the window, watching his every move. He hated talking to people, but one day he plucked up the courage and confronted her over the garden fence. He demanded to know why she kept watching him all the time.'

'What did she say?'

'She just told him it was a free country, and went back inside. A minute later she was at the upstairs window, looking down on him again.'

'The nosy cow,' says Ewan. 'That would drive me mad.'

Cody points a finger at him. 'Funny you should say that. Apparently this went on for months. Jack had no escape. She was always there. Even when her kids were fighting and screaming, she would ignore them so that she could keep watching what Jack was doing. At night, he would go to draw his curtains in his bay window, and he would look across and see her in her own bay, staring back at him. She was like an evil spirit, wanting to know about his every move.'

'Why didn't he call the police?'

'For one thing, what could we have done? Looking out your window is hardly a crime, is it? Besides, he wasn't that type of fella. Like I said, he had great trouble talking to people. He would never have come to us. One day, someone did, though.'

Cody pauses for effect. Checks to see that he's got the boy under his influence.

'Who?'

'Another neighbour. We got a call to say that Jack was walking up and down his street, and that he was covered in blood.'

'No!'

'Yup. So we went out there, and we found him, and we asked him what had happened. All he could say to us was the same thing, over and over again.'

'What? What did he say?'

'He said, "Now she knows what it's like to be watched all the time."'

'What did he mean by that?'

'We had no idea. Not until we went into the woman's house next door. That's when we found her.'

'Dead?'

'No. Actually very much alive. She was tied to a chair in her kitchen. But all around her, pinned to the walls, were the eyeballs of her husband and kids.'

Cody hears the gasps, both from Ewan and Webley. Ewan's mouth is wide open, bits of masticated toast still visible there. The room dances in the lights of the Christmas tree, but is deathly silent.

The knock on the door causes them all to bounce in their seats, Cody included.

'That'll be my dad,' says Ewan. He moves towards the door, but keeps his eyes fixed on Cody. Cody does his best to keep his face straight, so as not to shatter the illusion of truth.

When the boy has gone, Webley launches her elbow into Cody's ribs. 'What did you go and tell him that for?'

DAVID JACKSON | 191

'You saw him. He loved every minute of it. I bet he can't wait to get one up on his mate Jez with that story.'

Webley shakes her head in disbelief. 'For someone who's supposed to know all about the effects of trauma, you're not setting a brilliant example.'

'Don't know about that. I'm quite proud of myself. Reckon I'm a natural raconteur.'

'Really? Remind me never to ask you to tell me a bedtime story.'

Cody grins. 'I don't think that situation is likely to arise again, do you?'

She gives him another dig in the ribs.

From the hallway comes the sound of muted conversation. Then the door opens and Daley enters, his son behind him.

Cody and Webley stand up.

'Mr Daley,' says Cody. 'We're going to have to ask you a few more questions, I'm afraid. Now if—'

'Never mind that,' Daley interrupts. 'What have you been saying to my son?'

27

They escort Daley back to the police station on Stanley Road, but not before ensuring that he contacts a neighbour to keep an eye on Ewan. This is too serious a matter to conduct in the man's own house. They need more austere surroundings, more formality. They want to impress upon him that they will not tolerate further attempts to deceive or mislead.

They put him in an interview room. Sit him on the same plastic chair that Daley's young assistant occupied earlier.

Webley and Cody sit opposite him. Cody starts the recording of the interview. He makes it very clear to Daley that this interview is being conducted under caution. As he does so, he keeps his eyes on Daley, studying his reactions. Daley appears nervous. He keeps wiggling his chin from side to side, and scratching his nose.

Cody picks up a manila folder in front of him. Opens it. Pretends to scan its contents. Says nothing. He wants to let Daley sweat for a little.

Eventually Daley breaks the silence: 'Do you mind telling me what this is about?'

Cody closes the folder again. Places it back on the table.

'As I mentioned, we have a few additional questions for you.'

'Okay. That's fine, but . . . couldn't we have done it at the house?'

'I think we need to do this here, Colin. You don't mind if I call you Colin, do you?'

'No, but . . . This all seems a bit . . . official, like.'

'Well, murder is a serious offence, Colin. And we're dealing with two murders now.'

'Yeah. Okay. But I still don't see . . . I mean, have I done something wrong? You said I'm not under arrest . . .'

'No, Colin, you're not under arrest. But we need to clear something up. There's a slight . . . inconsistency in what you told us.'

Daley narrows his eyes. 'Inconsistency? What kind of inconsistency?'

'When we came to the school, we were led to believe that you had taken the day off sick.'

Daley nods. 'Yeah, that's right. What's the problem with that?'

'The *whole* day, Colin. The story we were given is that you were never at the school that day, and that you phoned Jamie Morgan to let him know you were ill.'

Cody pauses to allow Daley's brain to work on that. To give him a chance to acknowledge the error and correct it. But Daley says nothing. He just stares at Cody, his eyelids quivering slightly.

'The problem is,' says Webley. 'You were seen. At the school, on that very morning.'

Not a lie, thinks Cody. He *was* seen at the school. By Jamie Morgan. But phrasing it in this way doesn't drop Morgan in the shit.

Daley scratches his nose again. Pushes a hand through his hair. Then he blows out a stream of air.

'All right, it's true. I *was* at the school, but only for a short period of time. I felt crap, so I went home. It's no big deal.'

'If it wasn't such a big deal, why did you lie to us?' says Webley.

Daley raises a corrective finger. 'No, that's not right. I didn't lie to you.'

'You told us—'

'I told you nothing of the sort. I think you'll find it was Jamie who said that to you, not me.'

Technically he's right, thinks Cody. But this is not the right time to be getting bloody pedantic.

'Let's not start splitting hairs,' says Cody. 'You put him up to it. The thing we want to know is why did you do that? Why bother to make up a complete fabrication for what you've just been telling us is such a small matter?'

'Because . . . because it looks fishy, doesn't it? I mean, I disappear as soon as the law turns up at the school gate. Don't you think that looks a bit suspicious?'

'It looks even more suspicious now, Colin.'

Daley's shoulders slump. 'I know, I know. It was stupid. I'm sorry. I felt sick, and I panicked. There was no way I could have lasted even a few more minutes at the school. I was hot and I was sweaty and my guts felt like they were about to explode. I had to get out of there. Telling a little white lie was the least of my concerns at the time. I really didn't think it would matter.'

And perhaps it doesn't, thinks Cody. If Daley's story is true, perhaps this is just another cul-de-sac in an investigation that's leading nowhere.

'The Saturday before we came into the school, do you mind telling us where you were that day?'

Daley seems thrown by the switch in questioning.

'Saturday? What time Saturday?'

'Tell us what you did in the afternoon.'

'Okay. Well, we had a late lunch, and then I did some work in the kitchen, and then I listened to the match on the radio. After that, it was time to start thinking about tea, so I—'

'What work were you doing in the kitchen?'

'What? Oh. Well, I washed the dishes and then I did some odd jobs. I had to change a couple of the bulbs in the ceiling, and then I fixed a leak on the washing machine.'

'What was wrong with it?'

'Loose connection on the inlet. It wasn't hard to fix.'

'Okay, so then you listened to the match. Who was playing?'

'Liverpool were at home to Stoke.'

'What time was kick-off?'

'Three o'clock.'

'So the programme would have finished at about . . .'

'About five. Like I said, it was time to start thinking about the next meal then.'

'So, basically you were at home all afternoon and evening? Can your son verify that?'

Daley drops his gaze. 'Well . . . no. Not all of it. He goes out with his mates on Saturdays.'

'What about the following Saturday?' says Webley. 'What did you do on the Saturday just gone?'

'I went to town. I needed to buy some new clothes.'

'What time was this?'

'I left the house at just after two. Maybe two thirty.'

'How did you get into town?'

'I took the car. I hate public transport.'

'Where did you park?'

'At the multistorey on Mount Pleasant.'

'And which shops did you go to?'

'Ooh ... John Lewis, Top Shop, Hollister. A couple of others.'

'And then you went home?'

'Not straight away. I had a pint in the Big House.'

The Big House is a local name for a popular pub in the city centre. Its proper name is the Vines. As its nickname implies, its size makes it possible to hide away in a corner without being remembered by other customers.

'Did you meet anyone there?'

'Nope. Just had a beer, did the crossword and left.'

'What time did you get home?'

'I guess about six.'

'What were you wearing?'

Daley furrows his brow. 'Er, let me think ... Jeans, trainers, a grey sweater and a coat.'

'Describe the coat to me.'

'The coat? Well, it's like an aviator's jacket. You know – brown leather with a fur collar.'

Cody nods, though it's not the answer he would have liked to hear.

'All right, Colin. I'm going to show you a couple of photographs.' Seeing the concern on Daley's face, he adds, 'Nothing gruesome.'

He opens the folder in front of him. Removes the top photograph and slides it across to Daley. It's the grainy image of the figure at the Anglican cathedral.

'Do you recognise that person?'

Daley studies it. Takes his time about it, too, raising Cody's hopes.

But then he shakes his head. 'Nope. Is that . . . is that the killer?'

Cody doesn't answer. He passes the next photo across. The one taken at the Metropolitan cathedral.

'What about this picture?'

Daley gives this one short shrift. 'Same guy, isn't it? Hard to tell from these, though. This is the guy you want, isn't it? The one who killed the two women. Jesus.'

'And it's definitely not you?'

Daley looks appalled at the suggestion. 'Of course it's not me. I had nothing to do with it. Look, I admit I told a lie about being at home when I was ill. If I'd have known it would lead to this, I wouldn't have done it. Honest, this is nothing to do with me. I'm totally shocked anyone might even think it was.'

Cody hands him a third image. The web page depicting the coat in more detail.

'Ever seen this coat, or one like it?'

Daley is becoming more animated now. He looks to Webley, as if seeking help to end his ordeal. 'It's just a coat, isn't it? Lots

of people wear coats like that. How would I know if I've seen it
in the street?'

'But you don't own one?'

'No. Swear to God. I've never had a coat like that. Come and
search the house if you like. Ask my son, or people at the school,
or my neighbours. Nobody has ever seen me in a coat like that.'

And that's it. At this stage, there's nothing more they can
reasonably ask.

So they let him go.

'What do you think?' says Webley when they are alone in the
interview room.

Cody rubs his eyes, then draws his fingers down the sides
of his nose. 'I don't know what to think any more. Part of me
says the guy seems legit, and that he just made a mistake that
didn't justify us coming down on him so heavy like that. Then
another part of me says he's a lying git with no real alibi at the
time of either homicide. He was parked at the bottom of Mount
Pleasant. He could easily have stopped off at the cathedral on
the way home. He could have kept the coat in the boot of his car.
Switched it to do the murder, then switched back again before
going home.'

'We could request a search warrant. Search his car and his
house.'

Cody shakes his head. 'We need more to go on. It's all supposition at the moment. The only thing we know he's guilty of
is a slight deviation from the truth. And maybe that's the extent
of it. He could be a perfectly nice guy, doing his best to bring up
his kid as a single parent. Besides . . .'

'Besides what?'

'Our killer's too clever to be caught that way. He's not going to leave incriminating evidence lying around where we can find it.'

'If he's that good, how are we ever going to catch him?'

'God knows,' says Cody.

The irony of the remark escapes him.

28

He remembers . . .

Nine years old. Wanting to be an individual. Wanting to spend more time away from his mother. Wanting to go in search of his own thoughts and opinions.

Questioning things . . .

The questions crawl into his consciousness when he least expects them. They are like dark, scuttling insects, biting into his mind.

What if the Bible isn't true? the insects say. What if your mother isn't always right? What if there isn't a God? What if Jesus doesn't love you? What if nobody loves you?

He slaps them back with ferocity as soon as they appear. He screws up his eyes and grits his teeth and banishes the vermin to the blackness at the back of his head, where the unthinkable thoughts live.

But they always return, bringing with them their stings and their mandibles and their sucking mouth parts to feed on his brain.

He is at the barber's.

An innocent, mundane episode in a life, one would think.

The barber's name is Antonio. Or at least that's what's on his sign outside. It might not be his real name, but he has a black moustache to prop up the lie.

The boy's mother leaves strict instructions with Antonio. Nothing fancy, she insists. A straightforward boy's haircut. And no lotions, potions, waxes or mousses either. He's not entering a beauty contest, and he's not a poodle.

And then she exits the shop, off to round up pork chops or sausages or something equally unimaginative for their tea.

The boy settles into the hi-tech chair that makes him feel like the captain of a spaceship. He stares at himself in the mirror and wonders what Jesus has against unusual hairstyles.

Antonio begins his work. The clippers first. The boy feels the vibration against his skull, the buzz through his teeth. He watches the pieces of hair drop onto his shoulders like petals from a dying flower.

He closes his eyes as Antonio sprays scented water onto his head from a plastic bottle. Some of it runs down his face and tickles his neck.

With a flourish, Antonio raises his hands and displays the tools of his artistry: the comb and the scissors. His eyes take on the manic intensity of a sculptor or an oil painter, and then he launches his attack on the boy's head.

It stops within a few snips.

Antonio parts the boy's damp hair to one side, then the other. He peers at the boy's crown as he does so. The boy watches the puzzling behaviour in the mirror, and wonders why the barber has suddenly become so indecisive.

Antonio issues a short whistle to his colleague seated at the rear of the shop. The burly man abandons his copy of the *Daily Mirror* and comes to stand at his colleague's side. Antonio repeats his actions with the comb while the other man looks on. Some inaudible whispering ensues, accompanied by some nodding. The boy feels he should ask a question, but also that to do so would be getting above his station. Perhaps he has a particularly unusual head, he thinks. Or perhaps Antonio is considering a daringly radical haircut, despite the constraints laid down earlier.

The boy sits and awaits the outcome with interest.

But what follows does not seem right. It does not seem to the boy that this will in any way satisfy what his mother has ordered.

Antonio whips away the cape from around the boy's neck. Tells him he can't do any more for him. Asks him to sit on the bench at the back of the room until his mother reappears.

Confused, the boy does as he is told. He looks searchingly at Antonio as he drags his feet across the tiled floor, but gets no answers. When he perches his backside on the edge of the padded fake-leather bench, he wonders whether he has done something wrong. The atmosphere seems like a pale imitation of the situations he gets into at home, as though his mother has deliberately deposited an aura of dissatisfaction here in the expectation that he will undoubtedly do something to incur her wrath.

But surely he did only what he was told? He sat in the big spaceship chair and said nothing and did nothing except to look straight ahead. What possible harm can he have done with that?

Nothing, he tells himself. I've done nothing wrong. You can ask Jesus. He'll tell you. I didn't do anything.

But still he worries. He swings his legs above the floor, because if he tries to keep them still they will tremble. He feels sick, too. When he straightens his spine and cranes his neck, he can see himself in the mirror, and he thinks he looks the colour of old paper.

Something runs down his nose. He wonders if he is sweating profusely, but then he realises his hair is still damp. Why have they left it like that? Why is it that they can suddenly no longer bear to be anywhere near him?

It occurs to him to run away. To drop from his seat and dash across the shop and fling open the door and sprint down the street.

Will they run after me? he wonders. Will they try to catch me? And if they do, will they take me to the police for not paying for half a haircut?

Or will they not care? Perhaps they will simply be glad to be rid of me. Perhaps they will breathe a sigh of relief when this horrible little kid is out of their sight.

Because that's how he feels right now. Hated, unwanted, alone. It's a cocktail of negativity that comes readily to him these days. Self-esteem lost the battle a long time ago.

A tinkle of a bell as his mother steps through the door. There is already a scowl on her face, as though she detected the wrongness in here from fifty yards away.

She looks at the boy. He in turns says nothing, because he has nothing to offer.

Antonio moves away from his current customer. He approaches the boy's mother. More hushed tones and serious faces. His mother's face takes on a look of disbelief, embarrassment and anger. She pulls a purse from her bag, but Antonio waves away the offer of payment, then returns to his customer.

The boy studies his mother for further clues. It seems to him that she is turning redder by the second.

She takes his hand firmly in hers. Drags him from the bench and out of the shop. He doesn't make a sound, because he senses she is on that precipice again. She is on the verge of dropping into an uncontrolled free-fall of vitriol. He doesn't want that – not in a public place.

She pulls him quickly along the street, towards their house. He has to run to keep up with her pace. And then she begins muttering.

'I don't believe it,' she says. 'The shame of it. The embarrassment. They'll be talking about us, you know that, don't you? We'll be the local laughing stock. Everywhere we go, people will be pointing and staring at us. Oh, the shame!'

He decides to speak up, now that she has broken the silence. 'Mummy, I don't know what—'

'Shut up!' she says, and yanks his arm forward, hurting his shoulder. 'Keep that mouth closed, you disgusting little boy. I don't want to hear your excuses. Save them for your prayers, because I'll tell you what, God isn't happy with you right now.'

He wonders how she knows this – how she has received the message from God so quickly. But he decides it's one of those questions he must never voice. It's one of the insects in his head that must not be allowed to see the light of day.

He wishes God would talk to him, too, because he is still none the wiser.

What he does have, in spades, is fear. Wrath is in the air. He feels it building like an electrical charge in the clouds above. And he is the lightning rod, exposed and alone, knowing that the full force of that vengeance is about to strike him and burn him.

When she pulls him through the front door, it is with a force that causes him to lift from the ground. He lands in the hallway. Stares at the dark silhouette of his mother against the doorway onto the street.

She slams the door. Framed pictures on the wall jump as if startled. He is trapped in here now. Away from prying eyes. She can do what she wants with him.

'Turn around,' she orders.

He doesn't want to turn around. Doesn't want to be blind to what might be coming his way.

'Mummy, I—'

'TURN AROUND!'

The very energy in her words is enough to spin him on his heels. He stands shaking in the dim hallway. Ahead of him is the staircase. He wants to run up those stairs. He could race into the bathroom and lock the door. But he knows he won't.

A thick gloom sits at the top of the stairs. He can imagine figures hidden there in the darkness, watching. Grinning as they wait for their entertainment to begin. There are no good spirits up there. No angels to protect him.

The smacking of his bare legs ranks among her most ferocious to date. It comes in rapid bursts, in time to the accompaniment of her shrieking voice. His body moves forward without his conscious control, desperate to avoid the pain. He falls face forward onto the stairs, and still the slaps resound and burn his young skin. For a while, his screaming drowns out her words, but eventually they seep through:

'Cleanliness is next to godliness. Cleanliness is next to godliness. Cleanliness is next to godliness . . .'

And still he doesn't understand.

He suspects he will be sent up to his room not understanding. This whole lesson, ostensibly being branded on him with the rod of discipline, will for ever have failed to heighten his wisdom.

But his mother has not finished. Not by a long chalk.

Panting with exertion, she drags her sobbing child away from the stairs. Pushes and prods him to stumble ahead of her like a captured enemy soldier. In the kitchen she scrapes a wooden chair away from the table and leans on his shoulders to make him sit on it.

She moves around the chair to stand in front of him. Through the blur of his tears he can barely make out her form as she brings her face to within inches of his.

'Do. Not. Move.'

Her words act like glue, sticking him to the chair. It's as though he is under a hypnotic spell.

And then his mother is gone. Out of the kitchen. Out of the house, it seems. He hears the front door being slammed again, but still he is not convinced he is safe. He wonders if this is a test of his obedience. Wonders if she is standing in the hallway, waiting for him to break her commandment. God's commandment, too: *Honour thy father and thy mother.* The forces stacked against him are overwhelming.

And so he stays exactly where he has been put. He cries and he wails and he tries to overcome the red-hot pain through sheer willpower. He calls to God and to Jesus to help him in his hour of need, because that's what they do, isn't it? They are on the side of the weak and the innocent and the good of heart.

But perhaps he is not so innocent, not so good. His mother must know best, surely? She knows everything about the Bible. She knows what is right.

So where does that leave him? What does that make him? An irredeemable sinner, doomed to suffer for eternity?

Is he so utterly worthless?

When he hears her return, he wills his heart to stop. It would be a mercy, he thinks.

He is only nine years old.

She comes back into the kitchen. He starts to turn towards her, but she orders him to face forward, and his head snaps back into position.

She places a hand on his left shoulder. 'I have to do this,' she tells him. 'I have to fight the Devil. I don't know how you became so unclean, but we have to get rid of them.'

He sniffs wetly. 'Get rid of what, Mummy? I don't under—'

'The insects, boy! The insects in your head.'

The explanation shocks him to the core. He wonders how she can possibly have seen into his mind – how she can possibly know about the dark thoughts that scuttle around in his head. But there it is. She knows. She sees all. God must have spoken to her.

And then he hears the angry buzz. As though his mother is going to launch an attack on the insects with one even larger and more ferocious.

'Head down,' she orders.

He does as he is told. He expects the same sensation he experienced in the barber's: the soft vibration on the nape of his neck.

Instead he gets a violent scraping against his skull, as though she is trying to sand off his skin. And it is not confined to his neck: it carries up and over the back of his head, and right across to his forehead. Massive chunks of hair drop onto his lap.

'Mummy!' he screams. 'What are you doing?'

'Shush!' she tells him. 'You brought this on yourself. You're dirty. You could infest others. The insects could jump onto me. I have to get rid of them. Do you think Jesus would want anything to do with such a filthy boy?'

And so she continues. She tracks the clippers over every inch of his head, dragging the device so close against his scalp it sometimes chews a piece out of it. She seems deaf and blind to his signals of distress. He yells and he shakes and he pleads until it feels his heart will explode, but she carries on regardless.

And then it is done. The gnashing teeth of the clippers go silent. His mother goes silent, too.

The boy's head is still bowed. His eyes are closed. He doesn't want to move. Doesn't want to see. Doesn't want to exist.

'There,' says his mother finally. 'Now you're clean again.'

He notices a slight catch in her voice, as though she has just comprehended the atrocity she has perpetrated. But he doesn't turn to check. It doesn't seem to matter now.

He hears her leave the room. If he cared, he would call after her. But the caring has been driven out of him.

He doesn't know how long he sits there. The tears have dried to a crust on his cheeks. His throat burns with all the work it has done.

Eventually he stands up. His legs seem to move of their own accord, dragging him upstairs to the sanctuary of his bedroom. Throughout the short journey he keeps his eyes downcast, as though any reminder of his surroundings is too painful to bear.

When he gets to his room, he lowers himself gently onto the edge of his bed. From somewhere deep within the mattress, a coil pings his arrival.

He knows he is precisely opposite the mirror on his wall. He will have to look up at some point. But first he has to gather the strength.

Perhaps it's not too bad, he tells himself. Perhaps it seemed much worse than it actually is. Perhaps his mother has hairdressing skills of which he knows nothing.

He tells himself all these things. Positive thoughts to turn dark into light.

Slowly, he raises his head. Blinks his exhausted eyes to clarify the image.

A pale stranger looks back at him.

He rises from the bed. Again the mattress pings. He shuffles towards the mirror – closer, closer – until he is certain.

And then he screams.

He had thought he had nothing left in him, but these screams are long and loud and shrill. They could rouse the whole neighbourhood. His mother cannot fail to hear them.

But she does not come. She does not hasten to the side of her distraught nine-year-old child. She does not cuddle him or reassure him with soothing words. Instead, she leaves him to wallow in his misery, to bathe in the echoes of his cries.

It's all in God's plan, she will tell him later. He moves in mysterious ways.

She will say, *Blessed are those who are persecuted for righteousness' sake, for theirs is the kingdom of heaven.*

All this happens on a Friday evening. A small mercy is that he has the weekend to recover. In that time he does not leave the house. His cuts scab over. And he thinks, if he looks really, really hard, that his hair grows back a little. Not much, admittedly, but just enough to make it less noteworthy, less extreme. Perhaps he can get away with it now. Perhaps it is not such an attention grabber. Another week would be even better, but his mother isn't going to permit that.

And even if people do notice, doesn't he look like a hard-case now? Doesn't he look like someone who would smash your teeth in if you even look the wrong way at him? Isn't this the type of kid who has a bull mastiff and a fast temper and a fear of nobody?

He gets his answers on the way to school. Even with his mother at his side, the stares are not deflected. Children and adults alike turn towards him with wide eyes and wide mouths. Sometimes they point. Sometimes they wear wounding grins.

And when the shielding shadow of his mother is withdrawn as he crosses the school threshold, the hordes find their courage and approach. They do not see the tough skinhead he managed to perceive through his blinkered optimism. They do not see that his hair has miraculously blossomed into an inconspicuous style in the space of a weekend.

He knows this because of the taunts, the cruel jibes. They call him 'Jug Ears' and 'Belsen Boy' and 'Wingnut' and 'Slaphead'. These are not terms of respect or endearment. These are barbed spears that are meant to hurt.

Because being hurt is his lot, it seems.

It's the cross he is meant to bear.

29

He's missed something.

Cody stares at his computer screen. He flicks through report after report, statement after statement, but it's not jumping out at him.

It would help if he had some idea as to where to focus his attention, but he doesn't. He just knows that he has missed something. There is a set of neurons in his brain desperate to make a connection with another set, and yet he just cannot seem to stimulate the necessary spark of energy.

It's Thursday now. The middle of December. Almost two weeks after the murder of Mary Cowper, and seemingly still no closer to catching the killer. The police computers are bulging with masses of information, but none of it seems to be telling them anything of worth.

He passes an eye over a few more documents. Hesitates when he gets to the transcript of the interview with Daley. He keeps coming back to this, and he's not sure why. There's a magnetic pull there that should be telling him something, but he has scrutinised every word of it several times and still not discovered any hidden depths.

It doesn't help that his mind insists on wandering. Transporting him back to the phantom caller at his flat.

It makes him uneasy that he keeps being taken by surprise. The screaming over the phone was a surprise. The 'time to play' announcement was a surprise. And then the call at his door – Jesus Christ, that was a shocker!

So what will the next surprise be? He has no way of knowing, and therefore no way of preparing. And Cody doesn't like the sensation of being unprepared.

He also wonders whether he's handling this properly. He's a copper, and he suspects that the people responsible for these pranks are the same people who were responsible for torturing him and killing his partner. So why isn't he turning this over to the force? Why isn't he asking them to investigate – to put all the vast resources at their disposal to good use in catching these scum? Why not ask them to trace the calls coming in? Wouldn't that take the pressure off?

He knows the answers. Or at least he thinks he does.

This has become personal, on both sides. A private battle. His enemy wants to tease, to scare, to provoke, to entice. Any sign of a larger police involvement will cause the aggressors to lose interest and walk away. And Cody's chances of confronting them will vanish.

At the same time, Cody isn't convinced he wants to be shackled by the law and the conventions of police procedure. He needs the freedom to work in whatever way the situation requires. And that may mean doing things he would once never have dreamt of.

He has wrestled with this question a lot lately. What would he do if he came face to face with his enemy? What is he capable of?

What would he have done if he had managed to catch his mysterious caller the other night? Question him, certainly. But more than that? Beat him? Torture him? Kill him?

He doesn't know the answers. But neither does he want to go into this with one hand tied behind his back. His opponents will not be under any compunction to adopt Queensbury Rules, so why should he? When in Rome . . .

A thought flits through his brain, but evades capture.

What? What was it?

He focuses on the computer screen again. Daley's interview? No, not that. And yet . . .

The other chat with Daley! In his house, his living room.

When in Rome . . .

That's it! That's the missing link!

Cody jumps out of his chair. Grabs his coat. Raps on Webley's desk again on his way past.

'Come 'ead,' he says. 'Places to be, people to see.'

'Where are we going?' she asks.

'Rome.'

'I'd prefer Venice.'

There's nothing Italianate about Mrs Laplace's office in Oakdale School. Webley keeps throwing Cody questioning looks, but he doesn't want to explain himself just yet. Not until he's verified his suspicions.

Mrs Laplace leaves them to it. Reluctantly, it has to be said. She abandons her spacious office with a distinct inquisitorial gleam in her eye. Again, Cody refuses to explain himself.

Left with only the detectives for company, Andy Puckleton looks as though he's about to sit an exam himself. Cody thinks he's worse than he was last time. Not only does he keep adjusting his clothing, but there's a sheen on his brow and a redness in his cheeks that somehow doesn't seem healthy.

'I know we've dragged you away from a maths lesson,' says Cody, 'but this shouldn't take long. Is that all right with you, Andy?'

Cody prefers to use first names in situations like this, and especially now. Puckleton will spend most of his working days being called 'sir' or 'Mr Puckleton'. He will find Cody's familiarity in the workplace disconcerting.

Puckleton pinches the knot in his tie. 'I've left the girls some work to do. I'm sure we'll cope.'

'Yes. So you're probably wondering why we've come back to talk to you again.'

'It has crossed my mind. Was it something I said last time?'

'Kind of. It would probably be more accurate to say it was something you left out.'

'Left out? I, er, I'm not sure what you mean.'

'Well, you told us that you paid regular visits to Mary Cowper's flat.'

Puckleton runs his fingers down the seams of his trousers. 'Yes, that's right. I was perfectly honest with you about it.'

'And you also said that the reason you went there was to discuss problems you were having with your faith.'

Puckleton adjusts his wristwatch now. 'Yes. Again, it was the truth. Look, I don't understand . . .'

'We're not trying to implicate you in anything here, Andy. We're not even trying to be judgemental. What you do in your private life is none of our business, provided it doesn't infringe on anyone else's rights. It just helps us if we have all the facts. We like to know that people are being truthful, even when it's a little uncomfortable for them. But when someone deviates from the truth, even over an apparently trivial matter, it plants a seed of doubt in our minds about other things they might say or claim. Do you see what I'm getting at?'

'I . . . I think so. In a general sense. But I'm not sure how it applies to me.'

Cody makes a deliberate smacking noise when he opens his mouth. Leaves it to Puckleton to decide whether to interpret it as a tut of disapproval.

He looks over at Webley, as if inviting her to continue the questioning. But she looks as mystified as Puckleton. Cody realises he has been cruel in not letting her in on his suspicions. On the other hand, it's a lot more fun this way.

He turns back to Puckleton. 'Andy, when we first came to the school, we spoke to your head, Mrs Laplace, and the deputy head, Mr Beamish. When your name was mentioned as some- one who was closely linked to Mary, I asked if the connection was a romantic one.'

Puckleton emits a laugh like the tinkle of breaking glass. 'That's ridiculous!'

'Yes. That's what Mr Beamish said. Actually, I think he was about to make a joke about it, but he stopped himself.'

Puckleton rolls his eyes and shakes his head. 'That sounds like Tony. He lets his mouth run ahead of him sometimes.'

'Hmm,' says Cody, nodding in a thoughtful way that suggests there's more to come. Then he says, 'Later on, we spoke to Mr Daley, the school caretaker. Do you know him?'

Puckleton exercises his jaw a little before answering. 'Yes, of course I know him. But, well . . .'

'Go on.'

'To be frank, I don't like him very much.'

'Why's that?'

'I don't like his sense of humour. He can be a bit coarse, a bit vulgar. It's not really appropriate with all these girls around. Anyway, what's he got to do with this?'

'I mentioned your girlfriend to him.'

Puckleton looks as though he's about to levitate from his chair. 'What? Why? Why on earth would you do that? It's none of his business.'

'I was asking him about members of staff who might have been close friends with Mary Cowper. He named you. He also seemed fully aware of the reasons why you were having your regular sessions with Mary.'

The redness in Puckleton's cheeks seems suddenly to be sucked back into his body. 'What do you mean? What did he say?'

'Just that you were having problems with your beliefs.'

'My beliefs. Those are the words he used?'

'Yes,' says Cody. He turns to Webley. 'Isn't that right, DC Webley?'

'That's my recollection, Sarge,' she answers. There's a tinge of irritation in her voice. Cody tosses a smile at her, knowing that it will do nothing to pacify her.

Puckleton appears a little less agitated now. He's content with fidgeting again. He flicks something minute from his sleeve, then smooths the material.

'Still none of his business,' he grumbles. 'How did he know that anyway?'

'That was my thought,' Cody says. 'That's why I mentioned Laura, to see if he heard it from her.'

Puckleton raises his nose in the air, as if to sniff for another opportunity to get annoyed at someone. 'And did he?'

'No. You don't need to worry about that.'

'Right. Good.'

'He did seem a bit surprised, though.'

'Surprised at what?'

'When I referred to Laura as your girlfriend. He acted the way Beamish had done. Started to say something, and then changed his mind.'

Puckleton's mouth twists into a shape of indifference. 'Well, I don't know anything about that.'

'No. Do you think Laura would?'

Cody observes carefully as he puts this question in the most innocent way he can muster. He notices the rapid flicker of eyelashes, the rolling of Puckleton's tongue around his cheek.

Puckleton's voice is also seemingly guileless. 'Haven't you already interviewed her?'

'We have. We talked to her before we interviewed you. Bit weird, really.'

'Weird? What was weird about it?'

'She never mentioned you. Not once. Didn't say she had a partner, or was in any kind of relationship whatsoever.'

'That's not surprising.'

'No?'

'No. We work together, don't forget. It's never a good idea to let your personal life intrude into your work. I'll bet if you and DC Webley here had a thing going on, you wouldn't want your colleagues to know.'

This time, Cody steadfastly avoids looking Webley's way. He doesn't want to see what kind of expression she's displaying now.

He says to Puckleton, 'You, on the other hand, had no such qualms. In fact, you seemed incredibly keen to let us know that Laura was your girlfriend.'

Puckleton's shrug seems to travel down from his shoulders and through his whole body. 'I assumed it would stay between us. There didn't seem any harm in telling you. And, yes, maybe I did say it more than once. So what? I'm proud of the fact. Laura is a wonderful girl.'

'Yes,' says Cody. 'Yes, she is. But is she actually your girlfriend?'

The surprise in the room comes with its own shroud of silence. Puckleton's incredulity emanates from him in waves.

'W-What kind of question is that?'

Cody leaves his frontal assault in place while he launches a flank attack. 'Andy, when you visited Mary in her flat, where did you have your discussions?'

'In her living room. Why?'

'You talked about religion and faith, right?'

'Yes. But what has Laura—?'

'Did you refer to the Bible directly?'

'What do you mean?'

'I mean, did you and Mary open the Bible and read through sections in an attempt to help you with your problems?'

'Well . . . yes. Yes, we did. What's wrong with that?'

'Nothing at all. Do you remember which chapters you discussed in particular?'

Puckleton's hands are clenching along the seams of his neatly pressed trousers, crumpling the material.

'We hopped about. Mary knew the Bible inside out. She knew exactly which chapters to consult. She was a great help.'

'I'm sure she was. I've been to Mary's flat, Andy. I saw the Bible in her living room, the one that was used in your chats. There was a bookmark in it, so I opened it at that page. The chapter was Romans 1. Are you familiar with Romans 1, Andy?'

When in Rome . . .

No answer. Puckleton balls more material into his fists, causing his trousers to ride up from his shoes.

Cody says, 'Do you know what Romans 1 is famous – or should I say infamous – for?'

Still no reply.

'Andy . . . are you gay?'

Cody hears Webley shuffle in her seat, and then a sputter of forced high-pitched laughter from Puckleton.

'What? Is this a joke? What the hell gives you that idea?'

'Then you're not gay?'

'No. And why would it matter if I was? Is it a crime now? Because it's the first I've heard of it if it is.'

'No, it's not a crime. And, frankly, I don't give a toss if you're gay, straight, or you want to marry a chicken. Makes no difference to me.'

'Then why are you asking?'

'Because what does matter to me is the truth. If someone lies to me about one thing, then they may have lied to me about other things too. I like to know where I stand with people.'

'Well, I've told you the truth. You can choose to believe it or not. I don't care what you think, and I don't care what the others think either.'

'The others? Do you mean Mr Beamish? He thinks you're gay, doesn't he? That's what he was going to make a joke about before he thought better of it. Or do you mean Mr Daley? He suspects something too, doesn't he? When he was talking about the problems you were having with your beliefs, he didn't mean your religion, did he? He was referring to your sexuality.'

'How would he know? I barely even speak to the man. I told you, he's a nasty piece of work. He's a foul-mouthed idiot who likes to spread gossip. You shouldn't believe a word he says.'

Cody isn't sure he does believe everything that Daley told him, but he's not about to reveal that here.

'All right, Andy. Let's go back to the Bible. Romans 1. You know the chapter I mean?'

A tilt of the head from Puckleton. 'I know it.'

'And you know that many believers regard it as one of the clearest condemnations of homosexuality in the whole Bible?'

'Yes, I know that. But what I also know is that there are other interpretations of that chapter too.'

'Is this a conversation you had with Mary?'

'What? About whether God hates gays? No, Sergeant, I don't believe we had that discussion.'

'Did you talk about Romans 1 at all?'

'Perhaps. Mary would often quote passages from the Bible. She may have taken some of them from Romans 1. That doesn't make me a raging homosexual.'

'So then why the difficulties?'

Puckleton releases his grip on his trousers. Uses his hands in a theatrical gesture of disbelief instead.

'What difficulties? What are you talking about?'

Cody keeps his voice calm, his words measured. 'The difficulties you told us you were having with your faith. The whole reason for these sessions with Mary.'

Puckleton accepts the riposte of his own words. He lowers his arms, relaxes his posture.

'It's none of your business. My faith is a very personal thing. And even if it weren't, something tells me you wouldn't offer a particularly sympathetic ear.'

'Try me.'

'I'll pass, thanks. Now, if that's—'

'What if I ask Laura?'

The eyes that Puckleton now turns on Cody suddenly seem filled with hurt. Cody feels the stab of guilt.

Puckleton's voice is quieter now, as if he is acknowledging his defeat. 'Ask her what? About our sex life? About what we get up to when we're alone? About the fantasies I might have shared with her, or my desires? Is that the sort of thing you mean, Sergeant Cody? Is that the kind of question you intend to put to my girlfriend about me? Is that really how you see yourself making best use of your efforts to catch a murderer?'

It's a sharp reminder of the sometimes sordid side of being a police officer. It's not something Cody often reflects upon, but Puckleton has been articulate enough to bring it to the forefront of his mind.

When Cody speaks again, it is with what he hopes is a touch more compassion. 'Sometimes we have to ask questions like this. We don't do it to amuse ourselves. We don't get any kind of perverted kick out of it. We do it because we're trying to get to the truth. That's what our job is all about. To other people, some of our questions can seem ridiculous or totally unrelated to a case. And, to be honest, sometimes we have no idea where those questions might lead. We just know we have to ask them.'

Puckleton claws at his trousers again. His chest rises and falls as he considers his response. His gaze shifts back and forth between the two detectives.

He says, 'I'm a simple man, Sergeant Cody. Some people think I'm very old-fashioned. I have ideas and principles that are often very hard to stick to in the modern world. One of those is a belief in the sanctity of marriage, and that sex should be confined to those who are married. Laura, on the other hand, is more of a free spirit. She follows her impulses. She'll do what feels right to her at the time, whereas I have to turn things over in my mind first. I admire her for that. I wish I could let my hair down the way she does. But I can't. My beliefs are my beliefs.'

He looks down. Seems to realise he is ruining the appearance of his suit. He brings his hands together and interlaces his fingers – possibly to prevent further sartorial disruption, but perhaps also to help his words reach powers beyond this room.

'You can talk to Laura. She'll tell you that I have resisted the physical side of our relationship. But it's not for the reason you're suggesting. It's because I want Laura and me to be fully committed to each other first.'

'And have you explained all this to Laura?'

'Of course, but I don't think she fully appreciates how important my faith is to me. She lives for today and worries about the consequences afterwards, whereas I worry constantly about the effects of my actions.'

'And this is what you talked about with Mary Cowper? This conflict between what your girlfriend wants and what your faith demands?'

For the first time in the meeting, Puckleton smiles. It's the smile of a priest who witnesses enlightenment in a member of his flock.

He says, 'It's been tearing me apart. I want to keep Laura happy, but at the same time I have to stay true to myself. I'm not sure I can have both. But I needed to talk it through with someone. Mary was that sounding board. Now I don't know what I'll do.'

His last sentence is like a lament that could be uttered for a spouse or family member. Its sadness expands into the room.

And then the school bell breaks the spell, and everyone moves on.

Outside, as they leave the school grounds, Webley says, 'Quite a performance.'

'Wasn't it just?' says Cody. 'I'll lay bets he runs the school drama club. Hard to know what to believe.'

'I don't mean him, you numpty. I'm talking about you.'

Cody turns to her. Sees her arched eyebrows questioning his actions.

'Me? What did I do?'

'You know exactly what you did. You're the one with the flair for melodrama. You were hoping to put on a big show here, only the set kept falling apart and the props wouldn't work.'

'Megan, what are you going on about?'

'You were hoping for an Hercule Poirot moment, weren't you? Gather everyone around the table and announce the name of the killer to your gobsmacked audience. That's why you wouldn't let me in on it while we were driving here. Build up the suspense, and all that. Pity it turned into a bit of a damp squid in the end.'

'Squib. The word is "squib". Squid are characteristically damp, so it wouldn't be a very good analogy.'

'Whatever. I don't know what a squib is, so don't change the subject.'

'I don't even know what the subject is.'

'Yes, you do. I know you too well, Nathan Cody. You thought Puckleton was gay, but that he couldn't handle it, and so he was keeping it under wraps. But then, under your expert interrogation, he would out himself. And not only that, your persistent probing would cause him to reveal that Mary Cowper was using the Bible against him to make him feel like the lowest form of life on earth. She kept telling him how disgusting and depraved his thoughts were, until one day his mind snapped and he battered her to death. And then he began to think that all forms of sex outside marriage were evil too, so he found and murdered a prostitute, and next up he'll kill a nun for scratching her crotch, or a priest for looking at a choirboy. And while all this superb detective work was being demonstrated to us poor mortals, I was supposed to sit there all doe-eyed, wetting my knickers at the thought of learning the next important lesson on the knee of my magnificent superior officer. Go on, admit it – that's what you thought would happen in there, wasn't it?'

She stops for breath. Cody feels as though he has just spent a gruelling hour on a psychoanalyst's couch.

'Well, not exactly—'

'Pah! I can read you like a book, Cody. You're all the same.'

They reach the car. Cody gets out his keys and unlocks it. He says, 'Would have been quite impressive if it'd worked, though, eh?'

Webley stares at him across the roof of the car. Shakes her head in disbelief. 'No, Cody, it wouldn't. I was on to you from the start. Your plan was always doomed to be a waste of time.

If you'd wanted to know if Puckleton was gay or not, you could have just asked me.'

'What do you mean? Since when did you get gaydar installed?'

'I'm a woman, Cody. I know about these things.'

Flustered now, Cody says, 'Well, go on then. Is he straight or not?'

Webley taps the side of her nose with her index finger. 'That's for me to know, and for you to find out.'

'Megan. Megan! You can't leave it like—'

But Webley has the car door open and is sliding into the vehicle, leaving Cody to suck up the punishment for his arrogance.

30

Saturday evening. It's snowing again.

He likes the snow. Likes the peace it brings. It seems to muffle the unrest, the agitation. It slows hearts, mellows minds.

It will be Christmas soon. Joy to the world. Goodwill to all men.

He has the coat on again. The black one with the grey flashes highlighting the zips. It's nice and warm. Big hood to hide his face. Big pockets to hide his hammer.

Not that there's much chance of discovery here. He is on a quiet section of Allerton Road. There are no security cameras to worry about here, and in weather like this there are few passers-by. He is standing behind a chest-high sandstone wall, in the murky shadows created by a huge tree. If he sees anyone coming along the road, he can duck behind the wall. One time he didn't even bother doing that. He just stood there under the tree, watching as a woman in a white fur-trimmed coat walked by, oblivious to his presence mere feet away from her. He could easily have jumped out and smashed her brains in.

But she was not his target. His intended victim is across the road, in the tiny community hall.

They will be cosy in there, he thinks. They will have the heaters on, and a small place like that will soon be warmed up. They will glance through the windows at the flurrying snow, and they will smile smugly at how comfortable they are. They will smile, too, because of their shared happiness, their common understanding. Their eyes have been opened, and they know that everyone else in that hall can see what they see.

Let them rejoice, he thinks. Let them revel in their assumed superiority. Their time will come. For one of them, their time is nigh.

He hears the piano start up. It sounds slightly out of tune, but the playing isn't bad. And then the singing begins. *O Come All Ye Faithful*. He likes that one. Finds himself singing along in a whisper.

Later comes the chatter. He pictures the congregation splintering into small groups, then sipping from mugs of tea or mulled wine as they talk inane drivel about their plans for Christmas and their nauseating joy for everything in their pathetic lives.

Eventually the door opens and the voices spill out into the darkness. Bodies follow shortly afterwards, but nobody seems in a hurry. They trickle out in ones and twos, loitering in the doorway as they loudly proclaim their intentions to meet up again soon. And then everyone seems to feel the need to bless everyone else before the individuals finally manage to break away from the gravitational pull created by the concentrated mass of their like-minded acquaintances.

Some walk away. Others climb into cars and then drive off, quickly disappearing behind the curtain of snow.

And then it is quiet. It is his time.

He abandons his place beneath the tree. Moves out from behind the wall. The road is deserted. The only light he can see is the golden glow through the windows of the community hall.

He crosses the street without hurry. He has plenty of time. God is on his side. He has already proved that point.

He passes through the gateway. Walks up to the door. Reaches out a gloved hand and turns the handle. The door is not locked, and so he enters quietly and shuts it again behind him.

He was right about the warmth in here. It is almost stifling.

He is in a small reception area. There is a desk and a chair and a row of pegs on the wall. There is one coat and one hat and one scarf on the pegs.

He walks through into the hall proper. Not much here. A few tables and chairs, randomly scattered. A piano surmounted by a small artificial Christmas tree decked with too much tinsel. Gaudy paper chains are strung across the walls. At the far end of the hall, one of the tables has been covered with a paper tablecloth, bright red in keeping with the Christmas theme. On the table is a tea urn, some wine, an array of cups, and some plates of nuts, crisps and other nibbles.

There is nobody else in the hall, but from a doorway beyond the makeshift buffet table comes the sound of crockery being washed, and a woman singing.

O Little Town of Bethlehem, she sings.

He likes that one. Finds himself humming along softly as he traverses the hall with careful, deliberate steps.

When she stops singing in mid-verse, he realises he has been detected. He halts where he is. He doesn't want to alarm her.

She appears in the doorway. Puts a hand to her heart as she emits a small 'ooh' of surprise.

He sees the apprehension on her face. Quickly he pulls off his hood to reveal his biggest, most innocent smile.

'Sorry,' he says, showing her his empty palms. 'I didn't mean to shock you.'

He doesn't move towards her. He just lets her weigh up the situation.

After a few seconds, she finds a smile of her own.

'It's all right. What . . . What can I do for you?'

'I . . . I'm lost,' he says.

'Lost? Really? Well, you're on Allerton Road. Where are you trying to get to?'

'Heaven, eventually.'

She gives him a quizzical look. 'Heaven?'

'Yes. Sorry . . . I'm not being very clear, am I? It's just that, well, I walk past here a lot, and I see how happy you are. All the laughing and the clapping and the singing . . . it makes me feel really good every time. I just wanted to talk to you about it. To find out a bit more. Is that all right? If it's not – if this is a bad time – I'll go away and leave you in peace.'

He starts to turn away from her, but she takes a step towards him and reaches out a hand.

'Wait. You're serious?'

'Yes. It's weird. I get a kind of warm feeling when I hear you all in here. I don't know how else to describe it.'

Her own smile broadens now. He realises he has found her. He has made a connection.

'What's your name?' she asks.

'Matthew,' he lies.

He spent a long time choosing the fake name. Had to be one of the apostles, he decided. Most of them didn't feel right. He could hardly come in here and say his name was Judas. Matthew, though, is a good, solid biblical name.

'My name's Sue. Take a seat, Matthew. Would you like a cup of tea or anything?'

Sue. Not such a biblical name.

'No, thanks,' he answers as he slides onto the nearest chair.

Sue comes over and lowers herself onto the chair opposite him.

'Do you know who we are, Matthew? Do you know what we do?'

'Kind of. You're religious people, aren't you?'

'That's right. We're Born Again Christians. Are you a Christian, Matthew?'

Our Father, who art in heaven . . .

'I . . . I'm not sure. I think I am, but nobody in my family ever went to church. We never really talked about God and stuff. But now . . .'

'Now what?'

'I think I'm missing out. I feel like there's a part of me missing. Does that sound stupid?'

She shakes her head, and there is a mistiness in her eyes that is nauseatingly patronising.

'Not at all. I know exactly how you feel. Everyone who was here tonight has been through what you are going through right now. It takes some of us longer than others to realise what we're missing. The sad thing is that some people never realise it at all.'

Hallowed be thy name . . .

'So . . . what is it we've all been missing?'

'God. We were all missing God. But when we find Him, it's the most beautiful, perfect thing. That's why we're all so happy here, Matthew. We've found God. And I think you've found Him too.'

'Do you think? I mean, is it okay to find Him now, even if I didn't believe in Him before?'

'It's perfectly okay. In fact, I'd say it's better than okay. Because what it means is that you've made your own mind up. You're not believing because your parents believe, or because you've been brought up that way. You're doing it because you know it's right. And that has to be the best type of believing of all, don't you think?'

He makes a show of mulling over her words. In reality, her sanctimonious attitude makes him want to puke.

Thy kingdom come, thy will be done . . .

'I suppose so. But what if . . . what if someone does bad things before they find God? What happens then?'

She nods sagely. She has an answer, as he knew she would.

'That's the best part. You can repent. The Lord will cleanse you of your sins. You get a second chance, a new life. That's why we're called Born Again Christians. You can start all over again.'

On earth as it is in heaven . . .

'And what if you do bad things after you've been reborn? Is that still okay?'

'Well . . . what exactly do you mean?'

'I mean, what if you become a Born Again Christian, but then you do another bad thing?'

Her smile fades a little. He suspects some of her self-assuredness goes with it.

'God is forgiveness. God is love. If you truly have Him in your heart, then you will do everything you can to follow the path of the righteous. But, yes, sometimes we make mistakes. We're only human, and so we can't always be as strong as we'd like to be.'

Give us this day our daily bread . . .

She continues: 'But God is always there for us. He shows us what is good. We just have to listen to Him. When we fall by the wayside, we have to be honest about it and promise never to go that way again. If we can do that, we will be forgiven.'

'Do you ever fall by the wayside?'

The big question. The gigantic question. The most important question this woman will ever have to answer.

'Well . . .'

She smiles, shrugs. It's not an answer. Not a proper one. For a question of this gravity, it's an insult of a reply.

His mind searches for a way to edge her towards the truth without unsettling her. Her answer has to be supplied without duress.

'I think I would,' he says. 'I think I would do something wrong, and I'm afraid I wouldn't be forgiven.'

'Why do you say that? Why do you have such lack of faith in yourself?'

'I don't know. I suppose I don't have much confidence. I don't think I could be as strong as you are. If you never do anything wrong, you don't have to worry about being forgiven.'

She seems amused by this, which would irritate him immensely if it were not part of his plan.

She lowers her voice, as though trying to prevent God from overhearing. 'I'll let you into a secret. I've done a few bad things in my time.'

And forgive us our trespasses, as we forgive those who trespass against us . . .

'But not recently? Not since you were born again?'

She nods. 'Yes. I'm afraid so.'

'Seriously? What kind of bad things?'

Sue pulls away from the table a little. It's too invasive a probe from a stranger.

'Let's just say they're things that God might not have agreed with.'

He tries to appear mildly curious rather than disappointed by her reticence.

'So why did you do them, then?'

She chews her lip as she struggles with her answer to this one. He suspects that she has spent many hours wrestling with her conscience on this matter.

'Different reasons, I suppose. Sometimes because it seemed the right thing to do at that moment, even though I regretted it later. Other times because I was just weak, and I gave in to temptation.'

And lead us not into temptation, but deliver us from evil . . .

'And then what? How did you fix it after you did something bad like that?'

'I prayed. I asked for forgiveness.'

'As simple as that? But . . . how do you know He listens to you? How can you be sure that He has forgiven you?'

'Because that's what the Bible teaches us.' She pauses for a moment. 'Don't get me wrong. It's not easy. It's not like washing your face when it's mucky. You have to really mean what you say when you ask for forgiveness. You can't just carry on doing bad things, and then pray once a week to be made pure again. It doesn't work like that.'

'But . . . but you said you did more than one bad thing. You carried on doing them even though you knew they were wrong.'

A twitch of her upper lip tells him she's becoming irked by the direction this is taking. Well, good. She said it herself: it's not meant to be easy. She should practise what she preaches.

'Yes. But I also said that I'm weak. As humans we're all weak. God knows that, and He makes allowances for it.'

She affixes her most beneficent smile again. 'You have a lot of questions, and that's good. Would you like to come to one of our meetings to discuss it with other members of the group?'

Her words swim past him. He is focusing on what she said before that, about God making allowances. About Him knowing and accepting the mistakes of His flock.

He wonders where the allowances were for him. He wonders why everything had to be just so, from such an early age. Why wasn't he allowed to make mistakes, even back when he was far too young to avoid them? Why did he have to be punished for things that weren't even his fault? He couldn't help getting sick or wetting his bed or picking up head lice. Where was the understanding then?

And this woman – this smug bitch in front of him – what makes her think she gets off scot-free? She *knew* what she was doing. She *knew* it was wrong. How is it fair that she gets into heaven so easily, while he gets beaten and teased and humiliated and made to feel like a piece of shit under someone's shoe?

'I think you're wrong,' he says.

He sees the momentary puzzlement. 'Er, I'm not sure what—'

'About being forgiven. I don't think God has forgiven you. You're wrong.'

The smile disappears. The bewilderment gives way to irritation. She laughs. In his face.

'You seem very sure about that.'

'Yes. I'm very sure. One hundred per cent certain.'

He looks at her with ice in his eyes. Sees that she detects the change in mood, the tension in the air.

She says, 'I, er, I need to finish off here and get home.'

'Yes,' is his simple answer. But his hand is in his pocket now. His fingers are curling around the wooden handle of his lump hammer. This woman called Sue will not wash any more dishes. She will not go home. She has ensured this.

She starts to rise from her chair, but there is a hesitancy to her movement. She knows this isn't a proper end to things.

'If you don't mind leaving now,' she says. 'I need to lock up.'

'Yes,' he says again.

He gets up from his chair, too. He fastens his eyes on hers, and sees that she wants him to break away first. Wants him to go away from here and never come back. She needs to lock the door when he is gone and breathe out her anxiety. He can sense all that.

But he doesn't move. He just stands there in the warm, cosy room, staring her out.

She is first to blink.

'So . . .' She gestures towards the exit. 'If you'd just like to—'

He moves swiftly. Comes around the table as he starts to pull the hammer from his pocket.

But the head of the hammer snags on the material. It won't come out.

Sue yelps. She runs away from him. Flies into the kitchen and slams the door.

He hears the turn of a key in the lock. He manages to free the hammer. He tries the handle of the door, but it doesn't open. He pulls his right arm back. Lets fly with the hammer. The wood cracks but doesn't break. He hears screaming, and then her voice: 'Get away from me. I'm calling the police.'

He looks back into the hall. Sees her bag there. He doesn't believe she has her phone with her in the kitchen. It's a bluff.

But he can't be sure . . .

His actions become more frenzied now. He swings again and again at the door. More cracks appear, but still it won't budge. He realises then that he needs a new tactic, and he hammers instead at the lock. The sounds of fracturing metal and splintering wood mingle with the screams from the other side of the door. And then the cries suddenly fade, and he wonders why, but then he realises that they have not diminished but have been redirected.

She is shouting out of the window!

'Help!' she calls. 'Help me! Please!'

He takes several steps back. Runs at the door. Raises his foot. Slams it into the area just above the handle.

A huge cracking sound. Screws and other metal parts pinging away.

Step back again. Forwards once more. Slam!

The door flies open. He stands in the doorway, panting and taking stock.

Sue has climbed onto the counter. She has her head through the part-open window, and is struggling to squeeze the rest of her body through the narrow gap. One of her feet is in the sink, trying to get purchase, but it punches through the crockery, breaking it and turning the water pink with her shredding flesh.

He dives across the narrow room. Drops the hammer onto the counter while he grabs hold of Sue's cardigan and drags her screaming back into the kitchen.

For thine is the kingdom . . .

Her body slides across the soapy wet counter. Crashes hard onto the tiled floor. She tries to get to her feet, but slips in the water and the blood from her lacerated foot. She resorts to scrabbling away from him on her hands and knees.

The power and the glory . . .

He grabs the hammer again. Walks purposefully up to Sue's fleeing form. Brings the heavy mass of metal down onto the base of her spine.

The POWER and the glory . . .

She crumples. Moans. Tries to get up again.

But now he is on her. Now he is straddling her. Now he is putting all his reserves of energy into removing the stain of her from this earth.

THE POWER AND THE GLORY . . .

He hammers away.

For ever and ever and ever and ever and ever . . .

And when he is done, he looks down at his handiwork and sees that it is good.

Amen.

31

Slowly, they put all the pieces together.

Not of Sue Halligan, though. In that regard she is like Humpty Dumpty. All the Queen's detectives cannot put her back together again, with or without horses.

What they can reconstruct pretty well is what took place here. With the aid of the pathologist and the CSIs, they are able to build a fairly accurate picture of the sequence of events.

The scene tells its own story. The unlocked front door, the smashed internal door, the food and drink, the partly open window, the shattered crockery, the overflowing water, the bloodstains – they all set out their witness statements without ambiguity or contradiction.

And then, of course, there is the body. The most important witness of all. It cannot speak, but it can tell a compelling tale to the experts trained to hear it. Not yet in detail, though. It's a tease, is this one. Likes to keep its audience in suspense. It will hold some things back until it is on a cold table in the mortuary.

But some secrets she will never reveal. Those will be left to the living to divulge. And so that's where the detectives must turn their attention next.

The problem is that the living are numerous, and at least one of them will offer up lies when it suits. It's like the most complicated logic puzzle ever devised.

Still in their white protective outer clothing, Blunt, Cody, Webley and Ferguson stand closeted in the small reception area of the hall, staring out at the winter blankness beyond the open front door. They look like four snowmen who have decided to come in from the cold.

'All right,' says Blunt. 'Let's play similarities and differences again. Start with what this has in common with the other homicides.'

Webley is the first to reply: 'Method of killing is the same. Multiple blows to the head with a heavy instrument, probably a hammer. Then there's the victim. Female again. At forty-one, she's close in age to Mary Cowper, and we've already decided that Cassie Harris looked about that age too. All three had fair, shoulder-length hair.'

'Do we know what this woman looked like before her face was caved in?'

'Not yet. We're working on it.'

'What else?'

Ferguson now: 'Religion. Susan Halligan was a Born Again Christian. She ran regular meetings here at the hall. That's why she was here tonight.'

'How do you know that?'

Ferguson points outside with his pen. In the rear of a marked police car just pulling away from the kerb, a pale figure stares back at them.

'That's the husband. He found the body. He expected her home ages ago. When she didn't arrive, he tried her phone and got no answer. When he got really worried, he jumped in his car and came over to look for her.'

'Do we like him for this?'

Ferguson shakes his head. 'Not at the moment. He seems genuinely upset. Obviously we need to question him, though.'

Blunt nods. 'All right. Differences.'

Cody decides it's his turn to speak. 'She wasn't single, for one thing. And then there's the obvious difference.'

'Which is?'

Cody holds his hands out to indicate the space they are in. 'This,' he says. 'Not exactly a cathedral, is it?'

'Yes,' says Blunt. 'That's what was worrying me, too.'

Ferguson says, 'Worried, ma'am?'

Blunt looks at him. 'If we must have a serial killer – and personally I can do without them – I'd much prefer it if he followed a pattern. Our job is difficult enough without the occasional curve ball being thrown at us. We start off at a cathedral, we go to another cathedral, and now this. This isn't even a proper place of worship. The next time our killer strikes, it could just be in somebody's living room. The question is, why the change?'

The other three detectives get time to think about it when they have to shrink against the walls to allow a CSI to squeeze past carrying a bag of tricks.

'I'm guessing he thought it was too big a risk to go to a cathedral again,' says Cody. 'But I don't know why he didn't even go for a church. There must be plenty of blonde-haired fortyish women he could have chosen from.'

'Maybe that's just it,' says Webley. 'Maybe he wasn't spoilt for choice. What if there's something else connecting these women? Something more than their vaguely similar appearance. What if there are only a limited number of women who satisfy those criteria?'

Another technician comes through, and they all suck their figures in again.

'We're just in the way here,' says Blunt. She looks at Webley. 'You've made a good point, but we still don't know what this common factor is. Go back to the station with Cody and talk to the husband. The only good thing about an extra victim is that it gives us more of a chance to work out what it is about them that appeals to the killer.'

She turns to Ferguson next. 'Work up a list of whoever was at this meeting. We need to start rounding them up, even if it's only to rule them out. And don't take any bullshit from them about being too godly to do anything like this. In my experience, being a God botherer doesn't always stop you from being a vicious bastard.'

32

Adam Halligan looks like a man who hasn't slept for at least two days. His eyes are red and puffy. His dark hair sticks up from his head in random directions, like Stan Laurel. There is no element of comedy to him, however. The corners of his mouth, turned down almost as far as the line of his jaw, are a measure of his misery.

Cody starts up the recorder. Announces the names of those present. Checks for the umpteenth time that Halligan rejects the offer of a solicitor.

'Why would I need a lawyer?' Halligan asks. 'I haven't done anything wrong. Somebody killed my wife, and you should be trying to find whoever did it, not wasting time talking to me.' He plucks at the sleeve of his police-issued overalls. 'And why am I dressed like a bleeding convict? What have you done with my clothes?'

Cody nods sympathetically. 'As I think we've already explained to you, we have to do it this way. Look at it from our point of view. When the police arrived at the community hall, you were the only one there with your wife. You had blood all over you.'

'That doesn't mean anything. I was—'

'Let me finish. I agree with you. It doesn't make you a murderer. All we're trying to do right now is to confirm it. The sooner we do that, the sooner you can go home, and then we can go out and catch those responsible. What I'm also hoping, and I'm sure you are too, is that you might be able to give us some vital information that will help us.'

Halligan wipes a hand across his eyes. He seems mollified for now. 'Let's get it over with,' he says.

Cody looks to Webley on his right, handing the questioning baton to her.

'Tell us about tonight,' she says. 'Did it start off as just a normal Saturday evening?'

He nods, but struggles to hold back the tears, as though acknowledging the prior normality makes the ensuing horror even more difficult to bear. He so wants this to have been just another ordinary, boring day.

He says, 'I went to the match with some mates. I knew that Sue was having one of her meetings at the hall, so instead of rushing back, I went for a couple of pints.'

'With your mates?'

'Yes.'

'And they'll vouch for that?'

He raises his eyes, and Cody sees a flash of anger in them as Halligan recognises the stab of suspicion.

'I was with them all the way through the match, and then for an hour or so at the pub. We even travelled back home together. One of them only lives around the corner from me. I'll give you their names and phone numbers. You can ask them.'

Webley smiles at him. 'It's our job to check all the facts, that's all. What time did you get home?'

'Must have been about six thirty, six forty. Something like that.'

'And what time was your wife due home?'

'It's normally about seven. The meetings finish at about half-six, but then she has to tidy up and drive home.'

'How far is the hall from your home?'

'Only about a five-minute drive.'

'Okay. So you're at home. Your wife doesn't turn up at seven. When do you start to get worried about her?'

'I think it must have been about quarter to eight.' He checks the eyes of the detectives for more accusing glares, then hastily adds, 'That lot can talk the hind leg off a donkey when they get going. I thought she'd just be having a natter.'

'So what then? Did you phone her?'

'I texted her first. I waited ten minutes for a reply, and then I rang her. She didn't answer, so I went and found her address book. She keeps the names of all the group members in there. I picked one at random and phoned him. He told me he was one of the last to leave, and that was at half-six. So that's when I started to think something must've gone wrong. I never thought . . .'

His face contorts again, his aching painted there for all to see.

'I thought her car must've broken down or something. Do you know what I mean? A minor crisis. At the worst, maybe she'd slipped in the snow and had to be taken to A & E. Something that could be fixed, you know? Something that wasn't so bloody final.'

More sobbing and sniffing. Webley grants him time to recover.

'You're doing really well, Mr Halligan. Can you tell us what you did next?'

'I . . . I got in the car and drove to the hall. And before you say it, yes, I know I'd had a couple of bevvies. But to be honest, I don't give a toss. If you want to charge me for it—'

'We're not going to charge you for that, Mr Halligan. Tell us what you did.'

'There's not a lot to tell. I found her. That's it. I walked into the hall, and I called her name, and she didn't answer. I just knew something was wrong. Sue wouldn't leave the hall unlocked like that, with all the lights on. Besides, her car was still outside. She had to be close by. But she wasn't answering, so I knew. Do you understand what I'm saying? I knew it had to be bad. I just never thought . . .'

His words trail away, prompting Webley to speak again. 'What did you—?'

But Halligan hasn't finished. He suddenly opens the tap on a reservoir of thoughts and feelings that he needs to release.

'She wasn't human!' he yells. 'I looked at her and I thought, This doesn't even look like a human being. Her head was all . . . it was the wrong shape. All bashed in and spread out. I don't . . . I don't . . .'

He lets out a roar of primitive emotion that eventually dies and turns to tears. Cody feels the hairs on his arms standing on end, and he is sure that Webley must be similarly affected.

Webley's fingers slide a few inches along the table towards Halligan. 'Did you touch her, Mr Halligan? After you found the body, did you come into contact with your wife?'

'Yes,' says Halligan, but it comes out as a squeak, and he tries again: 'Yes. I wanted to be sure. I mean, I knew it was her. It had to be her, didn't it? But something in my head kept telling me to check. I suppose I still had a slight hope that it might be someone else. She was lying on her front, and I tried turning her to get a better look, but . . . it sounds ridiculous, but even then I wasn't sure. I mean, we've been married for sixteen years and I was looking straight at her, and I still couldn't tell it was her. That's how bad she was beaten.'

Halligan's gaze shifts to Cody, as if his next words are something only another man would understand. 'You've got to catch this bastard, because God help me, if I ever get my hands on him . . .'

'We'll catch him,' says Cody. 'Don't worry about that.' He delivers the promise with conviction, because it's what he believes. As devious as this killer is, Cody won't relax until the man is behind bars.

Webley clears her throat noisily, as though to remind the testosterone-intoxicated people here that she is just as capable of bringing the culprit to justice.

She says, 'This might sound like a silly question, but we have to ask. Did Sue have any enemies that you know about? Anyone who might have hated her enough to do this?'

A humourless smile creeps onto his lips. 'No. If you knew her, you wouldn't ask that question. Do you know what she was doing there in the hall tonight?'

'Tell me,' says Webley, and Cody wants to nod his approval. They think they already have the answer, but it's always better not to lead the interviewees.

'She's heavily involved with a group of Born Again Christians,' says Halligan, not without a lacing of sarcasm. 'They meet in that hall every week.'

'You don't approve?' asks Cody.

'Let's just say they're not my cup of tea.'

'Why not? You not religious?'

'I believe there's a God, but I don't go to church much. I've got nothing against anyone who does, but I don't go for all that happy-clappy nonsense.'

'So how did your wife get into it?'

Halligan shrugs. 'How does anyone? These people target the weak and vulnerable, don't they? They tell you how happy they are, and how they've solved all their problems. The thing is, it works for them. They really believe they've been given a second chance, and they're passionate about spreading the joy. You can understand how anyone who's a bit low might want a little bit of what they feel every moment of every day.'

'You think she was brainwashed?'

A sigh from Halligan. 'No. Not brainwashed. She just got caught up in it all. I can't deny it helped her. She just became . . . different. Not the Sue I used to know.'

Webley pitches in again. 'You said they target the weak and vulnerable. Are you saying Sue was like that?'

Halligan's lips shape several words before the sounds arrive. 'She had . . . problems. She lost a baby. It made her depressed. She . . . never mind.'

Cody realises there's something there that needs to be mined. He jumps in before Webley can take it elsewhere.

'What? What were you going to say?'

The sigh this time is heavier. More of a low moan.

'I suppose it doesn't matter now. She spoke about it openly anyway. She told everyone how being born again stopped her doing it.'

'Stopped her doing what?'

'She stole stuff,' says Halligan. 'She became a kleptomaniac. She was ill. She didn't know what she was doing. But on her really dark days she would sometimes pick things up in a shop and walk out without paying. Often, she didn't even remember doing it.'

Cody exchanges glances with Webley. A PNC check on Sue Halligan had not thrown up a criminal record.

'Was she ever caught?'

'A couple of times. She apologised, told them that she wasn't well, and offered to pay. She got lucky, I suppose. They let her go.'

'And what did you do?'

'Me? I knew nothing about it. The things she pinched weren't particularly expensive, so I had no reason to get suspicious. All this only came out afterwards.'

'Afterwards?'

'After she got all religious. She couldn't shut up about it then. Kept going on about how she used to be lost, but then she was found. She was always talking about repentance and forgiveness and seeing the error of her ways. To be honest, it got a bit much sometimes. Like I said, she became a different woman then. But at least she was happy.' His face creases in sorrow again. 'I'd put up with any amount of preaching now if I could have her back.'

They allow him some time to pull himself together. Cody sees Webley pick up the folder in front of her, in preparation to move on to the next topic. But for some unidentifiable reason, he's not ready to do that just yet. There is something in what Halligan has just told them – something that makes Cody want to follow this thread just a little more.

There are parallels here. Not with Mary Cowper – or at least not that he can see – but certainly with Cassie Harris. They were both committing wrongs. Both sinning, to put it in religious terms. And each of them turned to God for their salvation.

Is that important? Cody wonders. Or am I just making tenuous connections out of sheer desperation?

Says Webley, 'If you're okay, Mr Halligan, I'd like to ask you—'

Cody touches her arm. 'Just a second.' He turns to Halligan. 'What you were saying about your wife's kleptomania – did it simply stop when she found religion?'

Halligan stares at him as if the question was in a foreign tongue.

'Mr Halligan?'

'Yes,' he answers finally. 'Mostly.'

'Mostly? But not completely?'

'She had an occasional relapse. A couple of times – that's all.' Halligan suddenly finds his anger again. 'Look, Sue wasn't a bad person, okay? She had a few problems. The bad guy is the one who killed her, and he's still out there, and you need—'

'All right, Mr Halligan. Point taken.'

Cody lapses into silence then. Allows Webley to pick up where she left off. He's not sure why he asked the last question, or what he can do with the information contained in the reply. He just knows it felt important to ask it.

Webley opens her folder. Takes out a couple of photographs. She places one in front of Halligan.

'Do you recognise this man?' she asks.

It's a still frame from the video of the killer outside the Anglican cathedral. Halligan blinks away his tears and moves his face closer to the picture.

'No. Why? Who is he?'

'Here's another picture,' says Webley. This one at the Metropolitan cathedral.

'I still don't know who he is. Am I supposed to?'

Webley puts down a printout of the website displaying the killer's coat.

'What about this coat?' she asks. 'Look familiar?'

'No. It's just a coat. I don't understand.'

'You don't own a coat like this, then?'

'No. What are you getting at?'

'Mr Halligan, can you account for your whereabouts last Saturday afternoon, from about three o'clock onwards?'

'Last Saturday? I don't know. I was . . . yeah, I was with Sue. We went to the cinema with a couple of friends.'

'Which cinema?'

'The Odeon, in town. We watched that new Spielberg film. Then we went to Jamie Oliver's for a bite to eat.'

'What about the Saturday before that?'

'The week before? Christ, I don't know. We . . . London! We were down in London for the weekend, staying with friends. Look, what's this about?'

'I'll need you to give us the names of your friends from both weekends, if you don't mind.'

'Yes. I mean, no. I mean . . .' Halligan looks at the photos again, then at Webley, then at Cody. Cody can almost hear the tumblers in Halligan's brain clicking into place.

'Oh, my God.' He stabs a finger onto one of the photos. 'This is him, isn't it? The two killings at the cathedrals. This is him. And you think . . . you think . . .'

'Mr Halligan,' says Cody, 'let's not jump to conclusions here—'

'But you do. You think the same man killed my Sue.' He looks at the image again. Much harder this time, as though willing more detail to jump out of it. 'This is him.'

Halligan's mouth drops open, his jaw dragged down by the weight of grief. In his pain and misery, his questions are like the moans of the eternally damned: 'Why is he doing this? Why pick on Sue? Why her? Why?'

Cody's own mouth opens to reply, but no answers come, because he has none.

33

Sunday. Not a day of rest for Cody. In fact this is going to be one stinker of a day. He knows this. At some point today the shit will hit the fan. He will be asked a certain question, and he will give a certain answer, and that will be it. The explosion will be heard on the other side of the Mersey.

For now, he's trying to keep his head low and his mind focused on work. He has spent most of the morning interviewing those who were present at the Born Again Christian meeting the previous evening. He's already sick of it.

Nothing against the people concerned. They seem perfectly nice, and not at all suspicious. But, well, they will keep bringing God into the conversation. They will keep reminding Cody that higher powers than him will deal with those responsible. They will keep telling him that Sue Halligan is now at peace, as though the fact that her face was pummelled into something resembling raw steak is of no consequence.

He doesn't know why, but he would prefer more normal reactions. He would prefer them to get angry, to blaspheme, to swear vengeance. He would understand that.

Maybe it's me, he thinks. Maybe I'm just in a bad mood. And maybe that's not just because I know what's coming later, but also because I don't know what the hell is going on in this case.

Three victims. All blonde, and of similar build, appearance and apparent age. All religious. All killed at a site of worship. All killed on a Saturday, at around the same time of day. All killed in the same brutal way.

Is that it? Are those the only links?

Well, what are you expecting, Cody? Isn't that enough? Many serial killings are carried out completely at random, with no connecting glue whatsoever. You've got lots here.

Yes, but . . .

He thinks there should be more. Something he's not seeing. The missing link. But at the same time, he doesn't know why he feels that way. He'd call it intuition, but that just seems a bullshit way of confirming that he doesn't know.

Right now he's at his desk, studying the post-mortem report on Sue Halligan. Nothing illuminating here. Blunt-force trauma, just like the other two. Dispatched with a lump hammer or similar, just like the other two.

He reads on. The cold, clinical findings are all very well, but Cody finds himself more affected emotionally by the unrelated details, the things that turn lifeless corpses back into living, breathing people with hopes and fears and aspirations. He wants to know what she was wearing, what she carried with her, what scars she had, what earlier illnesses she may have suffered from. All the things that made Sue Halligan real.

To Cody, the list of Sue's possessions make particularly sad reading. They seem so trivial, and yet so revealing of the minutiae of her life. There is a used bus ticket here; a tube of lipstick that is almost empty; a till receipt from Asda (*the* Asda, he thinks); a small ornamental stone; a plasterer's business card; a keyring with a plastic Winnie-the-Pooh attached; a tube of sugar-free mints; a watch with a broken strap . . . The list goes on and on. Junk to most people, and yet of importance enough to Sue Halligan for her to hang on to them. It says a lot about who she was, and how her mind worked.

And yet it tells Cody nothing about the man who killed her.

Grace Meade sits quietly in her appointed spot at the back of the room, biding her time. She isn't as confident as the others here. She doesn't like to push herself into the conversation, to try to bend the thinking of the others while they are in full flow and perhaps defensive of the arguments they are making. She prefers to wait until the waters calm, and only then will she rise up from the depths and shake their boats.

She watches Blunt carefully as she draws out and gathers together the data from her subjects. The woman is masterful at that. Sometimes she has to tease the information out; other times she has to poke its hoarder with the sharp end of her tongue to release it. She knows precisely when to challenge, when to encourage, when to dismiss. She has skills that Grace could never hope to possess – an intelligence that goes beyond the mere cerebral kind.

And now there is Sergeant Cody. Clever little Cody. That enigma of a man who is addressed almost invariably by his surname. Like Inspector Morse, but without the crosswords.

Cody is telling everyone about Adam Halligan. Telling them that his alibis for the Saturdays on which Mary Cowper and Cassie Harris were murdered have been found to be as watertight as a duck's rectum. Telling them that, furthermore, there is no evidence to contradict his account of what happened on the evening of his wife's demise. In short, Cody concludes, there is no reason to suspect any wrongdoing on Halligan's part.

Which they all knew, of course. Nobody ever thought at any point that Halligan killed his wife, let alone the other two women. The detectives were going through the motions. Ticking boxes. Closing doors.

It brings them no closer to finding the killer.

And now Cody is saying more about Mrs Halligan. Interesting stuff, this. Stuff that makes Grace sit even more upright than usual. Surely he's not . . .

But he is. He is telling them all now. About Sue Halligan's kleptomania. And then about how her religious epiphany was her salvation. Or at least almost so.

Damn!

Grace can sense the wave of depression forming on her mental horizon. This was meant to be *her* news, *her* moment. Cody has stolen her thunder. She has no drum to bang, no fanfare to sound. The tightly stretched balloon of her contribution has been deflated to a flaccid irrelevance.

It's not Cody's fault. He's just good at his job. He got to the truth by other means, and kudos to him for doing so.

But still . . .

Grace's shoulders slump. She wants to quit work and go home. Nobody will notice anyway, she thinks.

Blunt thanks Cody. Opens it up to the floor for comments. She gets a few responses. Nothing especially insightful.

But then a question from one of the younger detectives: 'The stuff about Mrs Halligan's kleptomania. Okay, it shows she wasn't Mother Teresa, but other than that, do we think it's important? I mean, how would our killer have found out about it? I don't think her husband would have been shouting it all over the town.'

Cody seems stuck for an answer. Time for Grace to throw her hat into the ring.

'He probably wouldn't,' she says. 'But his wife wasn't particularly secretive about it.'

The heads turn. The eyes refocus. Her existence is registered once more.

'Grace!' says Blunt. 'I was hoping you might be able to shed some light on all this.'

Nice try, thinks Grace. But a false compliment. You haven't looked my way even once this morning, DCI Blunt. You had forgotten about me, as had all the others. But it's okay. I'm easily forgotten.

'She wrote a blog. Mrs Halligan, I mean.'

Grace presses a key. As the large monitor at the front of the incident room flickers into life, she notices Blunt's expression of surprise, and realises she probably should have asked for permission to take control of the display.

Sod it, she thinks.

The screen fills with a blog page carrying the title 'Finding My Way', and below that, in a smaller typeface: 'Jottings Along the Path to Salvation'.

Says Grace, 'Two things about these posts. First of all, she's very clear about where and when the meetings she attends take place. Anyone reading these would know exactly where to find her on a Saturday evening. The other thing is how candid she is about her life. If we jump back to one from a few weeks ago . . .'

Grace rotates the scroll wheel of her mouse. Pages of text fly past on the screen.

'Here, for example. I'll read out the relevant paragraphs.'

She clears her throat. Ups her volume as she reads: '"I'm going to be perfectly honest with you here, because I don't think it's possible to be true to God unless you are true to yourself. I'm not a saint. Quite the opposite, in fact. I've done bad things in my time. To be more specific, I have stolen things. That's right – I have taken things that didn't belong to me. I have picked things up in a shop, then walked out without paying for them. And I have done that not just once, but many times.

'"I don't tell you that because I'm proud of it. Actually, I believe I was quite ill at the time, and in a very dark place in my life. But I don't want to make excuses for my actions, either. What I did was wrong. I see that now, but only because God chose to shine His light on the correct path for me.

It hasn't been easy. I still wobble now and again. I still fall prey to the demons that stalk me. But always God takes my hand and leads me back onto the path. He will do that for you, too, if you let Him."'

There are a few seconds of silence while everyone digests this.

Blunt says, 'And this was a public post? Available to anyone to read?'

'Yes. Like the newspaper article about Cassie Harris, anyone could have found out that she had committed criminal acts. And that bit about having a wobble now and again suggests she continued to do so even after becoming religious.'

'Okay,' says Blunt. 'In that way, those two women were alike. But Mary Cowper still doesn't fit that mould, does she? Not unless there's something very big we're missing. Something the killer could see but we can't, despite all our digging.'

Blunt moves on to other things then, and Grace is left to feel she has just been dismissed. Cody's revelations about the victim's kleptomania removed the detonator from her bomb, so that instead of leaving a crater, she has barely disturbed the ground.

She sees only the backs of heads in the room now, as if their owners are sending her to Coventry.

She decides she needs to up her game if she is to get those heads to turn again.

And she has an idea as to how she might do that.

34

He bumps into Webley in the corridor. Nobody else around. An ideal moment for her to pose the question he's been dreading all day.

And he knows it's coming. He can see it on her face. She's all smiley and bubbly and excited at seeing him. And so his stomach lurches.

'Hiya!' she says. She's like a little kid. Happily innocent. Seems such a shame.

'Hi, Megan,' he answers. He tries to push the corners of his mouth up. An impersonation of a smile.

'Hectic day,' she says.

'Mad.'

'We're still on for tonight, though, aren't we?'

And there it is. The question. In a way it has helped him. If she hadn't asked it, he would have needed to approach her. This has brought things to a head. Doesn't help in the answering of it, though.

'Tonight?' he says. As if he doesn't know what she's talking about. Which is being rather cowardly, he thinks.

'The meal. Sunday roast, with all the trimmings. Whatever trimmings are. I've never really understood why the veg and stuff are called trimmings, have you? Anyway, I've got them. In spades. Gravy, too, because I know how much you like your roasties swimming in gravy. Oh, and Yorkshire puds. Can't have beef without Yorkshire puds, can you? And for dessert we've got— What's the matter?'

'About tonight,' he says, and hates himself for the effect it has on Webley. He is stealing her joy. He can see it draining from her face.

'What about it?'

'You said it yourself. About how busy we are . . .'

'Yes, we're all busy, but, well, we've got to eat, haven't we? We're allowed to do that.'

'I know, but . . . I'm really sorry, Megan. I'm not going to be able to make dinner tonight. Another time, maybe.'

'I don't understand. It was all fixed up. What's changed?'

'This case. The murders. I'm up to my eyes in it, and—'

'Forget it,' she says. 'I don't want to know.' And then suddenly she's pushing past him and marching down the hallway, and he's left staring after her, and when he calls her name she refuses to respond, and when he starts to follow, her walk becomes a run. He chases after her, follows her trail of anger and disappointment, past staring coppers who should have better things to occupy their minds, and then he's bursting through the exit, into the car park where there is cold fresh air and natural light and the sense that emotions can be set free.

'Megan,' he says again.

She has her back to him, her arms folded, hugging herself against the biting breeze. He can see clouds of her breath as she vents her frustration.

'Megan.'

She whirls on him. 'Don't,' she warns. 'Don't even try to fix this. It cannot be fixed, Cody. I'm not a car or a computer. You can't connect a loose wire or reboot me. Humans don't work like that. I sometimes wonder if you'll ever learn that lesson. Somehow I doubt it. But you know what? I've given up trying. Get back in there and work on your precious case, while I just stand here and freeze to death.'

'I can't help it, Megan. I'm a sergeant. I'm supposed to—'

'No. Don't even go there. Your stripes don't make you indispensable, Cody, much as you'd like to think you are. We're all in this together. We're all working our arses off. So don't start saying you're more important. That's just an excuse, and a shit one at that. And even if you were so vital to the case, you could have tried to meet me halfway. You could have suggested coming over just for an hour or so, and then going back to work. You could have made an *attempt*, Cody. But you didn't, and that's what's got me so bloody worked up.'

'Look, I'm sorry, all right? I don't know what else I can say.'

'You don't? You don't know what to say to the person who saved your life, and nearly got killed in the process? You don't know what to say to the person who listened to you and comforted you and didn't report you when you were practically having a breakdown on duty? You don't know what to say to the only person who knows you're in trouble and is doing everything she can to help? All that, and you don't even know how to respond to an invitation to a roast meal and a few fucking trimmings. Well, in that case, I'm sorry for you, *Sergeant* Cody, because I can't be there for you any more. You're on your own now. Have a nice life.'

And then she goes. Straight past Cody and back into the building. And as she goes, he sees the tears on her face, like melting ice, and something melts inside him too.

35

He's running.

He does it for the exercise, but also because it's often the only way he can relieve the tension. When he gets back to the flat he might do some weight training, too. With any luck he'll be so exhausted he'll get some sleep.

He pounds his way along Rodney Street in the dark. Most of the time he runs on the road, avoiding the slush on the pavement that is beginning to freeze into a perilous ice rink.

His eyes are drawn to the lights of Christmas trees on either side. He wonders how he'll be spending his Christmas. Not with Webley and her partner, that's for sure. Probably won't even merit a Christmas card from them.

He wonders if they've got a Christmas tree up. Almost certainly. Webley always loved a Christmas tree. They've probably already got presents under it.

He thinks he should probably buy Webley a gift. To make up for things. Something small but beautiful. He could leave it on her desk at work. He might even do so anonymously. Yes, that would be a good idea. She'd suspect, certainly, but she wouldn't know for sure. That way, he might avoid getting it thrown back in his face.

Not that it would really atone for what I did, he thinks. She had every right to be pissed off with me. I mean, Christ, it was only a dinner. I could have turned up, couldn't I? I could have tucked into the roast potatoes swimming in gravy, and hang the consequences. When was the last time I had a proper Sunday roast? For me tonight it was sausages and beans, whoop-de-whoop.

Not that easy, though. In the scheme of things, it's better this way. He can't tell her the truth, can't say what he really wants to say. It wouldn't be fair on her.

He runs. Heading up past the Anglican cathedral now. Mary Cowper walked this way many times. Will walk it no longer. Seems strange, that. Seems odd that a middle-aged woman who brought her little dog along this route thousands of times is suddenly no longer on this earth.

He looks through the railings as he jogs up the hill, his gaze not so much on the cathedral itself as the parkland beneath it, shrouded in darkness and mystery. What went on in there? Not physically – not in the act of violence itself – but mentally. What was going through the heads of those two as they acted out their parts in the drama? Did Mary have any inkling that her life might be in danger because of something she once said or did? Was she really as innocent as everyone seemed to think she was, or was her mother the only one who could see the truth? And what about the killer? Why was his head so filled with thoughts of violence and hate? What atrocity could Mary possibly have perpetrated that would make him want to grind her skull into the ground?

At the corner he takes a right turn, intending to circle the cathedral before heading back home. He notices the street sign fixed to the railings.

Hope Street.

What were Mary's hopes? And what was the killer hoping to achieve?

More puzzlingly, why did he move away from Hope Street after the first two deaths?

Why abandon Hope?

Waldo visits him that night.

He hasn't been for a while, but tonight he is here with a vengeance.

In his dream – his nightmare – Cody is locked in a room. There are no windows, no lights. He cannot see a thing. He can hear, though. Rustling sounds. Scraping sounds. Footsteps.

Cody wants to get out of this room. He wants that more than he has ever wanted anything in his life. But he can't find the door. He slides his hands along the smooth, cold walls, but he cannot find an exit. Cannot find any features at all on the hard surfaces.

Suddenly the texture beneath his hands changes. It becomes soft, yielding. Material of some kind.

He feathers his fingers upwards, trying to work out what this might be. Soft becomes hard again, but different from the wall. Much smoother. Plastic, perhaps, and thin, with a hollowness behind.

And then there is light.

Not for the whole room. That would be too much to ask. This is a narrow beam, a spotlight playing upon Cody's discovery.

And what Cody has found causes him to scream.

It's Waldo. The clown. The man who chopped at Cody's body and murdered his partner in the most horrifying way imaginable. He is here. His clown mask is what Cody's fingers have been exploring.

And what a mask it is. Unbelievably terrifying, with its rictus grin and its yellowish-brown serrated teeth and its patches of rotting flesh. And yet it also seems to move, to flex, to wrinkle. To alter expression just like a real face.

Cody screams and leaps back, just as Waldo's mouth opens and a foot-long forked tongue spits out at him. He back-pedals into the darkness, not thinking about falling or crashing into something. He wants to turn and run, but at the same time he needs to keep his eyes fixed on Waldo, to watch where he goes and what he does.

He hits a wall behind him. To either side is more blackness. The only light in the room is that reflecting off Waldo. The monstrous clown is closing in on him, and there is no escape, nowhere to go. Waldo gets closer, closer . . .

And then he stops, his snake tongue tasting the air for a few seconds.

Cody feels his pulse pounding in his own skull. He opens his mouth to speak, but cannot get any words out.

And then Waldo raises his hand. Brings it into the single beam of light. Shows Cody what it holds.

Advancing once more, Waldo presses the trigger on the power drill and it whirrs into life.

It's too much for Cody's brain. It takes him out of there. Snaps him back to his bedroom, where he finds himself sitting upright, panting for breath.

The dream was too lucid, too real. Even now he can easily imagine that Waldo is waiting in the shadows at the foot of the bed. He is standing there, drill in hand, ready to use it. Ready to—

Whirrrr!

And now Cody is crapping himself. Because that was real. That was a real sound.

And it was here, in the building.

36

Cody fumbles for the lamp switch. Turns it on. Nothing in the bedroom, but then he knew that. The sound was further away.

No, he thinks. Can't be. It's just the echoes of the dream. My mind playing tricks.

Whirrrr!

There it is again. Unmistakable now. What the hell?

Cody glances at his bedside clock. It's ten past three in the morning. There should be nobody else in the building.

He climbs out of bed. Hurriedly throws on some jeans, trainers and a sweatshirt. Picks up his police baton from the chest of drawers.

He goes out into the large hall. It's cold here. The central heating has been off for hours. He stands in the centre of the space and listens. The building complains to him of its age and its weariness, but nothing he hasn't heard before. He relaxes. Lets the baton drop to his side.

Whirrrr!

That was louder. Closer. Not up here in the flat, though. Somewhere downstairs.

HOPE TO DIE | 272

Cody feels his skin prickling all over his body. His mind is jumping to conclusions. Informing him that the occupants of his nightmare have somehow passed through a portal into his reality. Telling him that Waldo is waiting for him downstairs.

But that's ridiculous. It's not possible. There has to be a rational explanation.

So prove it. Go ahead, Cody. If you're so sure it's nothing to be worried about, go down there and prove it.

Okay, then. I will.

Although . . .

Perhaps it's not that absurd. Somebody very real was here the other night. Somebody very real has been phoning me up. Somebody very real played the sounds of my screaming over the intercom.

Why couldn't they be in the building right now?

Why couldn't a man in a clown mask be standing on the landing below, armed with a power drill?

That's feasible, isn't it?

So what do I do, then? Call for backup? Tell them I think there's an intruder in the building?

Sure, that'll work. Nobody will think any less of me when they get here only to find that I was scared of the dark. A story like that won't spread through the ranks like wildfire.

Because there really is nothing to worry about. And even if there is someone down there, you can handle it. You and your little baton there.

He begins to descend the staircase. The steps creak and crack as he moves. In the darkness they sound like gunshots. If anyone is waiting for him, they'll know he's coming.

He gets to the floor below. There's a heavy fire door here, separating his flat from the rest of the building. He reaches for the lock. Then he pauses.

Here we go . . .

In one swift motion he unlocks the door and pushes it open. He stands in the doorway, the baton on his shoulder, ready to strike. But he'd forgotten how dark it can be on this landing, and he can see little because he didn't think to bring a torch, and he's feeling pretty idiotic about it, as well as a little scared.

He squints. Tries to push his gaze into the shadowy pockets ahead. Cautiously he takes the first couple of steps beyond the security of his flat.

He knows that the light switch is in the middle of the wall, between the doors to two of the dental surgeries, but there are a few more feet to cover before he reaches it. Behind him, to the left of the door to his apartment, is the route to a small kitchen and some toilets. He glances that way, but it's pitch black. Best to get some lights on first.

He edges forward slowly, listening so intently it almost hurts. When he reaches the switch and flicks it on, the relief feels as instantaneous as the light itself.

Breathing easier now, he checks out the kitchen and the toilet stalls. Then he makes his way down to the ground floor, putting more lights on as he goes. There is no sign of anything untoward. The front and back doors are locked. The entrance to the cellar also seems secure. Cody shakes his head. Laughs at how worked up he was getting. He's still puzzled by the strange noise, though. Something outside, perhaps.

He's not going to worry about it. With any luck he might get some more kip.

He turns the lights off again. Trudges back upstairs. He gets to the first-floor landing. Lights off here, too.

And suddenly it's very black here. Even blacker, it seems, than it was before. Why is that?

The door. The one to his flat. It's closed. It's holding back the light in there.

He racks his brain. He thinks, Did I close the door? I don't remember closing the door.

He puts the landing lights back on. Moves towards his door and pulls on the handle. The door swings open with a high-pitched moan.

He puts his head through the doorway and looks up the staircase.

Shit, he thinks. Now I'm going to have to search my whole flat, otherwise I'll never get to sleep.

He touches the door gently with one finger. It slowly closes, again with a squeal of rusty hinges.

Okay, he thinks. Doesn't take much to close it. I might have brushed against it when I was searching. Even a slight draught might have been enough.

I'm still going to check the flat, though.

He goes back to the light switch for the landing. Turns it off again. He's not really worried now. Just needs that peace of mind that will come with one quick look into each of the rooms upstairs.

The whirring noise sends him flying backwards with shock.

The sound is coming from inside one of the surgeries on this floor. It's the noise of a dentist's drill, and it's not stopping. It goes on and on. Cody can practically feel the pain in his teeth.

There is a frosted-glass panel in the door to the surgery. The lights are off within the room. Cody decides he needs to leave the lights off out here too. Better that than make himself a target in the doorway.

He moves towards the door, baton poised. He has no idea what he's about to face, but he can't run and hide. He's got to confront whoever is in there.

He reaches for the doorknob. The drill continues to scream at him. He turns the handle, pushes hard on the door.

It rattles, but doesn't open.

The occupant has locked himself in. And now he knows Cody is coming after him.

Cody takes a few steps backwards. Runs at the door. Raises his foot and crashes it into the point just above the handle.

The door flies open, and Cody dashes in. But he's not familiar with this room, doesn't think he's ever been in here before, doesn't even know where the light switch is. And everything is a chaotic rushing mess as he shouts, 'Police, don't move!' and he fumbles for the light switch with one hand while keeping the baton ready to strike with the other, and he's trying desperately to hear beyond this godawful racket in case somebody in here is about to swing an axe at him or whatever. And then, mercifully, he finds the switch. Finds it and clicks it on and tries to absorb what he sees and hears.

Which is nothing.

The noise has stopped. There is nobody else in the room.

Cody sees the dentist's chair. He sees all the shiny white cupboards and steel trays and work surfaces and posters and boxes of equipment. He hears his own heavy panting and the hundred-mile-an-hour pulse in his head. He smells his own fear and the sickly odours of dental materials and antiseptic.

But what he doesn't see or hear or smell is another person, let alone a clown.

He traverses the room, just to be sure. But nobody is crouching below a table or hiding in a cupboard. The windows are closed and fastened.

He moves back to the dentist's chair and examines the drill. The power switch is on at the wall, but there's no sign of life in the implement.

What the hell just happened here?

A noise. A creaking sound. Not in here, but outside the room.

Cody raises his baton again. Starts towards the door. His body is beginning to ache with all the tension.

He steps out onto the landing. Looks left, then right.

And now another noise. Like the gentle click of the front door being closed.

Cody races downstairs again. Opens the front door. Finds only the empty night.

'Nooo!' he yells. He bangs his baton against the iron railings outside. Releases another roar of frustration.

He backs into the building. Shuts himself in with . . .

What?

What is, or was, in here?

Something that entered the building and passed through a locked surgery door? Something that was capable of operating the drill, and yet could not be seen or touched? Something that drifted undetected past Cody and then went downstairs and out of the front door?

A ghost?

Cody doesn't believe in ghosts. What he *had* been starting to believe was that his mind was slowly healing. The hallucinations and the violent outbursts have been much less frequent of late. But this . . .

If this was a figment of his imagination, then it was a doozy. It would suggest that his mind is more broken than he thought. And that's worrying.

Cody heads back upstairs. On the landing, he pulls the door of the surgery closed. It doesn't latch, because its lock is now in pieces on the floor. He's got some explaining to do in the morning.

All he can do for the moment is return to his apartment. There'll be nobody up there, just as there was nobody down here.

He's still going to search it, though.

37

The woman who bustles through the front door almost falls back into the street when she encounters the ghostly figure in the lobby.

Cody has been pacing up and down here for the past half-hour. He hasn't slept since his own encounter with the spirit world, or whatever the hell it was last night. Hasn't eaten breakfast either.

'Jesus!' says the woman. Then, recovering, she says, 'You bloody idiot, frightening the life out of me like that.'

'Sorry, Helen,' says Cody. 'I thought you might be Simon.'

The dental receptionist eyes him with suspicion as she closes the door and starts to unwind her seemingly endless scarf.

'What's up? You got toothache?'

'What? No. I just need to see him.'

'I can give you some ibuprofen.'

'No. Honestly, I'm fine.'

She flicks through the keys in her hand, finds the one she wants and moves towards one of the doors. As she unlocks it, she scans him from head to toe.

'You don't look well. Are you sure you're not in pain?'

'No. I mean, yes. I'm not in pain. Do you know what time Simon's coming in?'

Helen checks her watch. 'Well, he's got a nine o'clock appointment, and it's gone eight-thirty now, so—'

The front door swings open again. A man walks in. Tall, smartly dressed, good hair, square jaw. Looks as though he has money. Which he has.

On seeing Cody, Simon Teller raises an eyebrow in a Roger Moore-like expression of mild surprise. Then he flashes perfect teeth – his best advertisement for his services as one of the most sought-after orthodontists in the north-west.

'Cody! Haven't seen you in a while. You wouldn't think we occupied the same building. How are you? Have to say I've seen you looking better.'

Helen chips in: 'I think he's got toothache.'

Cody sees the immediate concern on Teller's face. 'I haven't got toothache. I just need to have a word.'

'A word? Sure. Let's go in here.'

Teller starts moving towards a door on the other side of the hallway, then calls out, 'Kettle on yet, Helen?'

Cody follows Teller into his treatment room. Bright lights flicker on. The ultra-modern interior belies the age of the building containing it. Lots of shiny surfaces and computer screens and equipment that looks as though it belongs in a spaceship. Perish the thought that anything as primitive as pain could be permitted here.

Teller waves Cody into a chair, then says, 'Which tooth is it?'

Cody sighs. 'My teeth are fine. It's not my teeth.'

'Well, you still look like crap. What's up?'

Cody has mixed feelings about Teller. He was introduced to the man by Devon, Cody's ex-fiancée, and never really warmed to him. Teller was married at the time, but even then he had a reputation as a woman-chaser. In fact, his only interests in life seem to be women, money, fast cars and golf. He has so little in common with Cody that conversations between them tend to fizzle out after a few perfunctory sentences.

That said, he did Cody an enormous favour by allowing him to move into the flat upstairs on a pretty minimal rent. It's a debt of gratitude that Cody wishes he didn't owe the man, but sometimes beggars can't be choosers. Another city-centre flat as spacious and as nice as this would be way beyond his price range.

'I didn't get much sleep last night,' Cody explains.

Teller nods. 'That could either be really good, in that there was a woman keeping you busy all night, or bad, in that there wasn't.'

It doesn't surprise Cody that Teller sees the situation in such blatantly sex-related terms. Teller tends to boil most things in life down to that.

'Bad,' says Cody.

'Okay, so . . .' Teller seems to struggle to bring his mind above gutter level. A look of surprise springs to his face when his brain succeeds. 'The flat. Is there something wrong with the flat?'

'No. Well . . . maybe. I don't know.'

'I don't follow.'

'I thought I heard things last night. Weird noises.'

'What kind of noises?'

Cody doesn't want to say. In the cold light of day, or at least the cold light of this treatment room, it seems ridiculous.

'I'm not sure. But it sounded like . . .'

'Yes?'

'It sounded like it was coming from one of your surgeries.'

'Which one?'

'Upstairs. The one by the door to my flat.'

'Okay. Can you be a bit more specific? What kind of noises? Do you mean like an intruder?' Teller looks a little alarmed now.

'No. Well, yes, that's what I thought at first. But it wasn't.'

'Are you sure?'

'Yes. I—'

'How do you know?'

'Well . . .'

There's a rap on the door, and Helen the receptionist breezes in. She is carrying a bunch of keys in her fist, and seems to be out of breath.

'Sorry,' she says. 'Upstairs . . . I think we've had . . . a burglar.'

Teller gets to his feet. 'Shit. So someone *did* get in. We should call the police.' He looks down at Cody. 'Wait. You *are* the police. I thought you just said—'

'I did. It was me.'

Teller gives him a look of confusion. 'What was you?'

'I kicked your door open.'

Teller stares at him for a few seconds, then returns his gaze to Helen. 'It's all right,' he says.

Helen starts to back out of the room, but with reluctance, her eyes studying Cody as though she suspects he's about to start murdering them all. Teller has to beam her a smile of reassurance to get her out of there.

Teller sits down again. 'Right. Let's get to the bottom of this. You kicked my surgery door open?'

'Yes.'

'Because you thought you heard someone in there?'

'Yes.'

'But when you got into the room, there was nobody there.'

'Correct.'

'Okay. I'm with you so far. The bit I don't get is what kind of noises an empty room could possibly make in order for you to believe it was occupied.'

Cody has to concede that this is an excellent point. What he's less certain about is how open he wants to be about the state of his mind.

'All right. Bear with me here, because this might sound a little crazy. I thought I heard a drill.'

'A drill.'

'Yes. One of your dentist drills. That's what it sounded like to me. I don't know, maybe I was dreaming it or something, but that's what I thought I heard. Whatever. It was my mistake. I broke your door, and I'll pay for the damage.'

Teller wears the face of someone who hears what he's being told and is trying to read between the lines. Cody would rather he didn't. He would prefer Teller to say, 'Fine, I'll send you a bill,' and leave it there.

Instead, Teller says, 'Show me.'

'Sure,' says Cody, knowing that some probing questions are about to come his way.

They step into the hallway. Teller says, 'Things going well at work?'

Probing question number one, thinks Cody. The sort of question designed to assess stress levels.

'Busy,' says Cody, keeping it minimal.

'You on those murders? The Bible Basher?'

'The what? Is that what they're calling him?'

'According to the tabloids. Not the stuff I usually read, you understand, but it finds its way into our waiting room.'

Cody isn't too surprised at the aptness of the sobriquet being used by the newspapers. The police have played their cards close to their chests, but too many people will have heard that at least one of the victims had her head caved in. Word soon spreads, and journalists have sharp ears for that kind of salacious gossip.

As they reach the staircase, Cody decides to change the topic. Ask some searching questions of his own.

'Have you seen much of Devon recently?'

He's hoping for a 'no'. He's hoping that this tall, wealthy, good-looking and now single guy is not buzzing around the woman who once unhesitatingly agreed to be Cody's wife.

Teller looks upwards as he searches his memory banks. 'Ooh, must have been at least a month ago. Maybe even six weeks.'

Good, thinks Cody. One less thing to be concerned about.

'Having a pre-Christmas drink with her next week, though,' Teller adds.

'Right,' says Cody. 'Great. Say hello to her for me, won't you?'

'Will do, mate,' says Teller, displaying his exemplary teeth again. I wouldn't have been in need of a torch if I had teeth like that, Cody thinks.

They reach the landing. Teller bends at the waist to examine the lock on the surgery door. 'Ah. See what you mean. Bit of a mess.'

'Like I said, send me the bill.'

Teller dismisses the offer with a wave of his hand. 'Let's take a look at this drill.'

Cody doesn't want to examine the drill. He doesn't want to stand there while Teller confirms that the only plausible explanation for the previous night is that Cody was off his rocker.

'Weird,' says Teller, fiddling with some switches.

'What is?'

'The drill is locked in the on position, the power at the wall is on, and yet nothing's happening.'

'Right,' says Cody, having no idea what this signifies.

'Bear with me,' says Teller.

He walks out of the room, leaving Cody thinking he must have gone in search of some tools. He'd like that to be the case. He'd like a practical, rational solution to all this. Anything that doesn't involve the spirit world or the loss of sanity would be most welcome right now.

When the drill suddenly bursts into life, he almost craps himself.

Teller jogs back into the room. Brings back merciful silence with a flick of the off switch.

'What the hell's going on?' Cody demands.

'I'll show you,' Teller answers.

He leads Cody out of the room, along the landing, and into the kitchen. There, he points to an electrical supply box high on the wall.

'The fuse that controls the power sockets in the surgery had tripped. All I did was to reset it. There must be a fault in the drill. A loose connection of some kind, causing it to go on and off. Eventually, it knocked out the fuse. I'll get someone out to take a look at it.' He laughs, and slaps Cody on the bicep. 'At least you know you weren't imagining things, eh?'

Cody returns a weak smile. It would be nice to accept Teller's version of events, comforting to disregard the things that don't quite fit them. A faulty appliance that just happens to declare its abnormality in the middle of the night – wouldn't that be a lovely coincidence?

But Cody has another, much more unsettling, explanation.

Someone was here last night. Someone with keys, or the ability to pick locks, got into the building. They went into the surgery and operated the drill until Cody woke up. And when Cody had finished checking the first floor and had gone downstairs, the intruder moved to the kitchen, waiting to operate the drill remotely from the fuse box. Then, once Cody had smashed his way into the surgery, the intruder slipped downstairs and out through the front door.

It wasn't a ghost, and it wasn't a figment of Cody's imagination.

Waldo the clown invaded not only Cody's dreams last night.

He was also in the building.

38

Damn him!

He's good, thinks Cody. Bloody good. A genius.

Waldo is here. In my head. Under my skin. I can feel him crawling around inside me, and I can't get rid of him.

It's what he wants, of course. Persecuting me is how he gets his kicks. I thought I was winning. I thought I was becoming myself once more. But this monster is tipping the scales again. He's determined to destroy me.

Cody is at his desk, staring with unseeing eyes at his computer. His brain is frazzled through lack of sleep and an inability to focus on anything but clowns.

Webley didn't help his mood when he arrived for work. He tried smiling at her, but she didn't want to know. And when he tried approaching her desk, she quickly stood up and went to talk to someone else.

Well, sod her, he thinks. I've got bigger problems to deal with.

One of those problems is solving the murders of three women, but even that has been relegated.

The silent phone calls. Then the screams. The music box and the eerie voice. The visitor at the door. And now the latest – an incursion into the privacy of his own home!

Jesus Christ, thinks Cody. Waldo was there. Actually *there*, in my house. If he'd wanted, he could have remained on the other side of that surgery door, just waiting for me to come in so that he could drill holes in my face.

And even when there are pauses in the actual bombardment, Cody's mind fills the gaps with its own cruel games. It creates the most fantastic and horrific nightmares, which don't end with coming awake.

He thinks back to how things were, a couple of months ago. He was at a crisis point then. The dreams and hallucinations were the worst they had ever been. He found himself losing control, lashing out at others. In that condition, he couldn't have lasted much longer in the force.

The clowns want him back in that state. He's certain of that. They are playing at psychological warfare. They want to turn him into a gibbering, drooling wreck. And probably for no other reason than that they enjoy it.

The problem is that they are succeeding.

He can feel his control ebbing away. His reason is being steadily sucked out of his body.

The only piece of driftwood left for him to cling to is the fact that the clowns have made contact. They say that, in a big city, you are never more than ten feet away from a rat. Well, maybe now he is never more than a few feet away from a clown. A terrifying thought to most people, but to Cody it brings hope. If they remain nearby, he might just have the chance of catching one. And then the tables might be turned.

It doesn't help that he has lost his only ally. Megan Webley played a vital role in dragging him back from the brink of insanity. Dragged him back from the brink of death, too. He owes her big time. He can't afford to shut her out completely. And yet isn't that the way things are going?

He sneaks a peek towards Webley's desk. Engrossed in something on her computer, she looks untroubled, and her beauty shines through. It seems to Cody that every time he crosses her path at the moment he causes that face to crease with lines of fury and sorrow. He isn't being fair on her.

He decides he needs to make it up to Webley. His mind rolls back to his thoughts of the previous night, before it was so violently disturbed.

An early Christmas present – that'll do it. He knows her well enough to find her something she will like. Something she will treasure. A piece of jewellery, perhaps. Earrings? No. Maybe a necklace, though. That would be—

Wait.

Why does that feel so wrong? Why does the idea of a gift like that stir up such uneasy feelings?

'Cody!'

He looks up at the sound of the bark from DCI Blunt. She is standing in the doorway to her office, beckoning him in. He gets up, crosses the incident room. Inches past Blunt's substantial frame, anxious not to come into contact with any part of her as he does so.

She follows him in, closing the door behind her. She comes around her desk and takes a seat. Invites Cody to sit down too.

'Are you all right?' she asks.

'Ma'am?'

'You look like death warmed up. Like you haven't slept in a week.'

'Oh. No. It's okay. There was a problem in the flat last night. Something to do with the electrics. Kept me awake.'

Blunt eyes him with suspicion. She has seen him like this before. She has suspected for a long time that he has been experiencing problems – of that he is sure. She never comes right out with it. Instead, she asks probing questions, or offers him opportunities to unload. He never takes her up on those offers. To do so would be the beginning of the end. Benevolent though Blunt might seem, her actions will be guided by the unchallengeable might of police procedure. The job he loves doing would be taken from him, to be substituted by months of psychiatric assessment and a role flying a desk in a dusty basement office. He's not having that.

'Is that all?' says Blunt. 'I've just been watching you. For the last five minutes all you've done is stare at your screen. You haven't moved a muscle. That's not just tiredness, Cody. Something's up.'

Here we go again, he thinks. Blunt playing the mother figure. She does this a lot with him, but not with any other member of the team. He often wonders why that is, but he won't dare ask her. That would be such an awkward conversation.

I could tell her, he thinks. Tell her what's really bothering me. Tell her about the clowns knocking on my door, the ghosts operating machinery in the middle of the night, the possibility that I'm getting into a deadly game I don't know how to play.

Could you help me with that, DCI Blunt?

'The case,' he says. 'It's getting to me.'

'It's getting to all of us. What in particular?'

Good question. Because actually there is something particular. He just doesn't know what it is. He has a feeling it was about to come to him, right before Blunt called his name.

'The lack of progress,' he says. 'I think I'm starting to take it personally.'

He doesn't mean this. He hates the fact that they seem to be making little progress in catching the killer, but he's not blaming himself for that. It's a plausible response to Blunt's question, however.

'Let me worry about that,' she says. 'It's my squad. The buck stops with me.' She pauses to allow her words of reassurance time to sink in, then says, 'How's our Megan getting on?'

Megan. Yes, he was thinking about her earlier, wasn't he? Just before Blunt's interruption, he was thinking about how he might appease her. Why does that seem so important?

'Fine,' he answers. 'She's fitting in really well.'

Except with me, he wants to add. Right now she hates my guts. Thinks I'm a total arsehole. Hence the idea of a small gift. Jewellery. A necklace. That's where I got to in my thinking. That's where my brain started to sound a gong. Why, damn it?

'Good to hear,' says Blunt. 'Keep her under your wing. She's been through a lot, but so have you. I'm sure you'll know the warning signs if she starts to wobble.'

Cody hears the latest unsubtle reference to his past history, but lets it pass straight through his head without interception. He needs to focus all his mental energy on—

'Cody, are you listening to me? I said—'

Cody raises a finger to stop her in mid-flow. He starts to rise from his chair, a smile forming on his face.

'Cody?'

'Sorry, ma'am. Gotta go.'

Blunt's expression clouds over. 'Cody!'

His smile broadens, defying her wrath, because he knows that he alone in the squad can get away with it. 'Got to check something. Hold that bollocking. If I'm wrong, you can give it to me later.'

And then he's heading out of the office and closing the door behind him, but not before he hears Blunt telling him that a bollocking is coming his way in any event.

39

He knows what it is now. Or at least he thinks he does.

He consults his computer again, but this time he doesn't scroll aimlessly through the files. He goes precisely to the pages he needs.

And this time he finds what he's looking for.

He scans the room, searching for someone to help him out. He catches the eye of a young and ambitious red-headed detective called Jason Oxburgh, or 'Oxo' as he's known to the rest of the squad.

Cody leaves his desk. Marches straight over to Oxo. 'Got a job for you,' he says.

'Sarge?'

Oxo always calls him Sarge. Everyone else usually calls him Cody, but Oxo has somehow never managed to move past the formality.

'I need you to round up the possessions of the three victims. Bring them back here.'

'Sarge?' says Oxo again.

'Not the clothes. I'm not interested in those. Just the stuff they were carrying on their person.'

It's obvious that Oxo is still mystified. 'Okay.'

'Right,' says Cody. 'Off you go.'

'What, now?'

'Now. Immediately. Without delay. Chop-chop.'

Oxo stands up. Grabs his coat and heads out of the incident room. Cody watches him leave. Then, as he turns, he sees several puzzled expressions among his colleagues. One of them belongs to Webley, who quickly looks away and pretends not to be intrigued.

Well, he thinks, let's see if she changes her tune when I hit everyone with the punchline.

His concentration doesn't improve while Oxo is on his mission, but at least now it's for more positive reasons. This is a significant development in the case. Has to be.

Gonna look an idiot if I'm wrong, though, he thinks.

If all I can do is say thanks to Oxo, then pack the stuff up and tell him to take it away again, I'll feel a right prune. The others will realise it, too. Webley will wet herself laughing at me.

But I'm not wrong. It would be too much of a coincidence.

He decides to step outside. Take a breath of fresh air.

When he gets to the car park, he nods to a constable on his way back in after a crafty smoke. Then he paces up and down a little, his hands in his trouser pockets to keep them warm. He hears the crunch of the rock salt beneath his shoes.

Should have put a coat on, he thinks.

He reaches into his jacket pocket. Takes out his mobile phone. Stares at it for a while.

What the hell. Can't make it any worse.

HOPE TO DIE | 294

He finds the number. Presses the green dial button. The call is answered after three rings.

'Cody,' says the voice. 'What's up?' There's a note of alarm there, which isn't the best start to the conversation.

'Hi, Devon,' he says. 'Nothing's up. Just thought I should give you a call. It's been a while.'

'Such a long time that you've forgotten I'm at work during the day?'

'No. Sorry. If this is a bad time . . .'

He hears a small sigh. 'No. It's fine. I could do with a break. What is it, Cody?'

'Well . . . it's Christmas in a few days.'

'Right.'

'And so I was wondering what . . . well, what we're doing about it. If anything.'

'How do you mean?'

'I mean . . . presents. Are we getting each other presents? I don't know what the protocol is here.'

He hears a few seconds of silence. Then: 'Protocol? Cody, life isn't defined by one of your police manuals. There's no protocol. You give at Christmas if it feels right, not because you're supposed to.'

'No. I know. But . . . I want to get you something, but I don't want you to feel awkward about it. I don't want you reading things into it that aren't there, do you know what I mean? And I don't want you feeling you have to get me something just because I get you something. That's why it's complicated.'

'You're overthinking it, Cody. As usual. Tell you what, let's just keep it simple, shall we?'

'Simple. Right. So . . .'

'So we don't buy each other anything. How does that sound?'

It sounds awful, he thinks. It sounds like another nail in the coffin of their relationship – a relationship he still has hopes of resurrecting.

'I suppose that would be simplest. Although—'

'That's settled, then. Feel better now that's sorted out?'

He doesn't feel better. He feels ten times worse.

'Have you . . . have you got any plans for Christmas?'

'Yeah. Off to stay with my folks for a few days, then skiing for a week. What about you?'

He had hoped her diary would be emptier than that. He doesn't want her to be sad, but he did hope for a void he might help to fill. The problem with Devon is that she refuses to sit in isolation and mope, like normal people. Her nature abhors a vacuum.

'Work, mostly,' he answers with fake jocularity. 'You know me.'

'Only too well.'

He waits for a follow-up tinkle of laughter from her, too, but fails to get one. Before the slight can penetrate too deeply, he makes his next move.

'But I can always find time to meet up. If you want to, that is. Lunch, maybe. Or a quick drink?'

Silence again. Which doesn't bode well. If she were keen, or even mildly interested in the possibility, the appropriate words would jump to her lips. What she's looking for now is a way out.

'I would,' she says finally, 'but I'm up to my eyes right now.'

Sure, he thinks. Except for Simon Teller. You can find time for a get-together with him.

She says, 'I have to clear my desk before Christmas. Before I disappear. You know how it is.'

He doesn't know how it is. His job isn't like that. His desk is never clear, because there are always major crimes being committed. Unfortunately, the killings and the woundings and the rapes and the abductions don't stop in the name of baby Jesus. Sometimes, such as right now, they worsen for that very reason.

'No problem,' he says. 'Just thought I'd put it out there. In case . . . well . . .'

'Yes. Thanks for asking, though.'

He allows her time to throw him a rope. Something along the lines of, 'What about the New Year? How are you fixed then?' But it doesn't appear. She's prepared to let him fall.

He thinks about asking her if it would be okay to phone her on Christmas Day, just to wish her a Happy Christmas. But he doesn't want to appear needy. Doesn't want to risk the pain and the humiliation of further rejection.

'Okay,' he says. 'Well, I should let you get back to work.'

'Yes. No rest for the wicked.'

'I'll send you a Christmas card. Something with robins on.'

'You remembered. Yes, please do.'

She doesn't say whether she will send him one.

'Great. Well, have a brilliant Christmas, won't you? Enjoy your skiing trip.'

'I will. You too. A good Christmas, I mean.'

He wants to remind her of previous Christmases. Wants to get her laughing about that time he mistakenly ordered a tree that was too big to get through the front door. Or when he left some posh chocolates next to a radiator, and watched her open the box to find a congealed brown mass at the bottom.

But he says none of those things. He leaves the past where it lies.

He says goodbye and hangs up. Stares at his phone again. He pictures Devon doing the same, but he hopes there is at least a tear in her eye. He hopes that how she just acted was tough for her, that putting herself across as cold and unfeeling was done with the best of intentions, since to lead him on would be cruel.

That's what he hopes. Because the alternative is that she really is over him – she really does have no feelings remaining for him. That would leave them without a future together.

He's not ready to accept that. Not yet.

He's starting to think that Oxo must have been involved in a traffic accident, it's been that long. But then the young detective enters the room, three cardboard boxes in his possession.

'Where've you been?' Cody asks him. 'I was about to send out a search party.'

Oxo tilts his head to see past the boxes stacked up in his arms. 'Sorry, Sarge. I went as quick as I could.'

Cody ushers him over to an empty table in the corner of the room, but makes no attempt to lighten the man's load.

'Put them on there. That's it.'

Cody studies the boxes. Sees that each is labelled with the name of a victim of the so-called Bible Basher. He takes a deep breath. Opens the first box.

Inside the box are a number of plastic evidence bags. Cody begins to search through them. These are the items that belonged to Mary Cowper. Cody recognises them from his attendance at the post-mortem. He knows exactly what he's looking for.

He finds it.

He lifts out the bag. Places it carefully on the table. Moves on to the next box, containing the possessions of Cassie Harris.

Unknown territory now. The doubts are returning. He continues to lift bag after bag from the box. Drops each one back in with a steadily sinking heart. It's not here, he thinks. I've made a mistake. This is where everyone realises what a tit I've just made of myself.

And then he finds it. The last bag in the box.

'Yesss,' he says.

Box three. Sue Halligan. Lipstick. Phone. Coins. Receipts . . .

And there it is.

Cody can hold back the grin no longer. It practically shines across the incident room, drawing the attention of everyone as he lines up the three evidence bags in front of him. Detectives begin to leave their seats to learn what profound discovery has just been made.

'What are they?' says Oxo, staring down at the table.

Cody claps him on the shoulder. 'These, my friend, are clues. We missed it, but our killer has been sending us messages since day one.'

40

Says Oxo, 'I still don't know what they are.'

Cody picks up one of the bags and holds it aloft so that the gathering detectives can see.

'It's a pendant of some kind. From a necklace, I suppose. I saw it when I was at Mary Cowper's PM, but thought nothing of it. Just looked like a broken bit of jewellery she'd stuffed into her pocket. Even when I started looking through the possessions logs of the other victims it didn't jump out at me. In Sue Halligan's case, for example, it's just described as a "small ornamental stone". Took me a while to realise that all three were carrying similar items on them.'

'Let's have a gander,' says one of the detectives, reaching out a hand.

Cody passes the bags around. Watches his colleagues as they peer at them intently. Each of the polished, speckled-brown objects is small and pear-shaped, and has a metal attachment loop at the thin end. Cody notices that Webley in particular finds them of immense interest.

'I don't get it,' says Oxo. 'What kind of message is this? What's it telling us?'

'That's the million-dollar question,' says Cody. 'These were placed in the victims' pockets, so they must mean something.'

Webley finds her voice: 'Before or after death?'

'What?'

'Well, did the killer put them there *after* killing the women, or were they already carrying them around with them?'

'Good point,' says Cody. Because it is, undeniably. And something he hasn't considered. 'We should talk to Stroud and the forensics guys. See if they can answer that. We should also ask people who knew the victims whether they have ever seen these pendants before.'

Webley holds her bag up to the light. 'Funny-looking things. I mean, they're not the most beautiful, are they? I wouldn't wear one around my neck.'

Cody isn't sure whether this is an attempt to shoot holes in his prodigious detective work.

'Yes, but you're not a serial killer trying to contact us.'

'If he's trying to communicate,' says Oxo, 'it's a bit subtle, isn't it? We nearly missed it completely.'

Cody throws him the glare that he wanted to send to Webley. 'Well, now we've found it, haven't we?' He turns to the rest of his audience. 'Can we all get a little bit more positive here, please? This could be crucial evidence. Anyone got any ideas about what it might mean?'

Blank faces turn to other blank faces. Some search for answers in the carpet.

'Something about worth?' Oxo ventures.

'Go on.'

'Well . . . something that's pretty, but is broken, and so not worth very much. Maybe that's how the killer sees the women too.'

Cody points a finger at him. 'Good. What else?'

He surveys the gathering again. Notes that there is patent scepticism on Webley's face. He wonders if being contrary is about to become her watchword.

Another figure arrives at the fringes of the throng. Taller than the rest by a head, he would have had difficulty joining them unnoticed.

'We having a seance?' Ferguson asks. 'Are things that desperate we need to talk directly to the dead?'

'They're already talking to us, mate,' says Cody. 'Take a look.'

Ferguson threads his way to the front. Stares for a few seconds at the table display. Picks up one of the bags and scrutinises it more closely.

'Where'd you get these?'

'They were on the bodies, only nobody noticed. A junk piece of broken jewellery doesn't exactly cry out for attention.'

Ferguson shakes his head. 'These aren't jewellery.'

'What? What do you mean?'

'They're not jewellery. They're lead fishing weights.'

'Fishing weights?'

'Yeah. I did a lot of fishing with my dad when I was younger. These are for carp and suchlike. They anchor the bait closer to the river bed. The speckled colouring is to make them look like stones.'

Cody stares at him open-mouthed. A bit like a carp.

He hears a splutter of laughter. Webley brings a hand to her mouth and attempts to disguise her outburst as a cough.

Says Cody, 'Why the hell would our killer want to place fishing weights on the bodies?'

Ferguson shrugs, but then Webley says, 'Maybe it's because they sleep with the fishes now.'

She gets a few chuckles, and Cody begins to wish he had never started this whole thing.

'I don't think this is the work of the Mafia, Megan. Seriously, what possible point can he be making here?'

More silence. When Webley raises a tentative finger, Cody is tempted to ignore it. He thinks he will explode if she makes another sarcastic comment.

His voice is practically a sigh: 'Megan.'

'Just an observation,' she says.

'All right. Observe away.'

'Colin Daley, the school caretaker. He's a fisherman. There's a photo of him in his living room, holding a bloody big ugly fish.'

The image flashes back into Cody's mind. He remembers the photo. Can picture it now. Damn it, why didn't he make that connection?

'You're right,' he says, unable to contain his mounting excitement. 'Colin Daley. The man who definitely knew Mary Cowper. The man who did a runner when we turned up at the school. The man who got someone to lie for him to cover his tracks. The man who had no real alibis for the times of the killings. And the man who knows more than most about fishing weights.'

'Hold on,' says Ferguson. 'Why would he draw attention to himself like this? So far he's done everything he can to stay off our radar.'

'He probably doesn't think he *is* drawing attention. Not in an obvious way. Like I said, we almost didn't notice the fishing weights at all. And he's probably so used to that photo being there that he's not aware we saw it. Far as he's concerned, we're none the wiser. I'll bet he thinks he's being really clever with his little guessing game.'

'Possibly,' says Ferguson.

'Do I sense some doubt?'

'Well, it's just that Daley is hardly the only fisherman in the world, is he? If we're basing our suspicions on that, you might as well include me, too. It's not exactly proof. It's not even enough to arrest him.'

Cody hates to admit it, but he knows Ferguson is right. It's not proof. Not by a long shot.

They need more.

41

She has watched all this with detached interest.

She didn't join the gathering at the front. It didn't feel right. She's not one of them. She worried that one of the detectives might have challenged her right to be there, and she would have found that really upsetting.

It's better this way, observing from a distance.

She needed to see it play out, from beginning to end. For a few unbearable minutes it seemed that Cody would beat her to it again, putting all her hard work to waste.

Clever man, is young Cody.

But it came to naught. Supposition at best. They need more. Cody needs more.

And I can give it to him, she thinks.

Grace can feel her heart thumping wildly, like an energetic animal trapped within her ribcage. This won't be easy, she thinks. I don't know how they'll react. Will they be angry or pleased?

But I have to tell them. It's important. No, it's everything.

She waits a few moments more while the detectives lose interest in the fishing weights and return to their seats. When all is quiet, she leaves her desk and moves unnoticed through the room.

She stops alongside Cody's desk. Waits for him to become aware of her presence.

'Grace,' he says. He appears a little surprised, a little mystified.

She whispers, 'Could I have a word, please?' then scans the room to make sure nobody is watching.

Cody clicks his retractable pen and puts it down. 'Sure. What's up?'

'In private,' she says.

Cody studies her face for a few seconds, as if inviting her to offer some clues, but she remains impassive.

'All right,' says Cody, standing up. 'Let's get a room.'

He smiles. She doesn't, because she's unsure as to whether he's messing about. *Get a room*. Something often said to people getting a bit flirty with each other.

But the room to which Cody escorts her is nothing like a luxury five-star hotel room. Nothing like a bottom-of-the-range motel room either, for that matter. Grace has poked her head into an interview room before, but never actually spent time in one. She finds it cold and bleak. There are no comfy armchairs here, no pictures on the walls. There are not even any windows: fluorescent strip lighting bathes everything in a harsh yellow glow. A single metal-framed table is surrounded by hard plastic chairs. On the table is a black recording device for taped interviews.

Cody beckons her into a chair. Takes one himself.

'Okay, Grace, what's with all the cloak and dagger?'

Oh, God, she thinks. Do I really want to go through with this?

'What you were saying out there, about Colin Daley. I think you're right about him.'

Cody nods. 'It's nice to know I have your support. Is that all you wanted to tell me?'

'No. Not quite. I've done something.'

'All right. What kind of something?'

'Well, you remember that online newspaper article about Cassie Harris?'

'Yes.'

'And you remember that blog post by Sue Halligan?'

'Of course. Where is this going, Grace?'

Okay, she thinks. Here goes.

'Well, I took a dump of all the recent Internet accesses to those two websites, and I did a cross-comparison of the IP addresses, followed by a reverse trace of the matching addresses—'

Cody shows her his palms. 'Whoa, Grace. I'm just a simple copper. Could you bring it down a level? What, exactly, have you found out?'

'That Colin Daley's computer account was used to access the web pages of both Cassie Harris and Sue Halligan.'

Cody's mouth drops open. It's a while before he can gain control of it to emit a simple 'What?'

Grace senses it's a rhetorical question, and doesn't repeat herself.

'Wait a minute,' says Cody. 'Lots of people will have accessed those pages, especially those intimately involved in the case. The names of the victims are all over the papers. All that's required is the ability to use Google.'

'Sorry,' she says. 'I should have made myself clear. The accesses from Daley's account were made *prior* to the murders.'

Cody's jaw turns to lead again. Grace finds herself wondering what's going through his head.

She gets her answer when he leaps from his chair, punches the air and shouts, 'Yesss!'

When he has finished dancing around the room, he says, 'Are you certain about this?'

'One hundred per cent.'

'Yesss! Grace, I could kiss you.'

The words shock her. She knows he is only joking, but even so . . .

'Come on,' says Cody. 'You need to repeat this in front of DCI Blunt.'

He heads for the door, but Grace stays put.

'Grace. Are you coming?'

'I, er, I can't. I can't tell DCI Blunt.'

Cody moves slowly back to her. 'Why? What's the problem?'

'She won't want to hear it.'

'Of course she will. You deserve a medal for this one.'

'I don't think DCI Blunt will see it that way. In fact, I think she might have me arrested.'

She sees how Cody's shoulders slump. 'What have you done?'

'I . . . I might have gained access to some computers that I shouldn't have.'

'Daley's computer?'

'No. The web hosting sites, so that I could get the IP addresses of the computers fetching the data. Then the Internet service providers, to reverse-map the addresses back to—'

'You were hacking.'

She looks into his eyes, hoping to find some forgiveness there. 'Yes.'

Cody turns away from her. When he turns back he has put on a mask of disappointment. 'Shit, Grace. You can't just go around doing stuff like that.'

'I know, but ... we needed answers. *You* needed answers. Don't worry. I was careful. I didn't leave any—'

'Yes, I'm sure you covered up your tracks, but that's not the point. The problem is, we can't use any of this stuff. Not if it was gained illegally. You do know we have computer techie bods we can go to for this kind of thing? People who use the proper channels?'

'Yes, but—'

Cody stops her again with a raised hand: 'Hang on. That's it!' He finds his smile. 'That's what we'll do, only we'll do it legally this time. We'll issue a Section 29 request, and get the same information that way.'

Grace says nothing. She doesn't want to be the one to dampen Cody's excitement. But the negativity on her face is clear to see.

'Grace?'

She takes a deep breath. 'Section 29 of the Data Protection Act specifies conditions under which information can be released about individuals without breaching their privacy rights. For example, if we knew that a certain IP address was used in the commission of a crime at a certain time, we could ask the Internet service provider who owns that address to tell us who it was assigned to. That type of very specific request isn't usually a problem.'

'But . . .' Cody prompts.

'In this case, we'd have to make a request on the pretence that we don't already know the outcome. First, we'd have to ask the hosting sites of the newspaper article and the blog to reveal all the IP addresses used to access those pages in a fairly general time frame. Then we'd have to ask each and every one of the ISPs who provide those addresses to give us the names and contact details of the owners of every computer on the list. You see the difference? Section 29 isn't designed for such fishing expeditions, and any data controller worth their salt won't furnish information on customers who have no proven connection with a crime.'

'They'd have to if we got a court order.'

'Same problem. I'm no lawyer, but I don't think any court in the land would issue a court order for such a speculative venture.'

She watches the information sink painfully into Cody's brain.

He says, 'So basically, what you're telling me is that we can't get the same information that you obtained, even via legitimate means?'

'Yes. I'm sorry. But I thought I had to tell you what I found. Did I do wrong?'

Cody breaks away from her again. Paces the room while he thinks.

'I can't let this go, Grace.'

She blinks. She didn't expect this. 'You're going to report me?'

He waves away her alarm. 'No, no. That's not what I mean. I'm saying I have to act on this. I can't just pretend I haven't heard what you told me.'

'I'm sorry. For putting you in this predicament, I mean.'

He steps up to her. Touches a hand to her forearm. 'Don't be. This is the best information we've had during the whole case. The circumstances aren't ideal, but I'll just have to work around them.'

'What are you going to do?'

'First of all, I'm going to ask you to forget we ever had this conversation. Are you okay with that?'

'Yes. Absolutely. And then what?'

'I'm going to bring Daley in. I'm going to lean on him. I can't use what we know about his computer accesses, but I can make him sweat. I can let him know that we're on to him. And if Daley is strong enough not to break under questioning, I'll watch him like a hawk until I've got enough to arrest him. One way or another, I'll get him.'

'Can you do all that without evidence? Won't DCI Blunt have something to say about it?'

Cody shows her his boyish grin again. 'Let me worry about the boss. She'll roar a bit, but she's just a pussycat really.'

Grace wants to support Cody. Wants to tell him what a great plan this is.

But something tells her it won't be as simple as he makes it out to be.

42

As he dashes back to his desk to retrieve his coat, Cody asks Ferguson if he's up for stretching his legs. Ferguson doesn't need asking twice, but Cody experiences a pang of guilt when he notices how Webley glances their way.

'Fancy some fresh air?' he says to her.

Webley raises her head again. Tries to appear as though she is unaware of the preparations for action.

'If this is a trick to send me out for coffees and sandwiches, the answer's no.'

'No tricks. And if this pans out, I'll buy the sarnies.'

Webley gets up. 'An invitation to a bacon butty with two blokes. How could I resist?'

Cody leads the way downstairs. Insists on driving the pool car.

Two minutes into the journey, Webley says from the back seat, 'Come on, then. Where are we going?'

'Wondered how long it would take you,' Cody answers. 'We're off to pick up Colin Daley.'

'Daley? What, on the strength of the fishing connection?'

'Not just that.'

'What, then?'

'Can't say.'

'Why not?'

'It's best if you don't know.'

Webley is silent for a few seconds. Cody can practically hear the steam coming out of her ears.

'Does *he* know?'

Ferguson twists in his seat when he realises the reference is to him. 'Me? No. Haven't a clue. I'm just going along for the magical mystery tour.'

Cody says, 'I've learnt something about Daley that we can't use against him. That's why I'm not telling you, because it would just get in the way. Just believe me when I say that it puts Daley at the top of our list. Our brief now is to pick him up, turn the thumbscrews, and see if he squeaks.'

There's another awkward silence. Cody is grateful when Ferguson clears his throat to speak.

'So . . . What did everyone do last night?'

And now Cody isn't so grateful.

'Well,' says Webley. 'I had a wonderful roast dinner. Beef, gravy, and not to forget the trimmings. It was delicious. What about you, Cody?'

'Er, I had sausages and beans.'

Ferguson looks at him. 'Pushing the boat out there, aren't you, mate? What'll it be on Christmas Day? Turkey Twizzlers?'

Before Cody can answer, Webley says, 'He's a busy man, Neil. Too busy to sit down and eat a proper meal like the rest of us.

That's how come he knows the guilty party is Daley, and we don't. Slackers like us spend too much time on our tuck.'

Ferguson opens his mouth to speak. Decides better of it.

It's a curious scene. A paradoxical one. Three detectives piling out of their car, business written on their features. Snowflakes swirling and dancing around them as they move with grim determination towards the school. And then the school itself, tall and majestic and evocative of a distant past. It is peaceful now. No shrieking or excited chatter or giggles. In its place, the sweetest sound: the notes of an all-female choir carrying the message of Christmas to the ears of these hardened police officers. Telling them of beauty and light and the promise of eternal happiness. It seems almost inconceivable to them that here, in the middle of this serenity and exquisite beauty, is a man who may have savagely ripped the lives from three women.

The detectives trudge up the steps of the school. They enter through the main doors. The singing is louder in here. Cody recognises the current song as 'Carol of the Bells'. It would lift his heart if he would let it. But he needs to remain focused on death, on violence, on righting wrongs.

Ahead is the reception desk. The deputy headmaster, Tony Beamish, is deep in conversation with the young woman behind the counter. It looks to Cody as though Beamish is flirting, but when Beamish becomes aware of the visitors approaching, he morphs effortlessly back into his professional sleekness.

'Is Mrs Laplace available?' Cody asks.

'She's in the main hall,' Beamish says. 'A practice for the Christmas carol service. Perhaps I can help?'

'We need to talk to one of your staff members. Colin Daley, your caretaker.'

Beamish sizes up the detectives in front of him. Senses the seriousness being emanated.

'What's he done?'

'We need to talk to him,' Cody repeats. He's not about to give details to anyone but Daley. He wants to make sure that any message reaching Daley's ears before the police get to him consists only of the news that he's a wanted man.

Realising he has just been slighted, Beamish tightens his lips, turning them thin and white. 'He's most probably in the work-shop, at the back of the school. Go back out that door, turn left, and follow it around.'

'I know it,' says Webley. 'Come on.'

She leads the way. Back into the cold crisp air. Along the drive-way until they hit a car park. They march under a brick archway and head towards a detached flat-roofed building. As they get nearer, a figure appears in the doorway. Cody recognises it as the caretaker's assistant, Jamie Morgan.

Morgan observes their approach as he dries his hands on a grubby towel.

'Your gaffer,' says Webley. 'Colin Daley. Where is he?'

Morgan's eyes flit over each of the detectives in turn. 'I-I dunno. He went to check on something a couple of minutes ago. He's— Wait! Here he is now.'

Cody, Webley and Ferguson turn in unison. They see Daley coming towards them from a side door to the main school building.

And then Daley slows his pace. Comes to a full stop. Cody realises that a crucial decision is being made in the man's head. He tenses.

And then Daley is running. Everyone is running.

Daley disappears back into the building. Pulls the door shut behind him. When the detectives get there, they find it locked from the inside.

'Neil, take the back!' Cody orders.

Cody and Webley race to the front door. They burst through. Beamish and the secretary have vanished, and there's no sign of Daley either.

'Shit!' says Cody.

He motions Webley to move one way along a corridor, while he heads in the opposite direction. He shoulders his way through a pair of swing doors. Pounds his way past a library and an art room. Slams through another pair of doors.

Nobody here. Cody starts to think he's made a mistake coming this way, but then he hears footsteps running towards him from an adjoining corridor.

He flattens himself against the wall next to the doors. The footsteps grow louder, drowning out Cody's heavy breathing.

The doors burst open. Cody leaps. Grabs hold of the man in front of him and starts to wrestle him towards the wall.

'It's me!' Ferguson protests. 'It's me!'

'Shit!' says Cody. 'Where the fuck is he?'

He realises that Webley is on her own, and starts sprinting back that way, Ferguson close behind.

When they get back to the end of the corridor, they see Webley appear on the other side of the lobby. She raises empty hands, indicating that she can't find him either.

Cody tells Ferguson to try the front of the building, then starts to jog over to Webley.

'Cody!' she yells, pointing over his shoulder.

Cody turns. Sees Daley appearing suddenly from a door behind the reception desk.

Daley makes a beeline for the front entrance. Catching sight of Ferguson on the other side of the door, he changes his mind and bolts up the staircase to the right.

'Neil!' Cody calls. 'Get in here!'

He takes the steps two at a time. He's not sure whether Webley is on his heels or not, or if Ferguson has heard his cry. He just knows he needs to stop the man up ahead.

Daley is fit, though. He gets to the upper landing way ahead of Cody, then does a quick reconnaissance. Making his decision, he runs straight at the double doors in front of him. Cody hears the doors crash open, a few high-pitched yelps, and then the singing falter and come to a juddering halt.

Cody gets to the top of the stairs. Ahead, voices build to a commotion.

And then the screaming begins.

Cody moves through the doors. Realises he's at the back of the gallery overlooking the main hall. Most of the school is assembled here. They have been listening to beauty, and now they are bathed in fear.

To either side of Cody, rows of girls yell and scream and clutch each other's hands as they try to come to terms with what is happening in front of them.

At the bottom of the aisle steps, Colin Daley has his back to the low rail of the gallery. Behind and below him, anxious faces look up and try to work out what is going on.

In the arms of Daley is a small, frail-looking girl. Tears are running down her face. She can't be older than eleven; this is probably her first year at secondary school. It could well be her last.

Cody sees the desperation in Daley's eyes. He's like a cornered animal. If something panics him now, he could act without thinking.

Cody puts out a hand to calm Daley's fears. Takes a step down.

'Stay away!' Daley yells at him, spittle flying from his mouth. 'Stay away, or it'll be your fault if she gets hurt.'

'It's all right, Colin. We just want to talk.'

Another step down. Daley turns slightly, makes a move as if about to throw the girl from the balcony. A collective scream erupts from the audience.

'Colin! Listen to me. This isn't helping. You're making things worse for yourself. Let the girl go.'

'I . . . I can't.'

Daley glances over the balcony again, down at all those fearful faces.

'You can, Colin. You know you don't want to hurt her.'

'Get away from me! All of you. Leave me alone!'

Cody assesses the distance between him and Daley. Tries to work out whether he can cover it quickly enough to stop Daley throwing the girl over the side.

'We're not going anywhere, Colin. It's over. There's no point to what you're doing. No point in harming this little girl. Look at her. Look at how frightened you're making her.'

Daley looks at the girl's face. Sees her tear-stained cheeks and quivering lips.

Then he looks back at Cody, and Cody knows something is about to happen.

'COLIN!'

Cody moves. Flies down those steps towards Daley.

Daley abandons the girl. Drops her like a sack of coal onto the floor of the balcony. Cody feels the relief flood through him.

But it's not over.

Daley jumps over the side of the partition.

Cody hears the screams, the loud bang as Daley hits the floor below.

And then Cody does something stupid. He follows Daley off the gallery.

In mid-air he realises that it's a longer drop than he thought. He decides this is going to hurt.

He hits the parquet floor with all the grace of a dead cod. One leg twists under his body, and he feels something go in his ankle.

He looks up from his prone position. Daley is heading towards the stage, while all around him screaming pupils are scrambling to get out of his way.

Cody gets to his feet. Pain fires up from his ankle, but he forces himself forwards. He keeps his eyes fixed on Daley. Sees him dodge around a knot of terrified girls, then crash into some discarded chairs and fly headlong into the front of the stage. He gets up again, starts to mount the short flight of steps onto the platform.

Cody tries to ignore the injury that seems to have set his whole lower body aflame. He puts all his energy into a final burst of speed, and then, like a lion seizing a gazelle from behind, he leaps and wraps his arms around Daley's trailing leg. He brings his quarry crashing to the wooden stage, then drags him back down the steps.

Kneeling over the moaning caretaker, Cody tries to find the proper words for arrest and caution, but the agony floods through his system, and all he wants to do is slip into the sweetness of oblivion.

43

'Right, then,' says Blunt. 'Care to tell me what the fuck has been going on?'

Cody meets the challenging gaze of his superior while he tries to assess how much of the truth she is willing to bear. He decides it's a minuscule amount.

'We went to talk to Daley again. He did a runner. He went up to the school balcony, then jumped off. I followed.'

'Yes, I have been apprised of the sequence of events. I know all about your little escapade. I know that a whole school population was traumatised, that a child was almost thrown to her death and that one of my detectives is now hobbling about like Long John Silver. What I don't know, Cody, is *why*. What on earth led you and your little mob to go on this rampage in the first place?'

'A hunch, ma'am.'

'A hunch.'

'Yes, ma'am. It was the fishing weights. Daley is a keen fisherman.'

'And that's all? That's what it took for the three of you to descend on the school caretaker like you were about to deal with a riot? It's a wonder you didn't take armed backup with you.'

'It all fitted. Daley ticked all the boxes. To be honest, I wasn't expecting him to react the way he did.'

'Hmm,' says Blunt. 'Well, it's probably a good thing for you that he did.'

'Ma'am?'

'What I'm trying to tell you, Nathan, is that there are a million unanswered questions in my head right now, the majority of which concern the things you are choosing to keep from me. Luckily for you, these questions are outweighed by the fact that Daley decided to do a runner from the law, and nobody goes to extreme measures like that unless they are guilty of something big. So, I'm going to make you an offer.'

Already Cody isn't liking the sound of this. 'An offer?'

'Yes. You for Daley. Nail him to the wall for me, and I'll forget about giving you the third degree to find out what was behind all this.'

Cody considers what's on the table, and tells himself that it doesn't seem too bad. It was always his intention to see this through. Daley has practically shouted his guilt from the rooftops, and so in theory all that remains is to tie everything up with a bow. Giving a guarantee of that to Blunt, though, is another matter.

'You're on,' he says. Then he adds, 'Not that I've anything to hide.'

'Hmm,' says Blunt again. 'Are you up to it? Physically, I mean?' She gestures towards Cody's foot, which is hurting like a bastard right now.

'I'm fine. It's just a sprain or something.'

'Pity you didn't land on your head. Might have knocked some sense into you. What the hell did you think you were doing?'

'It was a spur-of-the-moment thing. The balcony was higher than I thought.'

'Well, if you're going to start pulling stunts like that, we'll have to issue you with a parachute. How's Daley? Is he fit for interview?'

'He's fine. Whingeing a bit, but that's to be expected.'

'Has he lawyered up?'

'Yeah. He's got Prosser.'

'God, not Prosser the Tosser. He's such a weasel.' Blunt leans back in her chair and fixes Cody with an eye containing a glint of mischief. 'Who do you want on your side of the table?'

Cody thinks about this. Given the state of things with Webley, the obvious candidate to pair with in the interview is Ferguson. But then shutting Webley out for the foreseeable future wouldn't be fair on her. Personal problems can't be allowed to get in the way of the job.

'I'll take Megan,' he says.

Blunt looks a little surprised, causing Cody to worry that rumours have been spreading.

'Right then,' she says. 'Off you go, Hopalong. I want somebody's head on a plate, and right now I don't care if it's Daley's or yours.'

They take their places. Cody and Webley on one side of the table, Daley and his solicitor on the other. The duty solicitor is a man called Alan Prosser. He is short and bald and tanned, and his overly large grey suit and tiny eyes lend him the appearance of a mole peering myopically into the sunlight.

Cody doesn't feel comfortable at all. Despite being dosed to the max with some co-codamol he found in his desk drawer, it still feels as though his foot is resting in a furnace. Every time he shifts in his chair, new spears of pain shoot up his leg and into his torso.

Cody starts the recording and does the preliminaries. Announces the names of those present and the reason for the interview. He can see how nervous Daley is, but Prosser maintains a sneer of self-confidence.

'So, Colin,' Cody begins, 'let's get straight to it. Why'd you run?'

Daley scratches the side of his nose. 'I, er, I don't know. I panicked, I suppose.'

'Panicked? What was there to panic about?'

'You lot. Three of you, all coming after me.'

'What made you think we were coming after you? When you saw us, all we were doing was talking to your assistant, Jamie Morgan. It's not like we were battering down the front door of your house.'

'Jamie was pointing in my direction. It was obvious you were looking for me.'

Cody leans back in his chair. Shakes his head. 'I still don't see why you felt the need to leg it. You knew we were investigating a case involving the murder of a teacher at your school. We'd spoken to you before about it. It was only natural that we'd come back again, wasn't it?'

'I . . . I don't know. It looked like . . . You didn't look friendly. You looked like you were there to arrest me or something.'

'Arrest you? For what?'

'The murders, I guess. What else would it be?'

'The murders? Why would you think we'd be coming to arrest you for those? Did you do them, Colin?'

'No.'

'Is that it, Colin? You committed the murders, and you believed you'd been found out?'

'NO! I didn't do them. I had nothing to do with them. But I know how you people work.'

'How do we work?'

'You twist things. You bend the facts to fit your theories. You wanted to pin those murders on me.'

'So you ran.'

'Yes.'

'You ran because you thought we were going to fit you up for the murders of three women.'

'Yes.'

'Can you hear how ridiculous that sounds, Colin? You're telling us that you believed there was some massive conspiracy theory to pin three murders on you, and so you ran like a bat out of hell?'

Daley doesn't reply. Just rubs his hand through his hair.

'And you didn't just run, did you?' says Webley. 'You attacked a little girl.'

Daley snaps to attention. His eyes blaze as he fixes them on Webley.

'I didn't *attack* her.'

Webley is unfazed by the venomous glare. 'You snatched that girl out of her seat, and you threatened to throw her from the balcony. I'd say that was an attack, wouldn't you?'

'No. I would never ... I wouldn't have hurt her. I had nowhere to go, no way out. I was just trying to get you to leave me alone.'

'Hardly the right way to do it, though, was it? The poor girl was terrified. She'll have nightmares about this for a long time to come. Do you realise how much you may have damaged her?'

'No. Please. I ...' His voice fades out. He wipes a tear from his eye. 'It was wrong. What I did there was wrong. I know that, but I wasn't thinking at the time. It doesn't make me a killer, though. I could never do that to someone. You have to believe me.'

Cody speaks again. Despite the suspect's tears, he's finding it difficult to dredge up much sympathy for him. Daley is holding too much back. He's lying through his teeth.

'That's the problem, isn't it, Colin? Even if we believed what you're telling us – and I have to say that personally I think it's absurd – you need to ask yourself whether a jury would swallow it. Can you imagine it? Your day in court? You're there, telling a jury of twelve sensible people that the only reason you ran, the only reason you assaulted a young girl and threatened to kill her, the only reason you jumped from that gallery in the school assembly hall, was because you were afraid of being framed by the police for three murders you didn't commit. That's it, is it? That's the best you can do? Because I don't think any jury in the land would regard that as plausible. Do you?'

Cody doesn't give Daley time to answer. He hasn't finished yet. 'I'll tell you what the jury will think. They will listen to the account of how you grabbed hold of a little girl who is only eleven years old, and they will hear how you came within a hair's breadth of throwing her to her death, and they will say to themselves, "Yup, this guy's a killer. This guy could easily murder an adult female."'

'NO!' Daley slams his palm on the table, causing his solicitor to jump. 'I'm not a killer. I couldn't do that to anyone. You have to believe me.'

'We don't have to believe anything you tell us, Colin. It's the jury you'll have to convince, and right now I think you'll have a tough job on your hands. You need to come clean. You need to tell us why you ran away.'

Daley buries his face in his hands. Prosser, his solicitor, leans forward and says, 'I think my client has already answered that question. Can we move on, please?'

Cody waits for Daley to show his face again, then throws him a little shrug, as though to say, *It's your funeral, mate.*

44

Says Webley, 'Tell us about Saturday, Colin.'

Daley sniffs. Pulls out a tissue and wipes his nose. 'Saturday?'

'Yes. Saturday just gone. What did you get up to?'

'Not much. I did some cleaning. Ewan tidied his room. After lunch I went shopping, then I helped Ewan with some homework, and then I painted the bathroom ceiling.'

'What did Ewan do while you were painting?'

'He went to his mate's house to play on his Xbox.'

'So he wasn't around while you were painting?'

'No.'

'Did it take long to do the ceiling?'

'Yeah. There was a load of mould up there, because of the damp air. I had to wash it all off, then do a couple of coats to cover it up. Took me ages.'

'So what time did you start and finish?'

Daley blows air out of the side of his mouth. 'Started about half three, I suppose. Finished about seven-thirty, thereabouts.'

'Four hours? To paint a ceiling?'

'Like I say, I had to wash it all down first. And I had to leave it to dry between coats.'

'Still, seems like a long time to me. Are you sure you've got your facts straight?'

'I'm not making it up. Ask Ewan. First thing he asked about when he came in was the smell of paint.'

'Oh, I'm not denying you painted the ceiling. I do wonder whether it took as long as you said it did, though. I'm wondering whether you just gave it a quick going-over with a roller . . .'

'No.'

'And that maybe you then left the house.'

'NO! I know what you're trying to do. You're trying to say I could have killed that woman in Allerton. Well, I didn't, see. I was nowhere near Allerton. I was at home, painting my ceiling.'

Webley takes a deep intake of breath. 'I'd like to believe you, Colin. I really would. But here's the problem. Three women have been murdered, all on a Saturday evening. In each case, you've got no real alibi. Nobody to prove you were where you claimed to be.'

A snort of derision from Prosser. 'I'm sure I could quickly find a dozen people who can't prove where they were at those times. It means nothing. It certainly doesn't indicate any culpability for those homicides.'

Webley is quick to come back. 'And how many of those dozen have ever threatened to drop a young child from a great height, Mr Prosser? How many of them have already tried to evade questioning? How many have lied to the police about their whereabouts?'

'And,' Cody adds, 'how many of them knew at least one of the victims?'

'*Only* one,' says Daley. 'I knew Mary Cowper, and that's it.'

'Okay, so let's talk about Mary.'

'You've already asked me about her.'

'And now I'd like to ask you again. How well did you know her?'

'I told you. Not very.'

'Did you like her? Dislike her?'

'Neither one thing nor the other. She was just there. Just another teacher. I had very little to do with her.'

'And you never visited her flat?'

'No. Until it was all over the news, I didn't even know where she lived.'

'So how did you know about Andy Puckleton?'

'What?'

'You told us that he was quite close to Mary. How did you know that?'

'I saw them together. They were always huddled in corners, having quiet conversations. Sometimes they'd get in the same car together after school.'

'Did you think they were in some kind of intimate relationship?'

Prosser laughs. 'No.'

Cody keeps his face impassive. 'Why is that funny, Colin?'

'I just don't think they were friends in that way.'

'What do you mean? In what sort of way were they friends?'

'Well, not in a physical way.'

'How would you know? Andy Puckleton went back to Mary's flat on numerous occasions. How would you know what they got up to there?'

Cody knows the answer, of course, but he wants to hear Daley say it. Wants to know exactly how much he was aware of.

'I just . . . Look, I'm just guessing, okay?'

'No. No, you're not guessing, Colin. The first time we spoke, you mentioned that Puckleton was having problems with his beliefs. Only you weren't referring to his religious faith, were you? And then when I mentioned that he had talked to us about his girl-friend, it came as a complete shock to you. You knew something.'

Daley clenches his jaw a few times. 'Okay. So I knew about Andy. To be honest, most people did. He thought it was a secret, but it was all over the school.'

'What was?'

'That he's gay.'

'You know that for a fact?'

'Not exactly. But that's the rumour.'

'How did you hear it?'

Daley shrugs. 'Don't remember. It wasn't exactly earth-shat-tering news. It was just one of those things I heard.'

'He didn't tell you directly?'

'No. Why would he?'

'You tell me. I don't know how much of a friend he was to you.'

Daley's eyes darken for a fleeting moment. 'What are you trying to say?'

'I'm not implying anything. I'm just trying to get an idea of how much he talked to you about his personal life.'

'He told me nothing. Like I said, everything I heard was on the grapevine.'

'Do you think he told Mary about his feelings?'

'I don't know.'

'Because I imagine that someone as religious as Mary Cowper might have very strong views about homosexuality. Wouldn't you?'

'I . . . Possibly.'

'Possibly or definitely?'

'I—'

Prosser intervenes again. 'Where the hell is this going? It's already crystal clear that the police have established no motive whatsoever for the murder of Mary Cowper, or the other two victims for that matter. If you want to play amateur psychologist by conjuring up fanciful theories about the killer being on some kind of crusade against homophobic women, then feel free. But please don't try to shoehorn my client into that desperate scenario. Mr Daley is a family man. He has also told you repeatedly that he knew nothing about what went on in Mary Cowper's private life. He certainly wouldn't know what opinions or prejudices went through her head.'

'I just find it odd,' Cody replies, 'that your client seems to know so much about Andy Puckleton's personal affairs, and yet so very little about Mary Cowper. But I'll move on.'

Cody opens up a folder. Takes out a photograph and slides it across to Daley. It's the one of the killer outside the Metropolitan cathedral.

'For the benefit of the recording, I am showing Mr Daley photograph delta tango 713. Colin, do you recognise this man?'

Daley glances at it. Shakes his head. 'You've asked me this before. It's not me, and I don't know who it is.'

Cody passes him another image. 'This is image delta tango 717. It's a picture of the coat the man in the photograph was wearing. Does that look familiar?'

'Again, you've already asked me about it. No, I've never seen that coat.'

'Are you sure?'

'Certain.'

'You've never owned a coat like that?'

'No.'

'Colin, I should warn you that we are currently conducting a search of your house for evidence.'

Daley seems unperturbed. 'Go for it. You won't find a coat like that there. Ask around. You won't find anyone who has ever seen me wearing something like that.'

Cody puts the photos away. Then he says, 'Do you know what a lump hammer is?'

'Yes. Of course.'

'Have you ever owned a lump hammer?'

'Yes, I've got one. You'll find it in the cupboard under my stairs. Check it out. You won't find any bloodstains or whatever on it, if that's what you're thinking. Oh, and just to help you out, there are a couple of hammers like that in the school workshop. You might want to get those checked out too.'

The sudden display of cockiness irritates Cody. Puts a little dent in his own self-confidence that he can put this case to bed.

Cody picks up a large envelope. Slides three evidence bags out of it.

'For the recording, I am now showing Mr Daley evidence items delta tango 918, 406 and 212.'

He arranges the bags carefully in front of Daley.

'Do you know what these are, Colin?'

'They look like fishing weights to me,' says Daley. He looks up at Cody, puzzlement creasing his features.

'And you know that because . . . ?'

'Because I sometimes go fishing.'

'Do these weights belong to you?'

Daley looks at them again. 'I don't know. They're weights. Lots of people who fish have got them. Why do you ask?'

Cody ignores the question. 'So they could be yours? I mean, you have owned weights like these?'

'Yes, I've had similar weights. I don't know if these are mine, though. I've got a box full of them in my shed. Did you get them from there?'

'No, Colin, we didn't collect them from your home. These particular weights were found at the crime scenes.'

Cody watches as it dawns on Daley what he is being told. He makes a bloody good job of seeming surprised by it.

'Then they can't be mine, can they? I mean, what is this? What are you trying to say?'

'Yes,' Prosser says. 'What are you trying to suggest here? That my client killed three women and left his own fishing weights at the crime scenes? Why on earth would he do that?'

'That's what I'd like to know,' says Cody. 'Somebody left them there, presumably for a very good reason.'

Prosser slams the lid down on his laptop. 'Detectives, if this is the best you can do, then I think it's time we called this to an end, don't you?'

'We're not finished. We have—'

'You have nothing. Zilch. No evidence has been presented to suggest that my client played any part in the murders of these women. Fishing weights? I mean, come on, guys. The only ones on a fishing expedition here are the police.'

Prosser smiles at his own weak joke, while Cody starts to feel the case slipping through his fingers. He's fully aware that Blunt is observing him on the monitors – watching him make a complete hash of things. He promised her that this bit would be easy, and it isn't. He's looking like an incompetent fool.

Daley is literally about to get away with murder.

Cody tries not to show his anger as he formally terminates the interview. He sees the smug satisfaction on Prosser's rubbery lips, and wants to straighten them out with a well-aimed punch.

'Well, that was a waste of everyone's time,' says Prosser. 'Perhaps after a break we could deal with whatever charges you intend to press regarding the incident with the schoolgirl, and then we can call it a day. I'm sure you people have got better things to do, such as hunting a murderer.'

'We're not done,' says Cody. 'We haven't completed our search of Mr Daley's residence yet.'

'Well, good luck on that score. You've heard my client say that he will assist you in any way possible. He's got nothing to hide.'

Cody feels a familiar tingling. A kind of pins-and-needles in his face. It's a feeling he hasn't experienced in a long time. Not since his first case working with Webley. He knows this danger sign too well. Knows that it heralds a loss of control – that it could even be a prelude to violence.

No, he tells himself. Not here. Not with Blunt watching.

'Your computer,' he blurts out at Daley.

'What?'

Cody's mind races. He knows he cannot use what Grace told him, but at the same time he needs to re-establish some mastery of the situation before he blows a fuse.

'We'll be searching that, too.'

He stares hard at Daley. Sends a message to him: *Deal with that, you bastard. That's what will nail you. That's what will put you away for the rest of your life.*

Daley's mouth opens and closes several times. Cody waits for the fear, the denials, the confession.

'Fine,' says Daley. 'Knock yourselves out.'

And then Cody is on his feet. Fighting the pain that explodes up through his body, the tsunami of confusion that is swamping his mind, he takes himself out of that room before he can do physical damage to someone or something.

45

Cody moves along the corridor as fast as his gammy leg will allow, his eyes on the sanctuary of the washroom ahead. The sound of Webley calling his name somehow penetrates the cotton-wool fuzziness in his head, but he ignores it and ploughs on.

In the washroom he turns on the tap. Splashes ice-cold water onto his face to send the blood surging into the blocked vessels of his brain.

'Cody!'

He wipes the water out of his eyes. Turns his head to the left to see Webley standing over him.

'This is the gents,' he tells her. 'You're not allowed in here.'

She wrinkles her nose, and her dimples dance in time. 'Believe me, it's not out of choice. I'm more worried about the smells in here than the chance I'll catch sight of the Chief Super's todger.'

'So why did you follow me in?'

'I wanted to check you're okay.'

'I thought my welfare was off the agenda. After what you said—'

She holds her hands up. 'Fine. You're right. Forget I asked.' She starts to walk away.

'Wait,' says Cody. 'I'm sorry. I'm . . . not feeling great.'

She turns back to him. 'What's up?'

'My leg. It's killing me.'

'And?'

'The painkillers. I don't think they agree with me.'

'And?'

'Daley. He's making monkeys out of us.'

'And?'

'Isn't that enough?'

'You had a wobble back there, didn't you?'

He grabs a paper towel. Drags it across his face.

'Well?' she says. 'Didn't you?'

'Maybe. Okay, yes. A little one.'

'Shit. I thought you said you were better.'

'I'm better than I was. I'm a long way from cured, though. At least I didn't knock the smile off Prosser's face.'

A couple of months back, that's exactly what he would have done. Webley won't have forgotten what he was like then. She witnessed for herself how unbalanced he could be.

She says, 'Don't worry. You weren't the only one who felt like doing that. You think Daley's going to walk on the murder charges?'

Cody crumples up the paper towel, imagining it to be the head of Colin Daley, then tosses it into the basket. 'Not if I can help it.'

And then he's limping through the doorway, abandoning Webley to the dangers of the men's washroom.

She watches him go. Winces at the ache in her chest. She puts it down to her war wound, but it could be something else. It could be a reaction to the pain she saw etched on Cody's face. Pain that ran deeper than his injured ankle. Pain that betrayed an infection in his soul.

I shouldn't care, she thinks. He has hurt me too much, and so I shouldn't care. I told him as much. Stood outside in the cold and said so to his face. You're on your own, I told him. I wash my hands of you.

So what am I doing here? Why did I follow him into a room that smells like a pig-pen? Why did I ask if he was okay?

Because he's like a mistreated puppy. A dog that has been starved and beaten and tortured will react badly to other humans. It will growl and snap at them, and it will generally find itself unable to fit in.

That's the position Cody is in. He can't help acting the way he does. The damage done to him was too extensive.

And yet, she thinks, he brought me into that interview with Daley. He could easily have asked for someone else, but he didn't. He brought in the very person who tore a strip off him for not giving a shit.

Damn him.

Damn him for making me care about him.

46

Grace carries her mug of tea carefully back to her desk. It's Earl Grey, her favourite. She loves the delicate flowery aroma almost as much as the taste.

Nobody notices as she passes through the room. She's as ethereal as the steam from her cup. They don't know what a crucial contribution she has made today. They'll probably never know.

She's not sure how she feels about that.

Without her information, Colin Daley would probably not be sitting in an interview room right now, and MIT would still be flapping its wings over the meaning of a few fishing weights.

She has no idea what the weights might signify. Not her problem. The cops will sort that out. It'll be an easy ride for them now.

But only because of what she told them. That's the important thing.

And yet nobody can know about it.

It doesn't matter, she tells herself. You didn't do this for recognition. You did it because it was the right thing to do.

Crap.

Damn right it matters. I handed them the breakthrough on a platter. The squad should be writing songs about me.

Okay, so I cut some corners. I did some things that were technically illegal. I broke the law.

Shit. I work for Merseyside Police and I broke the law! And I told a detective sergeant about it! My God, what was I thinking?

A smile of wickedness breaks out on her face. She feels deliciously naughty all of a sudden.

Cody knows about her mischief. He's the only one privy to her wrongdoing. A shared secret. How exciting.

It didn't seem to bother him that much. Blunt would probably have thrown the book at her, but Cody wasn't prepared to chastise her. She recalls exactly what he *did* say, though. That memory will never be washed away.

Grace, I could kiss you.

That's what he said, I kid you not. His very words. Ask him. Go on, ask him.

Grace, I could kiss you. Grace, I could kiss you. Grace, I could . . .

'Grace!'

Her eyes flutter open, and he's there. All six foot of him. Well, near as damn it.

He's wearing an earnest expression, and for a second she worries that she was echoing his words out loud. Let the ground open up and swallow me now, she thinks.

'Cody! Er . . . yes? Can I help you?'

She thinks she comes across sounding like a hotel receptionist. But if he will go taking her by surprise like this . . .

'Grace, we need to talk again.'

'Okay.'

'In private. Again.'

'Okay.'

And now her stomach is fluttering. Her asking Cody for a private meeting was one thing, but the reverse situation seemed unthinkable. She is not used to being summoned to surreptitious liaisons with handsome, charismatic men. Not used to it with ugly, lacklustre men either, for that matter.

He leads. She follows. She glances behind her, to see if anyone is looking. This is supposed to be clandestine, but she wishes someone would notice. She is tempted to cough or stumble, just so they will look up and wonder why she is being led away so furtively.

Cody moves awkwardly across the corridor and into the same interview room they entered earlier. He holds the door open for her – such a gent, even though he must be dying to take the weight off that ankle.

I could look at that for you, she thinks. I did some first aid. I'm sure I could offer you some relief.

'Grace,' Cody says when they are both ensconced in the room.

'Yes?'

'About our earlier conversation . . .'

'Oh, God. I'm not in trouble, am I? You didn't tell DCI Blunt?'

'What? No. That stays between us. But I need something else from you.'

Something else? Something not work-related, perhaps? Would that be too much to hope for?

'Sure,' she says, trying to keep the tremble out of her voice. 'Name it.'

'It's Daley. He's proving a tough nut to crack.'

Ah. So it *is* work. Had to be, didn't it?

'Okay. How can I help?'

'That stuff you told us before, about Daley's account being used to access online material related to the victims – there's no mistake about that, is there?'

'No. If you've got time, I could explain exactly—'

'No, that's okay. I just wanted to check how sure you were.'

'I'm sure. I'd stake my reputation on it.'

Cody smiles. 'That's what I was hoping you'd say. And the evidence for this – it's out there in cyberspace somewhere, right?'

'Well, to be more specific—'

'Doesn't matter. But could it also be on Daley's computer?'

'I'm not sure what—'

'Could there be evidence of the same activity on Daley's computer?'

'It's possible. But I can't guarantee it – not without looking at the machine.'

Cody is beaming now. 'I was hoping you'd say that, too. Great idea, Grace!'

And then he's out of there. Like Webley before her, Grace is left alone in a room, wondering why there's an ache in her chest.

He finds Blunt in a monitoring station next to the interview room. As he enters, he sees at once that she is replaying the videos of the interview with Daley.

'Cody!' she says. 'I thought you might have gone into hiding after this.' She gestures to the screen.

'Yeah, I know,' he says. 'But to be fair, the camera hasn't caught my best side there. And I was never really clear about my character's motivation—'

'Stop pissing about, Cody. This isn't funny. Daley's dancing rings around you.'

'Well, I wouldn't exactly say that—'

'That's because you don't know whether you're coming or going. He knocked you senseless in there.'

'A minor setback. I'll come back in the next round.'

'I'm not sure there'll be a next round. You've got nothing left to hit him with. Unless he throws in the towel, we're beat.'

Cody raises his eyebrows. 'Are you a boxing fan, ma'am?'

'I've watched the *Rocky* films. But you're no Stallone, so let's get real here. Unless a miracle happens, we're going to lose this one.'

'Well, maybe we're due a stroke of luck. There's one place we haven't looked for evidence yet.'

Blunt narrows her eyes at him. 'What are you talking about?'

'Take a look at this . . .'

He leans across Blunt, causing her to pull back in alarm at the invasion of her personal space. Cody grabs the computer mouse, starts rewinding the video.

'Here,' he says. 'This is where Megan questions him about frightening the life out of the schoolgirl. What do you notice?'

Blunt pushes Cody out of the way and leans forwards again. 'He's irritated. Nervous.'

'His right leg. See that? See the way's he's jiggling it up and down? He does that when he's worried.'

'Okaaay. So where does that get us?'

Cody grabs the mouse again. Jumps to a point near the end of the video. 'This is just after I've suspended the formal interview.'

They both stare at the screen. They hear Cody telling Daley that they will be searching his computer. And they see Daley's leg bouncing up and down even more violently than it was before.

'Look at that,' says Cody. 'It's like his leg is plugged into the mains. His face and his voice are telling us one thing, but his body is telling us another. He doesn't want us searching his computer. He's worried we'll find something. I know it.'

Blunt waves him out of her space again. 'Fine. We'll take a look. If there's anything there, HCU will find it.'

HCU is the Hi-Tech Crime Unit. It's normally their job to analyse computers for evidence of crimes.

'Right,' says Cody. 'That's what I wanted to talk to you about.'

'Why don't I like the sound of that?'

'HCU have probably got dozens of computers on their waiting list. And even if we can get ours pushed to the front of the queue, they don't know what they're looking for.'

'Cody, they are the experts. We have to trust them to do their job. How else are we—?'

'Grace.'

'What?'

'We get Grace to poke around in Daley's computer.'

'Why on earth should we—'

'You've seen what she can do. She's incredible. Anything that HCU can do, she can do better . . .'

'Isn't that a line from *Annie Get Your Gun*?'

'And faster. If there's anything to be found, she'll find it. You know she will.'

Blunt thinks about it. But not for long enough. 'Absolutely not. It's not her job. It wouldn't be fair to give her that responsibility. Can you imagine the outcry if she messed it up?'

'She won't. She can do this. I trust her.' He pauses. 'Look, how about this? We bring the computer to Grace just for an hour or so, or whatever it takes to dump all the files onto another machine, and then we send it straight to HCU. Nobody even needs to know she's looked at it.'

'Not exactly true, Cody. I'm not covering this up. Chain of evidence. There are rules we have to follow.'

'Okay, okay. But you get the gist.'

Blunt rubs her hands up and down the arms of her chair. 'And she won't screw up the computer? Destroy whatever might be on there?'

'You've seen how she operates. The woman is at one with technology.'

'What if she doesn't want to do it? I'm not going to force her into this.'

Cody says nothing, and Blunt reads it for what it is.

She says, 'You've already asked her, haven't you?'

Cody finds a spot on the wall that suddenly seems fascinating.

'Nathan, why do I get the feeling that this is somehow connected with your sudden impulse to go after Daley?'

Cody looks back at her. 'Do you really want me to answer that question?'

Blunt shakes her head, more in disbelief than in response to Cody. 'I sometimes wonder who runs this team. There are certain members who seem to feel they can do whatever the hell they like.'

Cody shows her his best boyish smile. 'I'll take that as a yes to involving Grace. Thank you, ma'am.'

He starts to drag his body towards the door.

'Just a minute,' says Blunt.

Cody turns. 'Ma'am?'

Blunt hits a key on the computer keyboard, continuing the video, and Cody watches himself on the screen. Sees how he abandoned his chair so abruptly and stumbled out of the interview room, as if he felt an urgent need to throw up.

'What was that, Nathan?'

She does that sometimes. Calls him by his first name. Usually when she feels the need to be particularly motherly. He finds it disarming every time.

'I'm not sure what you mean.'

'That wasn't the graceful and professional exit I expect of one of my detectives. Looked to me like you lost it. And just before you asked Daley about the computer, it was as if you zoned out for a few seconds. Would I be wrong?'

Damn, thinks Cody. Was it that obvious?

He wonders if these final few seconds of the video are the bit on which Blunt was focusing her attention prior to his entrance.

'Yes, ma'am. You'd be wrong.'

'Nathan, we've been through this before—'

'The ankle, ma'am. And the painkillers. I started to feel a bit spaced out. I'm fine again now.'

She stares at him for a long time. He holds her gaze, knowing that a glance away will give her the truth she already knows.

'Go and talk to Grace,' she says quietly.

Cody turns and, for the third time in the space of less than an hour, unknowingly leaves a woman thinking long and hard about him.

47

Grace stares at the lump of metal and plastic before her. She knows how important it is.

'This is it, then,' she says.

'This is it,' says Cody. 'This is what might hold the key to putting a serial killer behind bars.'

Grace slides a finger gently across the closed lid of the laptop. It's an old, heavy, bulky model – a veritable dinosaur by current standards. But it'll do its job. More specifically, it can hold information – vast amounts of the stuff. And buried somewhere in all those binary digits could be the traces left by a murderer.

She finds it a sobering thought.

'You ran this past DCI Blunt?' she asks. 'She's okay with it?'

Cody – the man who said he could kiss her – says, 'One hundred per cent.'

'How? I mean, how did you manage to persuade her not to leave it to HCU?'

Cody shrugs. 'I told her the truth.'

'Which is?'

'That you're better than they are.'

And with that, he hobbles away again.

She waits until he is out of sight, and only then does she allow herself to smile. She smiles so hard that her face squeezes tears from her eyes.

This is it. Her recognition. Up until now, she has done all the pushing. Going against her nature, she made herself intervene whenever she could to make herself useful, to make people aware of her abilities. And now all that awkwardness and embarrassment has paid off. Someone has come to her. She didn't volunteer this time. She didn't draw attention to herself. Someone with a problem wondered who could solve it, and came up with the name Grace Meade. Ranked her even above others who would normally be the first to jump to mind.

It's a big moment.

And now she has to live up to expectations. Has to show that their faith in her has not been misplaced.

Cautiously, as if dealing with an unexploded bomb, Grace slides the laptop towards her and goes in search of darkness.

Blunt's office. Grouped around the desk are Blunt herself, plus Cody and Webley. Confronted by these expectant faces, Grace feels as though she's in a job interview. But she is more excited than nervous. She is ready to knock their socks off. Even Cody doesn't know what's coming. On the way in here, she gave him the thumbs-up to let him know it's good news, but she wants to surprise him most of all.

'As you know, I've been asked to take a look at Colin Daley's laptop computer, to see if I can find any incriminating evidence. Prior to this, information on two of the victims was found online. In the case of Cassie Harris there is a news article mentioning the fact that she was a prostitute who frequented the Metropolitan cathedral, while Sue Halligan put up several blog posts about herself. With this in mind, a natural starting point for my investigation was to search for any indication that Daley's computer was used to access those online sites.'

She pauses, and sees that Cody is nodding and smiling, clearly pleased that she has manoeuvred things into this line of inquiry without compromising its legality.

'Just so I'm clear,' says Blunt, 'you're telling us that by poking around inside Daley's computer, you can tell which bits of the web he has visited. Have I got that right?'

'Yes, to an extent. It's never complete, but a history of recent website accesses can often be found on a computer.'

'So your theory was that the history on Daley's machine might prove that he used it to read up about at least two of the victims?'

'That's correct, yes.'

'And you could tell whether that was done before or after their deaths?'

'Yes.'

Blunt looks to her colleagues, then back to Grace. 'Well, that all sounds pretty impressive. Of course, it wouldn't prove that Daley killed anyone, but it would certainly be valuable circumstantial evidence.'

Everybody is nodding and smiling now. Cody looks ready to start rubbing his hands together in glee.

'So,' says Blunt. 'What did you find?'

Grace waits a couple of seconds. Drum roll, please, she thinks. She sees Cody tilt his head towards her, urging her to deliver the devastating announcement.

'Nothing,' she says.

Cody's brow creases in puzzlement. The other two faces go blank.

'Nothing,' says Blunt.

'No. Unfortunately, I haven't managed to find anything on Daley's computer that confirms he accessed either the article on Cassie Harris or the blog site maintained by Sue Halligan.'

Cody's utter disappointment almost screams across the room at her. Sorry, Cody, she thinks.

'Wait,' says Cody. 'I'm confused. So Daley didn't access those sites?'

'That's not what I'm saying. What I *am* saying is that evidence of such accesses is not present on his computer, as far as I can tell. As I mentioned before, the historical record on a computer is never complete. If, for example, Daley did access those web pages but it was some time ago, the computer cache may have been cleared since then.'

She detects a darkening in Cody's mood – a suggestion that he is feeling duped and teased. Blunt and Webley also seem perplexed by the negative findings. It occurs to Grace that they're probably wondering why she went to all the trouble of setting up a computer next to her if she's not going to use it.

But it's what Grace wanted. Take them down, then bring them back up. Act like the magician whose trick seems to go disastrously wrong, but then turns into the greatest illusion ever. Much more of an impact that way. So here goes . . .

'So much for that theory,' she says, adding a slight laugh to make light of her own apparent ineptitude. 'But then I started looking elsewhere.'

The faces brighten. They understand the game here. It's dawning on them that they've just been softened up for the showstopper.

She continues: 'I found a number of files Daley had tried to hide. He moved them into one of the operating system folders, so they wouldn't be obvious if you looked in the normal places people keep their documents. To make them look more like system files, he changed their names and file types, but it was amateurish. It was pretty obvious to me that the files didn't belong there. He'd also encrypted the contents, but the algorithm he used was pretty old and insecure. It didn't take much to revert them back to the originals.'

'Grace,' says Blunt, 'please remember that some of us still have trouble finding the computer's on switch. What are these files you found?'

'It's easier if I show you,' she answers.

She turns to the computer next to her, then clicks the mouse, opening up a new window. It displays a video. Grace knows she doesn't need to comment now: the video will speak for itself.

The scene is the changing room next to the school gymnasium. It is obvious that the recording has been made from a fixed camera positioned high up in a corner of the room. The girls are blissfully unaware of its presence as they laugh and chat in various states of undress. Now and again, girls cross the room from the shower area, towels wrapped around them.

'Oh, Jesus,' says Cody.

He's uncomfortable with this, thinks Grace. He's a good, moral man who doesn't want to see these images. He would probably rather watch a post-mortem.

She decides to save him, and halts the video. 'There's a lot more,' she says. 'There are also videos taken in the shower room itself.'

Cody lets out a groan. Drops his gaze to the floor.

'I know,' says Grace. 'It's awful. But at least now you can throw the book at him.'

When Cody slowly raises his face again, she expects to see that he has managed to put his disgust behind him, and that he will be focused on the positives. We've got the bastard, he will be thinking, and we've got Grace Meade to thank for it.

But Cody's countenance is grim. It draws heavy clouds over Grace's optimism. Her preparedness for victory celebrations suddenly seems wasted.

He says, 'Grace, what you've done here is really valuable. We can make sure Daley never does this kind of thing again. But don't you see? It also gives him a reason for running away from us, a reason for being scared of us. A reason that's not related to the murders.'

48

They call Prosser in first, to disclose what they've found on the computer. Prosser gives nothing away in his expression; he knows how to play this game. He watches the videos and he takes his notes and he tells the detectives that he will need time to talk to his client. But Cody knows what's going through Prosser's mind. It's the same thought that won't leave Cody's mind – that this is a double-edged sword. It damns Daley, but it also exonerates him.

The detectives can only wait then. They pace and they drink coffee and they try to distract themselves with talk of the weather and Christmas and sport, while all the while their eyes keep drifting to the drab brown door of the consultation room, behind which Colin Daley and his lawyer are feverishly working on their strategy.

When they finally reappear, Cody feels a cramping in his guts. He has the sickening expectation that he is about to learn he has won a battle but lost a war.

He signals Webley. She comes over to join him, and then they escort Daley and Prosser back to the interview room.

Round two, thinks Cody, remembering Blunt's boxing analogy.

He sets up the recorder, makes the usual announcements.

'Colin,' he says, 'as I mentioned to you in our previous interview, we have seized your computer under the terms of our warrant, and I have to tell you that we have found some incriminating evidence on it.'

'That was very quick work, Sergeant,' says Prosser. 'One would almost think that you fully expected to find something there.'

'We have some very good staff,' says Cody. He looks at Daley again. 'Specifically, we found some video files that you had attempted to disguise. Would you care to comment?'

Prosser says, 'Let's not play guessing games. If you have something you want to discuss, get it out in the open and we'll discuss it.'

Cody opens a file. Takes half a dozen images out of it. Lines them up in front of Daley.

'These are stills extracted from just a couple of the many videos found on your computer. *Your* computer, Colin. Now, I'll ask you again, what would you like to tell us about these videos?'

Daley looks to Prosser. Prosser nods. Cody knows what's coming next.

'No comment,' says Daley.

He knows, thinks Cody. He knows we've got him bang to rights on this one. Going the 'no comment' route is his best chance of avoiding saying something that might trip him up.

'Really? You don't want to comment? I'm giving you a chance to explain all this away, and you don't want to take it?'

'No comment.'

Damn, thinks Cody.

'All right, Colin. On your head be it. I should tell you that we're sending some people over to the school right now. We're going to retrieve the cameras. Any idea how they might have got there, Colin?'

'No comment.'

'I mean, somebody must have put them there. Somebody with access to the changing rooms and the shower. Someone who had the skills and the opportunity to install the cameras so they couldn't be seen. Someone who could hide the wiring in the walls. Not many people in the school who could do all that, are there, Colin?'

'No comment.'

'*You* could, though. Piece of cake to a handyman such as yourself. Well, we'll take a look. Probably find your fingerprints everywhere, I would think.'

He leaves that with Daley, and notices how it sets the man's leg trembling again.

'And then there's the matter of how those videos ended up on your computer. I don't see how that could happen unless you did it yourself, can you, Colin? No, it's an easy one, this. You can say "no comment" all you like; all you're doing is making it easier for the jury to work out that you've got no defence.'

Daley wants to say something, but a sharp glance from his solicitor causes him to bite his lip. His leg continues to talk, though.

Cody leans forward. 'Have you always liked little girls, Colin? Always been a pervert, a paedophile?'

'I'm not a—'

'Colin!' says Prosser, shutting his client up.

Webley says, 'You don't have to do what he tells you. You do realise that, don't you, Colin? You can speak to us if you want. Anything he says is advice, that's all. You can choose to ignore it. You can choose to explain your actions.'

Daley stares at her, his eyes moist. He wants to cry, thinks Cody. He wants to let it all out. He wants an end to whatever monstrous forces are tearing him up inside.

So come on. Let it spill out. Open the floodgates. The videos first, to pave the way. Then the murders. That's how it went, isn't it, Colin? That's how it escalated. One bad thing leads to another, even more evil thing. Tell us about it, Colin. Make us understand.

'No comment,' says Daley.

Why does it always have to go like this? Why, when I think I've done something good, something really useful, does it all have to turn to shit again?

Grace sits at her desk, staring morosely at her computer screen. In her excitement she had failed to appreciate the implications of what she had discovered. She had thought that one thing would lead naturally to another – that clear evidence of Daley's nastiness could be used as a crowbar to prise open a door into an even murkier chasm.

But it had the opposite effect. Cody saw it immediately. He saw that door becoming firmly sealed. He saw how the route ahead became impassable.

They'll forget me again, she thinks. I did what they asked, but it wasn't what they wanted. They wanted more, and I can't always give them more. I can't give them what's not there. So my accomplishment will fade in their minds. I will go back to being that strange computer geek at the back of the room.

Out of desperation, she is trying one more thing.

There were hundreds of video files on Daley's laptop. Grace copied them all onto an external disk drive, but she hasn't got time to look through them all. That would take days.

What she can do, however, is run those files through her face-recognition software. She has already used it to scour many hours of CCTV footage, so why not these recordings, too? Mary Cowper worked at the school – perhaps she will have been caught on one of Daley's hidden cameras. Perhaps she will be seen taking part in satanic rituals, or shooting up with heroin.

It's an intensive process, even for a computer. There is so much data to analyse, so many faces to identify and compare.

She watches the display as each file is checked. Every time the computer moves on to a new file, she feels a surge of optimism. It's dashed again when a tiny cross is drawn next to the filename to indicate that no match has been found.

She wonders how things are going in the interview room. Perhaps they are having better luck than she is. Perhaps Daley is confessing all, including the murders. In which case her failings won't matter.

Only a few files left now. Look – another little cross. Ho-hum, no match. And what about this one? Go on, show me if you must. Cross it off your list, you unfeeling machine. Don't worry about the effect you're having on little old me. Don't bother to spare a thought for—

Beep.

This from the computer, interrupting her thoughts. A tiny electronic shout that changes everything.

No cross this time. A tick. A big fat green tick.

It has found a match.

Grace pounces on the mouse. Opens up the file. Watches intently as the video reveals its secrets.

It's a surprise, all right.

She's not sure what it means – only that Cody needs to know about it.

49

No comment. No comment. No comment.

That's all they were getting from Daley. Every question about the videos was batted swiftly away with the same two-word answer.

But now Cody has returned to the subject of the murders, and Daley has suddenly found his tongue again. He has, for example, just finished denying vehemently that he was ever a client of Cassie Harris.

All of which Cody finds a little puzzling. Why clam up on one set of charges, but be so loquacious concerning the others? Why not just refuse to respond to all of the questions?

Unless, of course . . .

Prosser is a clever bastard. He has probably accepted that his client is about to go down for the charges relating to the videos on his computer. He will have advised Daley not to make the job of the police easier for them. If they want to press charges, then fine, but don't run the risk of giving them extra ammunition to shoot you down.

The murder charges are less clear-cut. Prosser is well aware that the evidence is iffy to say the least. The problem with 'no comment' responses there is that they could count against Daley in court. A jury would be entitled to be suspicious about the fact that he chose not to defend himself at the first opportunity.

Yes, thinks Cody. That's what Daley is doing. He's effectively holding his hands up to one set of crimes to increase his chances of acquittal on the others. He's saying to the jury, *Look, what you need to know about me is that I say 'no comment' when I'm guilty. I haven't done that on the murders, though, so I must be innocent.*

Clever.

At least, Cody hopes the opposition is that devious. The unthinkable alternative is that Daley really didn't commit the murders.

Either way, it's starting to look as though Daley might well avoid conviction for the killings. What they need now is either some new evidence or for Daley to make a damning slip of the tongue. It seems a faint prospect.

'What about Allerton Road, Colin? Ever go there?'

'No. Why would I?'

'Ever come into contact with the third victim, Susan Halligan?'

'Nope. Never heard of her before her name appeared in the papers.'

'Are you a religious man, Colin?'

'Not especially. I believe in God, but that's about it. I don't go to church much.'

'What about the people you know – the ones you socialise with? Any of them particularly religious?'

Daley doesn't answer immediately. His eyes seem to freeze over, and a second later his knee begins its little dance. Knowing he's on to something, Cody leans across the table.

'It's a simple question, Colin. What's the problem?'

'I'm thinking. Going through people in my head.'

That's not it, thinks Cody. That's not what you're doing, Colin.

There's a rap on the door, and it opens before Cody can answer. Looking flustered, Grace Meade pokes her head into the room.

'There's something you should see,' she tells Cody.

Cody cannot hide his irritation at being interrupted at such a key moment in the interview.

'Not now, Grace. We're in the middle of—'

'I know. But it's important. Really important.'

Just how much this matters to Grace is written clearly on her face. Cody nods to her, then announces the suspension of the interview before halting the recording.

'I'll be back in a few minutes,' he tells the others. Looking directly at Colin he says, 'We'll pick up where we left off.'

He follows Grace out of the room and along the corridor.

'What is it, Grace?'

'I found something else. On Daley's computer.'

'What kind of something?'

'It'll be easier if I show you.'

Cody feels his impatience returning. He can't help thinking that he's going to explode at her if this turns out to be a waste of his time, when he could be in that interview room, turning Daley into mush.

Grace leads him over to her desk. Waits for him to take his place in front of her computer monitor.

'I found this video,' she says. 'It's not like the others, and it's the only one. I thought you should see it.'

She leans forward. Clicks a file icon on her computer. A video file opens.

Cody peers at the dark image. It's the school changing room again, but this time it's empty. A long line of tinsel has been strung through the handles of the lockers. Cody checks the time on the recording, sees that it was made almost exactly a year ago.

'Grace, what's this—'

'Watch.'

A rectangle of light expands across the image, then contracts again. A figure enters. Cody squints to work out who it is.

It's Mary Cowper.

Mary stops at the lockers. Turns and waits, her chest heaving as though she has just run a mile.

Another figure comes into view. She is wearing a paper party hat. Another string of tinsel hangs around her neck.

It takes Cody a few seconds to work out that it's the head teacher. Mrs Laplace.

He watches as the two figures come together. He sees Mrs Laplace reach out a hand to stroke Mary's face. Mary seems uncertain at first, but then she tilts her head to the side, pressing her cheek into the palm of the other woman.

And then they are kissing. It goes on for a long time. Mrs Laplace brings a hand to Mary's breast. Mary covers the hand with her own, keeping it there.

There is no audio on the recording, but it is clear that the women suddenly hear a sound. They rip away from each other, and both stare in the direction of whatever has startled them. Even in the dim light, the guilt and fear of detection are evident on Mary's face. She starts to move away, back towards the door. Mrs Laplace grabs her arm, but Mary yanks it away and disappears out of shot. Mrs Laplace's mouth opens in a guffaw that seems to surprise her. She brings a hand to her face to stifle the noise, then meanders drunkenly after Mary.

The rectangle of light grows again, shrinks again. The liaison is over.

The time span of the recording is only a few minutes.

But it's everything.

'Grace,' says Cody, 'that's two kisses I owe you.'

50

Cody is back in the interview room. Eyes locked on to Daley, frying him with their intensity.

I know you, Daley. I know what you are.

He sits down. Resumes the interview. And already the leg is doing its jig. Daley is dancing his way to hell.

Cody announces, 'I'm going to return to the subject of the videos.'

Prosser theatrically throws his hands up in despair.

'What? Okay, look – if that's the game you want to play, I'm going to advise my client to return to "no comment" responses. We've been doing our best to be helpful, Sergeant Cody, but if—'

'And also the murders.'

Prosser loses the thread, much to Cody's delight. 'I'm sorry, what?'

'This is about the videos, but more about the murders. We've linked the two. So what's your advice now, Mr Prosser? Talk or not?'

Prosser's face contorts as he wrestles with the logical dilemma.

He says, 'Let's hear what you've got.'

Cody reaches for the folder he has just brought into the room. The folder that holds the secret to ripping Daley apart at the seams.

He opens the folder. Uses his index finger to push the top photograph across to Daley.

'Recognise this, Colin?'

Daley's gaze strokes the photograph for a microsecond. He knows exactly what this is. Prosser and Webley, meanwhile, are united in their puzzlement at what the shadowy picture is telling them.

Says Cody, 'For the benefit of the recording, I am showing Mr Daley a still image taken from a video on his computer. The image shows Mary Cowper and Mrs Laplace, the head of Oakdale School, kissing and fondling each other in the school changing rooms.'

Cody hears a slight gasp from Webley, a more pronounced intake of breath from Prosser.

'Okay,' says Prosser angrily. 'I don't know what you hoped to achieve, but there was absolutely no need for this melodrama. You could have shown this to me first. But since you didn't, I have no alternative but to advise my client to resume his "no comment" replies.'

Cody keeps his eyes on Daley, annoying Prosser further by acting as though he's not even in the room.

'What about it, Colin? It's pretty damning, isn't it? It makes a liar out of you.'

'I'm not a liar.'

'Colin!' says Prosser.

'Really? You told us you knew nothing about Mary Cowper, especially when it came to her private life. This picture tells us you knew more than almost anyone else about her private life. I'd call that a lie, wouldn't you?'

'No. I couldn't say. How could I tell you about it?'

From Prosser: 'Colin, I would strongly urge you to—'

Cody turns Prosser into an irrelevance now. 'Well, that's just it. You couldn't tell us, could you? Not being as guilty as you are. You knew something about Mary Cowper. Something that you found disgusting.'

'No. Wait. I didn't—'

'See, I was wrong earlier. I admit it. I suggested that Mary might have been homophobic, and that she was doing her best to get Andy Puckleton to suppress his urges. But that wasn't it. She was trying to help him, because she knew exactly what he was going through. She was trying to get him to come to terms with what he is, to reassure him that it's okay. And you knew about that, didn't you? You knew she was gay, and you hated her for it.'

'No. I didn't hate her. I'm not like that.'

'It's over for you, Colin. You've lied to us from start to finish, and you've made others lie for you too. You sneaked off home when we came to the school the first time, and you ran away on the second occasion. You endangered the life of a child—'

'No.'

'You have no alibis for the times of any of the three murders. A hammer just like the ones you admit to owning was used to kill the women—'

'No. Please.'

'And fishing weights just like the ones in your possession were left at the crime scenes. And, to top it all, now we have evidence of paedophilia and an undeniable link with Mary Cowper that you refused to mention. Doesn't look good, does it, Colin? Looks to me like you need to think about how you're going to say goodbye to your son.'

That does it for Daley. The threat of being separated from his only child is the trigger. He leaps to his feet.

'NO! NO! NO!' he yells.

Cody gets to his feet too, ready for this to become physical. But Prosser grabs his client by the sleeve.

'Colin. Colin. It's okay.'

Daley pulls his arm away. Tears are streaming down his cheeks.

'I can't help it,' he says. 'I can't stop myself.'

Cody feels invisible fingers raking down the back of his neck. This is it. This is the confession. Come on, Colin.

The room goes deathly silent for a few seconds. Daley sits down again.

'I can't help what I am. It's . . . it's an obsession. I don't hurt anyone. I don't show those pictures to anyone else. And I'm not a murderer. I wouldn't hurt a fly. You have to believe me.'

No, Colin. Don't do this. The truth now. You owe us the truth.

But Daley presses on: 'I've never met the other two women who were killed. And the only thing I knew about Mary was that she was gay. But I would never kill her because of it. I swear to you, on my life. The videos, yes. I took them—'

'Colin,' says Prosser, because it's his job. But it's a meek attempt, which he knows Daley will ignore.

'I took them because I enjoy looking at them. And sometimes I hate myself for enjoying them. I feel dirty. It destroyed my marriage, and now I'll probably go to prison for it. I understand that. I accept it. But please, not the murders. Not the murders.'

More silence while everyone processes this. It's not what Cody expected, not what he wanted. It's only a partial confession. Why is he not yet ready to give them the full story?

And yet . . .

Something is bothering Cody. Something that Daley has just said in his rant. What the hell was it?

'I think,' says Prosser, 'that we could all do with a break. I hope that—'

'Wait,' says Cody. But he still doesn't know why he's asking. It's there, on the tip of his mind. What is it?

'Wait,' he says again. Because now he knows. 'What did you just say, Colin?'

'What about?'

'Your marriage. You said that your problems destroyed your marriage.'

Daley doesn't reply. It's clear he senses he's in a net.

Webley has caught on. She continues Cody's thought processes for him.

'When we first came to see you, at your house, you told us that your wife was dead.'

'Did I?'

'Yes. Cancer, is what you told us.'

'I . . . I had to make something up. I didn't want you talking to Kate.'

'Why not?'

'She knew about me. She caught me looking at pictures on my computer. I tried to explain myself to her, but she didn't want to listen. She was disgusted with me, and I don't blame her. She couldn't forgive me. She's very religious, you see.'

The fingers along Cody's spine again.

'Religious? So when I asked you whether you knew anyone—'

'Yes. My first thought was about Kate. But I could hardly say, could I?'

'Tell me about it,' says Cody. 'What happened then, after she saw the pictures?'

'Excuse me,' says Prosser, 'but is this relevant?'

Not for the first time in this room, Prosser is ignored.

'Tell me,' says Cody. He needs to hear this. This is important.

Daley shrugs, sniffs. 'Not much to tell. She left me. Took little Ewan away with her. Said I wasn't fit to look after him. Said I should never be allowed anywhere near kids. That really hurt. I'll look at pictures, but I would never . . . you know . . .'

'She didn't tell the police or the school?'

'I wasn't working in a school back then. And, to be honest, I don't think she wanted the shame of going public. She did say she'd report me if I ever tried to see Ewan.'

'So how come he ended up living with you again?'

'He turned up on the doorstep one day, a few months ago. He said he wanted to be with his dad again. I couldn't believe it. I was made up.'

'Did he say why?'

'Not really. He was upset about something. I tried to get it out of him, but he refused to talk about it. All he would tell me was that it was something his mother had done to him. He kept calling her a complete hypocrite.'

And then it's as though those invisible fingers dig their razor-sharp nails deep into Cody's flesh. He feels physical pain between his shoulder blades.

Webley is the first to notice. 'Cody, are you okay?'

'What?' says Cody, but to Daley, not to Webley. 'What did you just say?'

'A hypocrite. That's what he called her. In fact, any time she came up in conversation, he would only refer to her as The Hypocrite. He was really angry with her.'

Oh, God, thinks Cody. Oh, my God.

'Your lad's school,' he says. 'What primary school did he go to?'

'He was at Abbotsleigh. Look, I don't understand. What's this got to do—?'

But now it's Cody's turn to jump to his feet.

'Cody,' says Webley. 'What's—?'

'Your wife. Kate. She's about your age, right? About forty?'

'Yeah, but—'

'And she's got shoulder-length fair hair?'

Daley stares at him. 'How did you—?'

Cody pushes his notepad in front of Daley. Slams a pen down next to it.

'Write down her address.'

'Why? What's she done? What are you—?'

'Just write the fucking address!'

Cody has forgotten that this is still being recorded. It doesn't matter. He doesn't care that everyone in this room, plus Blunt watching on the monitors, thinks he's completely lost the plot.

Cody snatches away the notepad. Hops out of the room, leaving utter confusion in his wake.

In the corridor, Webley comes running up behind him. Blunt appears from a doorway in front of him. Both start firing questions at him.

Says Blunt, 'Cody, what the hell are you playing at?'

'The fishing weights.'

'What?'

'The weights. Dante's *Inferno*. Don't you see?'

'No. No, I don't. You're not making any sense.'

Cody doesn't want to stand here and explain himself. He needs to get out there and do something to stop what's coming.

He rushes his words out: 'The fact that they're fishing weights isn't important. What matters is that they're lead weights. They're symbolic.'

'Symbolic of what?'

'Hypocrisy. It's all described in Dante's *Inferno*. I have a copy at home. In the Eighth Circle of Hell, the hypocrites are weighed down by heavy cloaks that are gilded with lead. That's what the killer was telling us with the weights. That's what all the victims had in common. We thought Mary Cowper was spotless, but she wasn't – at least not in the eyes of some people. Not when she was doing things forbidden in the Bible. To her own mother,

Mary's sexuality was the work of the Devil himself, which is why she disowned her seventeen years ago. The killer thought Mary deserved an even more severe punishment. Same goes for Cassie Harris and Sue Halligan. They were both following God, but continuing to commit acts against His will, and that was unforgivable.'

'Okay, but why the panic?'

'Because it's not over.'

'What are you talking about? Daley's here, in custody. He can't—'

'It's not Daley!' Cody is practically shouting now. 'Don't you get it? It's his son! It's Ewan! Mrs Laplace told us that Mary Cowper came to her from Abbotsleigh Primary. Ewan would have been there at the same time. He knew Mary! And if Ewan went online to find his other two victims, he would have used his own computer. That's why Grace couldn't find a trace of any such activity on his dad's machine. And now we need to stop him.'

'Stop him from what?'

'The three murder victims weren't his real targets. They were substitutes – rehearsals for the main event. Ewan Daley was merely working his way up to killing the biggest hypocrite of all.'

51

He remembers . . .

At primary school. Sitting there in his damp trousers, praying that nobody else will notice the stain, the smell. But it seems that most of the class are already aware. Whenever the teacher is otherwise occupied, children turn to look at him and laugh silently. He dreads the upcoming break, when it will be much easier for them to tease and mock and jeer.

He cannot concentrate on the lesson. The teacher is Miss Cowper, and while the other children seem to have no problem with her, Ewan finds it difficult to be in her presence. She reminds him too much of his mother. Always talking about God. Always going on about the terrifying fate that awaits those who stray from the path of righteousness.

She even *looks* remarkably like his mother, especially now through his tear-filled eyes. It is as though, no matter where he goes, he is unable to evade his parent's judgemental, scornful scrutiny.

When Miss Cowper strolls slowly down the aisle of the classroom, reading aloud from a book, he finds himself praying for her not to notice his predicament. His embarrassment is intolerable enough already.

But she does halt alongside his desk. When he blinks away the blurriness in his vision and looks up, he sees that her eyes are on him, flickering from his stained trousers to his wet cheeks. And so he adapts his prayers correspondingly. He wills her to see his hurting. Pleads silently with her to show him that God-fearing people are not all like his mother: they can be compassionate and kind. They can offer love in a way that does not entail pain. They can enfold him in an embrace that will shield him from the many tormentors in his world.

And, for the briefest of moments, it seems to Ewan that she is about to do precisely that. He believes he detects the minute shift of her features into an expression of intense pity. He senses a slight leaning towards him, as though in preparation for stepping across the line that divides teachers from pupils.

But then something seems to provoke Miss Cowper to reassert her detachment. She tears her gaze away from his with the briskness of a plaster being torn from a cut knee, and it stings Ewan a hundred times as much. She moves on, continuing along the aisle as though she has already cast Ewan and his plight from her mind.

And now his shame is complete. Everyone knows of his state, and they all loathe him for it. Even Miss Cowper, who had the opportunity to turn it all around for him, chose instead to turn her back. She is exactly like his mother – she could almost *be* his mother – and he hates her for it.

At the age of six he does not understand much – he has no awareness of the complexities of emotional trauma and psychological transference – but he knows how it feels to want to hurt someone. And right at that moment he wants to hurt Miss Cowper. He wants something bad to happen to her. Something painful. He wants her to trip and break her leg, or to faint and smash her face on the floor. Or simply just to die.

That's it. She could just die. Something goes wrong with her heart or her brain, and she keels over and dies.

It's wrong to feel that way. He knows that. He knows he could never wish it of his mother, because children have to love their mothers.

But Miss Cowper is just a woman who looks and sounds like her.

So that wouldn't be as wrong, would it?

He remembers . . .

He has made it into the school building. The taunts are still ringing in his ears. Those oh-so-visible ears. With only a patina of hair remaining on his skull, his ears seem to jut out like handlebars.

He hopes he will be safer now. The staring will continue, of course, but perhaps the insults and the laughter will be stifled.

Please, Lord, let me get through this day. Don't make it any worse for me, please. Tomorrow will be easier if I can just get through today.

He ambles morosely along the school corridor. Most of the children are already in their classrooms, but he has dragged his feet. He would quite happily remain all day in this deserted, jibe-free corridor if he could.

But ahead, a door opens. Miss Cowper appears. In silhouette against the bright room behind her, she could easily be Ewan's mother. And even as she closes the door and heads his way, he still feels as though this is his mother by proxy. She looks out at the world through the same faith-tinted eyes. She has the same idea of where goodness and evil reside, and in viewing Ewan she will see the same wickedness and unholiness that his mother sees.

He has learnt to expect no interaction with this teacher outside the classroom, and his first instinct is to hang his head and avert his eyes to avoid her judgement. And yet, as they approach each other, some spark of rebellion ignites within him. He finds himself lifting his head and staring directly at her, challenging her for a reaction.

Her eyes find him. Ewan thinks he detects a glimmer of emotion there, but he's not sure what it is. And then she passes him without a word.

He knows he should let it go, but his defiant streak persists.

'Miss!' he calls. 'Miss!'

She stops. Turns.

'Ewan? Can I help you?'

He rasps a hand across his scalp. 'What do you think?'

Her eyebrows dance as her mind plays with a response. 'Very . . . fetching, Ewan. A little more extreme than your usual.'

'It was my mother's idea.'

Miss Cowper nods, seemingly unsure as to how to proceed. She starts to move away, but Ewan stops her again.

'She said it's what God wanted for me.'

Puzzlement now from Miss Cowper. 'God?'

'Yes, miss. Apparently he's taken an interest in hairstyles now. He used to be interested in my underpants, but now it's my hair.'

He doesn't know where these words have come from, and he hears the bitterness in his own voice. The shock registers with Miss Cowper too, and she advances on him, her face set.

'Ewan Daley, if that was an attempt at humour, then it was in very poor taste. You should never mock the Lord. I think that your mother would be appalled at what you have just said. Would you like me to tell her?'

He stares back at her, and feels the insolence being squashed out of him. Tears fill his eyes, and he hates himself for being so weak.

'No, miss.'

'No. I thought not. Now get to your class, and I suggest you think carefully about your behaviour.'

She spins on her heel then, and marches stiffly down the hall, her footsteps echoing. Just before she disappears around the corner, he wants to call out to her again, but the word that sits unused on his tongue is 'Mummy'.

He remembers . . .

The onset of puberty. Huge changes in his body, but also powerful changes in his emotions and urges. The world seems a more confusing, challenging place, and he is not sure how he fits in, how he should function. He needs guidance, reassurance.

He is at secondary school now. No more Miss Cowper. But his mother is still around, still demonstrating her warped love for him.

He had hoped the other pupils would accept him more at this school. But it hasn't worked out that way. Some of them will have heard the stories brought in by his contemporaries at Abbotsleigh. Others seem to possess a mystical ability to sense that he is somehow different. He is still isolated, still unhappy. He tries to focus his energy on his schoolwork, but his hormones provide distractions.

Once, his mother catches him in the shower when he is addressing those distractions.

He doesn't hear her enter. Is not even sure how she got in through a door he believed to be locked.

But there she stands, and he has never seen such disgust on her face before. Her very expression withers him, destroys his ardour.

But of course that is not enough.

She screams at him of his wickedness. Lets him know of the rotten core inside him. And while she emits her pious roars, she turns the shower to its coldest setting and aims the icy needles at his cowering body, his shrivelling genitals.

He remembers that lesson for a long time. With each period of arousal – and there are many at that tender age – he also experiences guilt, pain, shame. Sex becomes dirty, taboo. Pretty, flirty girls become teasing whores. The frustration builds.

It doesn't occur to him to question his mother. She is right. Like Mary Cowper, she has God on her side. Of course she is right.

And then it happens.

A water tank bursts in the school. The pupils have to be sent home early.

The first thing he notices when he walks through the front door is the noise. Coming from upstairs. The moaning and the groaning. And he knows what this is. He has done enough research on the Internet to recognise these sounds.

He mounts the stairs. Stands outside his mother's bedroom for a full minute, not believing his ears.

But he knows what this is.

Gently, with one finger, he pushes the door open.

She is there, naked on her back, a man's head clamped between her thighs.

She doesn't see him at first. She is too busy taking her private stairway to heaven.

He finds the scene impossible to process. This is lust. Carnal desire. And she is not married to this man. How can this be squared with what she told her son as she tortured him with ice-cold water in the shower? How does that work?

Is she not perfect? Can God truly condone this behaviour?

She sees him then.

The roar for him to get out hits him like a blast of wind. It rattles him, but he does not move.

Even when she casts her man aside like a broken toy and fumbles for a dressing gown and yells at him again, he does not move.

Even when she thunders across the room towards him, he stands his ground.

She asks him what in God's name he thinks he is doing.

And then he uses the word. The first time he has ever dreamt of calling her this.

Hypocrite.

It tumbles out of his mouth. It is so natural, so appropriate. It demands to be heard.

The slap is the hardest he has ever received. Her hand swings in a wide arc, and he decides later that he probably could have avoided it. But he lets it land. Lets it rock his head on his shoulders. Lets it leave an imprint on his face.

But still he remains where he is. Defiant. Hating. Perplexed. Saddened.

And knowing it will be the last time she ever hits him.

He remembers . . .

Living with his father now. He has good days and bad days. Mostly bad. His world has been turned upside down. He feels so full of loathing, so angry. He has a couple of school friends, but he hardly ever sees them. Often he tells his dad he's going to meet up with them, but he doesn't. He goes for long walks instead. Through the park, or into town.

He cries a lot, too. At night, into his pillow. And that makes him even angrier.

There's a poem he read. It's by Philip Larkin. It's about how your parents fuck you up. So, so true. Look at me, he thinks. What a mess they made of me.

He doesn't know about God any more. He thinks he believes, but he's not sure. He's been let down too many times. God has never seemed to care what happens to him. Nobody cares.

Sometimes the hatred makes him physically sick. He will replay events in his head, again and again, and he will feel the bile rising. He will feel the burning in his stomach, and then his throat, and he will have to rush into the bathroom to throw up into the toilet.

He decides he needs an outlet, and one day he finds it.

He's not supposed to use his dad's computer. His dad told him so, in no uncertain terms. But he's having problems with his own laptop, and it'll take only a few minutes.

So he enters his dad's bedroom. Brings the machine to life. There's a window already open, and in that window is a video that has been paused. And now he's curious. He can't stop himself. He needs to know what this video contains.

So he plays it.

It takes him a while to understand what this is, but the dawning is blinding. It is revelatory.

Hypocrite.

They are all fucking hypocrites. They ruin your life in the name of what they call right, and then they disobey all the rules themselves with impunity.

And why beholdest thou the mote that is in thy brother's eye, but considerest not the beam that is in thine own eye?

Well, they deserve to be punished too. Why not? Why should they get off scot-free?

Why should the monsters who make it their mission to destroy the youngest and weakest and most innocent among them even be allowed to live?

He remembers . . .

Mere weeks ago now. Searching the web for information on hypocrites and a fitting punishment for them. The lead weights are a nice touch. He'll use that. Nobody else will figure it out, but he'll know. He'll know that the reason for her punishment is in plain view, for all to see. His dad has some lead fishing weights in the shed; he won't miss one or two.

The lump hammer is easy. He simply buys one in a DIY shop on Smithdown Road. His appearance is more of a problem, though. There are cameras on every street.

He finds his solution at the local supermarket. Or, to be more precise, at the recycling bank in the car park. It's a simple act to saunter up to it one dark evening, pick up a bin bag dropped next to the clothes container, and walk away again.

In the bag he finds a coat with a hood. A little big for him, but it'll do the trick, and nobody will be able to trace it back to him. He already knows of a secluded wooded spot in Wavertree Playground where he can secrete the coat when he's finished with it. Perfect.

The days pass. He does more research. He remembers how Miss Cowper was always warbling on about walking her dog in the grounds of the cathedral, so it's not difficult to find her.

When the time is right, he does it.

He nearly chickens out, but he goes through with it.

It almost surprises him that, in the dim light of that winter evening, Mary Cowper seems more like his mother than ever before. In the tunnel, when he utters the single word 'Mummy', and she turns and faces him, and all he can see is the same burning in Mary's eyes that appeared every time his mother chastised or struck him, the urge to extinguish that light is irresistible. Every blow of the hammer is a blow into the skull of the woman who took away his happiness.

For a few days afterwards it is enough. His need for retribution is sated.

But then the hunger returns, stronger than before.

It is easier with Cassie Harris.

Easier again with Susan Halligan.

Killing his mother starts to become a habit.

He remembers . . .

This evening. Coming home from school. Seeing the police cars outside, the cops outside the front door. Realising it's all over. Realising his habit will have to be brought to its obvious conclusion.

He turns and walks away. Goes around the corner and calls at the house of Mr Oates. Explains to the old man that he can't find their key to the alleyway gate, and could he borrow one for a few minutes so that he can put the bin out?

Once he is in the alley, it's a simple matter to scale the back wall of his house without being seen by the police. Simple, too, to pick the cheap padlock on his dad's shed, and then collect the things he needs.

And now he's here.

Here in the middle of Dante's *Inferno*, with its bubbling cauldrons and hellish heat and smouldering flesh and skull-splitting screams.

Here is where it ends.

52

Even before Webley can bring the car to a halt, Cody can see that this is going to be a difficult situation. There are too many uniforms milling about, as if unsure what to do next.

Cody and Webley get out of the car, and one of the constables approaches.

'What's up?' says Cody. 'Is the boy here?'

The constable nods. 'He's here, all right, Sarge. You'd better come and take a look.'

Cody moves along the garden path. In through the front door. There is a curious smell here. A burning smell.

He crosses the hall to where several more uniforms are clustered at a doorway.

'Let me through,' he tells them.

They part. They let him see. And what he sees takes his breath away.

This is the kitchen. In the centre of the room is a dining table, and on that table lies Kate Daley. She is dressed in only her underwear. A long rope has been wrapped tightly around her, keeping her pinned to the table. In her mouth is a metal funnel, secured there with duct tape.

Behind his mother stands Ewan Daley. In one hand he holds a small frying pan; in the other, a lit blowtorch. To his left, something bubbles gently in a larger pan on the stove.

'Don't come any closer,' he tells Cody.

A moan from his mother. Cody looks at her again. Sees the blood streaming down her face, presumably from an initial hammer blow to subdue her. But what really turn his stomach are the holes in her body and the acrid odour of metallic fumes mixed with singed flesh.

Says Ewan, 'I liked your story about the eyeballs. It was an appropriate punishment. I know you made it up, but I enjoyed it all the same.'

He brings the blowtorch to the pan in his hand. Gives the content a long blast to ensure it remains liquefied.

'Ewan, listen to me—'

'This is appropriate, too. They used to do this in ancient Rome, did you know that? Apparently, they executed the Roman general Marcus Licinius Crassus by pouring molten gold down his throat. It was supposed to be because of his thirst for wealth. I haven't got any gold.'

'Ewan—'

'This is much better, though. Lead. It fits the crime. Did you find my little messages about that?'

Cody stares into Ewan's eyes. He finds them dead, soulless. For whatever reason, this young man has had the joy of life sucked out of him. He has moved beyond humanity, and into the realm of not giving a damn about the difference between life and death.

'We found them. The lead weights. Dante's *Inferno*. The punishment for hypocrisy.'

Ewan raises his eyebrows in surprise. 'Very good. I didn't think you'd get that. I'm impressed.'

'So what did your mother do? What makes her such a hypocrite?'

A flash of anger across Ewan's features. But at least he is still capable of feeling some emotion. It's the only thing Cody can exploit here.

'What did she do?' says Ewan. 'This. This is what she did. She turned me into this. Made a man out of me.'

He laughs without humour.

'You can still be a man,' says Cody. 'You can be a man by doing the right thing.'

Another blast with the blowtorch.

'The good thing about lead is that it has a low melting point. Just 327.5 degrees Celsius. Do you know how it kills you when it's poured down your throat?'

'No. No, Ewan, I don't know that.'

'They actually did a study, using a larynx from a slaughterhouse. It was in the *Journal of Clinical Pathology*. Look it up – it's fascinating stuff. One thing that happens is that the lead cools down quickly and plugs up your airways. But the other thing it does is to create lots of steam inside your body, and the high pressure causes your internal organs to explode. Nice, eh?'

Cody thinks he's glad he wasn't here to witness the torture of Mrs Daley. He can imagine the screams of agony and the sizzling sounds as the molten metal ate through her flesh. Looking at her now, he's not sure she will survive this ordeal, even if her son does no more to her.

'Ewan, that's your mother on the table. Your mother.'

'Yeah. Yeah, I know that. I'm not stupid. That's why I'm here. This is the woman who made every minute of my life a misery. With a little help from God, of course. Oh, He came in useful all right. He often comes in useful when people want to justify hurting somebody else.'

'She was wrong to do that, Ewan. But you'd be wrong to kill her. There's been enough killing already.'

Ewan shakes his head. 'No. Not enough. There's one more, and then I'm finished. Then you can do what you like to me. I don't care any more.'

The statement pulls at something deep inside Cody. A young lad like this, already sick of life. What could be sadder?

But he hasn't done it yet. He hasn't killed his mother. He could have. He could easily have poured that stream of death into her mouth at any point in the last few minutes. But he hasn't, and that means there is still hope.

'You care,' he says. 'I know you care. I know what you're going through.'

A bark of laughter. 'No, you don't. You have no idea.'

'Let me talk to you, Ewan. Just you and me. I'll send everyone else away.'

'Cody!'

The warning from Webley, just behind him. He ignores it. Keeps his focus on Ewan. He can see the boy wavering.

'I won't come any closer, I promise. I just want to talk to you, man to man. I want to tell you what I know about this. And then, if you think I'm wrong, you can do what you like.'

'Cody!'

Webley again, more firmly now.

Cody stares at the boy. Ewan reheats his bubbling cauldron as he considers the offer.

'All right,' says Ewan finally. 'I'll give you a few minutes. Get rid of the rest of them.'

Cody turns. Ushers the other cops away from the kitchen and back into the hall. He sees Webley look at him imploringly as he closes the door in front of her.

'Can I show you something?' he asks Ewan.

Ewan thinks about it, then nods. 'Okay. No tricks.'

Cody moves slowly, carefully. He bends down, starts to undo his shoelaces.

'What are you doing?'

'Bear with me. You'll see.'

Cody takes off his shoes. Strips off his socks. Straightens up again. He sees the puzzled awe on Ewan's face.

'What happened?'

'A man did this to me,' Cody explains. 'He tied me to a chair, and then he used a pair of garden loppers to cut away my toes.'

Ewan lowers the pan slightly. His gaze is entirely on Cody.

'Why? Why did he do that?'

'I don't know. I think he just enjoyed it. But that wasn't all he did.'

'No?'

'No. My partner was with me, also tied to a chair. The guy took a sharp knife, and he went over to my partner, and then he sliced off his face.'

Ewan almost drops the pan in shock.

'Shit.'

'Yeah, right?'

'So . . . so what happened then?'

Cody shakes his head. 'It's not a happy ending. It's not like the books and the movies. My partner died, and the guy got away, and I lived sadly ever after.'

More thinking from Ewan. 'So what's your point?'

'My point is that, just like you, I know pain. I know what it's like to suffer. I have had nightmares almost every night since that happened. I scream in the night. Sometimes I wet the bed.'

'Really?'

'Yes, really. The other cops out there, they don't know all this. I'm telling it to you because I think we're two of a kind. I reckon we can talk to each other because we think along the same lines. And that's what you need, Ewan. You need to talk to someone who understands you. I'm prepared to do that, but not if you kill your mother in front of me.'

Cody thinks, but he's not sure, that he sees a glistening in Ewan's eyes. If so, it's the first real sign of a crack in his protection against emotional infection.

Ewan nods towards Cody's feet. 'The guy who did that to you. What would you do to him if you caught him?'

Ah. A good question. A question that Cody has contemplated many times and never found an answer to. A question that, if things go as he hopes, he may soon have to confront.

'I'd arrest him. I won't lie, I might even kick the shit out of him while I was doing it. I'd enjoy it, too. But what I wouldn't do is kill him. And you know what? It's not because I'd be lowering myself to his level, or any crap like that. It's because killing him would end his suffering, and I want him to suffer. I want him to spend the rest of his life behind bars, knowing that I won. Every day he will think about what he did to me, and he will realise that he gave me the reason to take away his liberty.'

Ewan looks down at his mother, and it seems to Cody possible that he might be seeing her for what she truly is.

'That's right,' says Cody. 'Look at her. Look at the holes you made in her body. Think about her agony. Because *she'll* be thinking about it. For the rest of her life, she will be unable to stop thinking about the consequences of what she did to you. I think that's worth keeping her alive for, don't you? Dead people can't learn lessons.'

Ewan continues to stare at his mother. Cody gives him the time, hopes that he's done enough.

'So what's it to be, Ewan?'

Webley hates this. Hates being shut out. Hasn't Cody done so much of that already that he didn't need to resort to physically closing a door in her face?

She can't hear what's being said through the door, and that worries her. There's a homicidal hormonal teenager in there holding a blowtorch and a pan of molten lead, either of which could do serious damage to Cody if he's not careful.

And Cody isn't the most stable of people himself. What if he does something erratic? What if he freaks out again? What if—?

Fucking hell, why am I even giving a toss? If he wants to play the hero, then let him. I don't care if he screws this up. On his head be it.

Well, okay, maybe I care a little. Maybe I don't want him to die in there. Or to be horribly disfigured. Or injured a little.

Shit, Cody, what the fuck are you doing in there?

She gets her answer when the door opens.

It opens with painful slowness and solemnity. Everyone cranes to get a view inside.

It is with some relief to Webley that she sees Ewan with his head bowed and his hands empty. The pan and blowtorch have been placed on the draining board. He stands and waits for the inevitable.

An ashen-faced Cody beckons them in, and they pile through the door. While paramedics dash over to tend to Mrs Daley, Webley and the other cops zero in on Ewan.

'Don't hurt him,' says Cody.

For some reason, Webley finds herself turning her head to check on Cody. She alone sees him slipping his bare feet into his shoes. She alone sees him balling his socks and pushing them into his pocket.

She alone knows how much of himself he just sacrificed in this room.

53

It's a complex situation.

Long story short, they've caught a serial killer, which in itself is usually a cause for celebration and drunken revelry.

But keeping the story long, this serial killer is a kid. A kid whose mind has been fucked up. A kid whose mother is in intensive care and whose father is in custody on a child-porn charge. Dealing with the aftermath of a case like this requires the utmost tact and carefulness. It requires social services and mental-health counsellors. In the lead-up to a time of peace and goodwill to all men, the tabloids will have a field day with the contrast offered by this story. Some of them will paint Ewan as the spawn of the Devil. Self-professed experts will point to the case as a sign of all that's wrong with society. Politicians will wrestle with the ramifications. But at the centre of the storm is a mere child.

The processing and the paperwork take hours. But gradually the detectives start to drift away. For all of them it has been an exhausting operation, and many want to catch up on their sleep.

At some point in the evening, Ferguson drifts up to Cody's desk.

'Me and a few of the others are going for a beer. Up for it?'

Cody looks up at his lofty friend. 'Nah. Another time maybe. Thanks, though.'

Ferguson nods. 'You should give yourself some credit. It's a good result, you know.'

'Then why doesn't it feel like it?'

Ferguson nods again, then fades away.

Webley is the next to appear. She has her coat on.

'Calling it a night?' he asks her.

'Yeah. You should too.'

He points to his computer screen. 'Too much to do.'

'It'll wait. Besides, you need to go to the out-of-hours and get that ankle looked at.'

'It's fine,' says Cody. Although he knows it's not. He has just taken another dose of painkillers, and it's not helping.

'You did a good job in that kitchen.'

Cody merely shrugs in reply.

'What did you say to him?'

'Not a lot. He needed a friend. I was there for him.'

'A friend? He killed three women and tortured his mother.'

'Yes. Yes, he did. But maybe if he'd had a friend earlier in his life, he wouldn't have hurt a fly. There are times when we all need someone to talk to.'

Webley shakes her head in disbelief. 'Can you hear yourself, Cody? Can you hear the words coming out of your own mouth?'

'The kid has major problems. He—'

'Not the kid, you fucking idiot. I'm not talking about the case. Jesus!'

Cody stares at her. Wanting to say something. Wanting to take this where it should go. Not finding the words.

'Hey, Megs!'

This voice from a doorway at the far end of the incident room. Webley turns her head. Cody leans to look past her.

'Ready?' says Parker.

'Yeah,' she answers. 'Just coming.'

She turns back to Cody. 'We're going out for a meal. Then back to his place.'

'That's nice,' says Cody.

'Yes. Yes, it is. He's there for me. Just like you decided to be there for Ewan. And not at all like how you decided not to be there for me.'

He's about to tell her that there are too many occurrences of the word 'not' in that sentence for him to work it out, but she has already turned away. He thinks he senses anger in her steps as she walks off. He watches as she moves right alongside her fiancé. Sees Parker put his arm around her shoulder before giving Cody a knowing look.

And then they're gone. Out on the town for a slap-up meal and a few glasses of wine and a night of unbridled passion, during which all thoughts of Cody will be put aside.

He sighs, turns back to his computer. Forces himself to get on with his work.

He'll work until his eyes are too tired to focus any longer, and then he'll go home. Back to his empty flat and his empty fridge. If he's lucky, he'll have enough in there to put together a ham sandwich for his supper.

She watches him. He stretches, yawns. Then he stands up and puts his coat on. When he starts limping around the incident room, snapping off the lights, she feels she ought to announce her presence.

He almost jumps out of his skin when she coughs.

'Grace!' he says.

She gives him a little wave. 'Sergeant Cody.'

He moves towards her, wincing with the pain, bless him.

'I thought I was the last one here.'

'Then it's a good job you didn't start picking your nose or farting loudly.'

He laughs at that. 'Or worse. You've no idea what I get up to when I'm alone.'

No, she thinks. I don't know. I'd be interested to find out, though.

'I'm sure it's all very proper,' she says.

Cody quickly changes the subject. 'What are you still doing here?'

She gestures towards her friend the computer. 'I thought I'd catalogue the video files. They'll be needed for evidence.'

'Not joining the others for a drink?'

She hesitates. She doesn't want to tell him that she wasn't invited. Doesn't want his pity.

'Me? No. I thought about it, but . . . well, this seemed more important.'

She sees him nodding, but she's sure he has detected her lie.

'I want you to know,' he says, 'that you did excellent work on these murders. You did some really clever stuff I didn't even know was possible.'

She feels the blood rushing to her cheeks, and hopes the light is dim enough for him not to see it.

'Thank you. I try my best.'

'If you ever . . . if you ever want me to put that in writing or anything . . .'

'Thanks,' she says. 'It's nice to be appreciated.'

'You're appreciated,' he says. Then he adds: 'Do you like to watch a good film, Grace?'

She feels her pulse rate double. What is this? Is he about to ask me out to the cinema?

'Yes,' she squeaks.

'So do I. I like films that make me think – films that *move* me in some way. Do you know what I mean?'

'I . . . I think so.'

'And sometimes I come away and I think about why a film has had such an effect on me. I think about the excellent cast, or the direction, or the dialogue. But do you know what we always overlook?'

'What?'

'The film score. The music. It's there constantly, but we don't even know it. We don't realise how crucial it is to how we feel, how we react when we're watching a film.'

Grace finds herself holding her breath as Cody looks straight into her eyes.

He says, 'You're our music, Grace. Don't forget that.'

And then he smiles and leaves.

When she remembers to breathe again, Grace Meade decides that life doesn't get any better than this.

54

He is so relieved to get out of the car. It's not a long journey from the station to Rodney Street, but the air in that car was blue every time he had to press the clutch pedal.

It doesn't help that the nearest parking space he can find is about a hundred yards from his building. He just wants to get inside and plunge this bastard foot into some iced water. That's if he's got any ice.

He's glad that the case has been brought to an end. Always nice to take a killer off the streets. But at the same time he's worried that things will go quiet now. He could really do with a nice meaty case to take his mind off the Christmas festivities. Because, let's face it, it's not looking promising here, is it?

He wonders if he should just go away over Christmas. Go and stay in a hotel somewhere.

Yeah, because that wouldn't make him look like a saddo, would it? Sitting down to dinner next to some strange widow desperate for companionship – that wouldn't make him feel a little weird.

Fuck it, he thinks. It's just another holiday. I'll work all the hours I can get, and I'll read a few good books the rest of the time. Not a problem. It's one less chimney for Santa to worry about.

He puts his key in the front door. Goes inside. Closes the door again. Rather than blind himself with the hall lights, he spends a moment allowing his eyes to adjust to the moon-glow filtering through the window at the top of the stairs.

He limps over to the staircase. Looks up it as though it were Everest.

Shit, he thinks. This is going to be slow and painful. I could really do with a Stannah Stairlift now.

He takes hold of the banister. Puts his foot on the bottom step.

And then he hears the door buzzer.

He knows this isn't right. It's about eleven o'clock at night. Nobody comes calling at this time of night. Nobody except—

And then he's moving. Back towards the front door, as fast as his leg will allow. Because he's going to catch the bastard this time. He's going to yank open that door to see the fucker who isn't expecting the occupant to get there so quickly, and leg be damned, because he's going to kick the shit out of his night-caller, and then he's going to drag him inside and make him spill whatever he knows about the people who killed Cody's partner and made his own life such a misery.

And then Cody's there, at the door, pulling it wide and expecting to have to give chase, expecting to have to destroy what's left of his foot as he races after the deviant who has taken one risk too many, and who is now about to face the consequences.

But that isn't what Cody gets. What he gets is a dark shape that leaps at him through the doorway. A shape that grabs him in a tight embrace and pushes him hard against the wall and starts to suffocate him . . .

. . . with a kiss.

He pulls his face away. Stares with shock into his assailant's moonlit eyes.

'Megan! What—?'

'He told me,' she says, and Cody can now see the tracks of tears on her cheeks. 'He confessed. And now I know. Now I understand. You did it for me. You did it for me, you bastard.'

'Megan, I—'

'You don't need to pretend any more. He told me everything. Parker told me.'

'Told you what?'

'How jealous he was of you. How he asked you to not to visit me when I was ill. And the dinner. God, the dinner! I can't believe he actually came to see you and asked you to break off the dinner engagement with us. And you said nothing. You went along with it. Why did you do that?'

'Because . . . because he's the man you're going to marry, and I didn't want to get in the way of that.'

'Get in the way? Why would you be getting in the way?'

'I don't know, but it's what Parker believes. He thinks I want to take you away from him. I did it for him, but mostly I did it for you.'

Webley's tears flow more freely. 'Oh, Jesus Christ, Cody. You had me hating you. You had me thinking you didn't want to know me any more. I can't believe you were willing to sacrifice our friendship.'

'Your happiness with Parker seemed more important.'

Webley puts a hand on Cody's chest. 'Oh, Cody. What am I going to do with you?'

He smiles. 'Invite me to the wedding? I'll wear a disguise if it helps Parker.'

She shakes her head. 'There isn't going to be a wedding. I've called it off.'

'No. No, you can't do that, Megan. He wants you. He's obsessed with you.'

'He went behind my back, Cody. He tried to break up a friendship. I can't forgive him for that.'

Cody takes her hand in his. 'Look, just give it time, okay? Mull it over. Parker was scared, that's all. He didn't want to lose you. He realises how much of a magnet I am to women.'

Webley laughs through her tears. She slaps Cody on the chest, pushing him away.

'And still you're defending him. You're a good man, Cody.'

He thinks then that he could easily take her in his arms. He could easily return the kiss she planted on his lips. He could lead her upstairs. He could . . .

'And Parker's a good man, too,' he says. 'He will make you happy.'

Webley stares up at him, and for a few seconds he thinks that she is wishing he had said something else to her.

'Thank you, Cody,' she says. 'For everything.'

She pulls away. Heads back out onto the street. On the doorstep she pauses.

'It's Christmas in a few days,' she says. 'You *have* got plans, haven't you?'

He smiles. 'Yes. I've got plans. Don't worry about me.'

She nods, and he thinks he may have got away with it. They exchange soft goodnights. Cody closes the door and leans his forehead against it. He remains like that for a whole minute, just thinking.

Eventually he begins his ascent of the staircase. Drags himself up there like Quasimodo going up the bell tower.

When he gets to his flat, he goes straight into the kitchen. He finds some more painkillers and knocks them back with a glass of water. Then he slumps onto a chair. His plan was to eat something, but the pain in his foot has made him too tired. He needs sleep. Tomorrow he'll see someone about the foot. Jumping off that gallery was not the best idea he's ever had.

He stumbles through into his bedroom. Puts a light on.

And that's when he sees it.

A Christmas present. Right in the middle of his bed.

Suddenly he's wide awake. Someone has been in his flat.

He thinks back. The flat door was locked when he arrived at it a few minutes ago, he's sure of it.

But somehow there has been an intruder.

His first thought is that he should call it in. Get the bomb squad or whatever over here.

He rejects that option. This is a message for him, for his eyes only. Anyone wanting to kill him could have done so in a much less convoluted way than this.

He moves to the bed. Stares down at the gift. It's wrapped in green paper with pictures of Victorian toys on it: a jack-in-the-box; a rocking horse; one of those monkeys with brass cymbals between its paws.

Cautiously, he picks it up. It's light and irregularly shaped. There is no writing on the paper, no card attached.

He grabs hold of the paper, rips it apart. The thing inside falls to the bed.

It looks back at him. Stares with empty eyes set in rotten flesh. Grins with its yellow-brown teeth framed by blood-coloured lips.

It's the very mask worn by Waldo, the clown who snipped away Cody's toes and murdered his partner.

Cody stares at it for a long time.

And then he screams until it feels his lungs will burst.

Read on for an exclusive letter from David Jackson and a chance to join his Readers Club . . .

A message from David . . .

Dear Reader,

The Nathan Cody series of books is still a relatively new venture for me. My career as a published author began with an entirely different series set far from home – New York, in fact! There are currently four books featuring NYPD Detective Callum Doyle, the most recent of which (*Cry Baby*) has done phenomenally well.

So why the change? Two reasons, really. The first was that I reached a stage where I wanted to move to another publishing house. Publishers don't usually like to take on books mid-series, especially when the rights to the backlist are owned elsewhere. I knew that if I were to have any chance of stimulating their interest, I needed a new, fresh idea.

The other reason relates to local support. I discovered quite early on that by setting my books in New York I was missing out on the invaluable push that can be given by UK shops and media to local authors.

And so Nathan Cody was born. Given what I've just said, putting him in Liverpool was a no-brainer. It's the city of my birth, and I still travel there every day from my home on the other side of the Mersey. 'It's a city of contrasts – sometimes of turmoil, but sometimes of shining example – and I love it'. I hope that comes through in the books, with moments of intense darkness interspersed with the cheeky sense of humour for which Liverpool is famous. I like to think of this new series as '*Luther* with Scousers'.

I'm sure you'll have come to realise by now that Cody is much more than a detective who helps to solve mysteries. He's a complex character trying to cope with a traumatic past and an intriguing set of present circumstances and relationships. But what is even more interesting is what awaits him next (cue dramatic music) . . .

As the series progresses, we will see more evil clowns, more drama, more stress for Cody, and more of an insight into the lives of his colleagues and family. Characters like Megan Webley, Stella Blunt and Grace Meade have a lot more up their sleeves yet.

But I can't do any of this without you, the reader. My words are mere marks on a page until you breathe life into them. For me, one of the biggest delights of writing is making contact with readers, and not just through my novels. A huge thrill for me is when a reader makes the effort to write to me, either via the contact page on my website, www.davidjacksonbooks.com, or on Twitter, where I exist as @Author_Dave.

If you're interested in taking this a step further, I'd like to invite you to join my Readers Club. Don't worry – it doesn't commit you to anything, there's no catch, and I won't pass your details on to any third parties. It simply means you'll receive occasional updates from me about my books, including offers, publication news, and even the occasional treat! For example, sign up now and I'll send you an exclusive short story, completely free of charge. I won't bombard you with emails, but if you ever get fed up of me, you can unsubscribe at any time. To register, all you have to do is visit **www.bit.ly/DavidJacksonClub**.

One way or another, I hope to hear from you soon, and that you continue to read and enjoy my books. Thank you for your support.

Very best wishes,
David

Coming 2018

DON'T MAKE A SOUND

by David Jackson

You can't choose your family. Or can you?

Meet the Bensons.
A pleasant enough couple. They keep themselves to themselves. They wash their car, mow their lawn and pass the time of day with their neighbours. And they have a beautiful little girl called Daisy.

There's just one problem. Daisy doesn't belong to the Bensons. They stole her. And now they've decided that Daisy needs a little brother or sister.

D. S. Nathan Cody is about to face his darkest and most terrifying case yet . . .

PRE-ORDER NOW

Read on for an exclusive first look . . .

1

'What are you up to?'

The words startle him. But then Malcolm Benson finds the mental echo of the chuckle he failed to contain. He turns from his place at the sink, the amusement still written on his face.

Harriet is at the table, mug of tea cradled in her small hands. It's her favourite mug – the one with Snoopy on it. He made certain to give her that one on this special morning. She has her eyebrows arched in that endearing way of hers. One of the features that first attracted him to her thirty years ago.

He flicks soap foam from his Marigolds, then touches a finger to the side of his nose.

'Wouldn't you like to know?' he says.

Her suspicions confirmed, Harriet lowers her mug to the raffia coaster.

'You're planning something.'

'I'm always planning,' he says. 'You know that. Planning and plotting.'

Her eyes shine at him. 'What is it?'

'You'll have to wait.' He faces the sink again. Dips his gloved hands into the hot suds. He knows she will be staring at the back of his head, trying to read his mind.

'It's not my birthday for another month,' she says casually.

He remains silent.

'Is that it? Something to do with my birthday?'

He looks at her over his shoulder. In her fifties, and yet still full of such child-like innocence and wonderment.

'It's a present. But not for your birthday. It couldn't wait that long.'

'Malcolm. You're teasing me now. Tell me. Please!'

He had been hoping to draw things out a little longer, but it wouldn't be fair on her. Besides, he's as excited as she is to bring it into the open. He has kept it to himself for far too long.

'All right,' he says. 'Wait there.'

He peels off his gloves and removes his apron. As he heads towards the kitchen door, he sees how Harriet claps her hands together in anticipation.

He smiles all the way up to the tiny box room that is his study, and all the way back down again. This is a huge moment for both of them. The culmination of an immense amount of effort and patience.

He pauses before re-entering the kitchen. 'Close your eyes. No sneaky-peekies.'

'Okay,' she answers. 'I'm not looking. Promise.'

He walks through the door, his gift held out before him. Harriet has her hands tightly clasped over her eyes. There is a discernible tremor in her fingers.

'Right,' he says. 'You can look now.'

She parts her fingers. Slides them slowly down her cheeks. Her face registers puzzlement and then disbelief at the sight of the large, leather-bound book.

'It's . . . it's the album.'

He nods. He knows she's about to blub, and already a tear is forming in his own eye.

She lifts her gaze to lock with his. 'You haven't?'

'I have.'

'You've found one?'

He smiles.

'Oh my Lord,' she says. 'Oh my Lord. Show me, show me, show me!'

She leans across to drag one of the chairs around so that it's right next to hers. Malcolm sits down and places the album on the table between them.

'Are you ready for this?' he asks.

'Malcolm, you know how much I've wanted it. Open the book.'

He locates the silk tab inserted into the centre of the album. Opens the book at that position.

The reflected glow from the page lights up Harriet's face. Her hand jumps to her mouth. Tears spring from her eyes and run down the back of her hand.

'I hope those are tears of joy,' Malcolm says.

It's all she can do to nod her head as she continues to marvel at the contents of this treasure chest. This is better than any birthday.

She reaches out and turns the page. Emits a gasp. Malcolm studies her as she gets caught up in the dream. Watches her cry and smile and laugh as she turns page after page. He wishes he could do this for her every day.

The questions start to come then. Harriet wants as much information as she can get, down to the last detail. Malcolm is sometimes stretched to answer, but he does his best.

When Harriet reaches the last page, she goes back to the first. Gently touches a finger to the photograph affixed there. Malcolm knew she would love that one best of all.

And then a cloud of doubt seems to cross her features.

'This isn't just more teasing, is it, Malcolm? I mean, this is definite?'

'Oh, yes. You can see how busy I've been. Look at the photographs. It's all set.'

'All set? When? Soon?'

Malcolm strokes his chin. 'Well, that's the difficult part. These things take time. It's a question of logistics, you see.'

Her face drops. 'Oh.'

'So I thought ... I thought *tonight*. Would that be soon enough for you?'

Huge eyes now. Eyes brimming with ecstatic incredulity.

'Malcolm!' She throws her arms around him, pulls him into her warmth. 'Malcolm, you are an amazing man. I love you.'

She releases him finally. 'It won't be dangerous, will it? I mean, you're sure you can do it?'

He takes her hands in his. 'It won't be easy. I'm not as young as I used to be. But yes, I can do it.'

She hugs him again. Returns her gaze to the album. And then something occurs to her, and she glances up at the ceiling.

'Can we tell her? Can we tell Daisy?'

'I don't see why not, do you?'

*   *   *

Daisy hears them coming upstairs, so she puts down her pencil and sits up straight. She knows how much they like it when she sits to attention.

She has been writing a story about a mouse. She has never been much good at writing stories, and doesn't know much about mice, so it has been quite a challenge. She hopes they like what she has done. Later, she will do some more fractions, and then some reading. She has a very busy day ahead.

The door eventually opens, and as the adults enter she stiffens her posture even more.

She notices how much they are smiling this morning. In fact, this is probably the happiest she has ever seen them. She wonders what that might mean.

'Hello, Daisy,' says Malcolm.

'Hello, Daddy,' she replies.

Malcolm and Harriet sit opposite her at the small work table. They are still smiling.

'We've got some news for you,' says Malcolm. 'Something we're very excited about.'

Daisy doesn't reply. She's not sure how she is meant to answer. She sits and waits patiently.

'Don't you want to know what it is?' asks Harriet.

Daisy nods, although she's not sure she does want to know.

Harriet looks at Malcolm and nods for him to break the news. Malcolm leans forward across the table. Gets so close that Daisy can see the blackheads on his nose.

'You're going to get –' He breaks off, leaving a huge gap of expectation. Then: 'a little sister!'

Harriet flutters in her chair. Gives a little clap of delight.

Daisy, though, is still not sure how to react. She expects they want her to be as euphoric as they are, but somehow she cannot find it within her. Seeing their eyes on her, she opens her mouth, but no words emerge.

'What do you think about that?' says Malcolm. 'Isn't it wonderful? Just think of all the things you can share together.'

'You can show her your toys,' Harriet says. 'And you can read to her, and explain how everything works. Best of all, you won't be on your own any more. You'll never be lonely again. How fantastic is that?'

Not wanting to cause an upset, Daisy frantically searches her mind for something meaningful to utter.

'What's her name?' she blurts out.

Malcolm looks at Harriet. Harriet looks at Malcolm. 'Good question,' they say to each other.

'Her name's Poppy,' says Harriet. 'A flower name, like yours. And she's blonde like you, too. And only six years old. She's adorable, and I'm sure you're going to love her.' She turns to Malcolm again. 'Isn't she, Daddy?'

They get lost in each other's eyes again, giving Daisy a chance to formulate her next query.

'When? When is she coming?'

'Another excellent question,' says Malcolm. 'Hang on to your hat, Daisy – it's pretty fast! How does tonight sound to you?'

Something lurches inside Daisy, and she has to fight not to show it. 'Tonight?'

Too late she realises there is a tone of negativity in her voice. She sees how Malcolm's lips quiver slightly as they struggle to hold onto their smile.

'Yes, Daisy. Tonight. That's all right with you, isn't it?'

'Yes, Daddy,' she answers quickly. 'I mean ... I was just wondering where she's going to sleep.'

Malcolm looks across to the single bed. He frowns, as though the problem has not occurred to him until now.

'Well, I'm afraid you'll have to share that bed for a short while. We'll sort something out.'

'Details, details,' says Harriet. 'We don't worry about things like that in this house. It'll all be fine. It'll be more than fine. It will be the best thing ever!'

It seems to Daisy that Harriet could explode with joy. She could suddenly burst apart at the seams and splash onto the walls and ceiling.

She closes off the thought. Stares down at her story in an effort to distract herself.

'So,' says Malcolm. 'That's our amazing news. I knew you'd be pleased, Daisy.'

Daisy doesn't know the word 'sarcasm', but the tenor of Malcolm's voice tells her she is not reacting the way he wants her to.

'Don't worry,' she tells them. 'I'm a big girl. I'll look after Poppy.'

It's the most positive she can be, and the most truthful. It seems to do the trick.

'Well, we'll leave you to do your schoolwork now,' says Harriet. 'I'll pop up later to see how you're getting on.' She wags a finger. 'Don't expect me to be much help today, though. I don't know whether I'm coming or going, I really don't.'

They leave her then, almost floating out of the room on the cloud they have created. She watches them go. Waits for the door to close. For the familiar noise that always comes next. The grating sound that seems to reverberate in the centre of her chest.

The bolts being drawn.

She is alone again. She spends so much of her time alone. Because of that, a part of her really does think that it will be wonderful to have another child here.

But, if she had any choice in the matter, she would turn the opportunity down.

She looks around her bedroom. Sees it for what it really is. Not so much a room as a prison cell. The boarded-up window that means she constantly has to have the light on to see. The tiny sink in the corner, her only means of keeping clean. The curtained-off section hiding the manky old commode.

She has a television, but it isn't connected to the outside world. She can watch only carefully vetted DVDs.

She has learnt not to complain about any of this to the adults. To the people she calls Mummy and Daddy, but who are not her real parents.

This is not the place to bring another child.

It wasn't the place to bring *this* child.

She is not sure precisely how long she has been here, but she has a rough idea. She was forced to celebrate her tenth birthday recently. And she knows she was seven when she was snatched.

That makes it about three years that she has never set foot outside this room.

PRE-ORDER NOW

Want to read
NEW BOOKS
before anyone else?

Like getting
FREE BOOKS?

Enjoy sharing your
OPINIONS?

Discover

READERS FIRST
Read. Love. Share.

Get your first free book just by signing up at
readersfirst.co.uk